Dogwood Winter is a to in face of adversity, a story of heartache and healing that is certain to leave its mark on your heart.

— CYNTHIA ROEMER – AWARD-WINNING AUTHOR
OF *UNDER MOONLIT SKIES*

Dogwood Winter follows the wonderful friends we have made in Valley Creek through yet another masterfully crafted story. Two experienced souls reach for the promise of spring through great loss and longing, their love blossoming in an unlikely place and circumstance.

Moving and tender, this story explores hopes deferred and longings fulfilled in the rich and lyrical prose of this nuanced writer.

— KATHLEEN L. MAHER, AUTHOR OF THE SONS OF THE
SHENANDOAH SERIES

Happy Reading, Stephanie!

VALLEY CREEK REDEMPTION • THREE

A TIMELY BEGINNING
FROM AN UNTIMELY END

CANDACE WEST

Scrivenings
PRESS
Quench your thirst for story.
www.ScriveningsPress.com

Published by Scrivenings Press LLC
15 Lucky Lane
Morrilton, Arkansas 72110
https://scriveningspress.com

Printed in the United States of America

Paperback ISBN 978-1-64917-145-0
eBook 978-1-64917-146-7

Library of Congress Control Number: 2021942836

Editors: Erin R. Howard and Kaci Banks

Cover by Linda Fulkerson at bookmarketinggraphics.com

All scriptures are taken from the KING JAMES VERSION (KJV): King James Version, public domain.

"Never Alone" (1897) by Ludie Carrington Day Pickett, public domain.

*To Uncle Randall—an anchor, a rock, my second dad, whose voice
still whispers to me. You left us far too soon to enter God's glory, your
long-awaited home.
But not soon enough for you.
You never belonged to this world.*

ACKNOWLEDGMENTS

A special thank you goes to my family for their support and encouragement, especially with my long hours and days at the keyboard. They make the days bright and joyful. Words can never express my love and appreciation for them. A special hug goes to my son for his enthusiasm. Mama loves you to the end of the universe.

A huge shout out goes to Kathleen L. Maher, Lynn Watson, and Eileen Ward—my beta readers. Thank you for believing in George and Ella's story. Your critiques were beyond helpful. Kathy, I hope I learn to write like you when I grow up. Lynn, our phone conversations about our characters are always inspiring and fun. And Sister Eileen, thank you for being that extra set of eyes that I sorely need throughout the series!

To Dee Henshaw, thank you for your friendship and for allowing me to put your horses, Crockett, Grits, and Ginger, into my series. Knowing you is a joy!

I can't say enough wonderful things about the Scrivenings Press team—Linda, Shannon, and Elena. Thank you for your support of aspiring Christian authors, your tireless dedication, and your friendship. Each one of you has blessed my life. May the Lord continually bless and grow your endeavors.

And, as always, a heartfelt thank you to all of my readers, far and near. Some of you have become wonderful, personal friends, and all of you have blessed me with your eagerness for more. You keep me behind the keyboard. Thank you for every card, gift, email, every comment and post you make on social media, your reviews, and for spreading the word about this series. I couldn't do it without you. Hugs to you all. Know that you are loved.

I will restore health unto thee, and I will heal thee of thy wounds, saith the Lord. ~ Jeremiah 30:17

PROLOGUE

Tiptoeing barefooted through the fresh-fallen snow didn't
sting Ella's feet as she wound through Mother's grove of
dogwood trees.

A refreshing cold without the chill.

Ella's eyes flew open. Peering through the semi-darkness of
dawn unfurling within her bedroom, she clung to the receding
landscape within a hidden corner of her mind as she awoke.
Through the years, the scene had never changed—an elusive
riddle with no end.

A dream of such strange contradictions. The sunlight
caressing her face; the snow encasing her feet without burning
them; the warm, spring breeze sweeping over her bare,
outstretched arms, the sensations still lingering on her flesh
while she lay there awake. Always, Ella moved toward
something.

Always, she failed to reach it.

Instead, she remained in the haven of Mother's dogwoods.
The blossoms brushed against her pale pink frock. Against her
fingertips. Embroidered on the bodice of her dress, more

dogwood blossoms spread around her waist. Covered her aching heart.

Yet, the sunlight spilling onto her face radiated pure joy.

In the fading darkness, Ella rubbed her arms and blinked away the fragments of the scene. Mother once said happy dreams were promises carried to mortals on the wings of angels. No one had made promises to her, though.

Not in an age.

1

May 1912

Ella's head reeled but not from the headache pounding her temples. Dread bubbled up her throat.

"Are you certain?" she said, hating the waver in her voice.

"Unfortunately, yes." The doctor snapped his bag shut, the corners of his mouth set in tight lines. "I've seen my share of cases. You have all the symptoms." Shaking his head, he puffed out a breath and turned toward her brother Douglas who stood just inside the doorway. "Give this to her for the fever."

The wooden floor creaked beneath the Persian rug alongside her bed as Ella's brother moved closer to take the bottle from Dr. Weaver. Strange how she could still fret that his muddy boots, fresh from a newly plowed field, would soil it.

Douglas breathed deep, his navy-blue eyes peering into hers. "Will she get worse?"

"It's hard to say. Time will tell, though."

"Is that the best you can do?" Douglas tunneled a hand through his hair as he turned to Dr. Weaver.

"Douglas." Ella reached for his sleeve, but he jerked away.

"There's got to be something you can do." In two strides, he stood between the doctor and her bedroom door. "Is there a treatment, some kind of medicine? Anything?"

"Mr. Steen." A sigh edged Dr. Weaver's voice. "There's nothing else that can be done except wait."

The muscles in Douglas's neck tensed. "That can't be."

"Little is known about this disease. It affects some folks worse than others. Your sister may recover fully ... or not."

Hot moisture pricked Ella's eyes, threatening to sweep away her last ounce of bravado. She chewed her bottom lip. Perhaps the outward pain would erase the inner one, however momentarily.

Dr. Weaver plucked his hat from the settee. "Until then, you'd best move her to the main house where she can be cared for properly. Make her as comfortable as possible."

A hint of desperation flickered in Douglas's face. He spread his palms outward as though pleading. "Are you certain there's no place that can help her?"

"None to my knowledge." Dr. Weaver sidestepped Douglas and turned the doorknob. "I'll come tomorrow to check on her. All you can do is pray, Mr. Steen, if you believe."

His retreating footsteps clipped down the stairs and filled the silence between Ella and Douglas. Holding her breath, Ella waited for her brother's troubled stare to fasten onto hers. He took his time, rubbing the back of his neck. His glance bounced to the rose-patterned wallpaper, the crown molding, the floor.

Then her.

Ella felt her bravado crack. "Well, you always fussed about my living here alone."

Douglas's lips stretched thin. "Ella." His tone brooked no nonsense. Against her will, she gulped a shuddering breath and turned her head. A moment later, the foot of her mattress sagged under his weight as he sat.

"Infantile paralysis," he said, his gravelly voice barely a whisper.

The words nearly froze Ella's heart as she swallowed against the lace collar of her nightgown. "Do you think the doctor is right? That I contracted it from the river?"

"There's no other explanation. You should've never waded into it."

Ella's eyes stung, both from Douglas's words and the stabbing pain in her legs. "I'm sorry."

"I didn't mean it like that." Douglas shook his head, his voice thick. His sunburned hands gripped his knees. "I should've told Caleb no picnic, and there would've been no swimming."

"The day was warm and beautiful. Caleb needed to get out, especially after everything you've both been through. It was the first time in months he'd laughed."

Douglas pulled in a slow, deep breath, no doubt struggling to control emotions still too raw from his wife's untimely death during the winter. His shoulders sagged as he released it and cut a glance at her. "You're feverish. I've got to get you home now."

"But how?" Ella's words rose with another wave of pain.

Douglas rose and drew back the bedcovers with as much tenderness as their departed mother. "I'll carry you home in the buggy and send Mrs. Hawthorne to gather some of your things. Come now."

An unseen weight pressed against Ella's legs as she scooted them to the edge of the mattress. "I can hardly move them, Douglas. They feel so weak and heavy." Cold, icy fear wedged into her heart and reflected from her brother's darkened expression.

"Hold still. I'll carry you."

Before she could argue, Douglas scooped her up as though she weighed no more than a rag doll. The thud of his boots echoed through the silent house and down the staircase, shrouding the pounding of Ella's heart. What would happen to her? Would she die? Be crippled?

As he stepped out on the porch, the warm sunshine struck Ella across the face like an angry slap. Her eyelids pinched shut as she hid her face against his sturdy, broad shoulder. A few moments later, she felt him transfer her onto the buggy seat.

"Do you think you can sit up?"

"Yes, no farther than we have to go."

His calloused hand brushed her forehead. "Your fever's rising."

Ella gripped the armrest as Douglas jogged to the opposite side of the buggy and climbed up. A second later, the rig lurched forward. One of Douglas's arms encircled her shoulders and drew her closer.

"Lean on me, Ella Mae."

He hadn't called her that in years. She must be even worse off than she realized. Too tired to resist, Ella wilted against him and lowered her head onto his shoulder.

Slow, murky darkness surrounded her like a rising tide and swept her away.

"You killed her. You killed my baby." The distraught woman's voice shrieked along the corridor and raised the hairs on the back of George Curtis's neck.

Her husband lunged at him. A fist collided with George's jaw, snapping his head to the side. Everything dimmed while two hands clutched the front of his surgical gown and jerked him forward.

"You said it would be fine. Very little danger. You dirty liar." The father's hot breath blasted across Dr. Curtis's face.

"Thomas ... I'm sorry." His voice sounded far away, as though belonging to someone else.

Biting back a cry, Thomas pulled his fist back for another blow. Just before it smashed into George's face, three orderlies thrust between them and wrenched him loose.

The scene moved both with speed and slow motion. Claudia's screams and Thomas's threats clattered around him while the shouts of the orderlies, the push and swirl of the nurses around the distraught mother, anchored his feet to the floor. The only solid, stable thing in the corridor.

Dr. Curtis, will I see you in just a little bit?

George shivered at the memory of the little girl's voice, her last words before the ether closed those brown eyes full of trust and a touch of fear.

Was this really happening? A numb wave of shock rolled through him. No professional demeanor could brush it off, especially when it involved his two friends.

"Let me go!" Thomas twisted from their grasp and staggered toward his wife. "It just can't be. Lilith gone. God help us."

"My girl, my girl!" Claudia collapsed into a chair, wringing her hands. "Thomas. Our girl can't be dead."

Chin quivering, Thomas pointed at George. "You killed her, and I'll make sure you pay. You'll never practice again if it's the very last thing I ever do." Tears streaked down his face. "A simple surgery, you said."

What could he say? No words could bring Lilith back.

Dead. The little girl was dead.

Dr. Curtis, will I see you in just a little bit?

"Did you hear me, George?" Thomas stumbled forward, raw grief blazing in his face. An orderly caught his arm.

"Thomas, Claudia, I'm so very sorry. I—"

"You'll be even more sorry before this is over."

Behind George, the doors leading to the operating room

swung open as his fellow surgeon Alec Howard strode toward them.

"Dr. Curtis, you're no longer needed here. I'll take over." A touch of sympathy warmed the somber lines around his mouth.

He was only too glad to get out of there. The broken sobs of the mother pounded his temples with each hurried step he took away from the scene. Past the doors, down the hallways to the dressing room, he almost blindly ran.

Stripping off his surgeon's cap and gown, he approached the sink. Minutes earlier, before breaking the news to her parents, he had scrubbed away her blood, watched it wash down the drain. George reached for the soap and lathered his hands, scouring the skin until it stung. No matter how hard he had worked, he had failed to stop the bleeding.

Mechanically, George scrubbed his face next. Only then did he feel the throb in his jaw. He glanced into the mirror.

Dr. Curtis, will I see you in just a little bit?

His fingers clenched the sides of the sink. Water gurgled down the pipes, the sound filling the room. If only he could pour his life into that lifeless little body, trade his breath for hers.

George's gaze traveled down to his feet. On the toe of his shoe, a missed speck of her blood cried out to him like Abel's must have cried out to God.

Guilt seared his heart like the mark on Cain's forehead.

He was no better than a murderer.

2

Ｎew York City traffic whizzed past George as the exhaust fumes, the rattles of wheels, and honks from autos mingled together like smog. Drowning out the noise, his thoughts swirled into a numbness worse than emotion.

Rather than catch a taxi, he had chosen to walk home. Each step on the sidewalk only grew heavier. He passed the shops and weaved through the other pedestrians. Sweat beaded under the brim of his hat, yet it wasn't from the heat.

I've destroyed a family.

His steps quickened as though he could outrun the thought.

"Hey, you. STOP."

A hand seized his forearm and jerked him to a standstill.

George winced and blinked into a scowling policeman's face.

"Are you deaf? I yelled three times at you. You're about to walk into the traffic." The officer pointed a billy club under George's nose.

George's attention snapped into focus. Not ten feet ahead, automobiles rolled through the intersection.

"I'm sorry, officer. I wasn't paying attention."

"That's evident enough." His Irish brogue clipped the words. "I'll not be walking you home like a young lad, so keep your eyes open."

George pasted on a polite smile. "Thank you. I will."

The officer released him. "See that you do."

When the traffic stopped, George crossed to the next sidewalk. Past the streets and blocks, he traveled until he reached his neighborhood. Flatbush. Some of the finest, well-to-do families in the city lived here, their houses nearly crushed together.

As he lifted his head, his gaze unwillingly sought the last house at the street's end—Lilith's home. A mix of buggies and autos lined the curbs. Mourners gathering already.

It was bad enough it had happened, but why did it have to be someone from his neighborhood? Why did he have to be the cause? If he closed his eyes, he could see Lilith skipping toward him, her raven curls bouncing, her eyes sparkling with a greeting.

Pain twisted his heart.

A man standing in the yard turned toward him. Tucking his chin into his collar, George dashed up the steps to his home, thrust the keys into the door, and stumbled inside. With a firm click, he locked the door and released a breath.

"Dr. Curtis, you're home a bit late." Mrs. Taylor, his housekeeper, hurried toward him to take his hat and suit jacket.

"I walked." He failed to keep the strain out of his voice.

Mrs. Taylor put his things into the closet and turned. "I heard about what happened. I'm so sorry."

The sympathy in her eyes and voice almost overwhelmed him. In the years since his wife's death, Mrs. Taylor had become like a second mother to him. A rock in the household. A buffer between him and his son.

Stephen. No letter from him in three months.

George's heart constricted. "I don't know what to say."

She stepped closer and tilted her head to one side. "There's no use in telling you not to blame yourself. Words like that won't help right now. You're pale. You need to eat. Come—"

"I can't eat."

"I know. I made my broth instead. You'll have a bit of it with one of my rolls. You'll be ill if you don't."

George forced his feet to move. "I don't have the energy to argue."

"It wouldn't do any good this time, Doctor."

In the hallway, the grandfather clock chimed the half-hour. George entered the dining room to find the bowl of broth waiting. Steam curled upward. The aroma of chicken and vegetables filled his nose and failed to comfort him.

"Mrs. Taylor?" he called.

Her steps crossed the threshold. "Sir?"

"Would you mind joining me?"

"Not a bit."

Moments later, sitting at the other end of the table, Mrs. Taylor sipped a cup of tea, her gray eyes direct and incisive.

"Dr. Curtis, I wish there was something I could do."

"Nothing will help this." The warm broth rolled over his tongue but failed to soothe him.

"Only God above."

Wincing, George clinked the spoon against the bowl harder than he intended. "Please, Mrs. Taylor."

The teacup clinked in the saucer as she set it down. A sigh slid through her lips. "I know, but I'll be praying just the same. For you and the poor girl's family."

She meant well, but George couldn't bring himself to thank her. At every turn in his life, when he had needed God the most, he had been left alone. However, now wasn't the time to argue. Of all people, he would never want to hurt her.

Mrs. Taylor cleared her throat. "A letter from Miss Steen came today."

From Ella. George closed his eyes and pressed his thumb and forefinger against them. "You and she might be my only friends left."

"Nonsense, sir. I put the letter on your desk. Could be that it might lift your spirit a little."

George doubted it. "I've canceled all my appointments for the week. It's better if I stay out of sight for a while."

After another sip, Mrs. Taylor set the cup down. "I know you're trying to be respectful to her parents, but you can't stay inside forever. Your patients need you."

"My partner has things well in hand. To tell you the truth, I don't know how this is going to turn out."

"What do you mean?" A frown pinched the skin between her eyebrows.

"Thomas threatened to stop me from practicing medicine."

"Surely not. He's your friend."

"I killed his daughter." There it was. Stark. Brutal.

Mrs. Taylor cringed and yanked a napkin from the placemat. "Don't say it like that, sir." She dabbed her lips.

"I did. And that's exactly how he sees it." George pushed his bowl away. "Can you blame him?"

"I won't listen to that kind of talk." Mrs. Taylor stood and swept her hands across her skirt as if it would dismiss the thought. "You're one of the best doctors in the city. Your reputation is impeccable. He can't stop you. Nor should you let him, Dr. Curtis. Naturally, he's devastated and angry right now, but I can't believe he would try to destroy your life's work."

Unable to meet her confident gaze, George looked down at his feet. "You didn't see his face or hear Claudia's screams," he murmured. His glass clanked against the bowl as he pushed it away, his mind filling with the memory of Lilith's ashen, lifeless face. "I'm sorry, Mrs. Taylor. This is delicious, but I can't eat right now."

Like a blind man, George stumbled out of the room and

down the hall into his study. With his fingertips, he clicked the door closed while the other hand wrangled with his necktie. He whipped it off and tossed it on the desk. It landed on a white envelope, stained at the corners.

Ella.

After rounding the desk, he lowered himself into the chair and stared at it, a groan filling his tight chest.

Since they had parted in Valley Creek over a year ago, Ella had kept her promise to write. He smiled sadly at the memory of the awkward way she asked if they could correspond with each other. Every week her letters came, detailing life in that witty style so typically Ella. Presumptuous lass.

At first, he had no intention of answering. After all, she told him he didn't have to reply. Word by word, line by line, she tugged the way a fisherman lured a catch. Before long, he had found himself with a pen clutched between his fingers, firing back his opinion on ladies wearing trousers.

I think it's a grand idea. To be free of these heavy skirts would be invigorating. Ella's voice lived through the words.

Grand idea indeed. Where are your manners, woman?

Apparently, my manners are keeping company with yours, sir. Her tart reply still brought a slight twist to his lips.

Reaching for the envelope, George slid his thumbnail under the flap and opened it. Moments ticked away on the mantle clock as her voice breathed life into the words she had written. And in those moments, he forgot the anguish of the day.

ELLA TWIDDLED a fountain pen in her hand as the fringes of a headache settled behind her eyes.

"What good does it do, anyhow?" Her voice filled the empty bedroom. Even here, surrounded by trinkets and dolls from her childhood, cheer fled. Her legs, like heavy, wooden logs, lay stiff and immobile on the mattress. Even wiggling her toes required concentration.

Ella's throat ached, yet not from pain. From wanting Mother and Father. From craving for more than life had given her. Glancing down at the lap desk, she eyed the letter she had begun.

Dear Curtis,

And that was all. No more words, nothing else came. George Curtis was nothing more than a scrawl across a piece of paper and a bittersweet sting in her heart. An urge to wad the stationery and hurl it across the room needled Ella. Was it because of him, or her condition? Pulling in a deep breath, Ella laid the pen in the lap desk and snapped it shut.

Curtis didn't care about her, not really. More than a year of writing brought no change in his letters. Not one spark of feeling or emotion toward her.

He longed for someone else. For Lorena.

If Lorena weren't her best friend and sister-in-law, Ella would've despised her. How could she fight against unrequited love? Especially now?

She needed to clear her head. Ella flung the bedcovers away, but reality crashed into her as she remembered she couldn't go for a walk.

Someone tapped at the door. "Miss Ella?"

"Yes. Come in." Ella forced a smile as the housekeeper entered.

"A visitor is here to see you. The new minister's wife, Mrs. Calloway. Do you want me to send her away?" Mrs. Hawthorne fussed with the lavender bedspread and pulled it up around Ella, smoothing it around her feet.

Ella tucked a few wayward locks into her bun. "I'd like to meet her, especially since I've heard how young she is."

"A sweet child with much responsibility, I've heard." Mrs. Hawthorne tucked her chin with a nod. "I'll get her."

Minutes later, she introduced Mrs. Calloway and left the room with a promise to bring tea.

Ella gestured to the cushioned chair near the bed. "Please have a seat. I'm very glad to meet you."

The minister's wife smiled and crossed the room, a shy flush creeping into her cheeks. "Thank you, Miss Steen. I'm happy to meet you as well."

Her vivid blue eyes reminded Ella of the blue pools near her brother's Ozark home in Valley Creek. Deep, inviting, serene. Mrs. Calloway's golden hair glistened in the sunlight streaming through the window. My! She couldn't be a day over twenty.

Mrs. Calloway glanced down at her folded hands, then back at Ella. "I hope I'm not intruding. I hesitated because I'd heard about your illness. I didn't want to bother you, but when I learned your name, I couldn't wait any longer."

"My name?" Ella frowned.

Mrs. Calloway grimaced, a nervous laugh parting her rosy lips. "I'm sorry. I'm bungling this up." She smoothed her navy skirt. "I meant your last name. My best friend was a Steen before she married. I wondered if you might be related. Her name is Lane Steen."

Like a beam of sunlight through a thundershower, joy washed over Ella's heart. "Do I know her? She's my niece, and you must be Tabitha. I can't tell you how delighted I am to meet you." Ella held out her hands, and Tabitha grasped them, her nervousness dissipating in giggles.

Ella released her. "I should've known. Lane talked so much about you that I feel as if I know you already." Unexpected moisture burned her eyes as she watched tears well up in Tabitha's.

"I feel the same. Lane described you in her letters. It's almost like being home again."

"It truly is. What would I give to be in Valley Creek now to see my brother and all those dear people." Ella's smile dimmed. "Of course, I can't now."

"What does the doctor say, if you don't mind my asking?"

"I don't mind." Ella swallowed a sigh. "He isn't sure what will happen. Some people recover, some regain the use of their limbs, others don't. If I recover, it will take months at least. The fever is gone, but I still ache and feel weak. Dr. Weaver says it takes time."

"Time can be a friend. May I pray for you?" The sincere compassion on Tabitha's face soothed Ella's spirit.

"Yes, please."

As the young woman bowed her head, Ella grappled with her doubts.

For now, time was her enemy.

3

Sunlight sifted through the gap between the curtain and window where George peered out. A fine day, indeed, but not for a funeral. Another automobile puttered toward Thomas and Claudia's house. In the hallway, the clock chimed four. The services surely were over, and mourners were gathering to offer comfort.

George swallowed hard against the lump in his throat. For days he had choked on it. A terrible thing. It wouldn't go up and release as tears, and it wouldn't go down and dissolve into relief.

How many years had it been since he cried? He remembered the very hour—his wife's funeral and not since.

"I'd give anything to cry now," he murmured.

Lilith's last words swept like a breeze over his memory. Life was a strange phenomenon, hard to comprehend. Gone in less than a blink, a fragile thread snapped forever. Yet, other times, life seized every breath and kept going past the realm of possibility.

George dug his fingers into the curtain tighter while

another auto filed past. Lilith was gone before she had hardly begun. Here he was, middle-aged, still wondering why he was breathing. Where was the fairness in it?

Behind him, a man cleared his throat. Releasing the curtain, George whirled around.

In the doorway, Joseph Wallace stood. "Mrs. Taylor let me in. She told me I'd find you here."

Guilt mixed with grief at the sight of the older gentleman, the man whom he'd revered since childhood.

George gestured toward a chair by the empty fireplace. "Come in, sir. Please have a seat."

"Only if you'll join me." As he sat down, Mr. Wallace gestured to a chair opposite. "It's been quite a while since I've seen you."

Sitting, George avoided the direct, guileless gaze. In truth, he'd only seen Mr. Wallace a few times since his return from Valley Creek over a year ago. After Lorena's rejection, George hadn't the heart to keep up a strained friendship with her father. He had missed it, though.

George rubbed his chin, his mind grappling for a reply. "You know how it is. Work and all that."

"Yes, I know."

"Have you come from the funeral?"

Mr. Wallace sighed. "Yes. There's no need to go into all of that. I came to look in on you. I'm told you haven't left the house in days."

Surprise jolted George, but he covered it with a cough. Why on earth would Mr. Wallace care, especially after he had defied him concerning Lorena? George ventured a glance in his direction. "It didn't seem right under the circumstances."

"I understand." Mr. Wallace rubbed his knee. "I've been concerned about you. If there's anything I can do, George, please don't hesitate to tell me."

The offer was too much. Other than Mrs. Taylor, no one else had bothered. Once more, George gulped against the knot that seemed to grow larger with every breath he took.

"I appreciate it, sir."

Mr. Wallace studied his fingernails a moment before pinning him with a look. "Of course, I don't expect you to ask, but I'll be checking just the same. No matter what has happened between us, I'll always care about you. I ... I wanted you to know that. Especially today."

Heaven and earth. How could he speak after that? George dipped his head, unspoken words trapped below the knot, begging for release.

"Dr. Curtis, there's a police officer here to see you."

George looked up at Mrs. Taylor standing in the doorway as she folded her hands together, her lips forming a flat line. The leather chair squeaked as Mr. Wallace turned around to look.

"Excuse me just a moment." George rose, unsure whether or not to be relieved.

As George approached the entryway, the officer shifted toward him, his arms hanging stiffly at his sides. In one hand, the officer held an envelope.

"Dr. George Curtis?" The man raised his dark eyebrows.

"I am."

"I'm instructed to give you this." He held out the envelope, and George accepted it. "Good day, sir."

Mrs. Taylor shut the door and latched it. "Whatever is it for?"

"I'll know soon enough." As George reentered the parlor, Mr. Wallace stood.

"I'll see myself out while you attend to your letter."

Suddenly, without explanation, George knew he didn't want to be alone when he read that letter. "Wait, sir. I'd like you to stay a moment. That is, if you can."

"I will." Mr. Wallace sat down again.

With the edge of his thumb, George slit the envelope and drew out the papers. Unfolding it, he scanned the words, each one like a branding iron searing his heart. His mouth grew as dry as sand.

When he finished reading, George handed it over to Mr. Wallace and clasped his hands behind his back.

Knitting his brows, Mr. Wallace plucked his reading spectacles from his waistcoat pocket and scanned the pages. A dark frown tugged down the corners of his mouth, digging more deeply into his skin with every page he read.

At last, Mr. Wallace looked up with disbelief in his eyes. "Thomas Henderson is suing you?"

"He said he'd see to it that I'd never practice medicine again." George curled his fingers into a fist and planted them in the palm of his other hand. "The amount he's after will take everything I have."

Swiping a hand over his iron-gray mustache, Mr. Wallace peered closer at the papers. "I know he and his wife are grief-stricken, but this? It was an accident, a risk they took."

"Risk or not, the result is the same. Lilith is gone." George kneaded the taut muscles in his neck. "I'd feel the same if I were in their place."

Mr. Wallace folded the papers and handed them back. "Yes, but this doesn't make it right. I have a lawyer, a good man, who can help you. Allow me to contact him. Perhaps they'll settle instead."

George's mind swam, his thoughts too quick for him to keep up. "I'd appreciate it, sir, and thank you."

"You'll be hearing from me soon." Mr. Wallace rose and shook George's hand, his kind eyes crinkling in the corners while the frown dissipated. The familiar expression made George's heart ache.

Once he was alone, he took the papers to his study and laid

them on his desk. How could he fight it? Nearly every moment since the surgery, George had reviewed every detail of that day just as he would meticulously inspect every surgical tool.

He chafed his forehead with his fingertips. The goiter had been large, causing Lilith difficulty swallowing. The procedure was only one of many he had performed over the years. Yet somehow, his hand imperceptibly slipped, piercing the artery. Neither he nor his assistant could stem the bleeding that followed.

George opened his hands as though they would give him the answers. How did it happen? Why?

"MY LEGS FEEL LIKE LEAD. I have to concentrate as hard as I can to move them." Ella's bare feet touched the rug beside her bed as Dr. Weaver lifted her into a sitting position.

He placed the earpieces of the stethoscope in his ears and pressed the diaphragm against Ella's back. She took deep breaths as he moved it from one spot to another before listening to her chest. Although she scrutinized his face, the doctor's bland expression revealed nothing.

At last, he stepped back and removed the earpieces. "I'm pleased that the paralysis hasn't affected your lungs. Move your arms for me."

Ella obeyed.

"Grasp my hands as hard as you can." He held out his hands to her, palms extended upward.

She spied the swollen knots bulging between the joints of his fingers and hesitated.

"Don't mind those." Dr. Weaver's brisk command interrupted her thoughts. "They hardly hurt. I need to test your strength. As hard as you can now."

"I'm sorry." She squeezed until the blood fled from her

knuckles.

"That's good." A hint of a smile brushed the edges of his mustache. "You're maintaining your upper body strength. Now for your legs. Can you swing them while sitting there?"

A tremor tingled up Ella's spine. "I can try." Biting down on her lower lip, she closed her eyes and dug her fingers into the edge of the mattress. An invisible weight pressed against her limbs. First, she lifted her left leg only a few inches before dropping it. Then she did the same with the right one.

Dr. Weaver's gray eyebrows drew closer together. "I don't like this. The paralysis is affecting the lower half of your body. Are you in a lot of pain?"

"At times, yes. In my knees and hips. Especially at night."

"Hard to sleep?"

"Yes, sir." Ella's pulse throbbed in her neck. "What does it mean? Will I be crippled?"

Dr. Weaver's mouth disappeared for a moment under his mustache as he pressed his lips together.

"Doctor? Please, I need you to be completely forthright with me."

He narrowed his eyes, a hint of trepidation rippling across his face. "It's hard to know just yet. It sometimes takes months."

Hope seeped away from Ella the way a river recedes during a drought.

"Miss Steen, the worst thing you can do is give up. Little is known yet about this disease, but I can tell you this from my experience with sickness: you must push through it. No matter what might be ahead of you."

"And how do I do that?"

"You must exercise your legs, get out of bed—"

"How can I get out of bed when I can hardly stand?"

"Someone must help you. You must continue your normal routine as much as possible. Get dressed each morning and have Douglas take you downstairs. Exercise your legs several times a day. Rest when your body tells you. Occupy your mind with reading, sewing, whatever you can. Get fresh air on the front porch before the heat of the day sets in."

"Douglas is busy in the fields. He leaves before dawn."

"Then rise when he does."

"He can't possibly help me get dressed!" Ella's voice squeaked despite her self-control.

A hint of impatience edged his tone. "Then have him carry you downstairs. Nightgown and all. I suggest you move into the spare bedroom down there at once. Your housekeeper can help you dress."

"She has enough duties, especially since I can't look after Caleb."

"Miss Steen, save your stubbornness for recovery and nothing more." A wry smile softened the determined set of Dr. Weaver's jaw as Ella bristled. "Do what you can to look after Caleb, when possible. I don't care if he isn't still from morning till night. Perhaps he can help you exercise your legs."

"The very idea. A young boy exercising my legs?"

"You might as well tuck away your pride and conventions too. You don't have much choice."

The truth smacked Ella like a slap across the jaw and smarted with as much pain. "You're certainly right about that."

Without replying, he reached down and lifted her legs onto the bed. Using her arms, Ella lifted herself and scooted back against the pillows.

Stepping over to the dressing table, Dr. Weaver set his stethoscope inside his bag and snapped it shut. "I'll speak with Douglas about moving you downstairs." He lifted the bag and turned. "Chin up, Miss Steen. An ounce of optimism will do more than any medicine. You may recover the full use of your legs, but you must do everything you can."

All arguments fled before the deluge of doubts and questions rising within Ella. "I appreciate your words, doctor. I don't like them, but then, I don't have to, do I?" She forced her lips to curve upward. "I'll try."

"Don't try. Do instead." He moved toward the door. "I'll be back at the week's end."

After she heard the front door sweep open then shut, Ella tipped her head back against the rosewood headboard and closed her eyes.

Heavenly Father, what am I to do? How can Douglas care for me while working the farm? And Caleb needs a mother's hand, not mine. How can I be of use here? Father, I want to be a helper, not a burden.

"Aunt Ella?"

Her eyes flew open at the small, tentative voice. A pair of navy eyes peeked around the door.

"Come, dear." She patted the mattress, her heart filling with compassion. With his dark wavy hair and eyes, Caleb was a miniature of his father, coming to the family later in life and more like Douglas than his grown siblings. Caleb's lips turned down as he edged forward.

"Why the long face, love? You know my rule. Never enter my room frowning." She teased.

A ghost of a smile flitted across the ten-year-old's face. "What did the doctor say?"

"Nothing you need worry your head about." Ella gently pinched the tip of his chin between her thumb and forefinger. "I'll be running races with you before long."

"The Good Book says it's a sin to lie."

Wrapping her arms around the boy's shoulders, Ella drew him close and pressed a kiss into his unruly waves. "It's not a lie."

Burying his cheek onto her shoulder, Caleb pressed his nose against her neck, his voice muffled in her collar. "It ain't the truth either."

"Time will tell us." Ella schooled her voice light and nonchalant.

And I dread the answer.

4

At a bang of the gavel, the courtroom exploded with yammering voices as the judge entered his chambers. George flinched and rose on shaky legs. He pushed the dismay from his expression and steadied himself.

"How many more days of this, Mr. Delmar?"

Beside him, the lawyer scooped up notes and papers and thrust them into a satchel. "If we're fortunate, a couple of weeks."

The voices, growing more animated, bounced off the walls and pounded George's ears, the intensity stupefying. He resisted the urge to rub his face. If only he could be numb to this circus.

Turning to enter the aisle, George faced Mr. Wallace. Hat in hand and the crook of an umbrella hanging from his arm, the elder man tipped his head in greeting. "There's a downpour. I've a taxi waiting."

Together they pushed and wound through the massive crowd, the air thick and charged with heat. George fixed his eyes on the back of Mr. Wallace's coat, avoiding the stares and sneers that scorched his senses, each one pinpricking his conscience.

When they approached the outside doors, George froze on the top step and gaped at the scene awaiting him. Confusion slammed into his ribs like a gut punch. What on earth was happening? Lines of reporters on either side of the steps descended to the street. Their extended umbrellas bumped and swayed together as the rain splattered onto the pavement.

Donning his hat, Mr. Wallace opened the umbrella and handed it to George before continuing down the steps. "Time to walk the gauntlet."

"There he is! Dr. Curtis!" one of them yelled.

Their questions erupted like a volley of bullets, piercing his heart. The umbrella tipped as his grip slackened. Rain pelted the side of his face, a chilling sting.

"What do you have to say to the little girl's family?"

"What's a fair price for a child's life?"

"Why did you assure her parents that everything would go smoothly? Didn't you warn them about the risk?"

"Shouldn't you call it quits after such a deadly mistake?"

"Don't you feel responsible?"

A firm hand grabbed George's elbow from behind and thrust him forward. "Don't answer. Look ahead and keep walking." Mr. Delmar's voice barked in his ear, and George stumbled ahead. Near the bottom of the steps, Mr. Wallace turned and waved them toward the waiting horse-drawn carriage.

The three of them crammed into the seat. The reporters surged behind them, shouting above the clap of thunder.

"Do you think the parents are looking for blood money?"

George ground his teeth as Delmar shouted the address to the driver. The carriage jolted forward, and the driving rain against the roof overtook the sound of the yells trailing behind them.

"Complete madness." Mr. Wallace's gloved fist thudded his knee. "To get the press involved like this."

Delmar dabbed his rain-speckled face with a handkerchief. "We can try again to settle with the Hendersons. Though your offer was generous, doctor, you'll have to offer more."

Exasperated, George walloped his knee. "Generous offer? It's a little girl we're talking about, not a house."

"I understand that, Dr. Curtis."

"Do you?" Hot anger seared down his throat and pushed against his necktie.

A shadow clouded Delmar's eyes. "Believe it or not, I do. Unfortunately, they brought money into it, and that's how you must deal with them. They want more."

Mr. Wallace pulled his pocket watch from his waistcoat and checked the time. "You might be able to meet with them today if we forgo stopping at your office."

Delmar agreed. "I think it advisable to offer them 50,000 dollars."

A mist of cold sweat beaded across George's forehead. "That's more than half of what I'm worth."

"If you wish to stop this fiasco, you had better consider it. Did you notice the faces of the jurors as Henderson's lawyer described how the child died?"

A shudder nipped down George's spine. He'd relived every moment in clarity, feeling Lilith's fading pulse underneath his fingertips, her warm blood pooling against his hand while he applied pressure to her artery. Every eye on that jury had bored into him. Heaven above, he would've gladly given all his wealth right then to bring her back.

At his silence, Delmar pressed further. "If you don't put forward another offer, you could very well lose everything you have."

With all his soul, George hated the talk of money over a person's life. He worked his jaw.

"You must do it, son."

George raised his head. How long since the gentleman had called him son? Mr. Wallace's chest rose then fell as his shoulders dipped. He snapped the pocket watch shut. "You must."

What did the reporter call it? Blood money? It galled him to no end. Those reporters didn't care, and the crowd didn't either. The case was just another docket to the stone-faced judge, a sensation for the press, and an *unfortunate* incident to the jury. Meanwhile, two parents grieved, and he ached to take it back.

Yet nothing could make it right.

SUNBEAMS SPLINTERED through the branches of an ancient oak and spilled at Ella's feet. Usually, the porch swing would be swaying with a low creak, but it took too much effort to push with her feet. Shifting the lap desk, she repositioned her pen and reread her words.

Dear George,

Time moves slowly these days.

What an opening. Ella wagged her head. Even now, she didn't have the nerve to tell him about her illness. His indifference she could swallow but never his pity.

"I don't know why I even bother anymore."

"Miss Steen?"

Pressing a hand to her chest, Ella gasped. At the bottom of the steps stood Tabitha, a bemused look curving her lips.

"Excuse me. I caught you unawares." Her blue eyes sparkled.

"You might as well go ahead and laugh, Mrs. Calloway. It's begging to break free."

Rather than cover her mouth in embarrassment as Ella expected, Tabitha tilted back her head and laughed while her shoulders shook. The musical sound drifted across the yard and drew a titter from Ella—the first in weeks.

"Come up and sit with me." Ella patted the empty spot next to her. "It's high time someone brought me back to earth."

Tabitha climbed the steps, sobering. "I really didn't mean to intrude."

"Think nothing of it. I'm glad you did. My thoughts weren't very encouraging."

The swing wriggled while Tabitha sat. "Well, then, we'll call it Providential. My husband sends word that he'll be paying a call soon if that's all right."

"He's more than welcome." Glancing down at her lap desk, Ella folded the lid closed and set it on the wicker table beside the swing.

"Writing a letter?" Tabitha quirked an eyebrow with interest.

"Staring at an empty page is more like it." Ella shrugged, hoping her voice didn't sound as hollow as her heart.

"When I was going to the academy with Lane in New York, I hated writing papers. I became fairly adept, though. If you need a little inspiration, I might could help."

A cynical smile curved her mouth. "I'm not lacking inspiration, Mrs. Calloway."

Tabitha nudged the swing into motion with her tiptoe, a note of understanding touching her eyes. "You know, you look very much like Lane whenever she was troubled. The same expression deep in your eyes. I always knew. We may not know each other very well, Miss Steen, but if you need to talk, I'll listen."

A pang of loneliness squeezed Ella's heart. "You're very kind." Taking a breath, she fingered the locket brooch at the hollow of her throat. "I'm lacking courage."

"In what?

"Lots of things, I suppose. For now, I can't find the right words to tell my friend the truth about my illness."

"The one you're writing?"

Ella nodded. "And the funny thing is that I shouldn't be worried because Dr. Curtis wouldn't be very concerned."

Blinking, Tabitha sat straighter. "Dr. Curtis? You mean, George Curtis in New York City?"

A blush bit into Ella's cheeks, the heat prickling her skin until she was certain it matched the ginger color of her hair. "The very man. I forgot that you would've known him."

"He's a gruff, lonely man. A bit of a bear whose roar is worse than his bite. He was always very kind to Lane and me, though. You're friends?"

"I hardly know the answer myself. In fact, that's why I was complaining aloud when you first came."

For a long moment, Tabitha studied her folded hands, her lips pressed in thought. When she glanced up, a wistful look shone in her eyes.

"Dr. Curtis is fortunate to have a friend like you. I know what it is to be afraid to tell the truth. Honesty often hurts." Tabitha leaned closer and rested a soft, warm hand across Ella's. "But it will also set you free. Be honest with him."

Tears pricked Ella's eyes. "I never knew I could be such a coward. This illness has paralyzed more than my legs. It has seized my heart."

"No, never." Tabitha tightened her fingers. "I don't believe that for a moment. And I don't believe it will make a difference to Dr. Curtis."

"You have no idea how right you are." Ella's laughed ended with a sob. "I've a good mind to quit writing him altogether."

"Another thing I've learned. Never make a decision when you're upset." Leaning back, Tabitha fetched a handkerchief from her pocket and handed it over. "There now. Dry those lovely violet eyes of yours. Ever since we've moved here, I've heard tales about the famous Steen lemonade. Shall I go ask your housekeeper if we might sample it?"

A faint fragrance of rose petals wafted around the handkerchief. Ella blew her nose into it and laughed. "You've come to the right place. She always has a pitcher ready this time of year. Thank you, Tabitha. May I call you that?"

Tabitha smiled. "Yes, if you'll allow me to call you Ella."

THE GRANDFATHER CLOCK in the hallway chimed five o'clock, its deep bass tone reverberating through the house. In the study, George drummed his fingers on the bookcase and expelled a long breath.

"Delmar should be here by now."

Mr. Wallace glanced up from reading a newspaper. "Perhaps they're reconsidering."

Judging by Thomas's thunderous expression at court, George doubted it. For the hundredth time, he scanned the medical books lining the shelf. His life's work. His calling. At least, he once believed so.

A knock rattled the front door. Mrs. Taylor's skirts rustled past the study, the sound sweeping down the hallway. George and Mr. Wallace held each other's gazes as firm steps snapped toward them moments later.

Without looking at either of them, Delmar let himself into the room and shut the door. Crossing the Persian rug, he approached the desk and plopped his satchel onto it. He lifted his head, a hard glint in his eyes.

"They refused every offer."

Mr. Wallace slid a hand over his mouth and gripped his chin. Even though he half expected it, George felt the air whoosh from his body as though he'd been kicked in his side. He lowered himself into the chair.

"They mean to have their pound of flesh." Delmar folded his arms. "Nothing I said persuaded them. I'm sorry, Dr. Curtis."

"No need to apologize. You did what you could." Leaning back in the chair, George stared at the ceiling and focused on a small crack near the light fixture. If he stared long enough, perhaps the wretched knot in his throat would disappear. He blinked slowly, deliberately. "I'm finished."

"We can fight this." Delmar took off his round spectacles and wiped them with a handkerchief. "You might lose this one, but you can appeal."

"And drag it out further? It might take years. I haven't the means to go beyond this trial."

"I'll do my best, but it's going to be a hard fight. Again, I'm sorry, Dr. Curtis. This was a bad case from the start."

George squinted harder at the ceiling. "I understand. I appreciate your efforts."

Clearing his throat, Mr. Wallace stood. "George, I'll see you bright and early tomorrow. Delmar, I'll see you back."

Nodding, George watched them leave, a feeling of utter desolation pressing against his ribcage, rendering him breathless. His memory resurrected Lilith's rosy, laughing face as she skipped up the sidewalk to greet him. Many times, after a long, exhausting day, her cheer dispelled his gloom.

Dr. Curtis, can we trade something today? Some days Lilith held out a shiny rock, polished by her hands. Other times, a rose from her mother's bush. A marble. Other days she would be carrying a doll who needed a doctor's care. Inviting her into the study, George would inspect the ailing toy, tend the "wounds," and make it all better.

And always, Lilith would have something to trade. Ever ready, he would exchange it with a sack of gumdrops or a lollipop. With the recovered doll in hand and a lump of candy in her jaw, she would grin her thanks and skip away, her dark curls bouncing.

George jerked his head back and forth as though it might detach the memory. Groaning, he opened the top desk drawer. Several marbles rattled toward the back of it, then ricocheted toward him. The mellow fragrance of a dozen dried roses floated upward. Ten or twelve polished rocks lay amongst the roses, an assortment of shapes and colors. Tokens of friendship. Fragments of Lilith.

He opened the drawer a little further and peered into the shadow. Dismay seized his heart. "Oh no."

A tiny doll lay smiling at him. Tenderly, he pulled it out, its size fitting perfectly in his palm.

Rebecca's arm is broken, Dr. Curtis. See? Can you fix her? One of Lilith's playmates had been too rough with the treasure.

Her brown eyes had pooled and spilled over. How could he have not agreed to fix it?

Looking down at Rebecca, George fingered the torn, cloth shoulder, wishing he could forget Lilith's next words.

Can you keep her for me until I get back home? You'll bring her back all fixed up, and we can get better together.

Lilith's surgery had been the next day.

A sound rumbled within his chest and burst from his lips in a moan. He closed his trembling fingers around the doll and clutched it to his chest. Pain and grief wrapped invisible, icy fingers around George's throat, stealing away the air.

His shoulders drooped and shook.

In the silence of his study, for the first time in years, George wept.

5

"When you go into town, could you mail this for me?" Ella handed Tabitha an envelope.

Glancing down at the address, Tabitha settled herself on the swing. "Of course, I'll be glad to. Brother Calloway and I will be going today, in fact."

"I appreciate it." Ella breathed in the gust of morning wind sweeping across the Georgia fields. Fresh dirt and pine tinged the air. Dew glistened across the lawn speckled with Tabitha's dainty footsteps leading to the porch. Through the rising haze, Douglas led his team of mules to the waiting plow. Behind him, the sharecroppers led their teams as well. A busy, sweaty day waited in the fields ahead.

"Have you heard from Dr. Curtis?"

Ella pulled in another breath. "I had a letter from him a few weeks ago. It was barely a page. He sounded preoccupied, but then, that's not uncommon."

"I know he works long hours."

An ache settled in Ella's joints. Hiding a wince, she rubbed her arms. "Yes. He'll share his patient's cases with me at times." She sighed and fumbled with the brooch pinned just underneath her lace collar. "We've been writing for over a year, but I can't tell that our friendship has grown. Perhaps it's time to put it to rest."

"You're just going to give up?"

"I prefer to think of it as letting go."

Tabitha lifted a dark blond eyebrow. "Of what, Ella?"

"A silly dream." Ella bit her lip and scraped a fingernail along the peeling paint of the swing.

Tabitha crimped her lips together. Without a word, she slid the envelope into her skirt pocket

With a bracing tone, Ella stiffened her shoulders. "You can sweep all the romantic notions from your pretty young head. I'm a spinster in my prime. I might as well enjoy it rather than waste my time holding out hope for a crusty doctor. Besides, I've been thinking a great deal about what you said. I tried to tell him about my illness and ended up wasting half a dozen sheets of good stationery. And if I can't be honest, I must end it somehow."

"I see."

"No, my dear, you don't." Ignoring an inner warning to conceal the whole truth, Ella reached up and unfastened her brooch's latch. Tabitha's eyes widened as she slid it from the lace and held it out to her.

"What are you doing?"

Ella turned over Tabitha's hand and set the etched, golden piece of jewelry in her palm. "Open it."

Tabitha blinked several times. "Are you certain?"

"Please. Before I change my mind."

Ella scrutinized her young friend's apprehensive face as she opened it. Surprise and confusion swept over her features.

Tabitha's glance flew up. "It's Dr. Curtis when he was young."

Slowly, Ella whispered, "No, it's not."

"My stars. It must be." Dipping her golden head, Tabitha peered closer.

"It isn't." Hard, sharp memories blighted any further words.

When Tabitha looked up into Ella's eyes, understanding dawned in them. "I'm listening."

Months had passed since Ella had opened the locket, the memories and feelings colorless like the photograph within.

Ella's tongue felt brittle. "His name was Charles Gibson. My fiancé. He died of scarlet fever a few weeks before our wedding."

A gasp escaped Tabitha as she straightened, pressing a hand to her chest. "How terrible. Ella, I'm so sorry. I don't know what to say."

Ella shrugged. "There's nothing to say. How could you know? It happened a long time ago, not many months after Earl kidnapped Lane and disappeared. When I met Curtis in Valley Creek, I was stunned. It was as though Charles stood before me. I'd be lying if I didn't admit I was drawn to him for that reason at first, but it didn't take a full five minutes for me to realize that the resemblance was only physical. The two men couldn't be more different." Needing to remain grounded to the present, she filled her lungs with the humid morning air. "We crossed swords from the moment we first spoke."

Tabitha snickered and covered her mouth. "I can certainly see that."

"Being around Curtis brought back all the loneliness and heartbreak I had crammed away in my busy life. Until that moment, my heart held no room for anyone else. And then, when I saw his heartache through the aloof exterior, I cared— against my better judgment. Everything about him haunted me, especially his eyes. You know, that's the greatest physical difference between Charles and Curtis. Charles had merry, dark honey-colored eyes. Curtis's eyes are the deepest, cool blue. I wanted to soothe his hurt because I understood it. Then I began to yearn for more."

Compassion filled Tabitha's face as she studied Charles's picture once again. "It's uncanny. No wonder you're torn."

"Now you see why it must end. I have two secrets that I cannot share with him."

"I should've kept my mouth shut and minded my own business."

"No, you were right." She gestured to her legs. "This is bad enough, but how could I expect him to understand about Charles?"

"I truly don't know."

GEORGE'S TEMPLES throbbed on the taxi ride back to his home. On either side, Mr. Wallace and Delmar discussed the proceedings, their voices nothing but a steady drone jumbling with his thoughts.

Five days with no end in sight. Henderson's lawyers objected every chance they got, slowed the process until George was ready to hand everything over.

Of course, there were the reporters. Their questions grew ruder and more personal by the day. One of them dared go so far as to question if he enjoyed *carving* on children for the money.

Still itching to strike the man, George balled a fist. "This has gone too far."

"We have no choice since they refuse to settle, and it isn't right to just hand over everything you've got. The jury's decision doesn't have to be unanimous for you to win or lose. If I can sway several, however, the Hendersons will lose the case. It's the only chance you have."

"I've little hope of winning, and you know it, Delmar.

They're making me sound like a butcher." George ground his teeth.

"We've still got to fight." Mr. Wallace's knuckles turned white as his fingers closed around the armrest, the carriage hitting a bump. "Perhaps there are a few reasonable men on the jury."

"I doubt it."

When they arrived at his home, George said his goodbyes and watched the carriage turn around at the end of the street. Movement caught the corner of his eye. Across the way, his neighbors, the Ellsworths, paused mid-step on the sidewalk and eyed him.

George felt his heart skip. Swallowing, he raised a hand in a small wave.

As though he were a stranger, their faces showed no acknowledgment. Turning their eyes, they snapped their heads forward and continued walking. A few houses down, he glimpsed Mrs. Phelps peering from the window. The curtain dropped closed.

Never had he felt so alone—an exile among neighbors and former friends.

His front door whipped open, and Mrs. Taylor rushed down the steps. "You'd better get inside, sir. Don't give them the satisfaction." Bending, she scooped the newspaper from the step.

While he shut the door, his housekeeper scurried ahead toward the kitchen. Rather than take the paper into the study, she passed the doorway.

"Mrs. Taylor, might I have today's news, please?"

Turning around, she paled. "You haven't missed anything this week. I'll put it in the dust pin."

George drew his brows together. "What do you not want me to see?" He extended his hand, but she took a step back.

"My husband telephoned earlier. He saw it on our doorstep. It's nothing you need to read, sir."

"That bad?" He stepped closer and opened his palm. "I appreciate what you're trying to do. It's no use. I might as well know."

Mrs. Taylor laid the folded bundle into his hand. "Very well, Dr. Curtis. Bless you, I'm sorry." Eyes glistening, her face pinched. She buried her face into her apron and dashed down the hallway. A moment later, the kitchen door slammed shut.

Dread coiled around George's chest. Slowly, he unfolded the paper, his eyes drawn to the bold headline on the front page.

Doctor or Butcher? Wealthy Surgeon Poised to Lose Everything

George slammed it onto the side table. How much could a man take? Bile rose in his throat, burning and acrid. Would they strip him of his reputation too?

For the first time in months, he thought of his former best friend, Earl Steen. A renowned concert violinist, he'd faced mockery and scorn when his life fell apart, notwithstanding it had been his fault. No matter the reason, the feeling had to be the same.

And I also scorned him.

An intense urge to flee surged through him, to drop everything and leave it all. To go where no one knew him, to live a different life. To be anything other than Dr. Curtis.

The irony struck his core.

A rap at the door slammed him into the present. Turning, he shuffled to answer it, hardly caring who or what might be on the other side.

His fellow surgeon, Alec Howard, stood there. A good, talented young man, full of promise, Alec had worked tirelessly with George, trying to save Lilith's life.

Hat in hand, Alec took half a step backward. "I'm sorry to barge in, Dr. Curtis. You look as if you haven't slept in days."

"I'm managing." George stood aside and pulled the door farther open. "Won't you come in? I'll have Mrs. Taylor put on some coffee for us."

Alec shifted his feet and lifted his eyes no farther than the loosened, skewed cravat at George's throat.

"Thank you, no. I'll be brief." A red flush darkened his neck and flooded his face.

"Very well."

"Dr. Curtis, you've been a good mentor to me, the best. You've taught and shown me, led by example. You've been a model of integrity." Flexing his jaw as though the words tasted bitter, he rotated the hat in his hands. "I know we discussed a potential partnership. I was looking forward to it." Alec blinked and raised his eyes to meet George's. Regret and apprehension mingled there. "I have a wife and child to consider, especially now that—"

"Say no more, Alec. I understand. You must look after your reputation first." George held out his hand and tried to finish with a bracing tone. "I wish you well."

His flush deepening, Alec shifted his glance up and down the street.

George let his empty hand fall to his side.

"I bid you good day, Dr. Curtis." Jamming his hat on his head, Alec dashed down the steps and skittered away, his chin tucked into his collar.

Numb, George watched until Alec rounded the corner as if a legion of demons trailed him. The quiet street seemed to hold its breath.

Indeed, I'm an exile among my own.
And I no longer belong.

6

"You've got to move them, Aunt Ella. Dr. Weaver says you must push against my hand." A sheen of perspiration glowed in the afternoon sun from Caleb's face. Gripping the bottom of her foot, he pushed.

"I'm trying." Ella gritted her teeth. Pain burned through her hips and radiated into her back.

"I'm not even having to push back." Caleb frowned.

Puffing out air, Ella plopped back onto the quilt. "Give me a moment." The soft grass and firm earth underneath the spread cradled her shoulders and back. Above her, the breeze twiddled the leaves and whispered of childhood afternoons and forgotten tromps through the woods with her brother Earl. She closed her eyes, almost there.

"Am I being too rough, Aunt Ella?" Worry edged Caleb's voice.

Keeping her eyes closed, she cloaked the pain with her light tone. "Not at all, dear heart. You're doing wonderfully. My legs just can't keep up." In truth, she could hardly move them. Today seemed worse.

The rustle of grass beneath the quilt tickled her ears while Caleb settled beside her. "Are you trying to sleep?"

"No, just thinking of other times."

"Have you ever tried to see pictures in the clouds?"

"Have I?" Opening her eyes, Ella laughed. "We spent hours picturing wild elephants and old bearded men with funny ears. All sorts of things. Look." She pointed. "Right there is a cat with a pipe sticking out of its mouth."

Caleb laughed, the sound tangling in the branches overhead. "I see it!" Moments passed as they watched puffy clouds boil and swirl into other shapes. "Do you ever see people? I mean, people that you know?"

"No, darling. Just fanciful images."

Quietness settled over him like the stillness of a deep, shady creek. Caleb plucked a sprig of grass and tossed it. "Sometimes I look for Mother."

An ache throbbed Ella's heart, but she kept her voice light and gentle. "I'm sure she's smiling down from Heaven this very moment. You know, my mother is there too. Do you think they're wondering what we're doing? You tugging and pushing at my stockinged feet? Me falling back and yelping? I bet we make a funny sight."

Caleb's laugh drifted upward again, a balm to Ella's soul. "I bet we sure do."

"Shall we try again?"

"Yes, ma'am." Rolling to one side, Caleb sat up, grabbed Ella's foot once more, and pushed. Ella felt her knee bend. Pulling in a lungful of air, she held it and focused. Pushed only a little.

"C'mon, Aunt Ella, you can do better than that."

Ella pushed again, her muscles aching and quivering. "I'm … trying."

"Don't try. Do."

Despite her growing anxiety, Ella grinned at Caleb's use of

her maxim. "Indeed, young man." She threw all her upper body strength into her hip, willing it to travel down her leg.

"Aww, I can't even tell you're pushing."

A wide shadow spread across Ella's face. "Son, I think it's time to give your aunt a break."

Air whooshed from Ella's lungs as she blinked up at Douglas. The lowering sun dipped just beneath his shoulder.

"Well, Caleb, your father has come to my rescue at last."

Caleb leaped up and cast his arms around Douglas's waist. "Did you bring me anything from town?"

A half-smile curved Douglas's somber lips. "A lemon drop." He pulled it from his pocket and flipped it into the air with his thumb. Caleb caught the tart, sweet candy with his mouth. Grinning his thanks, he scampered to the house.

"And how are you faring?" Reaching down, Douglas's callused hand grabbed Ella's smooth one and pulled her to a sitting position.

"As you say, fair-to-middlin'."

Scooting an arm beneath her knees and bracing her back with the other, Douglas lifted Ella from the ground and took long strides toward the porch.

"I ordered a wheelchair today. It'll be a while before it gets here. I hope it'll help you."

"I hope I'm walking before then."

"Could be." The lack of confidence in his voice plunged Ella's hopes further away.

As he carried her up the steps, Ella noted the dark circles under his eyes. New lines carved deeper around his mouth, the etch of responsibility and grief aging the rugged, handsome face.

He lowered her into the wicker rocker before plopping wearily onto the swing. After brushing the dust from his knees, he reached into his pocket. "This came for you."

Guilt washed over Ella as she took the letter, Curtis's bold scrawl unmistakable.

"If you'd rather I go while you read, I'll head inside."

"There's no need." Ella lifted the edge of the envelope with her thumb and gingerly tore it open. "Besides, the breeze is nice out here."

Extracting the paper, she scanned the length. No longer or shorter than usual. A little more than one page.

His greeting and words filled the space methodically recounting small matters, here and there. A recent visit from Mr. Wallace, the weather, the quietness of his neighborhood, and a bit of politics. Ella rolled her eyes. Men and their politics.

Between the words, though, unease settled over her heart. His words seemed strained, forced. Perhaps he was working too hard.

The unease morphed into embarrassment. Something unsaid lurked behind the lines. Although he was trying not to say it, the tone was unmistakable. Fingers trembling, she switched to the last page and read his closing.

Here I am, sitting alone at the close of the day. The street is buzzing with the sound of autos and neighbors' conversations. Children scamper past the house laughing. I might as well be on an island, cut off from society. Maybe it's better this way. In fact, these days, I prefer it. I do better alone.

Friendship is a fickle thing. I hardly know any that stands the test of time. I have had my fill of it.

Take care with your own heart, Ella.

Heat scorched Ella's cheeks. Plain as plain, he was fed up with answering her letters. Weary of her friendship. Without thinking, she crumpled the papers into a ball.

"Ella?" Douglas paused in mid-swing. "What's wrong?"

Darting a glance at him, she tipped her chin to hide her trembling lips. "Nothing that a good night's sleep won't cure. I'm done with wasting my time being a fool."

Her mind began to compose a proper goodbye. The sooner the better, for both of them.

"THE PROCEEDINGS WILL RESUME TOMORROW." Delmar's voice came through the telephone's earpiece thin and tinny.

Relief surged through George. Illness had forced Henderson's lawyer to postpone; an entire week lost. Most of that time, he'd spent indoors away from his neighbors. Walking in the park was out of the question. Nothing but hostile stares met him, their anger fueled by gossip and sensational headlines.

"Good. I'm anxious for this business to end."

"This will be the toughest week yet, but I'm hopeful it will be the last."

"I'll see you tomorrow. Thank you." George rang off and replaced the mouthpiece on the telephone. Entering the parlor, he told Mr. Wallace the news.

The elder gentleman breathed out in relief. "It's high time. I rather wonder if Henderson's lawyer was truly ill or not."

Shrugging, George stroked his mustache. "These days, I don't know what to believe."

"The newspapers have been horrible and the gossip despicable."

George sank into the chair opposite Mr. Wallace and kept his face placid. "I haven't told you, but I appreciate everything you've done."

"Other than refer you to Delmar, I haven't done anything."

"You're the only one who has stood with me. No matter what they're saying." Uncomfortable, he swiped a hand across the back of his neck. "I don't deserve your kindness, especially after my conduct in Valley Creek, defying you over Lorena."

Sadness touched Mr. Wallace's eyes. "That's over and done, as it should be. We'll leave it there and speak of it no more."

"That's very generous of you. I'll never be able to repay you. I'm sorry for everything that happened between us." Lowering his head, George brushed at an imaginary piece of fuzz on his sleeve. "You've proven yourself to be my friend. I wasn't such a good one to you."

Mr. Wallace raised his iron-gray eyebrows. "My boy, you stood with us during our hardest times of trial after Earl took Lane away from us. How could I abandon you now?" His dark eyes glistened like a serene ocean in the moonlight.

No judgment. No condemnation. Only sincere affection.

Feeling his self-control melting under his kind friend's gaze, George sprang from the chair and dashed to the window. Moisture, hot and wet, pricked his eyes. Though he blinked and squared his shoulders, the tears split his defenses and streaked down his heated cheeks.

Silence pervaded the room. Ever the gentleman, Mr. Wallace would never encroach on George's boundaries. He was thankful for that. If his friend came and laid a hand on his shoulder, he would fall apart.

He pulled in a trembling breath and struggled to find his voice. "You know, by the week's end, I'll be ruined."

"We don't know that yet. Delmar will do everything he can to persuade them."

Gulping more air, George braced himself on the windowsill. "It won't work, Mr. Wallace. I can tell by their faces they believe I'm a butcher just as the rest of the city does."

When Mr. Wallace didn't answer, George turned and pinned him with a stare. "You know I'm right."

For a split second, Mr. Wallace looked older than a man in his sixties. Evidence of sleepless nights ringed his eyes. His shoulders lifted and sagged.

"I pray you're not."

The half-admission rattled George even more. He shoved his fists into his pockets, recalling the jury's hardened expressions.

"I've been thinking, trying to prepare. If Henderson wins, I'll have to sell the house and auction off everything to cover the suit and the legal fees. Will you help me with the arrangements? Put the house on the market?"

Mr. Wallace stared down at his polished shoes. "Of course."

Within his pockets, his hands clenched tighter. "I'll need ... a place to stay. Would—"

"Say nothing further, son. My door is always open to you."

A few hours later, when George sat alone in his study, he leaned his aching head against the back of the chair. Outside, an auto puttered by and honked. No doubt a group of children was waving at the driver. George closed his eyes, thrusting all thoughts of Lilith aside. His thoughts drifted slowly to nothing.

A light tap on the door roused him. Had he been sleeping? A glance at the mantle clock showed a full half-hour had passed.

Mrs. Taylor opened the door, a few letters in her hand. "The postman delivered these. Looks like one of them is from the lady in Georgia."

Ella.

George sat up and took them. "Thank you." He attempted a smile. "A letter from Miss Steen always diverts the mind."

"Well, sir, you need a bright spot these days."

As she closed the door, George waited until he heard her shoes clicking down the hallway. Tossing aside the other mail, he picked up the silver letter opener and slit Ella's envelope.

Only one folded sheet of stationery lay within rather than the usual three or four pages. George frowned and withdrew it. The faint scent of lemongrass and lavender met him, a smell that both calmed and refreshed his soul—like a drink of cold water after hours of thirst.

He unfolded the rose-colored stationery and frowned deeper. Only two paragraphs graced the page, short and brief, her usual perfect script hurried and a little cluttered.

Curtis,

Life always brings change. The seasons pass with time, and we must adapt to the changes they inevitably bring. I have enjoyed this season of friendship with you. Our correspondence was honest, sometimes heated, opinionated, but never humdrum.

However, I must say goodbye. This season of my life demands it. I know you are a busy man, and I thank you for tolerating my scribblings. I wish you well in whatever life brings you in the coming days and years.

Ever yours,

Ella

The mantle clock ticked away several long minutes as George stared at her words. He re-read them three times. Then once again.

Why?

A sharp pang of loss dazed him, slicing through his heart like a thief taking him unawares. Why was she saying goodbye? *This season of my life*—

What in blazes did she mean? Was it possible she had heard about his misfortune?

George bolted from his seat, knocking over his chair. A fierce desire to shake her shoulders seized him. Instead, he shook the stationery.

Steady, man. He took a ragged breath and rescanned her words. Surely she didn't know. He couldn't imagine her abandoning a friend.

Ever yours, Ella. She had never ended her letters in that manner. She closed with *Sincerely yours.* For someone saying goodbye, it certainly spoke things he'd never sensed from her. His throat tightened.

Other than Mr. Wallace, she was the only friend he had

remaining in the world. And now, she had ended it with the flourish of a pen.

Or had she?

Ever yours ...

The ending promised rather than severed.

George's heart pounded with a fragile thread of hope. Laying aside the letter, he righted the chair and opened a desk drawer. Refusing to consider what he was doing, he retrieved his stationery and pen. If Ella wanted to be succinct, he could be as well. His pen swept across the blank space.

No, Ella, the season isn't over. It has only begun.

And he wouldn't give her the satisfaction of signing it, either.

His hands tremored a little as he folded the letter and whisked it into an envelope. After addressing it and affixing a stamp, George pressed his back against the chair cushion and stared at the missive, unseeing. Instead, he imagined her violet eyes snapping up at him, her rosy cheeks flaming. Her soft Georgia drawl sharpened with a retort he suddenly ached to hear.

Had he taken leave of his senses? Closing his eyes, George kneaded his forehead. *The strain must be getting to me.*

He was being foolish. In the morning, he would discard the letter.

Hours later, just as the city skyline blushed with dawn and the streetlamps glowed through the fading darkness, George sipped coffee and tried to ignore the sinking feeling in the pit of his stomach. By the week's end, the jury would seal his fate.

The grumbling of the lock outside told him that Mrs. Taylor had arrived. A moment later, her heels clicked over the threshold. The swish of her dressing coat and the creak of the closet hinge told him that she was putting away her things.

"Good morning, Dr. Curtis." Her jaw stiffened to bite down

a yawn as she popped her head around the doorway. "A bit cool out there, but it will warm up soon."

"Good morning. I've put on the coffee if you'd like to help yourself to a cup."

"I might just do that. Thank you, sir." She paused mid-step. "I saw your letter to Miss Steen on the desk as I was locking up for the night. I took the liberty of dropping it into the letter box on the way home. One less thing you have to worry about today."

The sinking feeling swelled into a knot. The taste of coffee turned to mud. George set the cup down on the lace tablecloth. "Thank you, Mrs. Taylor."

Smiling, she clipped down the hallway, unaware of his consternation.

I must be a glutton for punishment.

7

"I received word from Lorena today." Ella fanned the humid air sticking to her cheeks. Her tendrils, loosened from the bobby pins, tickled the sides of her neck.

Ella noticed Douglas's shoulders stiffen when he pushed away from the porch post. The smells of the fields clung to him —sweat, dirt, heat, and mules.

"And?"

"She's doing well. They've finished the house."

"Using an inheritance he didn't deserve." Douglas hardened his jaw, his teeth gnashing.

"Father left it to him. Your brother spent years, just like you did, working the fields alongside Father. He earned every penny."

"He forfeited his right the day he deserted all of us." He slapped dirt from the sides of his overalls.

"Really, Douglas, I'm merely trying to tell you about Lorena's letter, not argue about *him*." She spat the last word since Douglas still refused to speak Earl's name. The two brothers had once been inseparable.

His features darkened, the twilight's shadow settling underneath his cheekbones and sharpening them.

Ella plunged ahead. "Lorena was distressed about my condition. She says I ought to consider coming to Valley Creek this summer to recuperate."

Douglas folded his arms. "And how does she expect you to get there?"

Without answering, Ella scowled and darted a pointed glance at him.

"Do you think for one moment that I'd set foot in that place? Not even for you, Ella." His eyes scoured her features. "You're actually considering it?"

"I might." Stiffening her back, she raised herself in the wicker rocker. "I'm not much good to you here. And I don't need you to take me if I decide to go."

Douglas sighed. "You and Caleb are my family. My home is yours, and I don't want you to think for one moment that you no longer have a place here. You do. Caleb needs you. And I—"

Abruptly, he pivoted on his heel and jogged down the porch steps. Ella raised a hand to her throat, fingering the etching on the brooch.

HOURS MELDED AS ONE, and days meshed until the arguments, questions, and sounds permeated all of George's thoughts. The hardnosed accusations from newspapermen chased his dreams.

And his friends? Those he'd welcomed and entertained under his roof treated him as less than a stranger, someone not worthy of even a second look. He had helped them in their hard times. Where were they now?

In the darkness of his room, George stared up at the ceiling. Anger and grief warred for dominance in his throbbing chest.

Another face, though, slowly took dominance. Violet eyes, lips quirked upward, waves of cinnamon hair, a smidgeon of fading freckles across her nose.

Strange how her face was still so vivid even well over a year later.

And now she had cut ties too.

With a growling moan, George sat up and tossed aside the bedcovers. Musing would do no good. He rammed his arms through his housecoat and trudged downstairs to the study. After sitting, he opened a bottom drawer.

The scent of lemongrass met his nose as he sifted through a stack of her letters. Confounded woman. *Since she refuses to write, I might as well divert myself from the present.*

Pulling out an envelope, he opened the familiar stationery. Ella's flowing, artistic handwriting possessed a soothing quality. Definite, unwavering, a thing of beauty. Something he desperately needed these days. His eyes drifted to the closing paragraphs.

A cold blast of air interrupted the warm days we have enjoyed this spring, unfurling gray clouds across the azure sky and blotting out the sun. Snow sifted downward on the unplowed fields and trees, outlining the distant hills.

Then I saw Mother's dogwoods, white with blossoms, the leaves like emerald jewels encasing each flower. Of all the trees on our place, these were her favorite as well as mine.

The flakes frosted each one like powdered sugar on a confection. Hardly a more beautiful sight you'll see than dogwoods in the snow.

And yet, I was tempted to hate the sight. The glistening blanket blights the flowers, cutting their beauty short. An untimely end. In these parts, we call it a dogwood winter—winter's ebbing grasp upon spring.

Dogwood winter feels like a broken promise.

Despite the sadness, her words poured a balm over his heart. He couldn't understand the reason. Right then, he didn't even care what it might be. All he knew was that he needed this calmness to see him through even rougher days ahead.

Several hours later, after putting her words aside, George straightened his cravat for the fifth time, peering at his reflection in the mirror above the parlor mantle. Dark circles ringed his eyes. Today would seal his fate.

Behind him, Mrs. Taylor rustled in the hallway like a nervous mouse. "Dr. Curtis, my prayers go with you." She clasped a handkerchief to her quivering lips.

It will do me little good.

Before opening the front door, George patted the elder lady on her shoulder. "I thank you for everything, Mrs. Taylor. Even your prayers."

"Bless you, sir." Her voice cracked.

After crossing the threshold, he stepped briskly to the waiting taxi carriage. Setting his foot on the step, he turned a moment and scanned the tall brick building that had been his home since he brought his bride all those years ago. Like everything else in the neighborhood, it seemed to glower at him, the shuttered windows blinded from memories of happier days.

The knot in his throat returned. Would that he, like Lot's wife, could turn into a pillar of salt.

"George, we must be going." Mr. Wallace's voice propelled him forward.

THE JUDGE BANGED THE GAVEL, and shouts erupted in the courtroom. Delmar's shoulders drooped. Across the aisle, Henderson's lawyer smiled while Thomas clapped him on the shoulder. Tears streamed down his face, each one like shards of glass piercing George's soul.

"An outrage." Anger tremored underneath Mr. Wallace's

mustache and yanked down the corners of his mouth. "An utter outrage." Crimson flooded his cheeks as he rapped his gloved knuckles on the banister just behind George's seat.

Very few times since he was a child had George seen Mr. Wallace angry. Despite all the commotion and the crush of people congratulating Henderson, a merciful numbness dulled George's emotions like a fog concealing a turbulent tide beneath.

It was over.

Thomas scanned the crowd before his eyes crashed into George's. Wiping his face with a handkerchief, he shouldered his way toward him.

"You'll never take another child's life, George Curtis."

Looking down at his feet, he focused on the numbness lest his emotions shatter.

"You have nothing to say?" Thomas hissed.

He forced his gaze upward, straight into the grieving father's. "Nothing can undo it. I hope you and Claudia find healing someday. If anything I have can aid it, then it's better this way." He filled his lungs and steadied himself. "Again, I'm sorry."

"You're finished here, Henderson." Mr. Wallace snapped, brushing past Thomas. He gestured to George and Delmar. "Let's go."

George closed his ears to the rumbling that echoed along the corridor. Rather than turning toward the entrance, Mr. Wallace quickened his steps. "The taxi is waiting at the back entrance."

They hurried through narrower hallways until they exited into the alleyway. Climbing inside the carriage, Mr. Wallace blotted his forehead with a sleeve. "They've gotten their pound of flesh, but they'll not get another ounce today. The newsmen can toss questions at someone else."

"I feel like I've been convicted of murder," George mumbled, the numbness dazing him.

"They certainly made it their business to do just that."

Delmar leaned his head against the seat, staring up at the canvas top. "I'm sorry, Dr. Curtis. Are you sure you don't want to appeal it?"

"I haven't the means. Besides, I'm finished here. No one trusts a doctor who is a *butcher* profiteering on lives." George scrubbed his sweaty palms against his trousers, taking on a businesslike demeanor. "Mr. Wallace, the house must be sold and my things auctioned off if I'm to cover the debt. Will you help arrange this?"

"I'll do everything I can, son." Mr. Wallace assumed a professional tone as well. "I'm confident the house can be sold quickly. It's a desirable neighborhood. The auction must take place as soon as possible. I suggest you pack the things you wish to keep." His tone wavered only slightly.

"I haven't much I need."

The carriage wheeled through block after block, farther from the chaos. When it arrived at the lawyer's office, Delmar paused before stepping down. He rubbed his clean-shaven jaw.

"In my line of work, I have to remain detached from my clients. But I want you to know, Dr. Curtis, what happened to you was a shame. An unfortunate accident. It's one thing to compensate and another to be robbed. You won't be receiving a bill for my services."

Shock filled George. "No, you did your job well. You—"

Retrieving his satchel, Delmar frowned. "I wouldn't be able to sleep at night. I can't take it. You'll hardly have two pennies to rub together after this." He held out his hand and grasped George's in a firm shake. "I wish you all the best, Dr. Curtis, wherever you go."

All the numbness melted like ice before a fire. George

couldn't find his voice, but he hoped his face expressed his thanks.

When they were alone, riding toward home, Mr. Wallace cleared his throat. "A good man, Delmar."

"He is indeed." Far better than he deserved.

"George, come and move to my place now. There's no need staying a day longer than necessary unless you wish it."

Oh, that the numbness would return. "I don't wish it. I'll pack tonight. You can expect me tomorrow."

"You'll stay as long as you need. The worst thing to do is make any hasty decisions, especially at a time like this."

George nodded his agreement. "I need the quiet. It sounds humorous, I know, because I've shuttered myself in my home for weeks."

"Say no more. I know what you mean. A different kind of quiet. What you need is respite."

Peace.

The musty, late afternoon air tasted of dingy streets, gasoline, horseflesh, and leather. Bitterness of soul accentuated the stench.

Tranquility had evaded him like a fugitive. Always hovering around the next corner, the next successful case, another accolade for work well done. Therein lay the trouble.

He failed to earn it.

8

Lowering her eyes, Tabitha climbed into the wagon and settled beside Ella. The seat jostled as she flicked the reins.

Ella smoothed her skirt. "I'm glad you asked me to ride to town. It feels like ages since I've been anywhere."

Casting her a glance, she guided the horse down the street. "You're looking paler. I think a little fresh air and sunshine is in order."

"Just because you're the preacher's wife doesn't mean you have to be honest in everything," Ella teased, nudging her with an elbow.

Keeping her gaze fixed on the road ahead, Tabitha raised her eyebrows. Her voice dropped to a mysterious whisper. "Does that mean I shouldn't tell you about the letter?"

Ella jolted. "What letter?"

"The one I picked up at the post office earlier. From Dr. Curtis, addressed to Ella Steen. Are you acquainted with her?"

Clasping the iron armrest, Ella choked on a gasp. On either side of the main street, the tall, false-front buildings receded as the wagon carried them out of town.

"As I live and breathe. Why would he write?"

Tabitha shrugged. "Perhaps to answer your last letter." Reaching within her skirt pocket, she pulled it out and plopped it in Ella's lap.

"It required no answer. I explained everything very nicely and said goodbye." She picked it up and felt the weight. "It's very light. Probably a cool, brisk assent. Do you mind if I open it?"

Turning to look at her, Tabitha's face filled with sympathy. "Of course not."

She didn't have to be told twice. Wriggling her finger under the corner, she ripped open the flap without tearing the whole envelope. Careful not to let Tabitha notice, she steadied her hands as she removed the stationery. As always, no particular scent accompanied it. The void was like him, withdrawn. She unfolded the sheet. Two lines in his bold, black script scrawled across the space.

No, Ella, the season isn't over. It has only begun.

She read it once. Twice. Again. Her breath thinned, her heart ramming against the stays beneath her dress.

"Well." Ella's hands drooped.

"Well ... what?"

"I can trust you to tell no one?"

"Of course." Tabitha frowned, her expression concerned.

After a brief explanation of her last letter, Ella thrust the paper into Tabitha's hand. "Here."

Seconds later, Tabitha handed the stationery back and grazed her own cheek with her fingers. "My gracious, Ella."

"He must have gone daffy."

"He sounds besotted to me." A girlish snicker escaped her lips.

Ella whipped out a fan and whisked the warm air across her warmer cheek. "Yes, go ahead and giggle. I don't find it funny in the least. He's never said anything like this. Not even close."

"Poor man. You must have given him quite a shock."

"The wretched man didn't even bother signing it." Ella fanned harder. The curls around her face flew back as if she were running.

Tipping her head back, Tabitha laughed until her shoulders shook. The bubbly sound curved Ella's lips upward despite her consternation. Reaching over, Tabitha squeezed Ella's hand. "Don't you see? Dr. Curtis must care for you at least a little bit."

The curve of Ella's lips eroded the way a sandcastle shrinks against the rolling waves as doubts swirled within her mind. Folding the letter, she slipped it into the envelope and plunked it onto her lap. "No, he doesn't, Tabitha. He might have written this out of shock or perhaps at the end of a long, taxing day. I can't believe he cares."

"How can you say that?" Her exasperated tone raised slightly.

For a long moment, Ella didn't answer. The truth wedged in her throat. She tugged her lace collar.

"Ella?"

"Because he loves someone else." She swallowed. "Lorena."

Tabitha winced. "That can't be true. While I was in New York, he acted like a kind, considerate brother to her. They grew up together."

Ella gazed across a peach orchard as a breeze rippled through the branches. Near the roadside, a pair of mockingbirds perched in one of the branches and twittered.

"Yes, but he learned to care for her after his wife died. He came to Valley Creek during my last visit, intending to win her hand, but her love for Earl proved stronger. I took him to the train station the morning he left. He was bitterly disappointed."

Holding the reins in one hand, Tabitha bent and flipped open one side of a basket sitting between their feet. After handing Ella an apple, she pulled one out for herself. "It helps to have a little sweet when digesting something sour."

"Perhaps." Ella sank her teeth into the tender flesh as juice unfurled over her tongue. "I don't believe for a minute his yearning for Lorena has changed."

After chewing a bite, Tabitha swallowed. "Time often dulls passions, though."

"And time often sharpens them. Look at this brooch." Ella lifted it. "I had no room in my heart for anyone else but Charles until ..."

"You met someone who looks like him." Dipping her chin, Tabitha pointedly raised her eyebrows. "Both of you have things you need to clear up."

Cringing, Ella snatched her fingers from the jewelry. "I think I'm the daffy one. Anyhow, I won't answer ... this ... whatever you want to call it. My mind is made up."

"My heart aches for you, Ella. You might ignore it, but it's far from over."

Ella's lips quivered as she swallowed another piece of apple.

ONE TRUNK WAS ALL he retained in the world. After discharging a tearful Mrs. Taylor from her duties, George wandered from room to room, taking only one or two things to keep. Photographs, his father's journal and pocket watch, a few of his son's childhood trinkets, his mother's diamond engagement ring set in emeralds—an heirloom of several generations past. Clamping his jaw as he packed the ring box, he hoped he'd never have to sell it.

Last of all came the study. Hands on his hips, George surveyed the shelved room that housed his medical books and the classics. He drew out a medical book and thumbed through the pages.

I wasted my time.

Years of dedication and study obliterated. His fingers

tightened along the spine. A fierce urge to rip the book almost overtook him, but his reverence to the profession quelled it.

I missed my calling.

To go far away and forget he was ever Dr. Curtis was paramount. Who would trust a ruined physician for treatment? Though he still possessed his license, it was as useful as wallpaper—mere trappings. Scowling, George shoved the book into its spot. As he turned, a book in a seldom-used corner caught his attention.

His mother's Bible. Almost twenty years had passed since he'd opened it. And he wasn't about to do it now.

Still, he heard her voice reading the passages aloud. Full of faith, a righteous woman, Mam would be more appalled over his lack of faith than his loss of career and wealth.

Tentatively, George drew out the Bible. Although his religious convictions had departed, something pricked deep inside. No. No. He couldn't, wouldn't open it, but he'd pack it in the trunk instead. Mam would want him to.

And so would Ella.

The thought crashed over him like a wave, angst drenching him. These days, the lass hovered even more in his mind, haunting every step he took. After laying the Bible under a stack of clothes, George went to the desk and opened the drawer containing her stationery.

Would he leave these behind? His collar tightened as he reached down and pulled out several. Like an anchor in a raging storm, Ella's written thoughts kept him grounded and brightened his lonely existence. He'd even started reading them over since no new ones came.

After finding a ball of twine, George bound the letters into several stacks and set them in the trunk. Only one last thing to do.

He opened the drawer of Lilith's things. Mechanically, he worked, choking down his grief and the sound of her lisping voice. One by one, he placed them into a waiting shoebox. Rocks, marbles, dried roses, and the tiny doll with a ripped shoulder. The ending of a chapter in his life.

An interlude he never wished to visit again.

Setting the shoebox inside the trunk, he closed the lid and secured the straps. His fingers brushed the wood. Everything remaining of his life and profession lay inside.

I'm finished being a doctor. I want no part of it. The sounds of Lilith's fading rasps of air shuddered through him. Another accident would be too much to bear.

The next morning brought him early to Mr. Wallace's doorstep. As the housekeeper ushered him inside, Mr. Wallace hurried into the foyer to greet him.

"My boy." He clapped a firm hand on George's shoulder. "Welcome. I'll send for your things in a while. Have you had breakfast?"

George smiled, feeling at home for the first time in weeks. "No, sir. I discharged Mrs. Taylor yesterday and was anxious to get here as soon as possible."

Nodding, his elder friend gestured toward the dining room. "I thought as much. There's a place already waiting for you."

"I marvel at you." George shook his head. "You always seem to know. It mystified me as a child."

Mr. Wallace chuckled as they entered the dining room. "I like to keep people guessing." After they took their seats, Mr. Wallace bowed his head and gave thanks. With respect, George closed his eyes and listened.

Ending the petition, Mr. Wallace reached for a napkin and spread it in his lap. "Now, while you're here, my home is yours."

George fought the waver in his voice. "I can't thank you enough."

"Say no more." Mr. Wallace salted his eggs. "I'm sure you'd do the same for me. Today, I thought we'd begin the process of setting up the auction of your belongings, draw up announcements, put your house on the market, etcetera. Just so you know, my firm won't take a dime on this. That way, you should be able to walk away with several hundred dollars. I hope."

Gratitude and relief eased the pang of losing everything. "It's more than I ever expected. I'll never be able to repay you. Thank you, sir."

Looking up, Mr. Wallace's dark, perceptive eyes met his, an unmistakable peace shimmering through the windows of his soul.

All at once, George's spirit felt like a blighted wasteland where the wind roared hot and wild.

THE DIAPHRAGM of Dr. Weaver's stethoscope trekked a slow circle over Ella's back. "Again." Dr. Weaver commanded, his face impassive. Ella pulled in another deep breath. Removing the earpieces, the doctor folded the stethoscope and placed it in his bag.

"Your lungs and heart are strong, I'm pleased to say. But your legs have gained no strength." He frowned, his eyebrows pinching a line across the skin between them. "I daresay they're weakening. Are you exercising them?"

"Caleb helps me every day."

"It isn't enough. You must push harder, or you'll lose the use of them altogether."

Goosebumps pebbled Ella's skin. "You're not known for your tact, are you, Dr. Weaver?"

"Tact doesn't get the job done in my profession." He folded his arms, his expression hardening. "I'm not unsympathetic to your plight, but the rest of your recovery depends upon you."

With a groan, Ella struggled to lift her leg, the weight heavier than ever. "I'm not looking for your sympathy. Believe me, I know. It doesn't seem to matter how much I exercise them."

His expression softened, allowing a glimmer of understanding. "As long as you're able to move them even the slightest, that's good. There's room for partial to complete recovery there. Whatever you do, no matter how frustrated you get, don't stop trying to use them."

"I won't."

The leather of Dr. Weaver's bag creaked as he shut it and grabbed the handles. "I'll see you in a week."

After the front door banged shut, Ella bit her lower lip to quell the throttling tears.

Heavenly Father, help me.

The moisture overflowed and spilled down her cheeks no matter how hard she chewed her lip. The flow paid no heed to her will. Just like her legs.

Not once since her illness had Ella allowed herself this moment, and it repaid her restraint with a vengeance. Her surroundings melded into a watercolor of hours and weeks of pain, weakness, regret, and frustration.

She longed to walk, to move freely. She missed the open fields, the peach orchard, running with Caleb, all the simple things.

Most of all, she missed those brisk, impersonal letters from a crabby, middle-aged widower whose heart belonged to another. Ella yanked a handkerchief from her pocket and scrubbed her face until the living room focused into view. On the rosewood side table lay her lap desk. The words she yearned to say about her plight and her secrets urged her forward, erasing all thoughts of her legs. She pushed herself up.

In less than half a step, Ella crashed onto the rug, the fibers searing her palms. The sound rumbled through the hallway and brought Mrs. Hawthorn's scurrying steps.

"Miss Ella! Miss Ella!" She knelt, wrapping an arm across her. "Are you badly hurt?"

Ella sniffed. "Only my pride, mostly. For a moment, I forgot about my legs and took a step." Turning over, she allowed Mrs. Hawthorne to help her sit up.

"Bless your heart, ma'am. You've scuffed your hands. I'll send Caleb for Mr. Douglas, then fetch the ointment." She stood and smoothed her apron.

Fingering her haphazard, coiled bun, Ella extracted a few hairpins. "Can you bring an ointment for foolishness while you're at it?"

A hearty laugh shook Mrs. Hawthorne's shoulders. "You beat all, ma'am. I would be bawling, and here you are, making a joke."

"Apparently, I do things backward." Holding the coil of hair in place, Ella pushed in the hairpins. "I bawl first, then fall."

"Oh, ma'am." Turning to go, Mrs. Hawthorne giggled and swatted her ample thigh. Moments later, her yells for Caleb to come down from a tree overflowed the yard.

Filling her lungs slowly, Ella closed her eyes and slowly released the air. At least she didn't break a bone.

Just a reckless wish.

9

I learned a long time ago that feeling sorry for myself stole joy more than any grief I bore. With the Lord's help, as the Apostle Paul said, I have learned to be content in whatsoever state I am.

Tonight, however, Ella's voice failed to soothe him. George closed his eyes and massaged them, easing the weary ache. On the table beside his chair, the dressing clock pointed to one o'clock in the morning. The plush pillows on the mahogany bed beckoned to him. For the first time in two weeks since moving to Mr. Wallace's, sleep tugged the corners of George's eyes. He yawned.

Still no word from Ella. The vexing lass must have truly meant it. All evening, his fingers itched to share with her the upheavals in his life— Lilith, the lawsuit, the auction of his possessions, putting his home on the market, and resigning from the hospital. At the same time, the thought of telling her made his blood run cold.

A flicker of pride and hurt throbbed until his heart stung. Well, if she wouldn't write him and if he couldn't summon the nerve, he would do the next best thing. Get it out of his system.

Rising from the chair, he crossed to the small desk, whisked sheets of stationery from the drawer, and plucked up a pen.

Dear Ella,

Words poured from the pen like a spewing geyser, starting from the beginning, sharing his friendship with Lilith and recounting the accident. Her death. One letter, two, three, four, and five. He sealed each one and scrawled Ella's name across the front. Every pent-up emotion flooded those pages while draining his heart. Every thought, every feeling, waited for her eyes only.

Yet she would never read them. The thought of it prickled a mist of sweat across his forehead. What would she think of him if she knew?

He stacked the letters into the trunk and glanced at the clock. Three in the morning. He was spent.

After trudging to the bed, George switched off the lamp, and darkness engulfed the room. He slid beneath the covers. Somewhere, blocks away, an automobile honked.

In the inky blackness, George saw Ella smile, her sparkling eyes easing the strain of the day. For the first time in weeks, sleep captured him and didn't release its hold until mid-morning.

The ten o'clock chime from the hallway clock jolted him awake. Throwing back the covers, George scrambled to get dressed. He dragged a comb through his thatch of thick, brown hair, donned his clothes, and hustled downstairs.

"Good morning, Dr. Curtis." Mrs. Reid smiled as she exited the dining room. "I heard you shuffling upstairs, so I set your breakfast on the table. Mr. Wallace gave me strict instructions not to wake you." She winked. "Let's see. If I remember, hash browns are your favorite, right?"

"You're a treasure, Mrs. Reid." George chuckled. "I'll eat every bite."

True to form, Mrs. Reid set a mouthwatering spread that

brought him back to his college years. Hash browns, eggs, and bacon graced the table alongside blueberry muffins. Immediately, he noticed there was no newspaper, which meant no disgraceful headlines to confront. Gratitude overwhelmed George. Mr. Wallace's thoughtfulness knew no bounds.

While he munched on the last bite of blueberry muffins, the doorbell rang. Wiping his mustache and lips, he pushed the chair away from the table.

"I'll get it, Mrs. Reid." He stepped into the hallway just as she bustled from the kitchen. A stab of apprehension struck George under the ribs. Suppose it was a newspaperman? He probably should've let Mrs. Reid answer it instead.

George touched the doorknob, his mind reeling with the memories of their shouts, their insolent questions.

Doctor or Butcher?

Shaking his head, he wrung away the thought and turned the knob. Dressed in a simple brown suit, a short, wiry man peered at him through round, tortoiseshell eyeglasses.

"I'm looking for Dr. Curtis. Could I have a moment of his time?"

George's heart shriveled up into a tight ball. "I'm George Curtis. What do you want?" He cared little if he sounded brusque.

Not a flicker of offense rippled across the man's face. "Dr. Curtis, I'm pleased to meet you. I'm Dr. Benson, not a reporter. May I come in?"

Masking his relief, George stepped aside. "Please come in. The parlor is this direction." Watching Dr. Benson cross the threshold, George cleared his throat, "I apologize for sounding abrupt just then."

"Think nothing of it." Dr. Benson hung his hat on the stand and followed George. "I'd avoid them too. The headlines were vile."

"So were the questions." George offered a seat before taking one himself.

"You're a better man than me. They would've hauled me to jail after the first day for punching one of them, especially that tall, loud one always at the end of the line."

George raised his brows. "You were there."

"I was. Every awful day, usually at the back of the room."

"But why?"

A sheepish look turned Dr. Benson's lips downward. With a squirm, he shifted the glasses on his nose. "I'd heard about the case and wanted to know what happened and why. Thomas Henderson's attorney no doubt swayed the jury, but it was clearly an accident. Could happen to any doctor, no matter how skilled. I'm a surgeon as well."

"I see." Crossing his arms, George narrowed his eyes. "What I'd like to know is why you want to see me."

"As I said, I'm a surgeon. However, I practice in a much less affluent part of the city. I mostly treat children." He leaned slightly forward, his gaze unwavering. "Most of their parents are too poor to pay medical bills, so my clinic relies on benefactors to cover the costs to help these families. Mr. Wallace is one of them. And, no, he didn't send me here. We need someone like you, Dr. Curtis."

"Now—"

"Of course, the salary isn't nearly what you're accustomed to receiving, but it's a start. The families would be fortunate to have you."

A needle could've tipped George over. He rubbed his chin, the stubble from a missed shave pricking his fingers. "Dr. Benson, I appreciate your offer. Truly, I'm honored by it. You must know, however, I made several mistakes. I diagnosed and treated the daughter of a friend. I should've referred her to a doctor who wasn't personally involved with her family."

"Most people won't hold you responsible for that. Her

family naturally wanted the best. But even the best can make mistakes."

The truth of the statement rankled George. "I can't go through that again. I've promised myself that I'll never pick up a scalpel, let alone practice medicine."

Dr. Benson spread his hands apart. "Your skill is badly needed, whether you like it or not." Sighing, he gentled his tone. "I ask you not to be hasty with my offer."

Sadness enveloped George, and he shifted his eyes from the eager man's face. "Your vote of confidence, especially during this time, means more than you'll ever know. To risk having me at your clinic might jeopardize the funding. I know several benefactors who would forget their *generosity* if I were there. I thank you, but I must decline. It's not because I don't want to. I can't. Instead of the patient, I would see Lilith, and that's especially dangerous."

Silence permeated the parlor for several long moments. Finally, Dr. Benson shifted to the edge of the chair and stood. George followed suit.

"What a shame. The medical field is losing a rare talent. I'm sorry." He held out a freckled hand.

George accepted the firm shake, a polite reply withering on his tongue.

"Thank you for hearing me out."

When they approached the door, Dr. Benson put on his hat. "One thing more. Promise me this. When the time demands for you to be a doctor again, you'll answer the call no matter where you are."

Wincing at the man's steady, knowing gaze, George opened the door and hesitated.

Dr. Benson crossed the threshold and partly turned. "No matter where you are."

George's mouth ran dry. "I promise."

"Godspeed, Dr. Curtis." Dr. Benson touched the tip of his hat and continued down the steps.

While the man turned the corner, George stood watching on the top step, motionless.

"Hey, mister." A young boy stepped around the corner of the house, his cherry cheeks bulging as he puffed for breath. He tucked a baseball glove in the nook of his arm. Shuffles and whispers skittered unseen behind him.

"Can I help you?" George descended a step.

"We was wondering if you're the butcher. The one in the newspapers. You look like 'im." He spat on the ground.

Despair locked its fingers around his throat and strangled him, rendering him bereft of words. Like a caged animal, George glanced around, seeking escape.

"Come on before he gets you." His friend dashed out and yanked the boy's arm, dragging him out of sight. The pounding of footsteps retreated between the houses.

The hasty words ripped through every defense and every wall, slicing straight to his soul. He was trapped, a spectacle for people to gawk at.

How could he possibly escape?

"Dr. Benson is an excellent doctor. Are you sure you won't reconsider his offer?" Mr. Wallace stretched his legs while sitting on the park bench.

George leaned his shoulder against an elm. Looking up, he focused on the aged, gnarled branches twisting and reaching upward, an emerald canopy over the rising heat. Shade or not, he shivered when he remembered the boys' taunts.

"Nothing can persuade me otherwise."

"A shame, but I can hardly blame you. Perhaps someday you'll reconsider."

A bitter laugh steeled George's resolve. "No, sir, not if I have anything to do with it."

"I telephoned you to meet me here because I might have a buyer for your house."

George glanced away from the canopy, his interest piqued. With a quick swipe, Mr. Wallace flicked a bug from his suit trousers. "A lawyer. He looked at it this morning. He's very interested. His offer was a little low, of course, but I think he'll come around."

A long breath seeped from George's lips. "He'll have to if I'm to cover my debts."

"The house is a sound investment in an excellent neighborhood. He won't lose anything by paying our asking price. And he knows it." Mr. Wallace removed his hat and wiped his forehead with a handkerchief. "I'm determined that you get at least several hundred dollars out of it. It's not much, I know."

"It's more than I expected, Mr. Wallace, and I'm grateful for it."

Not far away, a mail wagon clattered down the street, loaded with an assortment of boxes.

"Have you heard from Ella lately?"

Her name, spoken aloud after so long, zipped like a refreshing breeze through George's parched spirit. "No, sir."

"Ah, you'll get one soon enough, I'm sure. Might be on that wagon." Mr. Wallace's gray eyes twinkled, his affection for the lass evident.

Again, George tilted his head and listened to a twittering sparrow overhead. "I doubt it. She sent a polite note saying goodbye."

"Did she?" The gentleman's brow furrowed. "I wonder why. It doesn't sound like Ella."

"I sent a reply, but she hasn't answered." George laughed without mirth. "It couldn't have happened at a better time, could it? When your friends start abandoning ship, it's like watching dominoes topple."

"Did you tell her what happened?"

George swiped at a fly. "Not a word."

"Even if you had, I don't for a minute believe Ella would cut off her friendship. There must be something else."

"She said this season of her life demanded it."

Mr. Wallace blinked several times and scratched his temple. "It sounds like she's trying to tell you something without saying it."

Despite his calm exterior, George's frustration boiled to the surface. "The entire letter was like that. Every line."

"And do you care?" Mr. Wallace narrowed his eyes.

"I don't know." George folded his arms, ignoring the sting within his heart. "The lass baffles me, confounds me. She's a troublesome nuisance. I'm better off left alone."

"Yes, I can see that."

George glared at Mr. Wallace, whose solemn expression belied a twitch beneath his salt and pepper mustache. He vehemently wished he'd never met Ella Steen in the first place. Their correspondence had stoked a flame of friendship he'd never sought. She wormed her way under his thick skin then relinquished it. Why had she disturbed his existence?

"What are you going to do after the house sells?"

Taken aback by the shift in conversation, George's mind whirled. "I don't know. There's nothing left for me here."

"You need a fresh start. Although, without doctoring, I don't know what you'll do."

The taste of bitter helplessness recoiled George's tongue. "Maybe I could be a clerk somewhere. I don't know. I'm good with numbers. Perhaps an accountant. Or I could become a dentist. Pull teeth."

"It's possible." Mr. Wallace extracted his pocket watch and

checked the time. "Until then, I'd say you have some unfinished business to settle first."

"Have I missed something?"

"I think so, son. Her name starts with an *E*."

"You mean *exasperating*?"

Chuckling, Mr. Wallace snapped the lid shut and slid the watch into his waistcoat. "If you still possess your sense of humor, there's hope for you yet." He sobered. "Ella wouldn't stop writing unless the reason was serious."

The suggestion arrested him, and he covered his sudden concern with a cough. He ciphered her words through his memory. *This season of my life demands it.* Was she ill? Engaged?

His breath thinned. "What do you suggest I do? Pack up and head to Georgia? Just like that?"

Mr. Wallace studied him long and hard until George dug his shoulder a little harder into the tree's bark. "What else have you to lose?"

The question shattered his thoughts, splintering every argument like an explosion. Indeed, what did he have remaining? His reputation was destroyed, his career wrecked, his possessions divided among the highest bidders, his wealth dissolved, his friends vanished, and his home an empty shell.

The sounds of the city, teeming with activity and life, buzzed around him. A group of children shouted as they tossed a ball nearby. A few of them glanced his direction.

Icy dread cinched his chest, cornering him in places he craved to forget, and he turned away from their ogling eyes. "Absolutely nothing."

10

July 1912

"Write when you're settled, and please let me know how Ella fares." Clapping George on the shoulder, Mr. Wallace tightened his grip.

Returning the gesture, George struggled against the rasp in his voice. "I can't thank you enough for everything you've done for me."

"I'm glad I could."

Behind them, a loaded luggage cart rattled toward the train's baggage car. Loud voices and hurrying footsteps clattered throughout the station. The engine's shrill hissing blanketed the sounds of busy goodbyes. George's heart thrummed in rhythm with the noise.

"I'm in your debt."

Mr. Wallace shook his head, an apologetic look entering his eyes. "Nonsense. Just take care of yourself. I'm sorry you have only 150 dollars after everything was settled. Less than I hoped."

"I can assure you, it's more than I hoped to walk away with."

George straightened his black derby hat. "I'm free and clear. That's enough for me."

"Have you written Ella?"

"No, sir. I decided I'd take her by surprise. You know, a little turn about fair play."

A chuckle rumbled in his friend's chest. "I've no doubt it will be."

Calls of "all aboard!" rose above the organized chaos. George threw a glance over his shoulder at the train. Without warning, two strong arms engulfed his shoulders and pulled him forward. Mr. Wallace's voice wavered near his ear.

"Shake the dust off your feet, my boy. Look only ahead. My prayers go with you." He released him and stepped back.

Burning tears rushed to George's eyes. To hide them, he stooped and snatched up the briefcase leaning against his leg. "I'll not say goodbye, Mr. Wallace." The remnants of an Irish brogue from early childhood thickened. He and his parents had voyaged across the ocean to this grand city when he was a six-year-old lad. His father had become Mr. Wallace's employee and valued friend.

"Your family was the first to welcome my family here. Now, you're the last to see me off. Until our paths cross again, my friend."

Forcing his stiff lips to bend upward, George turned, climbed into one of the cars, and trudged toward the first available seat. From the window, he glimpsed Mr. Wallace waiting for its departure. One by one, as the cars filled with people, the knot in George's throat swelled.

A while later, the train whistled, and steam spewed across the platform. In his mind, George saw the black smoke puffing from the stack in time to the engine's chug, each one growing a little quicker with the turn of the wheels. As a child, he had been mesmerized by the swift, powerful machines.

Outside the window, the crowd waved to their loved ones

on board. Near the front, Mr. Wallace lifted his hat. George's heart shrank into a tight, throbbing ball. He raised his hand to the gentleman, the truest friend he'd ever known. They'd faced many things together. He'd seen Mr. Wallace come back from the brink of death.

Would he ever see him again?

As building after building slid past, George's eyes skimmed them. Many held memories of a lifetime. Then, beyond them, his mind rambled farther into the past, into a lush, flowered yard. A tea party between two little girls interrupted by a boy dangling a lizard. The lizard dropped onto the quilt, leaving behind its wriggling tail in his grubby fingers. Just as he knew it would.

The shrieks brought a soft smile to George's lips as he remembered Lydia and Lorena darting around while he gave chase. Mrs. Reid had scrambled into the fray, yelling, "George Curtis, you naughty boy! Stop this minute!" The memory of his stinging backside nearly brought an untimely laugh.

If I'd known I were chasing my future wife, I would've never dropped the tail into Lydia's apron pocket.

She never let him live it down. Nor did Lorena.

Shutting his eyes, George clamped down on the memories and leaned his head against the back of the seat. Both were lost to him forever.

A THROBBING ache stabbed behind Ella's left eye as she gawked at the contraption in front of her. A wicker back framed in wood, armrests, and two enormous wheels on either side.

"It's a wheelchair." Caleb rubbed a polished wooden arm. Beside him, Douglas laid a hand on his shoulder.

"Yes, I see that." Ella clipped the words constricting her throat. Even though she had expected its arrival any day, her reaction stunned her. Seeing it seemed final, like the thud of dirt spattering a coffin.

"Are you all right?" Concern sharpened the corners of Douglas's eyes.

"I'm fine." She twiddled with her brooch, skittering her glance away from the chair.

"I can see that." Douglas turned to his son. "Caleb, I'd like a word with your aunt. Go get some lemonade."

The youngster didn't have to be told twice. Ella only wished she could scamper away with him for a glass of the sweet, tart liquid.

"You act surprised. I ordered it with only the thought of helping you." His low, gentle tone did nothing to mollify her.

She sucked in a quaking breath. "I know, Douglas, I know. And I thank you, truly. Now that I see it, I feel like ... like ..." She whipped out a handkerchief and pressed it against her mouth, hating herself for crumpling under the pressure of his perusal.

"Here now, Ella Mae." The porch swing dipped under Douglas's weight as he sat and scooted closer to her. He patted her back awkwardly, remaining silent.

Ella gulped more air. "I'll never walk again, will I?"

Douglas shifted and turned his face away, the muscles of his jaw taut. "I don't know."

His hesitant tone plunged her emotions farther from self-control. "Oh, Douglas." The anguish she'd locked away gushed from her eyes. How could she do this in front of her brother? He had burdens and grief enough, yet here she was, falling apart.

Without warning, he gripped tight fingers around her shoulders, jerking her toward him.

"You can't do this. Not now, when you've come so far."

She wilted in his grip.

"Stop it." He gave her a quick shake. "Ella, I don't know

about your legs, but I know about you. You're strong. You'll see this through, walking or not." His voice lowered into a resolute whisper. "We all must."

The strength from his fingers fused into her spine. Blinking into Douglas's darkened navy eyes, Ella lifted her chin. "You're right. I'm sorry."

"Don't be. I know this isn't the time or place you'd choose." Releasing her shoulders and standing, he thumped the back of the wheelchair. "It's my clumsiness. I should've prepared you rather than carry it up the steps and plop it down in front of you."

A watery, overwrought giggle sputtered from her lips. "You've never been famous for delicacy."

"I wouldn't start pointing fingers if I were you." He quirked an eyebrow.

Ella blew her nose. "Tact thins with age." She pressed a hand against her warm cheek. "I do appreciate your thoughtfulness, Douglas. I know it'll help."

"And you'll continue your exercises?"

"As long as I'm able to wiggle a toe."

The screen door burst open as Caleb kicked the bottom while clutching two sweating glasses of lemonade. Water dripped from the bottom of the glass and splattered on the floor.

"Here you go, Aunt Ella." The golden liquid glinted in the sunlight passing through it.

Deep affection filled her heart. "You know how to refresh a soul, don't you, Caleb? Thank you, dear."

Caleb beamed, watching her take a long sip. "Just what the doctor ordered."

"And I couldn't ask for a better one." Smacking her lips, Ella winked and raised the glass for another, ignoring the memory of another, faraway doctor.

———————— ❧ ————————

DOGWOOD WINTER FEELS like a broken promise.

The rhythmic clacking of the tracks carried George into the present. Across the aisle, a man snorted and flinched in his sleep. Already New York City seemed a thousand miles away.

He folded Ella's letter and placed it within his briefcase. Minute by minute, the speeding steam engine carried him farther south away from his home and his life, away from everything he knew. Yet the familiar had transformed into an enemy.

Where will I go from here?

Without his calling, he was cut adrift like a raft in the midst of a swelling ocean on a cloudy night. A rolling darkness with nothing to guide him.

And what of Ella?

Striving to quench the anxiety that rose inside, George methodically laid out a plan in his mind. First, he would find out what happened. He would ask why she stopped writing. If she agreed, he would spend time getting to know her and Douglas better.

Also, he would look for a job and a place to live.

In that instant, the shock of a revelation bowled over his little plans. For the first time in his life, he was homeless. So caught up in Lilith's death, the betrayal of his friends, and the loss of his career, he'd barely stopped to think of it. Sure, he'd lost his house. He'd auctioned his possessions. But he'd been engrossed in the details.

Until now.

He had no home. He was alone.

George swiped his forehead with shaky fingers, glancing around the car. A little way down the aisle, a pale mother wrestled her squawking toddler onto the seat. A gentleman lowered his paper and glowered at them. An elderly lady gazed out the window as she knitted, unperturbed by the commotion. In a train full of people, he was alone. No place to go, no one to turn to.

No, never alone. No, never alone. He promised never to leave me, never to leave me alone.

His mother's singing drifted from a forgotten place, forging through the turmoil of his mind.

The world's fierce winds are blowing. Temptations sharp and keen; I have a peace in knowing my Savior stands between. He stands to shield me from danger when earthly friends are gone: He promised never to leave me, never to leave me alone.

His father's voice joined hers, the deep timbre of his Irish brogue melding with her soft melodious one. A sweetened pang filled the empty places of his heart where his faith once resided.

Ah, Mam and Da. What would you say now?

If only he could forget the words, forget everything. No matter where he turned, the rubble of his crushed faith confronted him everywhere. In the breeze skimming Lydia's daffodils during springtime. A singing sparrow perched on the eaves of the house. The quiet street of an early Sunday morning. Church bells. Lilith's smile.

To forget or remember? Which was worse?

Reaching into the briefcase again, he pulled out another of Ella's letters. Her lithe voice abated the gnawing of his conscience.

I have never been one to give up easily or to make a decision lightly. Actually, I should amend that last statement. When I was a child, if a task proved too hard, I would burst into tears and leave it unfinished. Also, Earl and I got into more scrapes from silly, imaginative ideas that would leave either one or both of us bruised and bleeding.

Mother cured me, though. If I gave up on a task, she put the knitting needles in my hand. Many afternoons I knitted, longing to be outdoors all the while. When I made a hasty decision, she put pencil and paper in my hand. Many an essay I wrote on the wrongs of haste.

Now that I think of it, it's a wonder I'm writing to you.

Indeed. Everything about Ella Steen was a wonder. Even now, he marveled he was on a train bound for Georgia. Why?

Because he was homeless? Curious? Or was it something more?

George sighed, weariness pressing heavily on his eyelids. Moving forward might be necessary, but he needed answers of himself and her.

11

W agons, buggies, and a few automobiles lined the circle
drive of the yard. George paused mid-step and inhaled
the thick, hot Georgia air, feeling the sunshine rake over his
shoulders. For the last half-mile, he had walked up the shaded
driveway, the tree branches an intertwining archway. He wished
to retreat into its cool relief.

Flanked on each side by an oak, a large, two-story, pale
yellow house with a steep roof commanded his attention. A
long porch yawned across the entire front. Somewhere from
under it, a dog barked, unwilling to leave the comfort of the
shade.

Other than the occasional stamping of a horse or the
swishing of a tail, the yard was eerily still. Silent. Like the
aftermath of a funeral.

The icy thought squeezed George's heart. Suppose
something had happened? Was Ella—

The briefcase clutched in his clammy palm dropped to the
ground. Without further thought, he sprinted across the yard
and the brick walkway and bounded up the steps. Yanking

open the screen door, he stepped unannounced into the entryway, all manners forgotten.

The hallway was vacant. A muffled sound drifted toward him, perhaps from the parlor. Was he too late?

He dashed toward the sound and burst into the room.

A collective gasp thickened the humid air. Ten pairs of eyes widened and fixed upon him. In the center of the room, ladies sat around a quilt fastened to a wooden frame. They held their needles suspended in mid-stroke, their jaws slightly ajar.

"As I live and breathe."

Following the voice, George's eyes fastened upon Ella sitting on the other side of the frame. Indeed, she lived and breathed, if not a little angrily. Her violet eyes glittered with, could it be, panic?

Unexplainable relief surged through him, sweeping into focus all the manners he had dropped outside the front door.

"Miss Steen, please excuse me. You see, I was passing through and thought to pay you a call."

One by one, amusement twitched the ladies' mouths as they relaxed their needles. One of them pushed back her chair a little and stood. Sunlight through the window gleamed through her golden tresses.

"It's wonderful to see you again, Dr. Curtis." She turned slightly to Ella, who was still sitting, her mouth slack. "Sister Ella, since I'm already acquainted with our friend, might I offer him refreshment while you continue entertaining your guests?"

As he lived and breathed. What in blazes was Tabitha doing there?

Ella blinked as though stumbling out of a fog. "Yes, of course, Sister Calloway. I thank you."

Tabitha stepped across the rug and brushed past him, beaming. "This way, Dr. Curtis. I'll show you to the dining room."

Struck dumb, he swiveled on his heel and followed her

across the wide hallway. On the wide floor planks, his shoes snapped louder in the silence, the sound undoubtedly sopped up by the ten pairs of ears in the parlor.

Once the dining room door clicked shut, Tabitha's hands flew to her cheeks. "Dr. Curtis!" she laughed. "You've no idea what you've just did. I mean, done."

Ah, so the girl still had lapses in grammar. He resisted a smile. "What are you doing here?" He reached out, took her small hand in his, and gave it a slight squeeze.

She flushed to the roots of her golden crown. "You're asking me?"

George released her hand, the heat roaring from his neck into his face. "You have me there. How's Frank faring?"

At the mention of her husband, her blue eyes twinkled. "He's doing very well. He'll be so glad to know you're here, which by the way, you still haven't explained."

"It's a long story. I'm sorry I bumbled in like this. When I saw all the buggies and automobiles, I thought something might have happened to Ella."

"You thought it was a funeral?" Her sandy eyebrows raised.

Grimacing, George shrugged and turned his palms upward. "I haven't heard from her in a while. I thought I'd look in on her while I was traveling through."

Tabitha moved to the oak sideboard and drew out a plate and napkin. As she filled his plate with goodies, she gestured for him to sit at the large table. "We're having finger foods today, but I daresay it'll fill you up. Ella doesn't do anything halfway."

"Like dropping from the face of the earth," George muttered.

Tabitha paused, half of a chicken salad sandwich poised in her hand. "Pardon?"

George cleared his throat and straightened himself in the chair. "I said, she's a lady of unparalleled worth."

Pressing her lips together, she added another half to the plate along with several ginger snaps and a rose petal drop scone. "Hmmm." She laid the blue china on the lace placemat in front of him. "Would you prefer tea or coffee?"

"Coffee, please." Glad to have an excuse to avoid her eyes, he admired the mouthwatering fare. Hours had passed since his last meal, and he'd had a long walk from town. His stomach rumbled low while he spread the napkin in his lap. "What did I just interrupt, by the way?"

The sound of coffee pouring into a cup reached him before the aroma. Humor tinged Tabitha's answer. "You've never seen a quilting bee, Dr. Curtis?"

"Not this city boy."

She neared and set the cup beside his plate. Steam curled upward. "A quilting bee is when ladies of a community get together to make a quilt while visiting."

"And eat delicious treats like this?" He took a generous bite of the sandwich.

"If they're lucky, yes." With a pat on his shoulder, Tabitha moved toward the door. "I'll be back in a bit and show you to the front porch. This time of day, the rooms are getting stuffy. There's a nice breeze there while you wait. You can sit in the swing or pick a chair. The ladies won't be much longer."

"Thanks, but I think I can find my way out." He shot her a sheepish grimace.

When she reached the door, she turned. "All right. And by the way, Dr. Curtis?"

"Yes?"

"It truly *is* good to see you again."

"And you as well." Returning her smile, George took a bite of the rose scone.

He hoped Ella felt the same way.

ONE BY ONE, the ladies filed past George, greeting him with polite nods and not a few curious, half-hidden smirks behind a handkerchief. The oldest, a lady in faded brown gingham who appeared to be well into her eighties, slid him a furtive wink. George ran a finger along his collar.

Without hurrying, they climbed into the buggies, wagons, and autos. As the last one sputtered down the lane, Tabitha stepped onto the porch and slipped a pair of gloves onto her hands.

"I'll take my leave now, Dr. Curtis." She held out her hand. "You'll find Ella waiting in the parlor."

A sudden nervous jolt sped his heart up a notch, but he kept his voice steady. "Give Frank my regards."

"I'll do that."

Jamming his hands into his pockets, he watched Tabitha descend the steps and climb into her buggy. After a parting wave, she urged the mare forward and entered the shaded archway. No sound but the pounding of his heart remained.

This time, he gingerly opened the screen door and stepped into the hallway. Strange that the distance seemed longer now. The floorboards whispered the sound of his approach.

He paused before appearing in the open doorway and listened. Silence. Pulling in a breath, he held it then let it drag out over his lips. He wiped his slick palms against his slacks.

Get it together.

George stepped into the room.

Ella sat on a chair near the window, clasping her hands on a quilt draped across her lap. Her cinnamon head dipped, eyelids lowered as she stared at her fingers. Her shoulders lifted as her chest expanded, then drooped when it shrank.

Then she raised those violet eyes and met his.

George's breath evaporated, and he gulped like a schoolboy caught for being naughty. My, but he'd forgotten how lovely she was. And yet, something didn't seem quite the same.

Her rosy cheeks were chalky and a bit thinner. The fading bridge of freckles across her nose stood out more than usual. Her shoulders and arms appeared thinner as well.

Ella lifted her chin. "Well, Dr. Curtis, are you quite done staring?"

George put a hand to his mouth and coughed. "Excuse me." He stepped closer, then stopped. "I know this is a little sudden—"

"Sudden?" Ella straightened her shoulders.

"Unexpected."

"Unexpected?" Her russet eyebrows shot up.

George thrust his hands behind his back and clasped them together. "I apologize for showing up unannounced, Ella. It's rude, I know."

"What are you doing here?" Her agitated tone quavered slightly.

In two more strides, George stood directly in front of her. "Is this the Southern hospitality I've heard so much about?"

"We haven't been talking two minutes, and you're already kicking up a fuss."

"A clumsy attempt at a joke, I'll admit." He offered a smile, but she didn't return it. Her round-eyed glare bored through him. This was going to be much harder than he thought. He gestured to a chair opposite her. "May I sit?"

Her fingers fidgeted with a gold brooch at her throat. "Of course. Now I'm forgetting my manners."

"Not at all." While he lowered himself onto the edge of the seat, George's mouth grew dry as sand. "You never answered my letter."

Ella recoiled. "I didn't see the need. My last letter explained everything thoroughly."

"Did it? I had more questions by the time I finished it."

"Such as?" Ella's tone dared him.

George scrutinized her long and hard. "Why?"

Ella's shoulders swelled then drooped. Dragging her gaze from his, she turned her head and focused on the scene outside the window instead. "I explained it."

Something in her profile, an expression both vulnerable and afraid, bridled his impatience. "You think so? It seemed like you were trying very hard not to tell me something. All this time, I've been wondering about it. What aren't you saying, Ella?"

She chewed her lower lip and blinked.

"Are you engaged?"

Ella's face turned to stone. "Hardly."

Frustrated, George pinched the bridge of his nose. No, the lass wasn't about to make it easy. "Are you ill?"

Her throat bobbed.

"Are you?" He leaned forward. "Ella?" *Please say no.*

Toying with the brooch again, she composed her voice. "Not now."

Her answer didn't relieve him. What illness could've stopped her from writing? He spread his hands out, palms upward. "I'm at a loss. I know something isn't right, and there's no use in hiding it from me."

Her lips quivered and parted. "Believe me, there's no hiding this." Her clasped hands trembled.

"What, lass? Tell me." He held his breath.

She turned her head, an unspoken plea cracking her aloof demeanor. Anguish cried out from those violet depths.

"This." In one swift moment, she flung the spread aside. It puddled onto the floor, uncovering two concealed wheels on either side of the chair. Ella buried her face in her hands.

A wheelchair. Confusion dizzied his brain. So intent was he that he had failed to notice the bulk under the quilt. "Ella Steen, what happened to you?" Not stopping to think, he reached out and gently pulled her hands down before releasing them. "Please tell me."

Two large tears spilled over. "I can't walk," she croaked.

An emotion hard to define slammed into his chest, knocking the wind out of him. "What do you mean?"

"She had infantile paralysis. And who are you?" a man's stern voice demanded from the doorway. In his hand dangled the forgotten briefcase. He held it up and scowled.

George winced, the interruption and shock rendering him speechless. The man stepped forward, his broad shoulders only inches from brushing the doorframe. His dark eyebrows drew down as he scoured George with a look that demanded an answer.

Glancing at Ella, then back at the man, George stood. "I'm George Curtis, a friend of Ella's."

The man's suntanned face mellowed a little. "Dr. Curtis? I'm Douglas Steen." He held out a hand. "I apologize for the cold welcome."

The firm handshake could crush bones. "There's no need. I apologize for dropping in without warning."

"Are you staying in town?" He handed George the briefcase.

"Yes, at the Inn."

"I'll have your luggage brought here, and my housekeeper will get a room ready. You're welcome to stay with us."

Ella wriggled in the chair, a look of dismay plastered on her face.

Infantile paralysis. George kept his voice even while his mind reeled. "Really, I'm fine at the inn. I don't want to intrude."

"Nonsense. I insist. You'll be far more comfortable here." Pounding footsteps down the hallway interrupted Douglas. A young boy skittered into the room. "Father! Mag's got loose again!" Breathing hard, he grabbed his sides. "She's in the corn, kicking up a storm."

"That good-for-nothing mule." Douglas rushed across the

room, casting a glance over his shoulder. "We'll get better acquainted in a while."

After a clattering of boots and the slamming of the screen door, both father and son disappeared. George released a breath and turned back to the object of his thoughts.

A wry smile twisted Ella's lips. "Welcome to Red Maple Plantation."

12

After her clumsy attempt at humor, Ella's lips crumpled. How could he? Seeing her like this? She pressed a hand against the squeamish feeling rolling inside her stomach.

Curtis pivoted toward her, seeming dazed. Dabbing her eyes with a handkerchief, she waited for him to speak. No words came, however. He rubbed his mustache and studied her from the top of her head to the tip of her toes. Not in a way to make her squirm and blush. Behind those bright eyes rose a storm of thoughts she couldn't decipher.

"Dr. Curtis, you're staring again." Gathering her battered dignity, she raised her chin.

Curtis blinked and lowered himself into the chair. "Pardon me, Ella."

The whole story spilled from her tongue easier than she expected. The unseasonably warm afternoon, the picnic, and the fateful swim. Her illness and loss of movement. His cobalt gaze never left her face, intent on every word.

"Have you attempted to exercise?"

"Caleb helps me every afternoon. My legs only seem to grow weaker."

Curtis rubbed his knees and pressed his back against the chair. "I'm so sorry, Ella."

No, she didn't want that. Bristling, Ella wadded the handkerchief and crammed it into her skirt's pocket. "I don't want your pity."

He sighed. "Not pity. I'd never feel sorry for you. You've too much vim and vigor for that." A ghost of a smirk softened the frown lines around his eyes. "I'm sure if I said just the right thing, you'd pop out of that chair and storm from the room."

The memory of her recent fall crowded into her mind. "I truly doubt that even you could accomplish that."

"Nevertheless, I'll try my best."

"Good luck to you."

Curtis stood and gazed out the window for a silent moment. Free of his probing stare, Ella took her turn scrutinizing him. His dark, chestnut hair faded into premature gray dusting his temples, no doubt from years of exhausting work. Dusky shadows pooled under his eyes. He looked somewhat thinner, his face a little wan and his stance weary.

Still, he was a handsome figure of a man. So like Charles. Immediately, Ella banished the thought like an unwanted phantom.

"Now you're staring."

The infuriating man didn't even bother turning to see, and she wasn't about to give him the satisfaction of denying it. "What brings you from New York? I don't believe the 'just passing through' bit for a minute."

Still staring outside, Curtis clasped his hands behind his back. His jaw hardened while the coolness of granite stilled his features.

"I've left New York."

"Left? Do you mean for good?"

"Precisely."

Shock jolted her. "Whatever for? New York is your home. You have a wonderful job there."

The muscles in Curtis's shoulders tensed. His throat bobbed. With the moments ticking between them, she watched his eyes rove the yard, lingering on the long driveway accented by the red maples Father planted so many years ago.

"Curtis?"

He blinked. "It was time for a change."

What kind of an answer was that? "You left your home, your friends, your career just because it was time for a change?"

"This season of my life demands it."

Ella's chest heaved. "Still rude and derisive, I see."

Curtis glanced over his shoulder, his eyes warming. "Forgive me. That line of yours has goaded me for weeks."

Her cheeks tingled. "I'm sorry to have caused you undue concern."

He turned and leaned a shoulder against the wall. "Undue concern? I came all the way to Georgia to find out."

The blush bit deeper into her cheeks and feathered down her neck. Fixing her interest on a painted landscape across the room, Ella lifted her chin. "And now that you have?"

"I'm in no hurry to leave. Ella, look at me."

Help. Warily, she regarded him.

"I hope we can resume our friendship. While I'm here, I'd like to help in whatever way I can. May I?"

His sincerity was nearly her undoing. Of all the things she expected from him, concern and gentleness never came close. Throughout their acquaintance, he'd been passively kind but often downright rude. Their correspondence had done little more than make the lonely hours bearable for them both.

Or had it meant more than she believed?

She pretended to smooth a wrinkle from her olive skirt. "As long as you promise not to pity me."

A pleased, relieved look erased the tension around his mouth. "I give you my word."

OUTSIDE, several owls called to one another among the maples. Their hoots resonated through the darkness into the walls of George's room. Crickets chirped in time to the frogs' croaking down by the pond. Somewhere, farther away in the fields, a pack of coyotes yipped, their cries raising the hair on the back of George's neck. Who said the country was quiet?

The high-pitched howls evaporated just as suddenly as they had begun. With a relieved grunt, George laid back against the pillows and linked his fingers together, cradling the back of his head in his palms.

Moonshine silvered everything in the room—the marble-topped bureau, the lamp, the armchair, his trunk. Beside the bed, an emerald and lavender garden rug forever bloomed with flowers.

So this was Ella and Earl's childhood home. Strange that he was occupying Earl's old room. Ella had whispered it when he wheeled her to her room, warning him never to mention Earl's name in front of Douglas. George had no reason to mention his estranged best friend. And apparently, his brother felt the same.

His thoughts bounced back to Ella. How could he help her?

The doctor within craved to find a solution, to bring strength into those weakened legs, while something else he dared not acknowledge yearned to comfort her.

Like a candle untimely extinguished, her eyes no longer sparkled the way he remembered. And here he was, a ruined man, a destitute physician without a profession. He was in no position to help Ella.

Yet how could he not?

George stifled a groan. From the instant he saw that wheelchair, he choked on every thought, every word he'd stored up for her. He'd be worse than a cad to burden her with his problems. She had more than enough to bear.

And it was growing harder to think about Lilith by the hour. He needed to focus on Ella instead.

Her loss of independence and her inability to help others were crippling her more than her weakened legs. She happily gave others her energy, her time, her talents. Her illness had severed these things from her grasp. She was adrift.

Like him.

George's chest rose and fell, his thoughts suspended. The realization dawned like the morning sun inching over a dark, obscure horizon.

She and I are alike.

Why had he never seen it? Perhaps he had been too proud, too wrapped up longing for something he never had any right to possess, and too busy to take account of himself. His conscience flamed. He was a first-rate fool. Both Mr. Wallace and Ella extended kindness and friendship when he least deserved it.

He had defied Mr. Wallace in seeking Lorena's hand while she was bound to Earl. Then he'd accepted Ella's offer of friendship like a man sentenced to the gallows.

No, he was worse than a fool. He was a blind wretch.

Turning over, he punched the pillow. He'd make it up to Ella if she let him. With time and hard work, she might regain her strength. Walk again.

And if she did?

He wouldn't blame her if she walked away from him.

DOWN THE SHADOWED stairway into another part of the house, dim lamplight wedged over a threshold of a closed door and scattered across the polished hallway floor. Inside the room, Ella stared at the Bible lying in her limp fingers. The words on the pages jumbled together and raced against other thoughts. After two chapters, she failed to recall a single word.

She set it abruptly on the nightstand. Tilting her head, she eased her aching back into the propped pillows against the headboard.

Her heart had dealt with enough turmoil. Just when she decided to forget Curtis, he burst into her life all over again. Despite herself, Ella smiled grudgingly. What a way for him to make a lasting impression on the ladies. And a Yankee, no less. They would clamor about it for weeks.

However, something was amiss. She could see the weight bearing down on him. The way he walked, head bent ever so slightly, whispered trouble. Something or someone knocked the wind out of him.

But who or what caused it? It wasn't because she ended their correspondence. Maybe it had unsettled him, yet it wouldn't cause such a change in his demeanor.

All through supper, Curtis kept the conversation polite. He anticipated her every move until she was tempted to ask if he'd like to spoon-feed her. She opened her mouth to say it, but Douglas, knowing her too well, pinned her with a look. Behind her brother's somber expression, a mix of suspicion and bemusement glinted. Curtis never caught on. His mind was too full. She could feel it to the marrow of her bones.

Whatever troubled him settled deep behind his eyes like still, quiet waters hiding an undercurrent. Why had he sought her out then refuse to tell her?

My legs. Underneath the bedspread, her legs stretched out like two strange branches no longer belonging to her. Her fingers dug into the bedspread. Of course. He wouldn't tell her because he thought she was weak. The chivalrous oaf. Perhaps she liked him better when he was curt and dismissive.

Father, grant me wisdom to know how to handle Curtis. I can do nothing else.

Ella kneaded her forehead. "Why do I bother loving him?" Gasping, Ella bounced a glance around the room and clapped a hand over her mouth.

Had she admitted aloud that she loved George Curtis?

Apparently, more than her legs were weak. Dr. Weaver needed to examine her head during his next visit.

Her attraction had grown far beyond his resemblance to Charles. In fact, it mattered none whatsoever. Beyond all doubt, she knew that underneath the hardened shell was a good man lost in a wilderness void of faith and love. A man that challenged and matched her wits. They were far more alike than different. In every letter, she had striven to win his regard, to break down the barriers. To convince him without saying that Lorena was never meant to be his match.

She had failed. And now?

I can do him little good.

Desperation to shield her heart warred with a selfish desire to detain him. Why shouldn't she, at the very least, enjoy his company for a few weeks? She would cherish those times for the rest of her life. He would depart never the wiser, and she could live on the memories the way a sparrow hungrily pecked crumbs. Since Charles's death, the years had taught her one thing: she could endure. She had lost once, and she braced herself to lose again.

Loss. An acrid taste filled her mouth, setting her teeth on edge. Deep down, a tremor of rebellion throttled her heart. Pressing a hand against her chest, Ella filled her lungs as though the air would expel the pain locked inside her soul.

She was tired of losing. Weary of enduring. Sick of feasting on the crumbs of love unrequited. Always yearning for something out of reach. Ending before beginning.

No, Ella, the season isn't over. It has only begun.

Ella gnashed her teeth harder and thrust Curtis's words out of her mind. Empty promises would do her no good. Here and now, she must face the truth. She had to send him away. The quicker the better for her own heart's sake.

He must go back to New York, and tomorrow couldn't be soon enough.

13

George buttoned the cuffs of his shirt and donned his waistcoat, catching himself humming. He paused. Since when did he hum? Reaching for the comb, he raked it through his hair. For the first time in many weeks, resolve pulsed through his veins, and he welcomed it.

And he suspected the reason was waiting downstairs.

After slipping on his shoes, George strode into the landing and hurried down the staircase, the beating of his heart matching the pace of his feet.

When he reached the dining room, the object of his thoughts was already primly waiting. His steps faltered on the threshold. Ah, but Ella was a lovely sight, her ginger waves crowned fashionably atop her head. A heightened rosy color tinted her smooth cheeks.

Those violet eyes lifted and encountered his.

"Good morning, Curtis. Come in. Mrs. Hawthorne set out breakfast not long ago." Her placid greeting made him feel strangely at home.

"Good morning, Ella. Thank you." The chair next to hers

scooted soundlessly on the rug as he pulled it out and sat. "I trust you slept well?"

Ella busied her hands by spreading a linen napkin in her lap. "I did, but not so well. And you?"

"The owls and frogs serenaded me for a while. After that, I slept better than I have in a long time." Following suit, George spread a napkin in his lap.

"I'm glad to hear it."

Starting with a platter of fried eggs, he served Ella first. While she poured the coffee into their cups, he filled his plate.

"Douglas headed to the fields hours ago, but he'll see you at dinner. Caleb also rises early to go with him."

"He seems like a good lad." George sprinkled salt on his eggs.

Ella cut into a piece of ham. "He is."

As George's eyes roved her face, he sensed tenseness in her movements. Her attention remained riveted on her breakfast, seeming to avoid his eyes. Was she in pain?

"Are you all right? You don't seem to feel well."

"I'm tolerable. I have quite a lot on my mind." She bit into a flaky biscuit.

Sympathy fringed his concern. "I can imagine. Is there anything I can do?"

Ella looked up then, those lilac depths piercing his. Without answering, she lifted a cup, but before it touched her lips he spied their trembling. She sipped a few times before setting the cup down.

"This isn't easy to say, and I don't want to sound rude, but I think it's best you go back to New York."

Years of maintaining composure under pressure rescued George from displaying his inward alarm. He, in turn, took a long sip of coffee before answering. Ella flattened her lips together, waiting.

He set the cup aside, his voice unperturbed. "You do?"

"Yes, I do."

"And here I thought you were thrilled to see me at last."

Ella jabbed a piece of ham with her fork. "It isn't funny, Curtis."

"No, it isn't. I have nothing to go back to in New York."

A few spiral tendrils grazed her cheeks while she cocked her head. "I find that hard to believe."

"Indeed." He swiped the napkin across his mustache. "Tell me, why do you want me to go when I've only just arrived?"

She stuttered over the answer. "I think it's best."

"For you or me?"

"For both of us. I'm not good company these days."

George heaved a sigh. "Lass, you've got to do better than that. Good company? You talk like you're ninety-nine when you're not a day over forty-five."

Ella's eyebrows thundered together. "I'm forty-four. The same age as you, and you know it. Please don't joke with me. I'm in earnest."

"I can see that." He reached over and laid his hand across hers, the warmth filling his palm. Before she could whisk it away, he captured it. "You still haven't given me a good reason."

With her free hand, she flittered with the brooch at her throat. "Curtis, please. I'm tired of this pretense of friendship between us. Our correspondence was entertaining while it lasted, but things change. I appreciate your indulgence. I know it was tiresome for you, and—"

"It was my lifeline." The admission escaped his tongue.

Whatever words were about to sputter from Ella's lips died. Her jaw slacked. "Your ... what?"

He gave her fingers a gentle squeeze, hoping to reassure her. "I admit that it was tiresome, at first. You know I'm a crusty grump set in my ways. But in time, it became more than I realized. When you stopped writing, it stunned me."

The color leeched from Ella's face. "I'm sorry. I never meant to do that. I find it hard to believe."

He stroked her knuckles with his thumb. "So did I."

A dumbfounded expression rounded her eyes. She opened her mouth as if to speak, then clamped it shut.

"Ella, I'll leave, but only if you look straight at me and say it. Is this what you want?"

She skimmed a glance over his shoulder. "I need you to go."

His thumb stroked the creamy skin of her knuckles again. "Do you *want* me to?"

She tugged her hand, but he kept it sheltered within his. Grimacing, she nibbled her lip. "Do *you* want to go?"

"Not a bit."

For a long minute, George dared not breathe while her thoughts ticked. Finally, Ella met his perusal and inhaled deeply. "You may stay if you wish."

Without trying to hide it, George beamed and released Ella's hand. "Thank you. I do wish it."

"Very well." Her quaking fingers lifted the cup to her lips.

"Have you lost your mind?" The mid-morning sun struck Ella's face as she whipped the newspaper shut. The wicker rocker jiggled against her stiffening back. "What are those?"

Unperturbed, Curtis studied her, seeming to calculate her size. He scanned her feet, then her waist, before dangling the trousers to study them.

"These are my trousers. I took the liberty of bringing them down for you to wear while you exercise."

Horrified, Ella swatted the legs away from her. "Well, you can take them right back up again. I'm not wearing those!"

"They're just clothes."

"They're yours. And trousers at that." She concentrated on lifting her foot. "I don't need them to walk."

"Actually, you do. For now." Curtis draped the offending article over his arm. "Ella, I spent most of last night thinking. Caleb is too young and not strong enough to help with your exercises. But I am. Your skirts are too heavy and hamper your legs' movement. Tell me, how are you going to hold them and take steps?"

Heat singed the back of Ella's neck. "I'll not wear pants, especially yours. They're indecent."

Curtis raised his deep voice a few octaves. "'I think it's a grand idea. To be free of these heavy skirts would be invigorating.' Your words, my dear, not mine."

Heavens above, they were. His vivid blue eyes gleamed, belying a much-too-innocent expression. Again, the chair wiggled when Ella shifted her weight. "I only wrote it to goad you. And I'm not your dear."

His deep laugh rumbled to the end of the porch and chipped away at her angst. Ella preserved her lips' tightness like a battleline.

"Lass, you'll be the death of me." He stepped closer and took her fingers in his.

Ella's breathing hitched. Had Curtis taken leave of all his senses? Holding her hand not once but twice in one morning? *Beware, Ella.* If a little hand-holding frazzled her now, she was a goner. However, goner or not, she didn't withdraw it.

"I don't wish to offend. Surely you can see the practicality. You probably carry at least ten pounds of skirts every step you take. How are you going to freely lift your legs?" His smooth fingertips tenderly squeezed hers. "If I didn't feel it was absolutely necessary, I wouldn't insist."

For good measure, he flashed a smile that dangled her heart over a cliff of fancy. *I should've sent him packing. What will be left of me when he is gone?*

Ella huffed, grudgingly returning a slight smile. "All right, doctor. As you wish."

Like a sudden cloud shrouding the sun, a shadow darkened Curtis's eyes and blotted out their twinkle. He dropped her fingers with an abrupt turn toward the front door. "I'll take these to your room and call Mrs. Hawthorne to help you change."

His wooden tone chilled her. What on earth had she said?

PERUSING a stack of books on the end table, George swiped his sleeve across his hairline, unsure if the southern humidity caused the prickle of sweat or the memory of Lilith's pallid face.

Poor Ella. He glimpsed her confusion before he turned away. Doctor indeed. What would she think of him if she knew? She'd question her faith in his abilities then.

He must do better controlling those rogue emotions, or she would ask more questions. George wandered to the mantle and stared into the clean, empty hearth. Focusing on Ella and her recovery was his priority now, not his troubles.

The door hinges creaked, and wheels rolled onto the hallway. She was ready. Shaking the memories loose, George strode from the parlor and watched Mrs. Hawthorne push the chair toward him.

With averted eyes, Ella's face blazed every shade of red. A thin shawl spilled over her lap and knees. His navy trousers peeked from beneath, cuffed several times until they skimmed the top of her pointed dress boots.

George snapped his fingers. "I didn't think about your feet. You need something flat with no heels."

Both ladies widened their eyes. Ella's cheeks nearly turned maroon.

"Sir, is this really necessary?" Mrs. Hawthorne huffed. "The poor lady is humiliated."

George shook himself mentally. He must proceed with caution, or Ella would lose her nerve. "If not today, maybe tomorrow. Those heels won't aid her balance. Her feet must be flat on the ground. I'm sorry I didn't think of it sooner. Does Caleb have an extra pair she might wear?"

Squaring her rotund shoulders, Mrs. Hawthorne narrowed her eyes as though ready to battle an ogre to protect the sensibilities of her lady. "Boys' shoes? I've never heard of anything so scandalous. You can take your Yankee airs back to New York where they belong."

"Mrs. Hawthorne." Ella's quiet voice slashed through the woman's irate pitch. "Dr. Curtis is right. Will you be a dear and fetch a pair of Caleb's shoes?"

"If I must," she growled, brushing past George with head held high. All the way up the stairs, her heavy feet clumped their protest.

George spread his hands wide. "I'm sorry, Ella. I'd never do anything to humiliate you."

Ella sighed, tugging the shawl farther down her legs. "I know. I trust you, Curtis."

Warmth spread through his chest. Although he didn't deserve it, he'd do everything in his power to honor it.

"Rest assured, if I hear someone coming up the lane, I'll whisk you inside before you're seen."

Upstairs a door clapped shut. Moments later, Mrs. Hawthorne padded down the stairway and thrust a pair of shoes into George's hands.

"Thank you, Mrs. Hawthorne. I'll take it from here." George handed the shoes to Ella and stepped behind the wheelchair. "Are you ready?"

"As much as I'll ever be."

The porch, however, presented another problem. Both

gawked at the steps as if they stretched miles. The grass yawned out in front of them, an emerald carpet broken by the latticework of shade from the oaks whose branches stretched high.

"What now, Dr. Curtis?"

What, indeed. George plucked up Caleb's shoes from Ella's lap and laid them aside. "You said you trusted me a moment ago."

Ella frowned, leaning farther away as he neared. "I don't like the sound of this."

He used his quiet, calming tone for patients. "We need to understand a few things. We're going to be working closely together. I've no intention of disrespecting or taking advantage of you, but I need your permission to physically help you, whether it be carrying you down the stairs or lacing up your boots."

"I can manage my boots." Chewing her bottom lip. Ella grazed him with a wary glance.

He knelt to be at eye level with her. "Do we have an agreement?"

Her glance skittered away. "I suppose."

To see this independent, headstrong lady vulnerable and anxious squeezed his heart until it hurt. How it must rankle her to depend on him or anyone else.

"I promise you, Ella. Everything will be all right." Standing, George pulled her from the chair and slipped her up into his arms. The scent of lemon with a hint of vanilla wafted around his head. Ah, just like the first time they crossed swords in Valley Creek. He savored a deep breath, the smell cleansing and comforting at once. So like Ella.

She fit perfectly, belonged. Blinking, he valiantly put that thought to rest.

Ella tucked her chin deep into the folds of her blouse. Alarm charged through him. Surely, she wouldn't cry. As

George navigated the steps, his mind grappled for something—anything to put her at ease.

Stepping into the yard, he cleared his throat. "Lass, what are they feeding you? Feathers?"

As her chin jutted, Ella's small but firm hand whacked the center of his back. "You rude creature."

A deep, relieved chuckle shook his shoulders. "It's always better to start off on familiar footing, don't you think?"

Silence stilled her but only a second. A gleam entered her eyes. With twitching lips, she tilted back her head and laughed, her hand resting on his shoulder.

How good to laugh and even better to share it with someone. He could stand there all day in the hot sun and hold her listening to the sound. What if he told her?

Indeed, what if?

14

Scarcely breathing as Curtis stepped into the shade and lowered her onto the grass, Ella twiddled a curl behind her ear. An odd sense of loss struck her when he stepped back. Catching herself, she resolved instead to pull her foot onto her lap. The boots must come off. Her fingers dug into the tight shoelaces. Without support, her spine burned.

"Allow me." Curtis knelt at her feet and undid the laces.

How was she supposed to be indifferent? His nearness was playing tricks with her mind and heart.

Curtis, on the other hand, was the perfect, unaffected doctor. "The first thing I'll do is work your feet, then each leg to warm the muscles up. After that, we'll build strength through resistance."

"Must you touch my foot?"

Did a grin ripple under his mustache? Curtis kept his eyes lowered as he tugged off each boot. "I must." His tone remained serious, brisk.

The breeze, cooled by the shade, slid over her stockinged feet, an invigorating feeling. She gasped. "You're right, Curtis! My legs do feel much lighter without those skirts."

"Good, good." He cupped the heel of her foot with his palm and pressed his thumb into the center of her arch—gentle at first, then gradually hard enough Ella winced.

"Do you feel this?"

"All too well." She tried to pull it away with no success.

He repeated the test on her other foot with similar results. "Very good." He stood and held out his hand. "I'll need your shawl so that I can fold and put it behind your head."

Handing it over, Ella cringed, the trousers fully unhidden now. She watched as Curtis methodically folded the shawl without a glance at her.

"You know, I'll give you one of my shirts tomorrow." Humor fringed his voice. He laid the folded shawl behind her.

"Whatever for?"

"Your lovely blouse looks rather silly with my trousers."

Chin brushing her collar, she examined the mix-matched pair. "Well, I have Caleb's shoes. I might as well complete the outfit," she muttered ruefully.

"That's my girl."

Shock hummed along Ella's spine. Looking astounded, Curtis paused. Their gazes mingled. Everything around them faded and hushed.

With a long breath, he broke the stare and sat down, concentrating once more on her feet.

The doctor's mask eradicated all emotion from his face. His tone switched to business. "If you'll lie back now, I'll work your legs up and down first."

For the next half hour, she took turns lying on her back and stomach as he worked her legs. Then came the push and pull of resistance. On their own, her legs couldn't do much pushing or pulling against his hands, but he urged her onward.

"You'll never gain strength to walk otherwise."

"My legs are screaming." She ground her teeth, putting her weight into her leg, pushing against his palm.

"That's a good sign."

"You think so?" Her tired voice brightened with hope.

"Your muscles are extremely weak but not useless."

With tender care, he set her foot down on the soft grass. "Let's rest a bit."

The cool blades cushioned her feet with delicious relief. Ella stretched her arms behind her head. "Thank you."

Even though her legs relaxed, they trembled from exertion. Ella's eyes slid closed. Around her, the sounds and smells of home amplified. The grass stirring, the men in the fields calling to one another, a mockingbird twittering somewhere in the canopy above them. Drifting from the garden, the sweet aroma of Mother's roses fringed the scent of an apple pie cooling in the kitchen window. Peace wrapped her like a soft quilt.

Such a feeling made her believe she could sit up and walk like the lame in the Bible.

Another sensation crept over her—an awareness of being studied. Her eyes popped open to discover Curtis watching. He flashed a sheepish grin, his face reddening.

"It isn't polite to stare at people, especially when their eyes are closed."

"Excuse me. I didn't consider you to be *people*. Only Ella." Mirth rippled through his eyes.

Something in the way he said her name, like a caress, tightened her rib cage. She must not let him wedge any farther into her heart. Whatever he felt now wouldn't last. He couldn't stay forever.

Could he read her thoughts? The way his gaze deepened was convincing. Stiffening, she broke her stare. "Anything else, Curtis?"

He plucked a blade of grass and flicked it her direction. Twisting through the air, it landed on her nose. Ella pursed her lips and puffed it away.

"One thing more." Grabbing Caleb's shoes, he slipped them on her feet. "Do these fit?"

"They're a little tight, but they'll do."

Nodding, he tied them. "I'll see about finding a bigger pair." He stood and bent, slipping his arms under Ella and lifting her from the ground. "Now, for just a moment, I want you to try to stand."

Fear laced through her. "What? I can't do that."

His voice, near her ear, held the right amount of assurance. "I'm going to hold onto you under your arms. You're going to hold my shoulders. I promise I won't drop you."

Slowly, he tilted Ella until her toes touched the ground.

The sensation of her weight pressing into her legs felt unfamiliar and strange. "Oh my." She clutched his shoulders, her breathing short and quick. The iron-like firmness of his arms steadied her.

"Can you lift your leg a little, as if you're taking a step?"

"I'll try." Over his shoulder, Ella concentrated on the orchard. How she loved to take walks there.

She raised her leg only a fraction of an inch. Her foot dropped onto Curtis's toes. "I'm sorry."

He didn't flinch. "Don't be. I'm fine. Now, try the other one."

Once more, she threw her mental energy into the movement with the same result. "I can do no more, Curtis." Sweat pebbled her hairline. Without thinking, she plopped her forehead onto his broad shoulder.

In a smooth motion, Curtis scooped her up, releasing the weight from her feet. "That's enough for today. You did well, lass."

Ella steeled herself against the ease of his steps and how natural it felt to be in his arms. "I doubt it, but I know one thing for sure. I've worked more today than I have since this started."

"If you can keep pace, we'll do this every day."

How could he promise when she didn't know how long he

intended to stay? Resisting the urge to nestle her chin into his neck, she muffled a sigh.

"Tired?"

"Yes, very."

After he ascended the steps, Curtis eased her into the wheelchair. Her limited sense of freedom ended, walled by its arms and large wheels. Stepping back, Curtis shoved his hands into his pockets, seeming unsure of himself. A wayward chestnut wave curled over his brow. Roguish.

Pain stabbed her temple, and she circled her fingertips on the spot. "I need to change and lie down. That is, if you don't mind being left alone for a little while."

"Not at all."

No conversation passed between them while he pushed her to her room. When he reached the doorway, he grazed her shoulder with his fingers. "I'll call Mrs. Hawthorne."

Nodding her thanks, Ella wheeled herself into the room and closed the door. At this point, she worried more about her heart than her body.

THE SCENT of peaches wafted through the orchard as George ambled among the trees. A clatter of wooden crates interrupted the tranquility when a wagon loaded with the juicy fruit jostled past him. He returned the workers' waves. Soon, the stillness lapped around him again. Pausing beneath the branches, he let it seep into his soul.

A beautiful place, this orchard. Golden sunlight mottled the green carpet from corner to corner. Dangling from the limbs, the yellow fruit blushed and swayed with the whispers of wind. In such a place, the forgotten yet familiar thrum of youth pulsed through his veins.

Was Ella the cause?

Even more than a beautiful face, he glimpsed a beautiful soul trying desperately to hide anxiety and hurt. Not to mention her heart. Why was she trying hard to conceal it from him?

The rustle of grass following a hiccup snagged his attention. George pivoted on his heel and crossed several rows. A branch cracked under his foot, and the sound hushed. Just a few trees beyond him, a shadow hunched low to the ground. Creeping nearer, George angled his head. The shadow swayed and shrank.

"Caleb?" As George approached the tree, Caleb jumped up and slinked farther away. "Hold still, lad. Are you all right?"

The boy kept his face turned away. "Yes, sir." He sniffed and swiped his sleeve across his nose. The side of Caleb's face glowed crimson like those candy apples he'd seen in a sweet shop window. A tear glided downward, and Caleb dashed it away.

"Here now." George turned the boy gently to face him. "What's the trouble? Are you hurt?"

Caleb shook his head, whisking one of his hands behind his back. "I didn't mean to, honest, I didn't."

"Didn't mean to do what?"

"Will you be angry if I show you?"

He gave Caleb a reassuring squeeze on his shoulders. "Not a bit. Now, tell me."

Two more tears gushed down his cheeks. "This." Tentatively, he brought his hand out. His fist clutched a tiny bluebird, its head limp and still. "I didn't mean to. I'm sorry."

For the first time, George spied a slingshot jutting from Caleb's pocket. "Were you aiming at it?"

"Only a little beside it. I wanted to see how close I could get without hitting it. Do you believe me?" He hiccuped and looked down at the lifeless bird. "I'm sorry, birdie."

The lad's distress sliced George's heart. The fragility of life had slapped the young child along with the terrible guilt that his hand caused it.

"My boy, hand the bird to me." Extending his palm, he waited as Caleb hesitated. Finally, he placed the soft, tiny body in George's hand. The breeze ruffled the feathers.

"I was gonna bury it here. I went to the barn and got a trowel." Gulping air, he pointed toward the tool propped against the tree. "Will you help me?"

Pain radiated from places George strove to forget. "Sure. Fetch the trowel, and we'll take care of it."

"Dr. Curtis, you're not angry with me?" His wide eyes pleaded for understanding.

How well George understood.

"No, not at all. It was an accident, and I know you'll take more care next time."

"I won't ever do it again."

In silence, George took the trowel, broke the ground, and laid the bird gently within the earthen bed. Caleb then used his fingers to drag the dirt over it.

A fierce desire to flee consumed George, but he was a man, not a little boy. Through the years, he'd seen death so many times and in so many ways. He'd weathered all of them. How could burying a little bluebird crush him?

"Dr. Curtis, can I say a verse?" The boy's raspy voice anchored him.

George steadied himself. "By all means."

The verses of the twenty-third Psalm drifted low and soft through the orchard, and George wrestled not to hear them. They mingled with the rustling leaves while a familiar Presence enveloped the place. No doubt reminiscent of olden times when God walked through the garden in the cool of the evening with Adam and Eve. But this time, George ached to hide instead.

When Caleb finished, they bowed their heads, and the boy

murmured a simple prayer from his heart. "Please, Lord, let Mother take care of the bird."

George clamped the back of his neck with his hand and inhaled like a man smothering.

"Dr. Curtis, will you walk to the house with me?"

He was only too happy to move. After plucking up the trowel, George circled an arm around Caleb's shoulders. The fragrance in the air soothed George. He heard the lad's deep intake of breath.

Soon they left the sun-dappled rows behind and entered the side yard. "Did the bird go to Heaven?"

An old, unbidden verse flashed into George's mind. *Are not two sparrows sold for a farthing? and one of them shall not fall on the ground without your Father.* Though his faith was absent, he couldn't harm the child's. He licked dry lips. "I believe so."

Relief smoothed the furrows of Caleb's frown. "Me too." He paused a moment. "Will I always feel this way?" he whispered.

How many times had George asked himself that question? Guilt was an unwelcome guest that stayed until it was good and ready to depart.

"With time, it'll ease."

"I hope so." He scrunched his sunburned nose.

When they reached the house, Caleb stopped and held out his hand. "Thank you, Dr. Curtis."

Such a big man inside a little boy. George's hand engulfed his. "I'm glad to be of service."

A slow, pleased grin stretched from one corner of his mouth to the other. "Friends?"

With a shake, George tightened his grip. "I'm counting on it."

Caleb released his hand and bounded up the steps. "I smell apple pie! I can't have any until supper, but Mrs. Hawthorne saves the leftover crust for me." The screen door swished open and smacked shut.

Grateful the storm had passed, George whistled low and rubbed the toe of his shoe in the grass. Already a full day and not yet mid-afternoon.

He rammed his quaking hands into his pockets while the broken places inside himself bled afresh. To face Ella like this demanded all his poise.

Between now and supper, he must dredge it up somehow.

15

From her corner of the swing, Ella eyed Curtis while pretending to read *Great Expectations*. With folded arms, he sat in the wicker chair, his head resting against the back. Although his eyes were closed, sleep evaded his face.

During supper, he had been quiet—not sullen or aloof. Though he answered politely, he wasn't present. She doubted he even knew what he'd eaten.

Caleb had told her about the bluebird. Surely, he didn't take it as hard as the child? Maybe she had upset him. Did he regret offering to help her? If that were the case, she could remedy that immediately.

"You'd do better to read that book rather than pretend." The exasperating man didn't bother opening his eyes.

Ella gasped. "Well."

"What is bothering you?"

"Me?" Even though he didn't see her, she pressed a hand against her chest. "It isn't me. I was wondering about you, though. You were quiet at supper."

Curtis's brow furrowed. "Was I? I'm sorry, Ella. I guess I didn't realize it."

His weary voice brought an ache to her heart. "You don't need to apologize. I'm only concerned." She ignored the nervous feeling tightening her throat. "Caleb told me everything. Are you all right?"

He remained silent long enough that she wondered if he'd ignored the question. His chest swelled and fell. "I never ask myself that question anymore."

"I sense trouble. I see it on your face at times. Something has happened to you, and you won't tell me. A man like you simply doesn't pull up roots and walk away from everything."

Opening his eyes, Curtis stretched his arms the length of the armrests and curled his fingers over the edge, his tone patient. "Ella."

"Don't you *Ella* me." She thumped the arm of the swing. "Douglas does the same thing, thinking I'm too weak or ill to handle anything."

"It goes much deeper than that."

Ella set aside the book on the wicker end table. "It isn't right for you to bear it alone, whatever it is. I'll listen and try to help in any way I can."

Curtis straightened and shifted toward her. "I know. I can't begin to tell you what it means to me. I promise you someday I will."

"Why not now?"

Pain, raw and intense, flashed through his eyes. "I can't."

His pain flew like an arrow into her soul. Shivers nipped her spine. Nodding, Ella averted her eyes and ran a thumbnail along the swing's peeling white paint. Only one question more burned on her tongue, and it wouldn't stay put. "Curtis, will there really be a someday?"

The rocker creaked as he rose to take a spot beside her. "I hope so, but it depends on you."

Still, she avoided looking at him. "You mean it depends on my legs." How it hurt to admit it.

Reaching out, he groaned and skimmed her jaw, his fingertips airy against her skin. "Lass, look at me. It has nothing to do with your legs." A frustrated scowl etched his lips. "I'm no good at this sort of thing. I only meant that I'm not going to push you."

Like you pushed Lorena. Yet she dared not speak the words. At her age, she didn't have time for half-hearted attempts. "And what about you? Where does George Curtis figure in all this?"

His gaze fixed on hers, unwavering. "Someday is a dream that's beginning for me. For the first time in a long while, I wake up each day with something ... someone to look forward to."

The earnest sincerity in his face tugged her heart, but she braced herself against it. How could she be sure of anything yet? "Whatever happened to you certainly must have addled your brain."

Rather than take offense, Curtis chuckled a little. His fingers gently squeezed her chin. "It did. I admit it. But if this is the result, I'm more than a little pleased."

Pleased but not happy? No matter her feelings, Ella resolved not to accept second best. No, life wasn't perfect, but she'd rather be alone than settle for lukewarm affection.

Searching her face, Curtis released her chin. "I see this doesn't please you, however." He rested his arm along the back of the swing and cradled her shoulders. "It's all new to me as well."

No, it isn't new to me. Not at all.

"I like the feeling, though." He edged a little closer, making her heart skip. From the corner of her eye, she saw him rub his jaw as though struggling with words. "Ella, I'm sorry for my rudeness when we first met."

A soft laugh escaped her lips. "Well then, I'll have to apologize as well. As I recall, I returned your rudeness with vigor."

With his free arm, Curtis turned Ella toward him and urged her closer until her head rested on his shoulder. Of their own accord, her arms slid around him. His firm, steady muscles solaced and strengthened her lagging courage.

His chin rested on top of her head. "You're a fine lady to do battle against. A part of me enjoyed it, I regret to say." His chest rose as he pulled in the evening air. "I no longer want war with you, Ella."

What, then? Love?

"I don't want war with you either," she whispered against the scratchy fabric of his waistcoat.

His arms tightened. "Once you've lost friendship and trust, you come to realize how rare and precious a thing it is. I used to think I was better off alone until I truly was."

He must have felt her spine stiffen at the word *friendship* because he rushed out the rest of his words. "Friendship and trust are precious things, and it ought to be the foundation for any relationship." He paused. Around them, the loud pulsing song of cicadas filled the silent gap between them.

His breath feathered her hair. "I'd be a fool if I didn't add I'd like more than friendship with you, Ella."

She relaxed, but only a little. Did he only want more than friendship because Lorena's rejection had left him alone and friendless? Could she endure being his second choice? Would it satisfy them both? Bleakness shrouded her emotions.

Ella tightened her hold around Curtis as an idea formed in her mind. There was only one way to settle her questions. A telegram ought to do the trick.

NO MORNING BREEZE cooled the heat emanating from George's head as he pulled Ella into a sitting position. A thin sheet of sweat glossed her face.

Wind puffed from her lips. "How much more?"

George yanked a handkerchief from his pocket and handed it to Ella. "Just a few more exercises. But for now, we'll rest a bit."

"Sounds good to me." Ella blotted her face, starting at her forehead, then circling her crimson cheeks and along her neck.

A wicked little smirk curved his mouth. He couldn't tell if his shirt was wearing Ella or if Ella was wearing the shirt. Baggy as a tow sack, it swallowed her frame. Even more uproarious, his pants looked like they were choking on the shirt, the belt cinched tightly around her waist. Ella's slender ankles peeked from the cuffs.

And yet, he'd never thought her more beautiful.

The thought smacked him with such unexpected force it stole his breath. Ella was an alluring lady with an exquisite soul. His own spirit, parched and dry, yearned to quench its thirst. With all her difficulties, peace graced every movement.

Ella held out the handkerchief to him. As her eyes snagged his, the crimson flush on her cheeks flamed deeper. Yanking her glance away, she reached up and fumbled with the top button of the shirt. With a gasp of realization, she whipped her hand away.

Her nervous quirk. It hadn't taken George long to notice she often fingered the golden locket brooch whenever she was troubled or upset. A dead giveaway.

"Missing something?" he teased.

She coughed a little. "I'm not used to this ... this attire."

George reclined in the cool grass on his elbow, relishing her blush. "You look as lovely as ever."

"Shush!" She twisted her head away from his perusal.

He chuckled. "I'm curious. Whenever you're uneasy, you reach up and touch your brooch. You're never without it."

Ella folded her hand together and set them in her lap. "No, I suppose I'm not."

"I can tell it's special to you. I have my father's watch. Was the brooch your mother's?"

"No." The words snapped a little too hard from her lips. Surprised, George lifted his brows. Judging from the agitation on her face, he knew she wanted to bolt if her legs only allowed it. And over a brooch?

"I'm sorry, lass. I didn't mean to pry."

She turned her violet stare upon him then. Without answering, she pressed her lips together as though to imprison any answer that might escape. George leveled one in return, hoping Ella felt it to the marrow of her bones.

Finally, she sighed. "It was a gift." Looking down, she stroked the cuff of the shirt sleeve with her thumb. "From my fiancé."

If someone had dropped half a dozen pans behind him, George wouldn't have been more shocked. He jolted upright. Ella's head flew up.

"He's dead. He died years ago." She held out a trembling hand. "I'm so sorry, Curtis. I didn't mean to startle you like that."

Like a thundering waterfall, relief deluged him from head to foot. So much he felt ashamed. He captured her outstretched fingers.

"I'm neither young nor old, Ella. I don't think my heart can take another shock like that." Squeezing them, he tried to lighten his tone with a weak laugh.

Guilt scoured the crimson from her face, leaving it suddenly ashen. Ella ducked her head and returned the warm pressure with her fingers. George inspected her expression for signs of remaining grief. Keeping his voice low and gentle, he pressed further, the need for the truth burrowing in his heart.

"And what happened? Can you talk about it?"

"It was long ago."

"Yet you still wear his locket. Is his picture inside?"

Squirming, Ella fixed her eyes on their entwined fingers. Imperceptibly, she nodded.

"I see." The sting of jealousy burned and ached deeply within his gut, but the guilt of those feelings pressed him harder. So she had loved and lost as well. And why ever not? George reprimanded himself. What an arrogant fool he was to assume otherwise.

He stroked his thumb over the back of her hand, but she remained still and quiet. "Lass, I'm listening."

Her lips parted. "Charles died a few weeks before our wedding. Scarlet fever."

In his mind, he imagined a young Ella weeping late at night while the rest of the house slept. How many years had she watered her pillow? Compassion overcame the ache of jealousy.

"That's a terrible thing. I'm sorry you had to go through it."

Still avoiding his eyes, she lifted hers to the clouds drifting above them. "I'm all right, really."

Yet she still wore the locket. "Forgive me for asking, but do you still love him?"

"No." Simply put, without hesitation. "Not for a long while now." A wistful smile fringed her lips.

"I understand how you feel."

To his surprise, she held up a hand, meeting his stare directly. "I'm sure your grief was much deeper since you were married."

"No, Ella. That's not so. When you keep vows you never had the opportunity to make, it testifies to the beauty and depth of your heart. You're a rare soul."

All the more, he thirsted for it.

George lowered his head and brushed his lips on the back of Ella's soft hand. Her low gasp reached his ears. His breath hovered over her skin as he searched her eyes for unspoken thoughts.

The luster of unshed tears brightened them

"You're a little pale this afternoon." Tabitha sipped lemonade and puckered her lips. "Did Dr. Curtis overwork you?"

The golden, tart sweetness trickled down Ella's throat as she sampled a taste. "He gives me a thorough going over, but he's always very mindful about my rest."

"Do you think it's helping?"

Ella flicked a ginger snap crumb from her skirt and watched it skitter off the porch. "It's too soon to tell. He's determined to do everything he can, so I'll work as hard and as long as it takes."

"That's the spirit." A serene smile highlighted Tabitha's eyes following Curtis and Rev. Calloway walking down the maple driveway. The grassy middle divided them as they ambled along the gravel ruts. Even from that distance, Curtis made Ella's breath hitch, the memory of his lips grazing the back of her hand a bittersweet ache.

"Ella Steen, I do believe you're distracted. Here I've been talking all this time while you make sheep's eyes at Dr. Curtis."

Blinking, Ella sputtered her lemonade, mid-swallow. Tabitha giggled, the musical sound dancing through the yard. With a clink, Ella set the glass down and thumped her chest.

"You're a dreadful tease."

"I couldn't help myself." Tabitha bit into the crisp cookie. "But I'll tease no more today. It's like old times seeing Dr. Curtis and Frank together. They're like two young boys."

"I can tell they're good friends."

"Frank grew up with his son Stephen. Frank respects Dr. Curtis deeply. I didn't know it until after we were married, but Dr. Curtis saved him from drowning when he was a child."

A sweet feeling of pride filled Ella. "He hasn't ceased to surprise me since he arrived. He possesses a tender heart under that shell."

Even though the men were out of earshot, Tabitha lowered her voice. "And how are things between you and him?"

"Better than I hoped. I still have doubts as to why. Something awful has happened to him, Tabitha. I think that's why he's here, but he refuses to tell me at present. He has quit being a doctor, has walked away from everything."

Tabitha's lips parted with a gasp. "That isn't like him at all. I can't imagine what would have driven him to it. It was his life."

"He isn't the only one not being forthright." Ella's shoulders drooped. "I'm having trouble as well."

"You haven't told him about Charles?"

The morning's conversation between her and Curtis spilled from her lips, the words tripping over each other like a babbling spring. Setting aside her glass, Tabitha listened intently. No judgment, no condemnation crept into her expression.

"I hate myself for being a coward. I was almost there. The words burned the tip of my tongue, but when those deep, hurt eyes looked into mine, I choked." Her hand pressed against her throat as she relived the moment.

"You must find a way to tell him, Ella."

"I know. I know. He'll get angry, and it will hurt him. Suppose he leaves and never returns?" The thought shriveled the truth into a dark corner of her heart.

Leaning closer, Tabitha gave Ella's arm a bracing squeeze. "I can only offer you my prayers for wisdom and God's timing. And a little sliver of my own experience. I kept a terrible secret from Frank, and it nearly ruined our chance for happiness. If it weren't for Lane, I would've never told him."

Ella lifted her head.

"He was more understanding than I ever hoped or

dreamed. I can't tell you what Dr. Curtis will do, but I firmly believe this: If he truly loves you, he'll find a way to accept it. It'll be a rough patch, no doubt, but he'd be a fool to let you go." Tabitha released Ella's arm and sat back.

"It sounds so simple."

As easy as rising out of her chair and walking.

16

"I received a letter from an old school chum of mine today." Frank Calloway stooped and picked up a long stick laying crossways in the path. "You remember William Gregory?"

An image of the spindly young man brought a smile to George's lips. "Good lad, William."

Frank swiped the stick through the long grass in the middle, sidling a glance at him. "He included a couple of newspaper clippings."

The gravel crunched beneath George's shoes as he halted. Frank stopped also, his green eyes full of understanding.

"I see." George rubbed his jaw, pain seeping inside as Lilith's face resurrected. "I don't know what to say."

"You owe me no explanation, but I wanted to let you know. I'm sorry, my friend. I wish there was something I could do for you."

"I can't escape it even here." Alarm charged through George when he remembered the ladies on the porch. "Does Tabitha know?"

Frank shook his head. "I was going to tell her this evening after we're home."

Dragging in a breath, George raised his gaze to the overhanging branching shading them. "I haven't told Ella yet. I will, Frank, but not now. I'd appreciate it if Tabitha wouldn't say anything."

The two resumed walking, their steps unhurried and laden with the heaviness between them. "She won't, but the sooner you tell Miss Steen, the better. Someone else might tell her before you have the chance."

"I've spent my life fearing very little. The thought of telling Ella makes my blood run cold."

"But why?"

"The words choke me; it brings everything back. And then, when I saw her, especially in her condition, it became even more difficult." Dread snaked along his spine. "I don't want to see the horror in her face. When I do tell her, she might think I'm a profiteering butcher too."

Frank tossed the stick into the ditch. "I truly doubt it."

"My lifelong friends, except Mr. Wallace, walked away. Every last one. I'd believe anything now."

"Do you believe I would?"

Although George knew the measure of the man, he kept silent.

"I'll always be your friend, Dr. Curtis, and I speak for Tabitha too. I'd venture to say Ella will be unmoved." Frank crossed his arms, a kind smile dissolving his somber expression. "Just because others lost faith in you doesn't give you the right to lose confidence in the friends you have remaining."

The unvarnished truth bolstered George's courage a little. "I suppose you're right."

"Whether you want it or not, I'll be praying for you."

His chest clenched. "At this point, it can't do any harm, lad."

MUSIC GLIDED FROM THE PARLOR, weaving its way down the hall, sifting through the screen door, and spilling onto the front porch where George and Douglas sat. Neither spoke much, but the silence was comfortable rather than tense. The dwindling, orange sunrays smattered the leaves, the grass, and the porch posts as it neared the horizon. In the yard below, Caleb shouldered a BB gun and aimed a rusty pail atop a wooden crate. A second later, the pail tanged.

The beginnings of a waltz pulled George from the porch and lured him into the house. Pausing on the parlor's threshold, he stole a minute to drink in the sight.

Sitting in her chair, Ella listened to the merry tune as the record crackled and popped from the Victrola, her eyes closed in concentration. A delighted little smile had erased the worry from her face. He knew, in that moment, she wasn't confined to the chair, but rather, she whirled around the room, lithe and free.

A few loose, cinnamon curls feathered the sides of her smooth cheekbones. Her index finger dipped and swiveled in time to the music.

"May I have this dance?"

Ella's eyes popped open wide and round. "George Curtis. Was that necessary?"

He stepped inside and moved toward her. "I couldn't help myself. It's a pretty piece of music, isn't it?"

The dreamy smile returned. "It is one of my favorites. The Blue Danube Waltz."

The pure joy on her face was hard to resist. George held out his hand. "May I?"

Ella chortled behind her hand. "You must be daft."

"I assure you, I'm in earnest."

Wide and unassuming, those eyes scanned his face. "Curtis, I simply can't."

"But I can." Without warning, he pulled her from the chair

and scooped her up in his arms. As Sousa's band performed the playful tune, George stepped in time. Her arms encircled his neck, her fingers lacing together.

Holding her tightly, he circled the room, his steps smooth and agile though he hadn't danced in ages. Shy at first, Ella kept her eyes down. As the tempo continued, a charming glow invaded her face until she could no longer hide the pleasure tugging her rosy lips.

Nor did George mask his delight, and the whirling continued. All too soon, the song came to a rousing conclusion, and he clutched her close and spun around for fun.

Ella squealed. George's booming laughter filled the room.

Their gazes tangled. All laugher melted away. At that second, George couldn't think of any other place he'd rather be.

He lowered his head, hovering his lips above hers.

Another breath passed between them. Closer.

Ella turned her head and buried her face in his shoulder. Keen disappointment dizzied George's senses.

"Well, now, what do we have here?"

George snapped around to find Douglas filling the doorway, his fists balled on his hips. Color blanched from Ella's face.

Gathering his poise, George steadied his voice. "We were sharing a dance." With ease, he neared the wheelchair and carefully lowered Ella into it, remaining by her side.

Douglas crossed his arms and stepped forward. "Looks like you were fixing to share a little more than just a dance."

Though Douglas only possessed a few years more than him, George felt like an adolescent lad caught red-handed. "There was no harm done. I meant no disrespect."

"Maybe not." His sharp glance bounced between them. "I'd like to know what your intentions are toward my sister."

Blazing suddenly alive, Ella rapped the arm of the chair. "Douglas Steen, I'm not a child. I'm a middle-aged woman."

"I'm well aware, but I've a right to know. I won't have him

taking advantage or hurting you, no matter who he is." His stare scraped over George.

Squaring his shoulders, he confronted Douglas's scrutiny head-on. "You should know that I care deeply for your sister."

"How deeply? Enough for a passing fancy or for all time?"

"Douglas!"

Her brother's stony face never flinched. Laying a gentle, restraining hand on Ella's shoulder, George dared not blink lest Douglas think him a rogue. "Ella and I are getting better acquainted. I don't dare presume what she thinks, but as for me," he pulled in air to steady the rumbling nerves in his stomach, "I'd like to share a future with her. My wish is to honor her."

Douglas uncrossed his arms, the rigid pinch of his mouth softening only a little. "Make sure you do, Dr. Curtis. I usually act first and ask questions later." He cut a glance at his sister. "You might as well quit looking daggers through me. I've looked out for you all these years, and I'm not about to hand you over to a man I hardly know."

Ella's chest heaved. "I'll have you know I haven't taken leave of my senses."

"Not yet. Take care, Dr. Curtis, that you don't either." After scorching George with another raking glance, Douglas spun on his heel. The screen door banged a few seconds later.

With a low whistle, George turned to Ella. "I'm sorry, lass. I've gotten us both into bad graces with your brother."

"Piffle tosh," she sniffed. "He blows up like a summertime thunderhead—dark, blustery then fizzles out in no time. Deep down, he likes you. I can tell."

George slid a finger around his tight collar. "If you say so." He sighed, a question burrowing under his skin, one that caused sweat to slick his palms. "And what about Ella Steen?"

The lips he had nearly kissed curved upward. "I like you too. Very much."

"Was I too forward? Did I misinterpret what happened between us a bit ago?" Although he loathed asking, he had to know. The last thing on earth he wanted to do was hurt Ella or take advantage of her.

A rose flush crept from her neck and bloomed into her face. She lowered her lashes. "No, you didn't. I was afraid."

His fingers skimmed her upper arms with a downward stroke. "I don't want to do anything to make you afraid."

She bent her head as if mortified. "It wasn't you, Curtis. It was me. I didn't want to turn away," she faltered. A sheen of moisture glimmered in her eyes like a purple sea.

He needed to stem those tears and quickly. "Well, in that case, the next time I get ready to steal a kiss, I'd better waste no time."

A charming sound filled the room. Ella's low, quiet laughter restored his waning confidence.

DISTANT SHOUTS BRIMMED over the orchard and raced through the garden, the barn, the outbuildings, and the yard. Caleb and a playmate were apparently not faring well in their battle against an imaginary foe. Tilting her head, Ella rested it against the oak and thought about the church services they had attended that morning. The timeless truths never failed to stir her spirit.

Beside her, Curtis had sat listening politely, but she sensed his closed heart. Rev. Calloway's words rolled off like rain on an umbrella. No matter how inspiring, he shielded the message from soaking into the depths of his soul.

And to what purpose?

With every day, they grew a little closer. As hard as Curtis guarded his heart against faith, she shielded her heart from his love. *Our struggle may well prove futile.* For Curtis stood to gain everything while she might be left holding the broken fragments of her heart.

Where did his devotion truly lie?

Above her, a few blue jays fluttered in the branches and fussed, their calls shrill and urgent. Ella's eyes popped open. The birds darted from one side of the tree to the other.

She scanned the ground in all directions. And then, her heart lurched. Not ten feet away, emerging from underneath a forsythia bush, a rattlesnake slithered into the open.

With trembling hands, she lifted herself slightly and tried to scoot away. The snake paused. Ella froze. Unperturbed, it inched forward. From the tips of her toes to the crown of her head, terror sparked along her nerves.

Against the garden gate leaned a hoe. It might as well have been at the end of the maple lane.

Father in Heaven, help me!

A scream exploded from Ella's lips. "Caleb! Caleb! Help!"

Among the peach trees, the laughs and shouts barred her cries. Her frantic thoughts turned to Douglas. He had gone on horseback through the fields. She had no way of knowing if he were near enough to hear.

The strength she couldn't summon into her legs, she threw into her voice. "Douglas! Help me! Douglas!"

The blue jays screeched louder.

Dropping her torso flat onto the ground, Ella rolled a few feet away. Again, the snake paused and raised its head. Her breathing thinned. The snake slid closer, unhurried. With her elbows and forearms, Ella dragged herself mere inches, her heavy skirts like fetters around the lower half of her body.

An icy cold tremor shimmied down her spine as the rattlers buzzed.

Inside the house, Curtis lay upstairs taking a nap. Never in her life had Ella felt more alone and afraid.

Father, grant me strength. Help someone to hear me.

She swelled her lungs with as much air as she could hold and aimed her voice toward the upper side of the house where she prayed Curtis's window stood open.

"Help. Me. Curtis! Help!" Again, Ella poured her might into a high-pitched scream. A cough wracked her burning throat. She dared not move lest she antagonize the snake further.

"Curtis!"

Perhaps moments passed, perhaps longer, but Ella never knew. The screen door crashed into the outer wall as Curtis burst onto the porch. Wildly, he glanced around then saw Ella stretched out on the grass.

"A rattlesnake, Curtis! The garden hoe is there, by the gate!"

He leaped from the porch. Within seconds, he seized the hoe and turned to approach the snake.

"Don't move, Ella." As he neared, he slowed his pace. Step by step, he crept until he stood within striking distance. Curtis inched his feet closer and raised the hoe, the blood fleeing his face. His unblinking focus centered on the snake. It drew back its diamond-shaped head within the folds of its body. The buzzing intensified.

Gnashing her teeth, Ella turned her head.

An instant later, the hoe thudded, and the buzzing ceased.

Air rushed from Ella's lungs as terror released its icy grip. Snatching a peek, she met Curtis's wild eyes. With the hoe, he dragged the limp body a safe distance away and hurried to her.

Deftly, he turned Ella over and gathered her up without bothering to stand. "Lass." His hand stroked her hair, unmindful of the pins. A few curls tumbled past her shoulders. "My lass. Are you all right? Forgive me. I should've been here."

Ella nuzzled her face into his neck, basking in the strength of his arms. "I'm all right now. It's no one's fault. I was the one who insisted on sitting out here. I never thought of the danger. Curtis, I'm so glad you heard me."

His arms tightened like iron bands around her. "It was

within three feet of you, no doubt headed for the tree and the blue jays' nest. You were in its way."

"You saved the birds and me. Thank God you came."

His lips grazed her temple. A tremor rolled across his shoulders. "If I hadn't opened my window ..."

"What ifs rarely do any good. All that matters is that you did open it, and you heard."

A hint of a tease entered his voice. "You do have a nice, shrill voice."

"Well, I take lessons, you know."

He chuckled, and the sound loosened the taut emotions binding them. Easing her back to look into her eyes, he tenderly squeezed her upper arms. "You lovely imp. I lost ten years of my life."

"You? How much do you think I lost?"

The sound of galloping hooves cut off any retort on Curtis's lips. Into the yard, Douglas and his mount charged, straight through Ella's flowerbed.

"My poor pansies."

Douglas reined in the horse and swung to the ground.

Taking in the scene, especially her soiled dress and mussed hair, he whipped off his hat and slapped his thigh. "I heard you scream. What's all this about?"

"Now, don't get your dander up. Curtis saved me from a rattlesnake. I couldn't drag myself away quickly enough. I was yelling for help, and he came."

Wrenching his scowling eyes from them, Douglas's stare hovered over the tops of their heads and spied the long, fat body. The lines around his mouth dug deeper into his skin.

"Thank God you're safe." He stepped around them to view the snake more closely. "Ten rattlers and a button. Dr. Curtis, I owe you a debt of thanks and an apology. I'm sorry."

Ella's eyes smarted. Although kind, rarely did her brother express regret.

"No need for apologies. I would've reacted the same way."

Douglas turned, his face relaxed but ashen. "Be that as it may, there's no need to hold her longer than necessary." He reached down and retrieved her into his arms. The fringes of a smirk teased his lips and eyes.

"Come on, Dr. Curtis. Dust yourself off while I carry our lady to get tidied up."

Agile as a young boy, Curtis hopped to his feet and did as he was told. The two men shared a chortle while Ella rolled her eyes.

17

Red-orange flamed into yellow gold as George struck a match and lit the kerosene lamp on the nightstand. Cold sweat ruptured from every pore on his body. He didn't know where Ella's screams ended and Claudia's began.

The nightmare had dragged George from the yard below into the hospital corridor with Lilith's mother and father. The blood, the child's ebbing breath, all too real. Goosebumps shimmied over his skin. The incident with the rattlesnake had poisoned his sleep and his dreams.

Shadows bulged on the ceiling, scattering across walls in every direction. Ramming his fingers through his hair, George scooted off the edge of the bed and shrugged into the robe draped over the chair.

Tonight the frogs reverberated the midnight air with their happy songs, refreshed by the late evening shower. Yet it did nothing to settle the hammering of his heart against his ribcage. He'd lost Lilith, and he'd nearly lost Ella.

What if he hadn't heard Ella? All evening a feeling worse than his grief over Lilith hemmed him in like a trap. What if the snake had struck?

Ella was right. What-ifs rarely did any good. They pricked like a needle into one's peace of mind.

Taking the lamp, George crept down the stairs toward the study. A little late-night reading might do the trick and settle his mind.

The library door swept open soundlessly to a high-ceilinged room lined with bookshelves. A gasp from a corner met his ears. With her feet resting on a divan, Ella sat in her chair with a book perched between her fingers, the soft lamplight accenting and tinting her hair. Her rouge tresses were tamed into a thick braid draping over her shoulder and past her waist.

"I'm sorry," George whispered. "I see you couldn't sleep." He gestured toward the book.

Ella marked the spot and closed it. "No, not after today. I hardly tasted a crumb at supper."

"Neither did I. May I come in and sit with you?"

"Of course." She shifted her feet a little to the side.

The gnawing feeling chiseled into his chest as he lowered himself. "Are you feeling all right?"

Ella shrugged. "A little shook up, I'll admit, but none the worse for wear. And you? You left most of your plate untouched. I think Mrs. Hawthorne was offended." The corners of her mouth lifted.

"I can't get through the day without offending Mrs. Hawthorne." He chuckled. "Maybe I'll win her over someday."

"Maybe."

Listening to the sound of her voice soothed him in ways that surprised him. He sobered. "And how about Ella Steen? Will I win her someday?"

Looking unsure, she tugged her robe tighter around her. "That remains to be seen."

"I deserve that."

Shock flickered across her face, but she said nothing.

George inhaled, noticing the spicy scent of kerosene meandering through the room. "I have to admit something else. The thought of something happening to you, of losing you, terrified me."

Although Ella didn't move, she stilled even further, so much that George wondered if she were breathing. What could he do but plunge ahead?

"You need someone to take care of you."

The lamplight glinted off Ella's eyes as she narrowed them. "I do very well, and Douglas takes excellent care of me."

"I know he does. I see how much affection he has for you. And he's always ready to knock my head off at a moment's notice." George darted a glance at her. Ella bit her lower lip to pin her frown in place but not quick enough to erase the twinkle of amusement. Gathering courage, he reached over and nestled her hand within his own. "But it's not enough."

"Whatever do you mean?"

"It's been eating at me for days. Douglas works tirelessly in the fields. Caleb is a young boy, splitting his time between the fields and the orchard. You're here. You said what-ifs do no good, but suppose I hadn't been here today. What then?"

"I don't know." She pinched her lips together.

The heavy shadow of his nightmare hovered over him. With a low, frustrated growl, George sprung from the seat. "I'm being clumsy again. Ella, I'm not very good with words. All evening I've thought of how I should say it, and I can't get it right. Forgive me for that. I'm trying to say I want to take care of you. If you'll let me."

Seconds ticked on the hallway clock. Had the lass turned to stone? No expression breached the stillness of her face. "If I'll let you?"

George gulped an unsteady breath. "I'd like to marry you, lass, if you'll have me." There. It was out.

Ella slowly twined her fingers together and folded them in her lap. "So you can take care of me."

"Yes. No." He groaned. "Ella, I don't go around proposing every day. What I also meant to say is I've learned to care a great deal for you." He laid a hand over his heart. "Something here draws me to you, and I'm tired of resisting it. You bring me more joy than I've felt in a long time. I want to do the same for you."

Still, her expression remained shuttered. She took her time scrutinizing him without a word. The pit of his stomach plunged to his toes.

"Ella, your silence is killing me."

Her lips parted. "The time has come to take the bull by the horns."

Dread curled up into a lead ball right in the center of his chest. He braced himself for her answer.

"Time is a luxury for the young, so there's no need in us beating around the bush. If I ever marry, it will be for love. I'm not looking for a nursemaid to tend me."

"I know you're not, and—"

She lifted her chin. "And I won't be second pickings either. I'm no consolation prize for a lonely man's battered ego."

She certainly didn't pull any punches. The knot in George's chest squeezed tighter. "No, lass, you're too precious for that."

A mist gathered in her eyes. "I appreciate the sentiment." She averted his scrutiny for a moment, chewing her lip. George kept his own mouth shut, sensing she was weighing her next words.

After a minute, she pegged her gaze on his. "I'll take nothing less than your love, George Curtis. Not Lorena's love, not your deceased wife's love. A love that belongs only to me. Just as fierce and just as devoted. I won't settle for less. I'd rather be emptyhanded and alone." Her voice quavered, making his heart ache.

Stunned, George blinked. Of all the things he expected her to say, he didn't expect those words. And spoken with such boldness. Or was it simply courage?

Like a thirsty man, he stood drinking in the sight of her in that shadowed corner. Her rigid jaw, that unyielding stare belying the fear and doubt lurking deep within, where she disguised her hurt. Her hands clutched together on her lap.

Did Ella have any idea what a remarkable woman she was?

George cleared his throat, determined to use the right words. "You should never settle for less, Ella. And I'm not offering less." He swallowed hard. "What I feel for you has the makings of something I never thought possible again. You may trust I don't use the word *love* flippantly."

She quirked her brow. "No? Perhaps in haste, then."

"You believe I'm moving too quickly?"

"Not toward me." She dabbed her eyes with the edge of her sleeve. "I believe you're evading something else instead."

Shock coiled around him. Did she know about Lilith? But how?

"What are you saying?"

Under the glowing light, Ella paled. "Lorena."

If Ella had leaped from her wheelchair and thrown a stick of dynamite at him, he would have been no less astounded. All his assumptions shattered to bits. Tilting his head to one side, he stepped closer. "Lorena?"

"Do you really think I believe you no longer harbor feelings for her?"

With an exasperated moan, he puffed out a breath. "What I felt for Lorena, I've put in the past."

"Have you?" Her voice rose the tiniest bit.

"I have."

Patience, man. George squared his shoulders. Minutes passed while they glowered at each other. Part of him burned to kiss her silly, but the situation was far too serious.

"Lass, I want no other future than one with you in it."

"Then let's put it to the test."

He didn't like the sound of it. "What do you have in mind?"

"I'll never be sure you're free of Lorena ... and I don't think you'll be either ... until you face her once more."

Yes, dynamite would have been preferable. He scraped his palm along the stubble of his jaw. "And how would you suggest I do that? Go to Valley Creek?"

Her flinty silence answered him. George's mind whirled back to the last time he saw Lorena, his goodbye. His final visit with Earl. The humiliation stung him. Stepping back to the divan, he eased himself down. "When I left, it was forever."

"Eternity is a long time, Curtis."

"Hardly." Leaning forward, he scrubbed his face with his hands. "I made a fool of myself, and I hurt those I cared about. You don't know what it'll cost me, Ella."

Ella's answer came softly. "Yes, I do. There's no other way you'll have me, Curtis."

So this was it. Years without Ella stretched through the rocks and valleys of his mind. The lonely, monotonous days of no companionship, her witty humor absent, no zest for living. No love.

Leaning forward, Ella rested a hand on his shoulder. "I'm not asking you to do it alone. I'll be with you every step of the way."

Incredulous, he glanced at her.

She gave his shoulder a heartening squeeze. "I took the liberty of sending a telegram to Earl and Lorena, asking if we might come. Lorena had already invited me not long after I told them about my illness. I received an answer yesterday. They said we could."

Flinching, George rose stiffly, his face hot. "I'd do anything for you, Ella, but I don't know if I can do that."

The quiver in her chin thrust a dart through his heart. "I won't be persuaded otherwise."

"Why isn't my word good enough when I tell you my feelings for Lorena are in the past?"

Her bravado crumpled, her vulnerability stripped bare. "As long as it's a part of you, you can't have any part with me."

All at once, words both fled and jumbled his mind. Memories of Earl and Lorena invaded the present, robbing his voice. He stepped away. What she demanded was too much.

"I'll say goodnight, Ella. I'm sorry."

Forgetting the lamp, he stepped into the dark hallway and clicked the door shut. The darkness shrouding the furnishings dwindled in stark contrast with the memories. Ella didn't know what she was asking.

Or did she, after all?

Pain jabbed Ella's back as sunlight spilled through the window onto her shoulders. Radiating into her neck, it stabbed her temple.

Scrunching her eyelids shut, she kneaded her fingers where the pain throbbed against the side of her head. For once, she was thankful because it nearly blotted the anguish of her heart.

All night she remained in that wretched chair, her tumultuous thoughts stealing away sleep. When she finally wheeled herself to her room, she merely sat by the dark window and stared at the stars as the hours chimed on the clock. She hadn't moved or uttered a sound. Indeed, the silence had choked her. To speak would open the floodgates of pain.

I should've known better.

She pushed Curtis too hard and demanded too much. She was selfish, asking the impossible. Perhaps a portion of love was better than none at all. Instead, she had staked her claim like a petulant child clutching a whole pie for herself. And she ended up with nary a piece of Curtis's heart. Well, the damage was done.

Upstairs, she heard him rummaging. He was surely packing. Her head pounded again, and she buried it in her hands. Never had she lived such an awful, wakeful night since Charles died. In truth, this feeling was worse.

If only crying would wash it away, but the quiet despair had strangled her tears too.

A light tap jiggled her door, and the knob creaked. Probably Mrs. Hawthorne, but Ella couldn't answer.

"You haven't been to bed all night? I was concerned when you didn't come to breakfast."

Ella whipped her head around to see Curtis filling the doorway. He stepped across the threshold, his brows shooting upward.

"No." She slid a hand over her disheveled waves. What a mess, although he didn't look much better. His rumpled waistcoat and slacks said as much. The dusky shadows under his eyes highlighted his wan features. Ella forced her voice to remain even. "I suppose you're coming to say goodbye?"

The lines around his eyes deepened with his frown. "Goodbye? Whatever for?"

Despite her pain, she hurled a glare at him.

Stepping in front of her, Curtis knelt to look in her face. "I don't ever want to say goodbye to you, lass."

Ella's heart thrummed to life, her hope gingerly rising. He laid a hand on the arm of her chair. "I didn't get a wink of sleep either, but no matter how I argued with myself, I always came back to that fact. You drive a hard bargain."

Ella winced. "I'm sorry."

"No, don't be." His thumb picked the edge of the armrest. "You're right. There shouldn't be anyone else between us. It isn't fair to you or me." He pulled in a bracing lungful of air. "And

I've given you plenty of cause to doubt my feelings for you. After all, you witnessed my folly with Lorena. It's better to settle it once and for all."

"You're willing to go to Valley Creek?"

His bright blue eyes burned into hers, resolute and unwavering. "If that's the only way to win you, then yes. And the sooner the better."

Of their own accord, her arms flung around his neck. With a muffled chuckle, he pulled her close and squeezed until she thought her ribs might collapse.

"Thank you, Curtis."

He pulled back enough to shift his feet underneath him and stand, lifting her. "Now that we've settled it, you should rest today. No exercise." Scooping up her legs, he carried her to the bed and laid her down as tenderly as if she were a babe. He pressed his warm lips briefly to her forehead and stepped back.

With deft movements, he crossed to the washstand, poured water from the pitcher into the bowl, and soaked a washcloth. Wringing it out, he folded it, approached the bedside, and laid it across her forehead.

"Do you have any aspirin?"

"Dr. Weaver left a bottle. It's in my top dresser drawer."

"I'll fetch a glass."

After a quick trip to the china cabinet, Curtis poured the water into a cup. After helping her sit up, he popped the aspirin onto her tongue and lifted the cup to her lips.

"There now." He sounded as though he were talking to a small child, his voice gentle and quiet. He set the cup aside and took great care plumping her pillows. Despite the pain, Ella suppressed a giggle. The crusty bachelor was nothing more than a lamb.

Circling her shoulders with his arm, Curtis eased her down onto the pillows. "Rest. I'll check on you later." He pulled the covers under her chin and backed toward the door. A moment later, it clicked shut.

Ella closed her eyes and sent a prayer of gratitude heavenward. For Curtis to agree was no less than a miracle and a promise of his feelings for her. Once he saw Lorena again, would his seeming devotion hold true?

Time enough for worrying later.

Within seconds, she drifted to sleep.

18

"You did what?" Douglas's book smacked the porch floor as he leaped out of his chair. Nearly dropping his guitar, Caleb twisted around and gaped from his perch on the steps.

Ella restrained the impatience goading her. "I said I sent a telegram."

"How?"

"Tabitha was kind enough to take it to town and send it."

Douglas bent and plucked up the book. "Was that necessary?"

"It was." Glancing at Curtis sitting beside her, she detected a glimmer of humor on his sober face. His eyes were far too quiet and guileless.

Douglas leaned his hip against the porch railing. "I suppose you're going to tell me the reason?"

"Naturally." She shifted her eyes to Caleb sitting far too still, his hand immobile on the guitar's neck.

Douglas followed her glance. "Son."

"I'm going, sir." Caleb stood without a backward glance. "And just when it was gonna get interesting, too." His mumble caught their ears as he sprang around the corner of the house.

Beyond him, the last sliver of the sun disappeared behind the distant trees. A trace of a smile softened Douglas's face.

"I'm pretty interested myself, Ella."

"You know Lorena invited me weeks ago. I asked if I could still come, along with Curtis. He was an old friend of theirs, you know."

Along the back of the swing where his arm rested, Curtis lightly tightened his arm around her shoulders.

Douglas tapped the spine of the book against his palm. "So I've heard. But if you think for a minute I'm going to let you travel unchaperoned on a train to Arkansas, you've got another thing coming."

Ella bristled. "I traveled alone and unchaperoned to Arkansas once before. What's the difference now?"

Ever the maddingly protective brother, Douglas pinned Curtis with a stare. "What's the difference? Are you engaged?"

"Douglas Steen!" Ella's jaw slackened. "That's none of your business."

"Isn't it? Are you engaged or not?"

The pompous bore. Squirming a little, Ella fumbled with the brooch, caught herself, and thrust her hands into her lap. Curtis coughed over a chuckle.

Ella cleared her throat. "After a sort."

"After a sort?" Douglas crossed his arms.

A deep flush roared up her neck and scorched her face. "Will you quit repeating me? You're being tiresome, and you know it."

"Yes, we are engaged." Curtis broke in, as unruffled as the motionless trees in the yard. Both brother and sister gawked at him.

"Yippee!" The sound of Caleb's feet scampering toward the orchard padded through the tension. For a moment, no one breathed. No doubt to hide a smirk, Douglas dropped his stare to his feet. Ella busied herself by straightening the cuffs of her blouse. When her brother did lift his head, his face remained immobile.

"That's news to me, and I can tell by looking at Ella that it's news to her too."

Curtis never blinked, as if he weren't dazed in the least. "We've made promises to each other, but the decision is up to Ella. I'd marry her today if she would have me, but she has reservations which I understand and respect."

Thunderstruck. Through the years, Ella had heard the expression, but never did it apply to her. Until that instant. "Today?" Her voice cracked.

"That's right, lass. Today." His freshly trimmed mustache curved upward while his unabashed appraisal tingled the tips of her toes.

Douglas cleared his throat. "Well, whether she says today or not, it'll be no. I don't want to offend, Dr. Curtis, but I'm not acquainted with you well enough. I'm too old to bother about polite niceties when it comes to my family. Has she told you about her inheritance?"

An anxious look swept the color from Curtis's face. Douglas's keen eyes sharpened. "She didn't, I see. That's encouraging. At least your feelings don't stem from that."

Ella sighed. "I think this is quite enough for one evening."

"So do I." Douglas uncrossed his arms. "But I'll leave y'all with this. Whether you're promised or engaged—whatever you want to call it—you won't be traveling alone together to Valley Creek. I'll make arrangements to accompany you."

As he jogged down the steps, Ella gasped. "Well, I never. Narrow-minded and high-handed! You and I will discuss this later, Douglas."

His stride lengthened as he jogged toward the orchard, no doubt to corral his son.

———————— ❦ ————————

GEORGE FELT Ella's eyes inspecting his face. If Douglas had punched him in the gut, he'd be just as winded. He'd never given a thought to an inheritance. Here he was, destitute and homeless, courting a lady of means. He truly was daft. He'd better start learning to think like a poor man. Ella would be much better off without him. Yet his soul craved to devote himself to her and build a future.

"Curtis?" The concern in her voice tore at him.

He took a breath. "Your finances never crossed my mind."

"Nor mine." Her shoulders rose then fell with a sigh. "Maybe I shouldn't say this, but I have complete faith in you, Curtis. I know it means nothing to you."

Guilt coiled around his throat. What would she say if she knew about Lilith and his ruin? "Ella, you know I'm no longer a doctor." Withdrawing his arm from her shoulders, he scrambled for the right words. "And it's only fair to tell you that I'm no longer a man of means."

Ella cocked her ginger head. "You've lost your wealth?"

The words twisted his gut even worse than Douglas's. "Everything. I've nothing to offer you."

"And why haven't you told me?"

Anger and frustration at himself shook him. "Because I'm a coward, plain and simple. What happened in New York is difficult to relate. I will tell you when I'm able. But you deserve to know this much now." He stared into the deepening twilight as the purple shadows enveloped the trees. "Will you trust me in this? I'll understand if you won't. You don't owe me anything."

The gentle whisper of the evening breeze rustled the bushes, soothing the silence between them. Fireflies twinkled like ethereal golden stars. A balm for memories he longed to forget.

Ella's skirt swished as she shifted on the swing. "I trust you, Curtis."

Her tone, low and gentle, eased the turmoil churning within his mind. He turned toward her. Her face, though still ashen from the sleepless night and headache, possessed a serenity he lacked.

"Do you know how beautiful you are right now?"

A bashful smile lowered her eyelids. "Since I'm asking a hard thing of you in returning to Valley Creek, I think it fair to trust you in this. I'll spend time praying about it." She met his eyes then. He waited for her to suggest he pray as well, but she didn't. The bashful smile turned impish. "God is bigger than you or me. He'll deal with you accordingly."

Despite himself, he grinned as relief washed through him.

DOUGLAS DRUMMED a pencil on the edge of his desk while Ella crossed her arms and leaned forward.

"You don't have to go with us. I'm safe with Curtis. He'll take care of everything I need."

"It's not his place. Yet. I don't care how old you are—"

"I take exception to the word *old*."

Impatience pinched his mouth. "I don't care how *grown* you are. No sister of mine is going to travel alone, unmarried, with a man."

Though fed up with her brother, Ella tipped back her head and chortled. "You know, sometimes you can be such a prig. Here I am, over forty, and you insist on treating me like a little girl."

Not a flicker of amusement splintered his stern expression. "You can laugh or argue as much as you like, but it won't change my mind. When and if you say *I do*, I'll hand you over but not a moment before." He whacked the edge of the desk with the pencil. "Going to Valley Creek is a ridiculous idea anyhow."

"It's important."

Douglas lifted a brow. "Care to enlighten me?"

Ella restrained her fingers from fumbling with her collar. "Now, that's a very personal matter between Curtis and me. Believe me, he's no more thrilled about it than you are. And will you please put away that pencil?"

Sighing, he relented and thumped it across the desk. "I'd do better reasoning with Mag than you."

"Comparing me to that knot-headed mule won't do any good." Stiffening her back in the chair, Ella braced herself. "Douglas, you're blustering about this when there's actually something else that's eating at you. It's Earl, isn't it?"

There. She had spoken his name. Now she'd really done it.

Douglas's dark navy eyes raked her. He sucked in a breath as though a stinging slap caught him broadside.

"Ella, you're treading on thin ice." His low murmur nearly shattered her resolve, but she must see it through. Straining on a gulp, she swallowed slowly and hard.

"No, you're the one who's treading. You've sworn never to speak of him; no one can even mention him to you, and yet you insist on taking me there. Why?"

Douglas ground his teeth, his jaw muscles swelling on the side of his face. Ella twisted her fingers in her lap, venturing further.

"When Father left Earl his part of the inheritance and entrusted it to me, you flew into a rage that simmers to this day."

A dark crimson stain swarmed his face. His fingers, resting on the desk, curled into a fist. "The harm he inflicted on our family took Mother and Father to an early grave."

Undeterred, Ella continued. "When Earl became a Christian, you refused to believe it. But since that day, it has eaten at you bit by bit until here we are now." Try as she might, Ella couldn't bridle the quiver in her voice. "You want to see him ... your brother. The one who shadowed every step you took when we were growing up. The one you fiercely loved. And you still do."

Douglas erupted from the chair, spilling it across the floor. Ella caught her breath.

As though chased by a phantom, he bolted from the room, the air sweeping across Ella as he passed. Within seconds, the front door slammed, rattling the windows.

Forgive me, Father, but I had to do it.

Curtis's hurrying footsteps skidded into the room. "Ella, what happened? Are you all right?"

His sturdy hand grasped her shoulder while his anxious eyes searched her bleary ones. Nodding, she rested her hand across his and absorbed his strength. "I was flushing out old haunts."

A grimace crinkled Curtis's eyes at the corners. "You have a knack for it."

"A flair I could do without, to be sure." A jittery snicker parted her lips.

Drawing a handkerchief from his pocket, Curtis dabbed her eyes as tenderly as if her mother were present. The passing years had eroded days and countless hours since she felt this cherished. Not for any possession or beauty she might possess. Simply for herself. It was a feeling worth dying for.

A feeling worth treading fire.

THE RAILROAD CAR swayed as it rounded a curve, the clacking tracks nearly lulling Ella asleep. With a gloved hand, she smothered a yawn. Beside her, Douglas stared out the window. His hooded gaze roved the rising Ozark foothills. Across from her, Curtis hid his face behind a newspaper. Next to him, Caleb battled with a set of toy soldiers along the windowsill.

If only she could see Curtis's expression and read his thoughts. Ever since morning, he'd hardly spoken a dozen words. No doubt the pressure of seeing Earl and Lorena was building. In truth, she didn't want to brave it herself.

What if I see love in his face when he sees her?

She wriggled her shoulders against the plush cushion and ignored the roiling of her stomach. Through the years, she'd weathered battles—Lane's kidnapping, Earl's disappearance and betrayal, Charles and her parents' deaths—and she must handle this too. *I'm thankful Lorena understands.*

The train disappeared into a tunnel, plunging them into pitch-black darkness. The rumbling of the train, compressed inside the walls, reverberated through the cars and rattled her teeth. A much-needed distraction to redirect her thoughts.

Since that evening on the porch, they hadn't spoken of his troubles. Without any mooring, Curtis drifted on a troubled sea of memories. A doctor without a vocation. Whatever happened stripped him of his faith in himself.

The railroad cars emerged into the sunlight once more, and Ella released a breath she hadn't realized she was holding.

The newspaper crinkled as Curtis peered over the top edge at her. His regard brightened, melding with hers, the message shining abundantly clear.

The tension unraveled inside her. With one hand, Curtis fished in one of his pockets and withdrew an envelope. Holding it out to her, he deepened the look and gestured for her to take it.

Ella took the letter, her eyes questioning. He merely sat back, smiled, and lifted the newspaper.

Not wishing to disturb her brooding brother, Ella shifted a little sideways, slid a thumb beneath the sealed flap, and opened it. Her breath thinned.

My Lass,

By the time you read this, we will be well on our way. There will be no time for private conversations nor time to alleviate your anxiety.

While I write you, it is well past midnight. My few belongings are packed, and I cannot sleep. The clock ticks away the minutes, and my thoughts fill with you. I am worried about what we will face, but I am even more worried for you. Though your physical well-being is important to me, your heart and your tranquility are foremost.

Above all else, I am devoted to you. Whatever comes, if you will bear with me, I have no doubt that what you desire of me will become yours forever. Please remember this.

I have discovered a treasure in you that I never want to lose. Stay with me, Ella, and I promise you we will come through this together.

Ever yours,

Curtis

For the first time, he referred to himself the way she alone did. Though Ella's eyes burned, the ache in her heart faded with his promise. Closing her eyes, she folded the letter and brought it to her lips. If he indeed felt this way, she could wait forever.

Furtively, she peeped through her lashes and glimpsed his caressing perusal of her face. The tenderness she saw in those depths snatched her remaining breath.

19

"I feel like I'm still rolling down the tracks." Ella clung to George's shoulders as he carried her down the aisle of the immobile railroad car.

"In a little while, you'll forget all about it when you bump around in the wagon," George joked. "You know, I could get used to carrying you around like this." He clasped her a little closer.

"Hush, Curtis." She gave him a quick, smarting pinch on the shoulder, but he didn't miss the twitch of her lips.

Behind them, Douglas and Caleb trailed, lugging a few plump carpetbags. After descending the steps of the railroad car, George stepped briskly onto the platform. The clean air whisked away the stale, heavy smell of fabrics, tobacco, and passengers.

"How much farther?" Douglas roved his glance from one end of the depot to the other. Stretching, Caleb rubbed weary eyes, sprigs of wayward hair standing atop his head. The hot, humid breeze tousled his black curls.

"Five miles. Well, less than five since we're stopping at Earl and Lorena's." Ella twisted her head to look over at her brother.

A second later, George felt Ella's eyes on him, but he kept his straight ahead. "Lass, the time hasn't quite come for you to start looking holes through me."

She pinched him harder this time. "Are you nervous?" she whispered.

"I'd be made of stone if I weren't. And you?"

"Right now, I'd rather be made of stone." The trepidation in her voice made him crave to press a reassuring kiss onto her temple.

But he wasn't quite so sure of himself. With all his heart, he hoped the old feelings wouldn't resurrect when he saw Lorena. If he were a praying man ...

As they rounded the front of the building, George spied a wagon sitting under the shade of a hickory tree. In it sat a woman with a flowered sunbonnet, her auburn hair peeping from underneath the brim. A babe, kicking chubby legs and laughing, squirmed in her lap.

"Lane. Lane!" Ella waved. "Curtis, Douglas. It's Lane."

Lane gathered the babe more closely and clambered down the wagon. As soon as her boots hit the ground, she hitched up her skirts with one hand and jogged to them.

"Aunt Ella. My, but it's good to see you." Laughter rippled across Lane's face as she took Ella's outstretched hand into hers. She looked at George then, her smile not dimming. "I never thought I'd see you again, Dr. Curtis. Welcome back." The sincerity in her tone buoyed him.

"Thank you, my dear. I thought so too. It's always good to see you."

"And is this Abby? She's even more darling than the picture you sent. Look, Curtis, she has her mama's fiery hair and her daddy's hazel eyes. She just turned a year old last month."

Indeed, a few ruddy waves beneath the miniature sunbonnet curled around her forehead. For a second, it carried

George back to the time when Lane was that size. The old, familiar whisper of happier times drifted around him like an elusive mist. There one minute, then dispelled the next.

Then quiet descended as Douglas took a tentative step nearer. Ella gestured him closer. "Lane, this is your uncle Douglas and cousin Caleb."

Douglas removed his hat, an unreadable emotion on his face as though words clogged his throat.

Lane held out her hand. "I'm pleased to see you both. Welcome."

Douglas engulfed her hand with his muscular, work-worn one. Her clear blue-green eyes held no recognition of the uncle she once knew as a wee toddler, but Douglas's eyes brimmed with it. He cleared his throat, his words husky like dry leaves.

"I'm glad to see you too. Pardon me for saying, but you're the image of our mother."

"I'm so very glad to know it." She blushed, shifted Abby, and looked at Caleb. "I have a boy just about your age. You'll enjoy one another. Y'all come on and get in the wagon."

After George settled Ella on the wagon seat, he helped Douglas load their luggage into the back. A few quilts were spread on the wagon bed for sitting. As the men climbed in, Lane turned to Ella. "Would you mind holding Abby while I drive?"

"Mind? I'm dying to." Ella reached across and plucked the babe into her arms. As she cooed at Abby, a glow of pure joy lit Ella's face.

Would the lass never cease to grow lovelier? Delight filled George as he watched the happy interaction between them. Abby squealed.

"She's a talker, my Abigail." Lane snapped the reins across the team's back.

"I remember someone else who loved to talk at that age."

George shifted his spine away from the jostling sides of the wagon.

"So I've heard."

As the ladies' conversation flowed, George filled his lungs with the clean, mid-afternoon air. The trees spread their limbs high and thronged the hillsides like sentinels guarding the inhabitants against the outside world. Not far from the road, winding like a shimmering, azure ribbon through the trees, Valley Creek gurgled and tripped over the smooth stones.

George ventured a look at Douglas. He, too, seemed mesmerized by the sights. Caleb's wide eyes missed nothing, from bird's nests to critters vanishing into the brush.

This place was a world away from New York City. What a refuge for an exile like him. The thought seized him. Lost years filled his mind while he pictured Earl trudging up that very road, angry and alone. An outcast of his own choosing.

George saw his thoughts echoed in the simmering of Douglas's eyes. How well he understood, but time and troubles had quelled the anger. Swiping the perspiration from his forehead, he hoped time had quenched other feelings also.

Lane turned partially around and looked at George. "Pa and Mother no longer live at the old place. It took about a year to build the new house. It's a little closer to mine."

"I'm interested to see it."

"So am I." Ella cuddled Abby closer. "Lorena described it in her letters. It sounds like a beautiful place. I'm so happy for them."

Crossing his arms, Douglas squirmed and glowered at the wagon bed. No longer than George had been a guest in their home, he sensed the undercurrent in Douglas's life. He understood all too well and, frankly, he was weary of it.

Would this time in Valley Creek set him free?

The miles jostled onward. Over hills and shaded vales until the land nestled down and flattened, encompassed by the rising mountains. Valley Creek. Pastures and fields dotted homeplaces often hedged by split rail fences or low rock walls.

Dropping clothes into a steaming iron wash pot, a woman straightened and shaded her eyes with a hand, warily watching them pass. Only a few steps away, leaning against the log cabin, a shotgun stood ready for use. When she recognized Lane, she waved.

In a place like this, George's past seemed like a different lifetime. Except for the memory of Lilith. Every time he closed his eyes, she was there.

They clattered across a short wooden bridge and soon turned into a clearing.

"My, my." Ella breathed, raising a hand to her mouth.

A large, wide whitewashed house reposed on stone pilings in a well-swept yard. A serene sight. Across the length of the house, a long porch stretched and rounded the sides. Four long, green trimmed windows winked from beneath a steep, sloping roof with a dormer window centered perfectly above the steps. The new wooden shingles caught the light, honey-colored in the sunshine. Near the backyard, a huge vegetable garden thrived, its rows clean and meticulously kept.

And at the bottom of the front steps stood Earl Steen.

Removing his hat, he shaded his bronzed face with his hand. The movement hid any expression, but he stood straight and firm as though nothing could uproot him.

After the wagon neared, Lane reined in the team, threw on the brake, and waved. "Hi, Pa!"

Earl raised a hand.

Ignoring his stiff muscles and icy dread deep inside, George climbed out. With brisk strokes, he dusted his arms and legs.

After standing, Douglas jumped over the side of the wagon. He didn't bother dusting his britches or admiring the place. He leveled his attention on his younger brother for the first time in many years.

He moved forward, each stride lengthening and falling quicker than the last one. Earl's hand dropped from shielding his eyes. Closer Douglas strode until he was within arm's reach. He halted, stood stock-still for a mere heartbeat.

In a flash, his fist swung out and cracked Earl across the jaw.

Earl's head whipped around, and he stumbled back several feet. The ladies gasped while Caleb ducked down in the wagon.

Blood-red anger broiled into Earl's face. In two strides, he dashed to his brother, his eyes glinting. Douglas raised his fists, ready for the brawl.

"I promised myself long ago if I ever laid eyes on you again, this would be the first thing I'd do."

Time suspended around them. Earl balled his fists, his chest heaving. As George watched, he spied another emotion, akin to anguish, overshadow the anger in Earl's face.

Flexing his jaw, Earl unclenched his fists and lowered them stiffly at his sides.

"If it helps, here's the other side, Douglas." He turned his other cheek toward him and closed his eyes.

Douglas reeled backward as though he'd been slugged. Spinning on his heel, he tramped from the yard and entered the rutted, dirt road. He kicked a limb without breaking stride, soon lost to sight.

Earl approached the wagon, rubbing the rising lump on his jaw. He looked from one to the other, his eyes finally resting on George.

"While we're at it, does anyone else want their turn?"

"Pa." Lane reached across and placed Abby into his arms. Earl gathered her close as he laid a swift kiss on her head.

The words jammed in George's throat as his former friend surveyed him, the shadow of anguish lingering in Earl's face. He must say something. Swallowing, George reached for Ella.

"Thank you for having us."

"You're most welcome." Peace quickly overtook the anger flashing in Earl's eyes moments ago.

As George slipped his arms around Ella, he swung her down and brought her closer to her brother.

Tears threaded her voice as she gingerly reached out and fingered the crimson mark on Earl's face. "This wasn't the way I wanted to say hello. I'm sorry. The pig-headed brute."

"Ah, we'll have none of that." Earl smiled as Abby nuzzled her head against his shoulder. "No tears. I didn't expect him to meet me with a bear hug. I know Douglas." He stepped closer to the wagon and peered over the side at the crouched boy. "And who's this young fellow come for a visit? You must be Caleb." He held out a muscled hand.

Grimacing, Caleb shook it as if shaking hands with a lion. "Yes, sir."

"I'd know you anywhere. You're the image of your father. Welcome to my home." He released the boy's hand. "Come now; there's a boy around back—Jimmy—who's excited to meet you. He's down at the creek just beyond the woodshed yonder. Why don't you go make friends."

A relieved grin brightened Caleb's face. "Yes, sir. Thank you, Uncle Earl." Jumping up, he sprang from the wagon and scampered around the house.

"They'll become fast friends, I know it." Lane climbed from the wagon. "Where's Mother?"

"Hanging clothes on the line. I expect she'll be around in a minute. You arrived a little sooner than we expected."

"The train was early." George's voice box cracked like a rusty, inflexible tool.

"And I, for one, was glad. I've had enough clackity-clacking."

Earl chuckled and turned toward the house. "Let's get you settled, then I'll help George with the luggage."

From the back of the house, a lady swept around the side,

carrying a large, empty basket. No one had to tell George who she was.

Dark golden hair. Firm, lithe steps. Lorena's blue eyes cautiously met his. He never thought he'd see her again.

She set the basket on the porch and stepped forward, smoothing her apron. "Ella, darling, I'm happy you're here."

Ella's voice rasped. "I'm truly happy to see you, Lorena." She held out a hand.

Lorena neared and gathered it within her own. Hesitantly, she turned her glance to George.

Like darts hitting a target, he felt every eye fixated on his face. "Lorena, I appreciate you and Earl for allowing me to come."

The tightness around the corners of her eyes relaxed. "You and Ella are always welcome here."

As she stepped toward Earl, an unexpected relief seeped into George. The old feelings he dreaded didn't surge into his heart. Rather, at the sight of her, the strongest emotion shaking him was profound regret for his past conduct. Strange, but after days of dread, he welcomed the feeling.

He turned and met Ella's scouring stare hunting any covert emotion lurking behind his expression while she tried to cloak her vulnerability.

George peeped at the others. For a moment, they were occupied with a cooing Abby. A perfect diversion.

Leaning in, he planted a swift kiss on the end of Ella's upturned nose. Her quick gasp filled him with unexpected mirth.

"Shhh, lass. Behave yourself," he murmured.

She stammered soundlessly, looking trapped between annoyance and being mesmerized.

"Earl, what happened to the side of your face?" Lorena's rising voice snagged their attention. She grasped his elbow.

"Douglas."

"Where is he?" She whirled on her heel, hands flying to her hips.

"He took a walk." Ella's voice was slightly breathless, and the roses blossoming in her cheeks belied her calm demeanor.

"Well, let's hope he simmers down before he returns." Sighing, Lorena compressed her lips.

20

Music spilled from the long, wide porch after a satisfying supper. Earl's fingers danced on the bridge of his violin while Harley Ray picked the jaunty tune on his banjo. Beside him, Guy kept time with a guitar, his fingertips skipping between the frets.

Despite her exhaustion, Ella ached to tap her feet but couldn't keep pace. A fresh breeze swept the curling tendrils from her cheeks. She caught Lane's eyes and smiled. A slight grin parted Lane's lips as she glanced over at Edith's pronounced middle. Stretching, Edith straightened her back and drew a breath, folding her hands over her stomach. Next month, two little ones would join the family. Ella lifted a silent prayer for the babies and their mother. *Lord, please be their shield. Let this time be different.* Against her will, she remembered Edith's wee lady in the graveyard on a hilltop not far away.

Down at the end of the porch, as far away as he could sit, Douglas glowered at the hills. He crossed his arms over his chest as though oblivious to the music.

But Ella knew better. His ruminations mirrored a haunted ache hovering deep inside. All through supper, he'd kept his gaze fixed on his plate while the lively chatter buzzed around him.

In the yard, Caleb and Jimmy tossed a baseball back and forth while twilight unfurled dusky shadows over the hills and vales.

Beside Earl, Lorena rested her chin in her palm and hummed the tune. Other than polite, cordial glances at Curtis, she had managed to keep the mood light around the table. Affection filled Ella's heart. What a treasure, her sister-in-law! More than anyone else, she understood how important this visit was to Ella.

As Earl slid into *Kathleen Mavourneen*, Curtis enveloped Ella's hand with his. With a surprised glance, Ella encountered his slight smile. Had he sensed her thoughts? Her cheeks tingled. She certainly hoped not.

With all her heart, Ella yearned to turn her palm over to meet his and intertwine their fingers, but she resisted the urge. Not yet. Not until she was sure of him.

Will I ever be?

Ella swallowed a sigh and returned the smile, allowing his warmth to seep deeper into her heart than was wise.

"Do you think there are dogwood winters here?" Curtis mused.

Ella scrunched her brows. "Pardon?"

He dipped his head closer. "Dogwood winter. 'Winter's ebbing grasp upon spring.'"

Realization dawned over Ella. "Ah, yes. Laughing at me, are you, Curtis? Have you been reduced to memorizing my letters?"

Without missing a beat, Curtis tightened his fingers over hers. "'The snow blights the flowers, cutting their beauty short. An untimely end. In these parts, we call it a dogwood winter—winter's ebbing grasp upon spring.'" One side of his mustache ticked upward. "Are you surprised I remembered?"

"I hardly know what to think." Ella's fluttering pulse thinned her breath.

Curtis sobered. "Neither did I. All I know is that it has stayed with me ever since. Why do you feel it's a broken promise? I've often wondered about it." His gaze captured hers, earnest and intent for the answer.

Had anyone ever looked at her with such yearning? The answer faded from Ella's mind and melted somewhere in the music. "I can't say."

"Can't or won't?"

Couldn't the wretched man see that her wit had suddenly abandoned her? "Curtis, please. Everyone is watching."

"No, they're not. They're watching Douglas trying to ignore the music."

Ella managed a quiet giggle. "I'd hate to be him right now."

"A nice way to change the subject, but I'll not let it go that easily." His fingers brushed the tops of her knuckles. "Tell me why."

Sighing, Ella squirmed at unwelcome memories. "This isn't the time or place. I'll tell you sometime, but not today."

"Very well. I'll hold you to it." Turning his head to watch the boys, Curtis broke their gaze. Immediately, emptiness deluged her. What would he do when he learned the answer?

Interrupting her thoughts, Douglas spewed a low growl as he shoved himself from the chair. He hopped to the ground and stalked toward the backyard.

Ella snagged Earl's glance as he raised his chin slightly from the violin. *My brother, I know how you feel. Take heart.* Earl answered her with a tiny nod, resting his chin once more on the instrument.

After another half-hour, the music dwindled to a stop, and the men put their instruments away. Goodnights were said and embraces given while Guy and Harley Ray readied their wagons. When the young folks drove away, the crickets chirruped, drowning out the sound of the wagon wheels. Beside Ella, Curtis cleared his throat.

"Earl, Lorena, I'd like to thank you for letting me come and offering your other place while I stay."

Earl nodded. "It's been standing empty since we finished building here. We freshened it up a bit for you. I know it's small, but it's private."

Ella remembered Earl's small, three-roomed house that he had built after the tornado almost destroyed Valley Creek. Yes, Curtis would enjoy the privacy, and it would give her a little time to breathe and think.

"It's exactly the thing I need." Rubbing a hand across the back of his neck, Curtis scooted to the edge of the chair. "Before another day passes, I have to say something."

"There's no need." A wary look stole into Earl's eyes.

"But there is." Curtis's gaze bounced between Earl and Lorena. "It's no easy thing for me to apologize. I've thought of little else on our way here, but I don't know what to say. No words are good enough to tell you how much I regret my past actions. Lorena, I hope you'll forgive me and consider me the brother I once was. Earl, I ridiculed you and did everything to stand in your way. I'm truly sorry." His voice wobbled when he turned to Ella. "And Ella. I made a fool of myself and was unkind to you. I'll always regret it."

Ella pressed a hand against her throat, stemming the rush of moisture to her eyes. As though unable to speak, Lorena dipped her head, her eyes shimmering.

Earl offered his hand. "It's forgiven, George. Let's speak no more of it."

The former best friends clasped hands with a hearty shake. A relieved smile vanquished the angst in Curtis's face. "I don't deserve it. Thank you all."

When the handshake ended, he shifted toward Ella and

intertwined her fingers with his. The promise in his face was solely for her.

Ella forced her quickening breath to slow. It seemed too good to be true; however, time would prove the sincerity of his devotion.

"Dr. Curtis, this is a pleasant surprise."

George waved while Doc Brown shouldered a hoe and trudged out of his vegetable garden. Morning dew and dirt splattered the legs of his overalls. After nudging up the brim of his straw hat with a finger, he slapped his gritty hand against his thigh and held it out to George.

George pumped his hand. "It's good to see you again, Doctor."

"Missed me so much you couldn't stay away, eh?" Doc released George's hand and leaned the hoe against a pine tree.

Chuckling, George rested his hands on his hips. "Something like that."

For a few seconds, the two men regarded each other, and George felt the same kinship he remembered with Doc during his last visit to Valley Creek.

"I never thought I'd see you again." Doc brushed a ladybug off the sleeve of his flour-sack shirt, his sharp focus never leaving George's face.

"I certainly never thought I'd return."

"The Lord works in mysterious ways. Come on." Doc gestured toward the backyard. "The creek runs behind my place. It's cooler there, and there's a spring running right into it. Best tastin' water around. We'll talk there."

"Lead the way."

The trees closed around them and banished the hot summer

sun as they neared the water. The cadence tripped and gurgled over the rocks as if whispering to itself. The sound eased the turbulent emotions within George. Another nightmare had stolen his sleep. This time Lilith had come, asking him to help her find her way home to her mother and father. He'd taken her cold hand, and they searched until they found her parents' graves in the cemetery. Her frantic cries had shaken him awake. Even now, the memory slammed George's heart against his ribcage.

The cool, moist air skimmed his face. The birds chirped overhead while a few others splashed in a shallow pool a safe distance farther down the bank.

A world apart from New York City. The Promised Land after wandering in the wilderness of guilt.

With a relieved groan, Doc squatted then sat on a large flat rock. He patted the space beside him. "Here's the spring." Water bubbled up from the ground and meandered a twisting, pebbled path downward. He scooped a handful of water into his palm and lifted it to his lips. His Adam's Apple bobbled. "Hits the spot. Refresh yourself, Dr. Curtis."

If only I could. Sitting, George dipped his fingers into the frigid, swirling water. "I've never drunk water straight out of the ground."

"There's a first time for everything."

Scooping up a handful, George lifted it to his mouth. The crisp water glided down easily and cooled his insides. "You're right, Doc. I've never tasted anything like it." He dipped his hand into the water again and took a long drink.

"For something that's odorless and colorless, it satisfies like nothing else." Doc removed his straw hat and fanned his face. "What brings you back?"

Heat pricked the back of George's neck. "Personal matters. I'm here to prove myself to Ella Steen."

"I'd heard she was coming." A roguish grin twisted Doc's lips. "Good. She's a smart gal."

"She is. I hope I succeed."

"I reckon you stand a good chance." Doc reached into the water and scooped himself another mouthful. "And while you're here, I'd be obliged if you'd accompany me on some of my calls. It's not often I get to keep company with another doctor."

Dread snaked around George's heart. He hesitated, searching his mind for a safe answer. "I appreciate it, but I'll be helping Ella most of the time. She's had infantile paralysis and can't walk. My time is taken up trying to help her regain strength."

"I hated to hear of her misfortune. I'm sorry." Doc sighed. "Maybe you could come with me on my early morning calls before you see Ella."

"I don't think I can this time."

"Can't or won't?"

"A little of both. I'm sorry." He spread his hands wide, palms upward.

Doc squinted as if trying to decipher George's excuses. "Care to tell me why? I see the look on your face. Dread and something else. When you visited before, you were more than willing to go."

His something else was guilt. Pure and simple. To keep from clenching his teeth, George swiped another drink from the spring. Doc's perusal never wavered.

"You can trust me, Dr. Curtis."

Trust. A word that could destroy or build. A word that had become a stranger. Frustration choked him.

"Dr. Curtis?"

"I'm not a doctor." Before George could yank them back, the words escaped. Saying them aloud felt like a knife thrust under his ribcage.

"What do you mean?" Doc tilted his head to one side.

"I can't do this."

"With any other person, I'd stop right there. But not this time. Whatever you say won't go any further than me. Please. Tell me."

An unspeakable feeling juddered through George as he tried to blink away Lilith's face. He sucked in a quick breath. "There was an accident. I ... I killed a little girl."

"How?"

"In surgery. She bled to death." His squeezed his eyes shut.

Compassion filled Doc's voice. "That's a tragedy, and I'm sorry for you and her family." He sighed. "But you've lost other patients, surely. It happens to all of us."

Opening his eyes, George pressed his palm against the cool, hard surface of the rock as though it might anchor him. "Yes, but this was different. She was a family friend, a neighbor of mine."

"I can relate. Doctoring here in this valley, I know all my patients. Some too well. I've made mistakes."

George raised his head and drilled into Doc's stare. "What did it cost you?"

"Folks here understand that life is fragile and hard. Survival is never guaranteed and always Providential. They know I'm not a miracle worker. When it's all said and done, it's up to God. Although I've suffered many sleepless nights wondering if I could've done more. Or if I'd done the wrong thing. What did it cost you?"

"I had to leave the city, leave my profession. The girl's father sued me and won. It took everything I had."

"No, it didn't."

A frown pinched George's mouth. "Pardon?"

"You still have your skill."

"No. The thought of ever using a scalpel again sends chills down my spine. While tending patients, I would be fighting memories of Lilith. A doctor must be focused, able to think clearly to make decisions." He rubbed a rough hand over his eyes. "I can't."

"Dr. Curtis, I can't tell you the times I've wanted to quit. This has knocked you sideways, but you've got to push through."

Unable to take any more, George sprang up. "I'm sorry. I appreciate your words, but I'm too old to start over. I don't know what I'll do in the future, but I can assure you, I won't be Dr. Curtis ever again."

Doc rose, a steely determined look dinting lines around his mouth. "If the calling is genuine, it won't ever leave. And it'll keep you awake nights even longer than the memory of Lilith."

George's eyebrows rose. He doubted it.

21

The bedcovers flew back as George bolted upright. His heart thundered within his heaving chest. The scene had been too real—Lilith's marble-white face, her fluttering pulse, her blood.

George shuttered and scraped the palm of his hand over his clammy face. The moonless night cloaked the little house with an inky blackness infusing the marrow of his bones. Shifting to the edge of the bed, he snatched a match from the side table and struck it.

Immediately, a small golden flame flared to life. His quaking fingers hovered above the wick of the kerosene lamp, gliding the match over it. With a puff of air, he extinguished the match as light drove the darkness into the corners.

Everything within and outside the house was silent with a deafening stillness. The table clock showed 4:30 a.m. Mechanically, he rose and made the bed. The simple squares of the faded, patchwork quilts spoke of lean times in Earl Steen's past.

And here he was in the same boat.

With stiff fingers, George dressed. After setting aside the

comb on the dressing table, he carried the kerosene lamp through the tiny living room and into the tinier kitchen. The warm, golden glow wedged a beam of light through the shadows. Beside the stove, stacked on the floor, Earl had left enough wood to start a fire, along with the kindling inside a pail. He set the lamp on a narrow, wooden countertop.

George hadn't started a fire since he was a young boy in Ireland. A good thing he still remembered helping his mam prepare one in their cottage. After checking the air valve, he took a sheet of old newspaper and set it on top of the bed of ash inside. Next, he set the kindling on top of it.

In a few minutes, the crackling fire radiated a warmth that settled George's throbbing pulse. After rummaging through the cabinets, he found a coffee tin along with the percolator. On the countertop, in a box, lay a slab of cured, smoked pork belly. George's mouth watered. He imagined the bacon sizzling in a skillet. A large stoneware bowl beside it held a dozen eggs. The little pantry shelves held mason jars of preserved fruit and vegetables. There were even a few loaves of sourdough bread. Earl and Lorena had spared no details for his needs. Gratitude and shame warred with each other. He didn't deserve such kindness.

A while later, he sat at the small table in the living room, sipping fresh coffee. Outside the window, the gray, shadowed trees slowly donned their color in the crimson dawn. His gaze meandered the unvarnished plank walls, the practical red gingham curtains, and the hearth with stones no doubt pried and hauled from the nearby hillside.

The sharp, bitter coffee nearly set his teeth on edge. A wry smile tipped the corners of his lips. He had plenty of time to master coffee making. From now on, wherever he lived, he would have to get used to living simply. Making do. Although the thought wasn't galling, it didn't appeal to him either. The main problem was figuring out how to survive. What he needed was a trade. A town where he could make use of himself, especially if Ella would be willing to have him.

Hard work didn't frighten him. Finding his place in life did.

"Halloo!" A voice from outside shattered his thoughts.

Scrambling from his seat, George hurried to open the door. A buggy with a sorrel mare stood in the yard. Doc Brown held the reins in his tanned fingers.

"Are you ready, Dr. Curtis?"

Dumbfounded, George clenched the doorframe. "What's this about?"

Doc raised the reins just a bit. "Time for house calls." Quirking an eyebrow, Doc's expression dared him to argue.

"Not this time or anytime, Doctor. I know you mean well, but I'm not one of your patients."

"Thank the Good Lord for that." Doc guffawed. "Get your bag. I know you have it. No doctor leaves anywhere without it. No matter what."

George forced down his rising bile. "You're wasting your time."

"No, sir. You are." Doc pointed a finger that burned into George's gut. "I need your help today, and I won't take no for an answer."

"You've gotten along without my help all this time. I'm sure you'll be fine and dandy."

"Not now, Dr. Curtis." A stony glint stole into Doc's lean face. He drew in a deep breath and slowly exhaled. "Do I have to hogtie you to this buggy, or are you coming nice-like?"

George opened his mouth to say no, but Doc's flinty countenance froze the words on his lips. Clamping his mouth shut, George pivoted inside and tramped to his trunk in the bedroom. He swung open the lid.

Next to his clothes, nestled to one side, lay his bag. He curled a fist. Maybe it was better to go and show Doc how inept he truly was. He would never ask George again. Reaching down, he grasped the cool handle and tugged it out. After he came into the living room, he plucked his hat from the peg on the wall.

"Very well." George snapped the door shut behind himself and descended the steps.

Scooting over to give George room, Doc quipped, "About time."

Without bothering to answer, George climbed inside, and Doc snapped the reins lightly against the mare's back. Before he could settle into the seat, the buggy rolled forward and flung him against the cushion with a firm bounce.

While long miles passed, the quiet morning enveloped them, the muggy summer air thickening as the sun beamed its first rays over the mountains. The smell of sawdust spiced the light breeze. In his mind, George pictured the sawmill buzzing as the men in Valley Creek unloaded logs from wagons. A horsefly bobbled between the mare's ears, and she tossed her head.

"Steady, Ginger." Doc made a nickering sound while lifting a whip.

The horsefly hovered above the mare's head. Before it could dip down again, Doc snapped his whip and hit it. The mare never broke her stride.

"Well, you won't be bothered by that one again." Doc scooted back, pleased.

Forgetting his irritation, George blinked. "Incredible. I've never seen anything like that in my life. And your mare didn't spook."

Doc chuckled. "We've ridden a lot of years together, Ginger and me, and we've seen our share of horseflies. I've learned a lot of tricks on these long rides, and she has learned to trust me. All I have to do is give her the word, and she knows."

"It's amazing."

"When I had no other recourse, I improvised." He cut a glance at George. "You will too."

George grunted.

"And sooner rather than later." Doc tilted his head up and watched the pink, wispy clouds suspended high above them. "I'm leaving Valley Creek."

George straightened, alarmed. "Whatever for? You can't leave here. People depend on you."

"Be that as it may, I'm still going." Doc's raspy voice thickened as he pinned George with a look. "I'm dying."

Blunt. Stark. The words hurtled into George with a force that knocked the wind out of him. He stared back at his friend and noticed for the first time a yellowing of Doc's eyes. George gritted his teeth. "What is it?"

"Cancer of the liver most likely. It's hard as a rock, and I'm getting more yellow by the day. Put your fingers here." He pointed to his upper right side.

George pressed and felt the firmness of Doc's liver. He removed his hand and stared forward as a dreadful knowledge seized him.

"That's why I need your help."

How could he refuse his friend? He rubbed his tight jaw. "As long as I'm here, I'll do what I can."

"That's not what I mean." Doc winced and shifted on the seat as the buggy hit a rut. "I've seen a lot of things in my time, and I've never been much of a believer. Until the last few years. I reckon what happened with Earl is what brought me around to the Lord."

Frowning, George shifted as well but not from any tracks in the road. Doc continued as if he hadn't noticed. "My wife and I have been praying for months that the Lord would send a doctor to replace me. The moment I saw you, I knew God provided."

Could this conversation get any worse? George grasped the

armrest and schooled his voice. "You have it all wrong, Doc. I'm not the man. I said I'd help but only as long as I'm needed."

"Like it or not, you are. I feel it deep in my bones."

"No. I appreciate your confidence, but you're wrong. I'm only here for a little while, and then I'm moving on."

"Argue if you like, but when I have a hunch, I'm always right."

"You don't know what you're asking of me."

"Don't I?" Doc's sharp scrutiny narrowed, a hint of impatience kindling them. "Do you think I've never had long days when I wished I'd never touched a medical book? That I get tired of the endless hours and scant pay? Do you think I've never lost a patient by making a mistake? I've seen babies die before they took their first breath, and I've fought to keep their mamas from following them. Sometimes I failed." His chin quaked. "But I never quit. And neither will you. I daresay God won't let you."

George turned his head away. "We'll see about that." The determination in Doc's sallow face pained him almost physically.

"We certainly will, Dr. Curtis."

Though no one else was nearby, Doc lowered his voice. "Other than my wife, no one else knows about my condition. I'd like to keep it that way. Folks have enough troubles without havin' to bother about mine."

With a burning throat, George riveted his gaze on the rhythmic bob of Ginger's head as her hooves plodded down the road. Helplessness and the familiar taste of grief swept over him. Leaning forward, he rested his elbows on his knees and hauled in as much breath as his lungs could hold while Doc talked of his patients as if nothing had happened.

THE EARLY AFTERNOON sun spilled into the yard, breached by the shade above Ella and Lorena. While Lorena mended one of Earl's shirts, Ella darned his socks.

"Has the adjustment been hard for you?"

"I've found it difficult at times because of the lack of conveniences, but I'm finding my stride. It's been good for me. I can't imagine any other life without Earl." Lorena's nimble fingers dipped and pulled the needle through the material. "I've been more at peace here than at any other time in my life."

"You've come into your own."

"I never thought it possible. When I look at Earl and this place, I'm looking at a miracle." Lorena's gaze roved over the yard and house, contentment lighting her profile. She glanced at Ella. "It pains me to see your restlessness. I hope you'll find some respite here."

Ella finished Earl's sock and dropped it into a basket beside her wheelchair. "I just want to be useful again, and ..."

"And?"

"You know, Lorena. Curtis is trying hard to win my heart and confidence, and I wonder how I can look after a husband." Reaching down into the basket, Ella plucked up another sock and prepared to mend it.

"With God's help, you'll find a way. Have you told George about Charles?"

Ella's fingers stiffened. "Yes."

Lorena rethreaded a needle. "What about Charles's picture?"

"I'm a coward; that's what I am." Disgust and anxiety soured her voice.

"Ella."

"Don't *Ella* me. Believe me, I know." Ella nearly pricked her finger. "It's getting harder by the day. I've let too much time pass. I know Curtis will be hurt, and I'm scared he won't understand. My feelings for him have nothing to do with Charles."

Setting the shirt in her lap, Lorena sighed and laid a hand on Ella's arm. "If George was willing to return to Valley Creek for your sake, it'll take more than a photograph to shake him."

Ella studied Lorena's face closely. "I hope you're right, but I'm more concerned about other things sidetracking his affections."

Without flinching, Lorena met her direct scrutiny. "I know you are. When you asked about his coming, I confess I was nervous too. After watching him with you, though, I was greatly relieved. What he feels for you is real."

Embarrassed, Ella dipped her head, her cheeks heating. "Forgive me for saying this, but I don't want to be second best."

Lorena's hand tightened on her arm, her grip gentle and reassuring. "Of one thing I'm certain: George never does anything halfway. If he loves you, Ella, you can rest assured his devotion is with every fiber of his being. No one else will reside in his heart."

Ella's eyes smarted. "Thank you for being patient and understanding with me."

"You're my dearest friend. Never forget you can tell me anything."

"Likewise, Lorena. Thank you."

Lorena's eyes sparkled as she picked up Earl's shirt once more, her voice becoming teasing. "This should be an interesting summer."

The heat bridging Ella's cheekbones crackled "The spring has been more interesting than I anticipated. In more ways than one." She gestured toward her legs.

Sympathy fringed Lorena's lips. "I know." She glanced around the yard as Jimmy's and Caleb's shouts exploded from the woods. "Those boys are already having the time of their lives."

"Caleb needs this badly. I'm hoping Douglas will get himself out of the way long enough to let him stay for the summer."

"I suppose Douglas intends to spend most of his time here wandering the woods." She pushed the needle through the cloth. "Still as stubborn as always."

"And it hasn't mellowed with age." Sadness wrapped around her shoulders, sagging them. "I'd hoped—well, anyhow, since he leaves tomorrow, there'll be no time for him to soften toward Earl."

"It's a shame, though I understand. So does Earl. He must love you very much to be willing to come."

The rattling of wheels interrupted their conversation. Doc Brown's buggy soon rolled into the yard. Beside Doc sat Curtis, who waved while Doc reined the mare to a stop. Curtis's eyes sought Ella's and found them, a hint of weariness darkening them.

"Hullo, ladies." Doc tipped his hat. "I trust you're doing all right this fine afternoon." More whooping in the woods overflowed into the yard. A grin crinkled Doc's face. "I can tell the boys are fine."

Both Lorena and Ella laughed. Lorena folded Earl's shirt. "It's good to hear them. Doc, would you like to get down and have something to drink?"

"Thanks, but I'm heading home. My wife will have the coffee waiting."

"Give Mrs. Brown our regards."

"I'll do that. And I bet she'll have a fresh loaf of raisin bread for you on Sunday." He winked.

"We'll be looking forward to it."

While they finished exchanging pleasantries, Curtis stepped over to the porch. The bag clutched in his hand caught Ella's notice. After he set it aside, he dipped some water from the pail dangling from a peg. He took a long drink. No doubt he was washing away the heat and dust.

After he hung the dipper back on its nail, he came to stand behind her underneath the shade. He rested a hand on the back of Ella's wheelchair. "Thank you for the visit, Doc."

Doc touched his fingers to the brim of his hat. "Same time tomorrow?"

Ella heard the whisper of a sigh in Curtis's answer. "I'll see you then."

With a nod, Doc waved goodbye. After flicking the reins, he turned the mare around and headed toward Valley Creek.

Ella glanced over her shoulder at Curtis. "Did you go with Doc on his house calls?"

"Not willingly. With his powers of persuasion, he should've been a politician."

With a smile that included them both, Lorena lifted her wide-brimmed hat from the grass and rose. "I'll leave you two to visit while I take some water to Earl in the field."

"There's no need to hurry off, Lorena." Ella clamped down on the nervous stirrings within her stomach.

Donning her hat, Lorena's smile widened. "Tell that to George."

A dusky scarlet crept up George's neck, darkening at his collar. "Has country living worn out your subtlety?"

With a snicker, Lorena shrugged. "Perhaps. Or maybe it comes with age. Beating around the bush becomes a waste of time."

As she went to fetch the water pail, Curtis stepped around Ella's chair and lowered himself on the vacant one. He glanced at the sock still lying in her hand.

"And how's my lass today?"

His lass. Ella's pulse galloped, but she covered it with a cough. "We've had a busy morning. Cooking, tidying the house, and mending. It feels good to be useful."

"You're a treasure, Ella. And more."

Now that he was near her, Ella eyed the shadows rimming his eyes. "I can see you're tired. Did you not rest last night?"

"Only part of it. Did you?"

"Only part of it."

A chuckle loosened the tension around his mouth. He tweaked the tip of her nose with his knuckle. "No matter how difficult your day, you manage to make those around you smile."

Not knowing what to do with such a compliment, Ella fingered the lace at her throat, the brooch now absent. "I can't say how."

"It's one of your gifts."

Anxious to turn the attention from herself, Ella peeked over his shoulder at the bag sitting on the porch. "How was your morning with Doc?"

Curtis's shoulders rose then sagged. "Difficult."

22

George watched the lovely blush fade from Ella's cheeks. She blinked, obscuring her disquiet for an instant.

"I thought you said you'd never doctor again."

"And I still have no intention of it."

"Then why did you take your bag?"

"Doctor Brown demanded it."

Ella squinched her nose. "Demanded it?"

Nodding, George dusted the legs of his pants. "He showed up at the house this morning, wanting me to go with him. He wouldn't take no for an answer." His bottled-up frustration overtook his patience. "I'm in a bit of a jam."

"Tell me, Curtis."

For a few long seconds, he peered into the depths of Ella's eyes. Oh, he had much to tell—much more than he could say, especially concerning Lilith. Though the unspoken thoughts staggered over his tongue, he crammed them to the back of his mind. Better to focus on the present instead.

But he couldn't keep this from her, and he sorely needed someone to help him bear it.

"I know I can trust you to keep this to yourself. Doc doesn't want anyone to know, and he'd be angry if he knew I was telling you."

Alarm spread across Ella's features. "I'll not breathe a word to anyone."

The words tasted like chalk on the tip of his tongue. "Doc is dying. He has cancer of the liver."

Ella's hand flew to her mouth. "How terrible. I'm so very sorry, Curtis."

"So am I." In more ways than one. Torn between grief for his friend and his predicament, George closed his stinging eyes.

"His wife will be devastated. Valley Creek will be at a loss."

"I know."

George felt her small, warm hand cover the top of his. "I know there's more."

What a lass she was. So perceptive and understanding. Reaching over, he clasped his other hand over hers, clinging to it like an anchor in tumultuous waves.

"He wants me to take his place."

A ridge of furrows puckered Ella's brow. "Permanently?"

"Permanently."

"Gracious me." She searched his face as though trying to decipher his thoughts.

George tightened his grip on her fingers. "I've agreed, under protest, to help while I can, but I won't be staying."

He could see the thoughts ticking within her ginger head. "Perhaps it's wise not to make any hasty decisions, but I wouldn't discard the idea altogether. I firmly believe you must continue practicing medicine. It's as much a part of you as walking."

"No. I'm finished with it."

"Are you?" One eyebrow quirked upward.

"I am." He stroked her fingers. "And what about us? I'm a

poor man. A doctor can't make a decent living here. How could I take care of you if I stayed? Where would it leave us?"

A challenge kindled in her eyes. "Do you think I'm incapable of adjusting to life here?"

"Incapable isn't the right word. Impracticable is more like it."

Flattening her lips together, Ella snapped her head away. George scrubbed a hand over his face. He had blundered again. "I'm not referring to your condition, only my ability to provide for you."

She raised her chin. "I'm not destitute."

"I'm thankful you have it to help, but I won't depend on it. What kind of man would I be otherwise?"

"I feel the rumblings of a quarrel starting, and I don't feel like bickering with you." Withdrawing her hand, she lowered her head, her tone low and rankled. "Would you wheel me to the house?"

"What about your exercises?" The warmth he had relished from her touch dissipated.

"Perhaps tomorrow."

"We cannot waste even one day, lass."

The stubborn ridge in her jaw hardened. Sighing, George rose and pushed the wheelchair across the yard, watching the waves of her hair jiggle and bounce with every bump. Indeed, life in the country would prove harder for Ella if she didn't recover the use of her legs. Her ability to move freely would be hampered.

And he'd not stand for it. Her comfort would come first, whether she liked it or not.

When they reached the porch, George stopped and lifted Ella into his arms. Her arm circled his shoulders lightly, hesitantly, as he climbed the steps. When he reached the top, he paused.

"Look at me, darling. Please. Will you allow me to help you exercise later today?"

George watched the stubbornness war with reason while she chewed her bottom lip. In that moment, she had no idea how lovely she was. Despite his irritation, he yearned to gather her closer. He refrained, though it took all the resolve he possessed.

Finally, Ella raised her downcast eyes, and his breath hitched. Their gazes mingled, a mix of willfulness and angst between them. And something else much more powerful.

Ella's lips parted. "If I must."

Relief coursed through him. "Thank you."

After taking her inside, he fetched the wheelchair and transferred her onto it, careful not to jostle her. With averted eyes, she pressed a hand to her cheek. George knew he must do everything to shield her from feeling like a bother. She would never be that to him.

He stepped back. "I'll see you in a while."

Still without looking, Ella waved her fingers. After backing away, George turned and exited the house.

GEORGE FOUND Earl in the cornfield just as Lorena was leaving. After a small wave, she shifted the water pail into her other hand and continued down the row. Watching her tread lightly over the clods, George feared his unrequited feelings might rebound, but the sight stirred nothing. Thankfulness abounded within.

He spied Earl's eyes fastened on him and shrugged, grimacing. "I may as well be blunt. I was only thinking how relieved I am to be free of any untoward feelings for Lorena."

"Truly, George?" Earl's scrutiny probed into his soul, and regret brimmed within it.

"Truly."

Nodding, Earl seemed to accept his answer. For a silent minute, the two men regarded each other, the ghost of their former friendship rising from an ash heap of memories.

Around them, the corn stood chest-high, their deep green leaves shimmying in the feathery breeze. A strap lay across Earl's shoulder and connected to the plow where a mule stood swatting flies with his tail. A sheen of sweat covered Earl's face, though his wide-brimmed hat shaded most of it. Dirt clung to his shirt and overalls.

A question burned in George's gut. "Tell me, how does a successful concert violinist wind up in the hills cultivating corn?"

Earl pushed up the brim of his hat. "Tell me, how does a successful doctor wind up in a cornfield with him?"

A wry grin twisted his lips. "You've got me there."

"I'll tell you anyhow. Pride and God." Earl's face clouded a little, like the billows drifting over the afternoon sun and scattering the light. "My ego and shame drove me miles away from my family. No need to rehash it with you. My sins took me farther than I ever intended. But God took all the wrongs and brought good out of it. I'm here in this cornfield now simply because of His mercy." Earl brushed a sleeve across his forehead. "Now, why are you here?"

Indeed. Why?

"There are two reasons. First, a terrible mistake I made in New York. It cost me all I had—my home, my practice—everything."

Intent, Earl widened his eyes. "I'm not one to pry, but I'm sorry to hear it."

Trying not to glance away, George found it hard to hold Earl's steady gaze. "Thanks."

"What's the other reason?"

George filled his lungs with the clean Ozark air. "Ella."

No expression changed the serious look on Earl's face. No surprise. No approval, either. George plunged ahead. "We've been writing for well over a year, and I've learned to care for her deeply."

"How deeply?"

"More than I've cared for anyone in a long time. I intend to marry her if she'll have me."

A hint of a smile flashed through Earl's eyes. "It could be a big if."

"I'll never be worthy of her, but I'll do my best to try."

"Love her the way she deserves, and it'll be enough."

George gazed over the tops of the corn, moving like green waves. "Strange how things turn out, isn't it?"

Earl took a minute to watch the swaying corn. The sun silvered the flecks of gray at his temples. "I know this probably doesn't make sense to you, but I'd rather be here than anywhere else in this world."

The sting of loss panged George. Waking or sleeping, it hovered over him no matter how far he fled. "At least you belong somewhere, Earl. I no longer do."

"Then put your plow down in the earth."

"What?"

Earl removed the strap from around him and motioned George nearer. "Come here. Stand behind the plow."

Hardly knowing what to think, George did as he was bidden. The next instant, the strap looped around his shoulder, angled sideways across his chest, and curved around his back as Earl brought it over him.

"Grab the plow."

George hesitated. Then he stepped closer. The mule swung his head around and looked at George as if he couldn't believe it either. Looking ahead, George closed his fingers around the wooden handles, worn smooth from years of use.

The row stretched out in front of him, a narrow path

waiting to be stirred after the battering of the rain and elements. To be cultivated fresh and new once more.

Stepping nearer, Earl clapped a hand on George's shoulder. "You ready?"

"No, not exactly. You know I've never done this in my life."

"I'll walk alongside you. Keep in step with the mule." Earl stood beside the animal and looked over his shoulder. "Do you know the secret to plowing, Dr. Curtis?"

"Hardly."

"Don't look back."

With a command from Earl, the mule pulled forward. For the first time in George's life, he felt the earth move as the plowshare bit into it. The shafts vibrated within his palms as the soil flipped and crumbled. As they stepped, George summoned his strength to hold steady while keeping pace with the mule.

His shoes sunk into the fresh earth as he plodded in the furrow. A few times in his life, when he'd sailed in a ship, he learned how to move with its dip and sway. In this field, he understood a whole new way of walking. Ahead, the mule's head bobbed in rhythm with its steps.

The moist scent of fresh soil touched George's nose. He drew it inside and savored it. It was honest, simple, and clean. Who would have thought dirt could feel or smell this way?

Down one row and into another they went. Then another. Sweat trickled down the sides of his face and beaded along his back. For the first time, it dawned on George that his troubles hadn't plagued him. His concentration on the task had banished it. Awe-struck, he welcomed the aching back and burning shoulders. Better than the distress he'd borne for weeks.

After the fourth row, Earl grabbed the mule's bridle and stopped him. Turning around, he appraised George and chuckled. "You're a sight, all right. You did well, but I think you've had enough."

Satisfaction filled George. Though he was tired, he relished the feeling. Far different from fatigue.

Earl lifted the strap over George's head. "You'd best get a drink at the house."

George stepped to the side, his chest heaving. The vibrations still buzzed along his arms and legs. "I'll do that."

As Earl took his place behind the mule, George paused. "Thank you, Earl. I needed this."

THE LADIES TITTERED when they saw George rounding the house. His gaze swung toward the airy sound. Ella and Lorena sat on the porch swing with a wide, round bowl between them, snapping an early picking of green beans. Over each of their laps draped a large, bleached cloth piled with the fresh vegetables.

With a confused frown, George halted. "What, may I ask, do you both find so funny?"

"Curtis," Ella pointed at his person. "Did you roll like a hog in the field?"

The ladies cackled again.

Looking down, George observed his dirt-splattered pants from his thighs to his toes. The moist dirt had crusted around the soles of his shoes, rendering them unrecognizable.

As he had walked to the house, his preoccupied mind forgot about his appearance. A droll grin split his mouth.

"I do look a mess, don't I? Earl was teaching me how to cultivate."

Though their eyes widened, their busy fingers didn't pause as they snapped the beans and dropped them into the bowl.

Ella started on another handful. "Really? And how did it work out?"

Moving closer, George rested one foot on the bottom step. "The mule pulled the plow while I held on. It was hard but surprisingly satisfying."

A pleased look sparkled in Ella's eyes. "You might become a country boy, after all."

Seeing her joy obliterated the doubt crowding around him. Almost.

"I'd better get cleaned up. It's a good thing I have another pair of trousers." He held up his foot. "I see what will occupy my evening. These shoes weren't made for the fields."

"You'll need to get a pair of boots at Huitt's store," Lorena observed. "They'll prove useful here."

His chest tingled at the thought. He didn't want anything to tie him there longer than necessary. Even a pair of boots.

With an obligatory nod, he turned toward the road. "I'll go get cleaned up, then see you all at supper."

As he walked toward his place, another thought tumbled around in his mind, one that struck him when he finished plowing. So occupied by the idea, he had forgotten his soiled appearance. Deep down inside, George knew it had to work. It must.

He lengthened his strides toward the small house a quarter of a mile away. The July sun pounded the earth and radiated around him, but George hardly noticed. He couldn't rest until he put it to paper.

After he arrived and tidied up, he retrieved a notepad from his trunk. Sitting at the table, he drew, the idea flowing through his pencil strokes.

His fingers trembled slightly. Would this prove to Ella once and for all how much she meant to him? In truth, whether or not he won the lass, he wanted to do it for her.

After several more details, George straightened and

observed his simple drawing. For the first time in a long while, the fringes of hope dawned.

"It's possible. With this, Ella might walk again."

Folding the paper, he slid it inside his pocket and rose from the table.

Now to implement it.

23

"Can we do it?" Curtis watched Earl study the paper. For another countless time, Ella resisted the urge to huff because she couldn't see what they were discussing beside the fireplace, especially since it dealt with her. With a furtive wink, Lorena smiled as she reached inside a basket for an unfinished baby's quilt. With her needle and thread, Lorena began stitching.

Ella ran her hand along the padded upholstered sofa. Her legs ached from the afternoon exercises that Curtis put her through. Oh, to be able to stand.

"It's straightforward. It won't be hard." Earl lifted his head. "It's a good idea."

"When can we start?" The anxious expression on Curtis's face made Ella's fingers itch to thread through his hair.

"There's plenty of daylight left." Earl folded the paper and handed it to Curtis. On the opposite side of the room, Douglas squirmed in his chair. The newspaper rattled as he turned the page. His pinched expression hadn't dissipated yet.

"Since this concerns me, I'd like to know what you two are doing."

A placid smile curved Earl's lips and relieved Ella's nerves somewhat. To see him at complete peace still awed her every time she beheld him. He indeed was a miracle.

Beside him, Curtis put the paper into his trouser pocket. "You'll see in time."

Ella summoned her sweetest, most persuasive voice. "But I'd like to see now."

Affection twinkled in his eyes, but he shook his head.

"Please, Curtis."

"You're hard to resist, but I want to surprise you. Call it a late birthday present."

"You don't know when my birthday is."

As if brushing away a smirk, Curtis smoothed his mustache. "May twentieth."

Ella drew in her bottom lip.

Chuckling, Earl stepped away from the darkened fireplace toward the hallway. "We're wastin' daylight. Ella will argue till the cows come home if we don't get moving. Let's grab a couple of axes in the barn."

"Lead the way."

Curtis hesitated as he passed Ella. Pausing, he lightly caressed her shoulder, a hint of apology on his face. "I'm not trying to be highhanded, lass. I want to surprise you."

Well. When he looked at her with such adoration, her irritation fizzled and breathing quickened. "All right."

His fingertips gently squeezed before he stepped away to follow Earl.

Without a word, Douglas folded the newspaper, flung it on the side table, and followed them. Ella waited until the screen door banged shut.

"Douglas is going to help. I just know it. Even if he doesn't say anything."

Rolling her eyes, Lorena pulled the needle through the

material. "I love you all, but the Steens are the most stubborn lot of people I've ever known."

"I can't disagree with you, though we try not to be." Ella glanced around the large parlor whose beaded board walls stretched over twelve feet high. Lorena's baby grand piano graced one end of the room opposite the fireplace. Two long windows framed a view of the front yard. Most of the furnishings, simple and stylish, came from Lorena's former home in New York City.

"I think George cares for you more than you realize."

Startled out of her thoughts, Ella glanced sideways at Lorena. "How do you know?"

"It's obvious, especially in how he treats you. It's a beautiful thing to see."

Ella rubbed her aching knees. "When the newness wears off, will it last? I'm afraid of what I can't see deep within his heart."

Lorena sighed, her nimble fingers never losing rhythm with each stitch. "Sometimes love comes in a blinding flash, knocking a person sideways. Other times, it seeps into one's heart and fills it without notice. You know, real love is an act of faith. Whether it strikes suddenly or builds over time, it can't last without placing complete trust in the other person. Even if it requires stepping out on nothing. Whatever is past is past, Ella. George is moving on from it."

Ella reached over and fingered the edge of the colorful quilt. "If only life could be pieced together as beautifully as this."

"It is, mended beautifully by a Master hand."

Another thought darkened Ella's heart. "What about when I show him Charles's picture? It could ruin everything."

Lorena paused stitching, and regarded her. "I'm praying about it. It will be George's turn to put his faith in you."

"I haven't thought of it that way." Ella thumbed through the catalog on her lap, a feeling of shame and nervousness swirling inside. How foolish of her to have waited. Ella shivered despite the raised windows and warm breeze circulating through the house.

THE MULE BRAYED as he pulled the load from the woods into the clearing. He stopped, though Earl urged him forward. George wiped the dripping sweat from his jaw and watched Earl tug the animal's bridle.

"Huldy, I've seen stubborn mules in my time, but you take the cake." In a few quick strides, Earl returned to the edge of the woods and snapped a stick from the nearest tree. As he waded through the knee-high grass, he caught George's stare.

"Don't worry. I'm not going to hurt 'im."

A flash of embarrassment intensified the heat emanating from George's face. Beside him, Douglas stood like a rocky hillside, rigid and unmoving. The entire time they worked felling the trees, Douglas never spoke one word even though Earl included him in the conversation.

Once more, Earl grabbed the mule's bridle. He showed Huldy the stick and tugged. "Now gittup."

The mule stepped forward.

"That's it, Huldy. Good boy." Tossing the stick aside, he lightly slapped the mule's neck. Earl caught George's stare again. "Huldy's a bit lazy, but he doesn't like getting rapped across his hindquarters. All I have to do is show him, and he's ready to work. Country life isn't all pretty. Sometimes you do what you have to do to make things happen—within limits, of course."

George tromped through the grass until he fell in step beside Earl while Douglas followed behind the load.

"You didn't have to explain yourself to me, Earl."

"Sure, I did," Earl replied good-naturedly. "I saw the look on your face, and I don't blame you." His face sobered as he guided Huldy. "I take no pleasure in striking anything, and I avoid it. Huldy is a good mule. I've rarely used a stick, and when I did, it was no more than a few strikes."

Thirst scorched George's throat, but he ignored it. "Do you ever get tired of explaining yourself—or proving yourself?"

"Sometimes." Earl sidled a glance toward his older brother. "But I did a lot of damage. I remind myself that though God has forgiven me, it doesn't grant me a free pass in this life. There are still consequences."

George swallowed down the sting of despair. "How do you bear it?"

Earl studied George's face, his blue-green eyes placid. "Day by day. By His grace."

"Putting one foot in front of the other." George focused on the path ahead of them.

"With God."

God. Although far away from everything, George couldn't escape Him here. Indeed, He seemed nearer—much too close for his comfort. He cast the thoughts aside.

"I think Ella will be surprised, don't you?"

"As much as one can surprise Ella," Earl chuckled.

The thought sprung an unbidden grin across George's lips. Her quizzical face hovered in his mind. When she saw their load, she would be more mystified. Huldy pulled four logs, roughly fifteen feet long and slim in diameter. At the thickest part, they were about as big around as George's arms.

He imagined her scrutinizing their every move, the questions burning the edge of her tongue.

He gulped against the dust sticking in the back of his throat. He hoped she wouldn't be disappointed. Ella was accustomed to nice things, not the crude handiwork of a city doctor who hardly knew how to nail two boards together.

Doctor.

He was no doctor. As Doc's words replayed in George's thoughts, he forgot his thirst, the heat, and the dust.

The moment I saw you, I knew God provided.

Resisting the burn of anger, George rolled his shoulders. No, he wasn't the man for the job. His focus was on starting a new life with Ella.

Like it or not, you are. I feel it deep in my bones.

No, he wasn't. He would help Doc until—

The thought choked George. He wasn't ready to lose his friend. And Valley Creek wasn't either.

For the rest of the trek to Earl's place, George chased away those thoughts, grappling with his calling and his conscience. When Earl finally led the mule into the side yard, George exhaled his relief.

Turning toward the house, George's eyes snagged on the sight of Ella sitting near the end of the porch, watching their arrival. Like he'd imagined, a quizzical expression lit her face.

His throat suddenly tightened with something stronger than thirst. Nearly stumbling over his feet, George rushed to the side of the house and filled his gaze with her.

Ella tilted her head to one side, a laugh lilting her voice. "Is this my surprise, Curtis? Is it the mule or the logs?"

George pulled off his hat and felt the fingers of the breeze thread through his hair and cool his temples. "The logs."

Ella leaned forward, reaching a hand toward him. George captured her slender fingers within his and lifted them to his lips. They brushed the back of her hand and lingered before he lifted his head. Ella's cheeks tinted like the fiery sunset fringing the hillsides.

"I brought you water," she said, her voice turning wispy. She glanced at the pail and dipper beside the wheelchair.

In his need to see her, George had failed to notice it. "So you did, lass."

After releasing her hand, he lifted the dipper out of the water and brought it to his mouth. The cool water trailed down his parched throat, washing away the dust. Nothing else had ever tasted so good. After draining it, he took another dipperful.

With the last swallow, George caught Ella's gaze tracing his face, soaking in every detail.

His heart leaped. Did she feel the same as he did?

Then Ella met his eyes. With a tiny gasp, she ripped her glance away and skittered it to her brothers unhitching the mule. "Um. You're welcome."

George set the dipper in the pail and snagged her hand again. "I didn't say thank you." He kissed it quickly this time. "But I do."

Stepping back, he turned and joined her brothers to start unloading the logs. He felt her bemused stare right between his shoulder blades.

While he and Earl sawed the logs, Douglas took a post hole digger and dug four holes about a foot deep. By the time they finished this first step, nightfall had seeped over the landscape.

Earl hoisted one end of the hewn stob while George lifted the other end. "We'll be needin' a little light, Douglas."

Without a word, Douglas turned and paced toward the barn.

"He could find his way blindfolded through a barn," Earl smirked as they hauled the stob to one of the holes and lowered one end inside. Grabbing a nearby shovel, George filled in the spaces with dirt.

"I guess he truly means not to speak to you while he's here."

"I expected nothing less."

No ire rankled Earl's voice, and George marveled over it. Standing upright, he wiggled the log to test its stability. "I'd say it's not going anywhere."

"No, I don't think so." Earl took his turn testing it. "I have a feeling this might work, George. I'm obliged to you for doing this."

With a glance toward the porch, George saw Ella's silhouette still sitting, the lamplight from one of the windows puddling behind her. In front of her, dangling his legs while sitting on the porch's edge, Caleb watched.

A strong emotion swept over George like a whistling gale, thickening his throat. His gaze flicked down to the toes of his shoes then into Earl's face. In the dimness, he couldn't see it clearly, and his courage bolstered a little.

"I'd give both arms if it would help Ella walk again."

"I know you would."

The full realization slammed into his chest. As if he'd been running for a mile, George heaved in a long breath and exhaled. Over the course of their correspondence, his heart had drifted closer to Ella's through the rise and fall of his existence. These weeks with her had driven him nearer. Somewhere, in the upheaval of his life, he'd lost his heart. To her.

He loved Ella and Ella alone.

The shovel he was leaning against quaked in his hand. Bending methodically, George set it on the grass, grateful to the deepening nightfall for obscuring the truth plastered all over his face.

A twig snapped as Douglas neared, carrying three lanterns in each hand. After lighting each one, he took twine and hung them on the tree branches above them. Though dim, they glowed enough for them to continue their tasks.

Earl and George set the other three stobs into the post holes while Douglas took an axe and chipped a wide notch into their tops. Each stob, four altogether, stood opposite of each other about ten feet apart like a rectangle.

Once Douglas was finished, they stood a few minutes and observed their work thus far.

"It looks good." George blew a few wood chips from one of the notches.

"Now for the two logs."

First, they used the axes to chip a notch on each end to fit into the corresponding ones. Then, the three of them hefted the logs one at a time. Straining against the weight, they lowered one end into the notch on one stob before affixing the other end into the notch on the opposite side. They did the same with the next one, the weight pulling George's muscles tight.

Again, they stepped back and observed their work. The width between the two long logs was about three feet, just enough room for a person to walk between and brace themselves with their hands, like a railing.

"Now for the straps." Earl's pleased voice belied the weary shadows pooling under his eyes, the long workday unfinished. He fetched the long strips of leather from beside the tree.

"George, I'll show you how to secure the logs." He handed Douglas several with hardly a glance.

George helped Earl fasten the log to the first stob, pulling it firmly and tightly into the notch.

"We don't have to worry about it budging for sure." Earl handed a few more straps to George. "Are you ready to try the next one by yourself?"

"I'll give it a go."

Under Earl's watchful eyes, George secured the other end of the railing. When he straightened, Earl appraised his work.

"Couldn't have done it better myself."

Douglas finished the last one and approached George. He clapped a hand on his shoulder. "If this doesn't work, nothing will."

A tremor of nervousness prickled George's spine. "Let's hope it does."

Earl rechecked one of the leather knots. "With God's help."

He dipped his head toward the porch and cut a sideways glance at George. "She's waiting. Go get your gal and show her. We'll put up the tools."

"Thanks, both of you."

Douglas gave his shoulder a final squeeze and turned to help Earl.

With his heart in his throat, George approached Ella, sitting with her face obscured by shadows.

24

Ella's pulse hammered as Curtis drew near, his stride purposeful against the porch planks. He stood looking down at her, a gleam in his eyes that the dark couldn't hide.

"Are you ready?"

Unable to trust her voice, Ella reached for him instead. The next moment he lifted her into his arms and carried her down into the yard. While owls conversed in the woods, neither of them spoke. The groaning of the barn's door hinges reached their ears. Side by side, Douglas and Earl were walking in stoic silence toward the backdoor. Ella's heart ached for them both.

When they reached the spot, Curtis's voice, low and deep, brushed Ella's cheek. "What do you think?"

He stepped between the two log railings. Overhead, the lanterns flickered while lightning bugs pulsed around them.

The fringes of a smile upturned her lips. "What exactly is it?"

Without taking his eyes from hers, he tightened his arms around her. "This is to help build your strength. A ten-foot-long walkway. You can stand here and place your hands on each rail, holding yourself up while practicing steps."

For the first time in weeks, hope rose over the horizon of Ella's heart. Her chest burned and tightened as she drank in the sight of Curtis's surprise. For her.

"Lass?"

I haven't said a word. What must he think? His anxious look pricked her. "Curtis." She stroked his shoulder, struggling to steady her voice. "This is the most beautiful gift I've ever been given."

Surprise curved his mustache. "Truly?"

"Truly."

A pleased, satisfied emotion relaxed Curtis's face. "I don't know what to say. You must've received many beautiful gifts through the years."

Ella blinked against stinging tears. "None so wonderful as this. Do you know what it means to me?"

"I think I do." He carried her a few steps farther between the railings.

"I'd like to try for a few seconds."

"All right. But only a few." Lowering the arm cradling her legs, Curtis allowed her feet to touch the ground. "Brace your hands on either side."

She did as he said while he circled his hands around her waist. She palmed the smooth bark of the logs. Stiffening her arms, Ella rested her weight against them.

Supporting herself was more challenging than she imagined, but she was on her feet for the first time in an age. Though they felt like strangers to her body, she relished the feel of them touching the ground.

Ella's knees quivered. Instantly, Curtis scooped her into his arms. "I think that's enough for now."

She couldn't stop the grin from spreading over her face. "I did it, Curtis. I did it." The joy of her small accomplishment dizzied her senses. "Thank you, thank you." She flung her arms around his shoulders tightly, her cheek resting against his. The light, evening stubble of his firm jaw rasped her skin.

"You're a brave, amazing woman, Ella Steen. I'm proud of you."

Pulling back, Ella stilled under his steady, bright blue gaze. "Are you?"

"That and more."

Everything around her hushed as Ella lost herself in his eyes roving over her hair, her eyes, her cheeks, and chin. Her lips.

"You'll never know how much you mean to me. Whether you walk or not."

The fervor of his gaze fastened on hers and dizzied her further. Yearning to touch his face again, Ella threw aside her restraint and fingered his firm, prickly jaw.

Curtis closed his eyes and leaned into her palm. Turning his face, he planted a kiss into the center of it. Then another.

His tenderness robbed Ella's breath. Again, his eyes roved her face, and he dipped his head towards hers. He'd called her brave moments ago. Did she have courage enough to meet him this time?

Before she could decide, Curtis's lips captured hers. Ella wrapped her arms around his neck as he tightened his hold around her. His lips caressing hers seemed to whisper of his love. Dared she believe it? Casting aside her doubts, she surrendered herself to this moment.

"It's about time to bring her inside, don't you think?" Earl's amused voice broke them apart.

Heat flamed Ella's face as she whipped her head around to glare at her brother. "Really, Earl."

"I still have the lanterns to put up." Earl ambled down the steps. "I'd say you thanked him right and proper." He winked at Curtis.

With a chuckle, Curtis pressed his lips against her brow and murmured, "He's right, you know. You did do a right and proper job of it. Maybe you could thank me tomorrow too?"

Ella smacked his shoulder and hid her burning face against his shirt collar. She felt him shift and turn toward the house.

Curtis's chest rumbled with laughter. "Earl, you have impeccable timing."

Hearing her brother's footsteps approach, Ella ventured a peek. His usually somber eyes sparkled with mirth.

"I intend to."

As Curtis carried her, she relished the solid strength of his shoulders and arms holding her, not to mention his firm stride. Though she would rather be nowhere else, Ella wondered if she would ever walk beside him.

After settling her in the wheelchair, he took her inside. No one else was in the wide hallway. Bending forward, Curtis framed her face between his hands. "Till tomorrow."

Breathless, Ella could only nod. As he straightened, he stroked her jaw then turned toward the door. Butterflies swirled in her stomach. She couldn't remember the last time she'd felt this way.

Hours later, Ella shifted beneath the bedcovers and propped herself on an elbow, peering through the window. Stars pinpricked the cloudless night and shimmered like jewels. Was Curtis awake as well?

Did she dare believe he might love her? He seemed devoted, but was it partially out of pity? Or need? Except for his son in Europe, he was alone in the world. Whatever happened to him in New York had shaken him to his core. Once he gained his bearings, would his commitment remain?

His kiss still tingled on her lips, bringing a sweet ache with it. While her heart told her one thing, her logic warred against it. Somehow, with God's help, she must learn to walk, to show

Curtis she could face anything alongside him. After all, he had given her the means to try.

In the dark, she saw the outline of the railed, narrow walkway he and her brothers put together. His gift touched her beyond her ability to express.

Then the brooch on the side table caught her glance. Guilt stalked into her thoughts and raveled the joy as though it were a threadbare garment.

She must tell him. She had waited much too long, but she couldn't keep it from him anymore. Would he forgive her? Suppose he didn't believe her?

Whispering a prayer, Ella sank onto the pillow and closed her eyes. The thought of hurting Curtis wedged like an icy blade beneath her ribcage. Lorena had said it wouldn't sidetrack him.

With all her soul, she hoped Lorena was right.

"LET CALEB STAY, Douglas. He's more than welcome for the rest of the summer," Lorena urged.

Ella reached out and took Douglas's thick, work-hardened hand in hers. "Look at him and Jimmy out there, hoping against hope that you'll let him. He needs this."

With one hand gripping the screen door, Douglas hesitated, a pained expression dimming his face while he watched the boys loitering near the roadside, their heads down and hands jammed into their pockets.

"He's my youngest, the only one still left at home."

Ella knew it was his way of saying how lonely he'd be without Caleb. She tightened her grip on his fingers. "I know. His siblings are too old to understand how he feels. They have their own lives. Right now, he needs a friend, someone his age like Jimmy. And it will only be until September."

His jaw ticked as he flung a glance at Lorena. "I don't know."

Folding her arms, Lorena sighed. "Whatever your feelings are about Earl, don't let it keep you from letting Caleb stay. He'll be safe here. And happy."

At the word *happy*, Douglas stared hard at the floor. "I know, Lorena, and I thank you, but it's best he come home with me." Dropping Ella's hand, he stooped to pick up the suitcase and shoved open the screen door.

With a defeated shake of her head, Lorena shrugged at Ella as they followed him onto the porch. Ella wheeled her chair through the doorway, wishing she could thump Douglas over the head with one of its wheels. Pig-headed man.

Just as Douglas descended the steps, Earl rounded the house with his team, Crockett and Grits, hitched to the wagon.

"How about a ride to the station, Douglas?"

Douglas halted. "We'll walk."

Earl frowned a little. "It's a bit far for a youngin'."

"We'll manage." Douglas turned his attention to the boys. "Son, it's time to tell your aunts goodbye."

With his chin tucked, Caleb shuffled past his father and stopped at the bottom of the steps. Jimmy straggled behind him, listlessly twirling a stick between his fingers.

Staring at the ground, he rubbed the toe of his shoe in the grass. "Goodbye, Aunt Ella, Aunt Lorena."

"Don't you goodbye me, young man. Come here and give us a hug." Ella spread out her arms.

Caleb's chin quivered as he climbed the steps. When his arms rounded Ella's shoulders, he burst into tears.

"Darling, shhh." Ella tightened her arms around him. Peeping over Caleb's shoulder, she eyed Douglas.

At the sound of Caleb's outburst, Douglas pivoted and reached his son's side in two strides. The suitcase dropped from his grip. Watching helplessly, Douglas swallowed hard.

Sighing, he lifted his hand and stroked the boy's black curls. "Son, does staying mean that much to you?"

Caleb shoved away from Ella's embrace and swiped a sleeve across his nose. With the back of his hands, he dashed the tears from his flushed cheeks. "I won't leave you, Father. I'll come."

Douglas's eyes misted. With an expanding chest, he knelt on one knee and took Caleb by the shoulders. "My brave boy. When I get home, I'll be busy in the fields from daylight till dark. Why don't you stay until September?"

With a hiccup, Caleb blinked. "You mean it?"

For an answer, Douglas rumpled his son's head.

"Will you be all right?"

"Yes, don't you worry."

Caleb lurched forward, flinging his arms around Douglas's neck. "Thank you, Father."

Douglas gathered the boy close for a moment then stood. Though he smiled, Ella saw the grief swelling behind his outward façade. "Mind your manners and do your share of the chores."

"I will."

He dipped his head toward Jimmy. "Go skedaddle with Jimmy while there's daylight. I'll see you soon."

With another tight embrace, Caleb bounded off the porch. The two boys whooped and scampered toward the woods.

Douglas released an unsteady breath as he watched them go. Blinking, he glanced at Lorena. "I'm obliged. I know he'll be well cared for."

Sadness turned down the corners of Lorena's mouth, her voice low and earnest. "Douglas, I do wish you'd at least have a word with your brother before you go."

Douglas's brows thundered close together. He lifted himself from his knee and yanked up the suitcase. "You've let it go, and that's your business, Lorena. I appreciate your feelings, but the day he turned his back on all of us is the day he died to me."

Knowing he'd heard, Lorena flicked a glance at Earl and bit her lower lip.

Ella stiffened her back. "Have a safe trip home."

Douglas met her stony glare with a haunted, stricken look that begged for help. As though his stubbornness held his heart captive. Ella's chest ached.

He tipped a finger to the brim of his hat and descended the steps. With straightened shoulders, he passed the team and wagon without a glance at Earl. The three of them watched in silence until he disappeared down the path leading to the depot.

Both women turned their attention to Earl. He dropped his gaze to his hands holding the reins and clenched his fingers around them. Hurt and frustration mottled his face. Ella watched the emotions war until resignation hunched his shoulders.

When he raised his head, he spied them watching and cleared his throat. "It was foolish to expect anything different. Some things are too much to ask. Since the team is hitched, I reckon I'll head to Valley Creek and get some supplies we need." He cracked a rusty smile at Lorena. "I'll be all right, dear heart."

Popping the reins across Crockett and Grits, Earl drove from the yard.

"You brought a Yank to me? What do ya expect me to do with 'im?" The older woman swished a wiry strand of white hair out of her eyes.

Doc scowled and leaned across the crude, work-worn table in the center of the dim cabin, flattening his palms against the surface. "Now, Sal, you've got to give him a chance."

"My pa never gave a Yank a chance, and I ain't about to start."

"Sal," Doc growled. "Your pa is dead and cold in his grave along with the Confederacy."

"And more's the pity." Cramming a fist onto a thin, sharp hip, Sal nailed George with a heated glare.

A knot from one of the cabin's logs dug deeper into the center of George's back as he leaned against the wall. Though he was the subject of the argument, an odd sensation of being a mere bystander overshadowed him.

Sal withdrew her dagger-like stare and aimed it back at Doc Brown, her flinty brown eyes reminding George of a glinting bayonet blade.

"Get 'im out. Now."

"See here just a doggone minute, woman." Doc brandished a finger, but she never flinched. Instead, she slid a speckled hand into her skirt pocket, drew out a flintlock pistol, and leveled it at George.

"Now."

Petrified, George held his breath and for once wished himself back in New York City. Unruffled, Doc grunted. "Dr. Curtis, give us a minute, please."

Gladly. George pushed away from the wall and trod softly. The last thing he needed was a hole blown through him. He lifted the handmade latch and stepped into the fresh air. After shutting the door, he sidestepped it in case Sal decided to fire anyhow.

Sal's voice rattled the hinges.

"There ain't been a Yankee on this place since Lee threw down his guns at Appomattox. I oughtta shoot you where you stand."

"And end forty years of friendship?" Doc's brittle voice sounded amused. "Put the gun down, Sal."

"If you expect me to work with him, you've got another thing comin'."

"I've never asked you a favor since I first set foot in Valley Creek when I was twenty-five. But I'm askin' you now."

"If he's such a good doctor, why does he need me?"

"You know as well as I that we ain't in the city. There's not an apothecary around every bend in the woods. You've got to teach him the medicines that grow right here."

"When dogs talk and people bark."

"Do I have to beg you?"

"You teach 'im. I've taught you all I know. Wish I hadn't now."

Something smacked the table hard. Probably Doc's hand. "You've got to do it."

"Over my dead, cold body."

"Well, it'll be over mine."

Doc's quiet voice shrouded the cabin in silence. George angled his head toward the door and closed his eyes. After a moment, a shuffling sound dissolved the quiet. Had Sal moved closer? Her voice told him that she had.

"Let's have it, Doc."

The huskiness of his voice deepened. "They'll be laying me to rest by the end of the month, if not sooner."

More silence followed before Sal made a soft growl. "I shoulda known. It's right there in your eyes."

"Whether you like it or not, Dr. Curtis is a Godsend. I don't have the time or strength to teach him. He's the best doctor Valley Creek could ask for. You've got to do it. Just like you did for me all those years ago—a wet-behind-the-ears doctor who didn't know his head from a hole in the ground. I'm obliged to you."

"Shut up."

"And I'm going to owe you more before it's over. But I'll never be able to repay."

More shambling sounds. "You'd have me break my vow to my pa on his deathbed, to have no dealings with Yankees?"

"It was a foolish vow. And I recall you once made a promise to me as well. You said you'd always help me in any way you could, and I need it. Sorely."

"You always did drive a hard bargain."

"Are you agreeable, then?" Hope lightened Doc's tone.

While the cabin seemed to hold its breath, George imagined the grudging look Sal was giving Doc. Maybe she was still holding that flintlock pistol.

She huffed. "I ain't agreeable, but I'll do it. For you."

"Thank you."

The door yanked open, and George skittered three or four steps sideways. Sal poked her head out, her brows drawn together as she raked him with her eyes. "A doctor, a Yank, and an eavesdropper. You might as well be a carpetbagger while you're at it."

The cabin roared with Doc's laughter. Thumping himself across the chest as he stepped outside, he wiped at a tear. "Now that you've been thoroughly insulted, Dr. Curtis, I think we can begin the business of learning Ozark medicine."

He gestured toward the scruffy-looking woman. A drab homespun dress swallowed Sal's sharp, wiry frame. Her salt and pepper hair was gathered in a bushy knot, untamed strands framing her swarthy face.

"Dr. Curtis, meet Sal Scarbrough. She's a medicine woman. Knows every tree, bush, and herb in all these hills. She'll teach you everything you need to know. Sal, this is George Curtis."

Sal crossed her arms and harrumphed.

In that instant, George knew he must make a snap decision. Tiptoe around her or be the charming Yank she loathed. He resisted the urge to gulp and schooled his face into a wide smile at the lion-like lady.

He gave her a courtly bow. "Pleased to meet you, Miss Scarbrough."

Sal bristled. "It's Sal, Yank. May God help you, 'cause you're gonna need it." Uncurling her arms and stiffening them at her sides, she whirled on her heel and stormed into the cabin. The door banged shut.

"I'd say that went rather well," Doc chortled.

25

"I'm not going to stay, Doc. I wish you wouldn't bother." George popped the reins across Ginger's back. "Gittup."

"Soundin' like an Arkie already. You don't know it yet, but you're staying."

From the corner of his eye, George noticed Doc rubbing his side. Wincing, Doc squirmed in the seat.

Dread cinched like an iron chain around George's heart. Though neither of them commented on Doc's discomfort, unspoken understanding dangled like a heavy cloud over them. The worst kind of truth.

Doc removed his hat and fanned his face . "I've known Sal Scarbrough for forty years. Smart gal. Kind of a wild spirit. She was widowed too young, lost a babe in childbirth." The memory darkened Doc's face. "I delivered her. Her Pa, Hezekiah Keys—we called him Hez—watched over her. Taught her everything about plants and how to take care of herself. And Hez hated Yankees so much he wouldn't let Sal wear blue. He was almost killed at Gettysburg, and his brother, John, was killed at Sharpsburg. Folks up North call it Antietam. His remaining brother died at Camp Douglas, a prisoner-of-war camp in Illinois."

"That's a hard thing." George loosened his collar as the morning heat rose. "I'll keep it in mind."

"Don't go easy on her. That's the worst thing to do. She won't respect you otherwise. I just wanted you to understand the prejudice."

"And will I face more like it?"

Doc shrugged. "There're all kinds of prejudices around the world. Mostly, the hardest time you'll have is being accepted as the doctor. You'll need determination."

"The only thing I'm determined to do is leave Valley Creek and marry Ella." George's tone brooked no argument, but Doc merely quirked one side of his mouth upward.

"Next stop is the Weatherford's place. We'll look in on Granny Weatherford. She's blind and has rheumatism. While we're there, we'll check on the mare. She's due to have a foal any day, and she might have trouble. It's her first one."

George swung his head around to look at Doc more fully. "A mare?"

"Welcome to country doctoring. Be prepared to wear many hats."

And I thought I was stubborn. The elder gentleman refused to let it go. George bit his tongue. Even though it rankled him, he didn't want to hurt his friend. Perhaps it was better to stop arguing and let him think otherwise.

As the buggy rolled and shuddered down the rutted, dirt road, Doc shared the stories of his patients: their personalities, their quirks—the dos and don'ts of dealing with them. Despite himself, it piqued George's interest.

"That's Zeke Martin's place," Doc pointed as they drove by a small, whitewashed house with a rock chimney. A picket fence bordered the yard. "Keeps his place as neat as a pin. Looks quiet and peaceful, doesn't it?"

"It does."

"Don't let it fool you. He keeps a gobbler that will flog you if you go through the gate before Zeke calls him off."

"A gobbler?"

"A turkey. Just you step through that gate without Zeke's permission. He will come 'round the house gobbling, fluffed up, headed straight for you."

George laughed, and Doc joined him. "Don't ask how I know."

A half-mile farther, the Weatherford place peeped from among a grove of trees. As they wound into the yard, an elderly lady sat in her rocking chair on the porch, her eyes closed and chin tucked into her collar. A limb snapped under the buggy's wheel. The lady jolted upright.

"Granny Weatherford, hallo!" Doc's deep voice smoothed the tense lines around her wrinkled face.

George reined in Ginger.

"Doc Brown, you've no business scarin' the living daylights out of me like that." Her sightless eyes twinkled.

"It'll keep you young." Doc climbed from the buggy while George followed.

"Not this old woman." A toothless smirk crinkled the folds of her cheeks. She tilted her head just a bit. "I hear two sets of feet. Who ya got with you?"

"A friend of mine, Dr. George Curtis of New York City."

Granny Weatherford held out a blue-veined, gnarled hand. "Pleased to meet you, Dr. Curtis."

George took her thin, cool hand in his warm one. "I'm glad to meet you, Mrs. Weatherford."

"Granny will do. Everyone calls me that. What brings you to these parts?"

"I'm here visiting friends, the Steens."

Nodding her approval, Granny winked. "Good folks, the Steens, though Earl was quite a rounder for a while. God finally caught up with 'im, though." She patted his hand with her other one. "If you're a friend of the Steens and Doc's, then you're a friend of mine."

Such unexpected, ready acceptance from a stranger filled George with gratitude he couldn't express.

"I'm glad to be yours as well."

"And I bet you're as handsome as your voice."

Doc pulled a glass, brown medicine bottle from his pocket and set it in Granny's lap. "Granny is a bit of a shameless flirt, Dr. Curtis. You'll get used to it."

Granny released George's hand with a swat at Doc's. "At my age, I'm entitled to it." She fingered the bottle. "I'm obliged for this, Doc. I've been out of medicine for a few days, and my bones are tellin' me. Arnold has a dozen eggs waiting for you."

"Granny's son," Doc explained to George.

From the corner of the house, several hens clucked and scattered as a middle-aged man rounded it.

"Thank the Lord, you're here, Doc! The mare's having her foal, but it's not laying right."

"We're coming, Arnold." He gestured for George to follow. "There's not much time to lose."

As they jogged to the barn, George uncuffed his sleeves and rolled them up. The same cluster of hens scattered and clucked as they invaded the barnyard.

A little while later, George stood and watched the new mother lick the warm, trembling foal in the bed of hay. Beside him, Doc leaned against the stall and mopped sweat from his face with a handkerchief.

"Congratulations, Dr. Curtis. You've done a first-rate job."

"I couldn't have done it without you." Stooping, George swiped sprigs clinging to his legs and chest. Splatters of blood dotted his clothes as well as his arms. With all his might, he forced thoughts of Lilith to the back of his mind.

"Thankee, Dr. Curtis, Doc." Arnold shuffled through the hay toward them. "Come out and get washed up."

Arnold's thick forearms flexed as he pumped while Doc and George scrubbed their faces, arms, and hands with homemade lye soap. The ice-cold, clean water splattered over George's skin, setting his teeth on edge. Once the blood was scrubbed away, Arnold handed them a fresh flour-sack towel to dry themselves.

"Ma baked bread this morning. I'll get you both a loaf." As he straightened a twisted overalls strap, Arnold took the towel and strode to the house.

"I hate to take their food. They'll need it." George whispered.

Doc blotted the trails of water dripping from his face. "Whatever folks offer you, take it. Money's scarce, but they'll give their best. To refuse any form of payment would deeply offend them. These people are self-reliant, determined not to be beholden to anyone. Also, it's the surest way to build trust. You help them. They return the favor."

When they reached the buggy, Doc thrust his hand under the seat and dragged out a box with an empty basket inside. "Always be prepared."

Wonderment struck George as Arnold hurried out of the house, banging the door behind him, armed with two wrapped loaves of bread and a basket of eggs dangling from his arm.

"Much obliged to you both." Arnold's somber face held no trace of a smile, but the gratitude shone through his eyes.

Doc transferred the eggs from Granny's basket into his, gently packing each one for the ride. "My wife will be glad to have these. Granny's hens lay the best eggs in these parts."

The gleam in Arnold's face shone brighter. He handed the loaves to George. The buttery smell tickled his nose and made his mouth water.

"Thank you. It smells delicious." George placed the loaves alongside the basket in the box.

Arnold nodded. Listening on the porch, Granny raised a hand. "Son, go fetch Dr. Curtis some of my butter. He'll need it with the bread."

"Thank you, Granny." George grinned, feeling like a little boy using such a personal name. "I didn't do much to deserve it, but I'll enjoy it."

With a cluck of her tongue, Granny waved. "If you're with Doc, rest assured you'll earn your keep."

Doc hoisted himself into the buggy. "That's right. From now on, George, you'd best remember to keep a fresh change of clothes under the seat at all times. A country doctor always needs it." For good measure, he winked.

Surveying his splattered slacks and shirt, George grimaced without argument.

"THE LAST STOP OF THE MORNING." Doc plucked his pocket watch from his vest. "It's nearly noon. I spend the rest of the day at my office. I daresay, starting out at five o'clock every morning is startin' to take its toll on me, but you're young enough to handle it."

Doc had grown paler since the last few stops. His hand, sagging on the armrest, tremored a bit. George caught himself lifting a silent prayer and stopped. He and the Lord weren't on speaking terms.

"This here is the Mahans' place." Doc's mouth twisted with evident pain as he scooted from the seat and climbed down.

"Doc, let me get something to ease you." George reached for the black bag, but Doc gestured for him to follow instead.

"No, not now. We've gotta check Henry Mahan's leg wound.

He miss-licked and hit his leg with an axe. I stitched it up nearly a week ago."

George hopped down. "Miss-licked?"

"That's Arkansan speak. It means he swung wrong. He was chopping stove wood, missed, and hit his leg instead."

The front door of the house swung open, and a younger man came out. His brown suit was simple and threadbare. As he donned his hat, he glanced up, saw them, and waved. Immediately, George remembered him from his previous visit. The preacher of Valley Creek.

"Parson Crandall," boomed Doc, holding out a hand. "I see you're making calls too."

The man shook Doc's hand, his eyes sincere and friendly. "I am." He then offered a hand to George. "Hullo. I believe I remember you. Dr. Curtis, right?"

"Right." George accepted the handshake, although unease knotted in his gut. "Nice to see you again." He hoped the lie didn't show in his face.

"I'm glad to see you back in Valley Creek. Hope we'll see more of you." Glancing at Doc, his pleasant expression faltered. "Henry seems worse."

"I ain't surprised. He won't do what I say." Doc's lips flattened together. "I reckon we'd better go and see about him, George."

After saying their goodbyes, Doc rapped on the door. "Henry."

"C'mon in."

The tiny, weathered house choked on the hotter air inside, despite the open windows. George dipped his tall frame through the low doorway. The acrid smell of body odor and whiskey cuffed him across the face. He bit down on the inside of his lip to stem the rising gag.

Doc, however, seemed unperturbed while he crossed the room.

Through a back window, George spied a woman tending a cast iron pot over a fire. The steam boiled upward. With an apron, she dabbed her browned, taut cheeks—a face too soon robbed of youth. George wrenched his attention back inside the room.

A middle-aged man sat in the corner, his foot propped up on a three-legged stool. A bit of a flush crept above his dark, chest-length beard. Smoke curled up from the corn-cob pipe sticking out of his mouth.

"Henry, I'm here to check your wound. This is Dr. Curtis, a friend of mine."

Wary gray eyes inspected George as Doc knelt and unwrapped the dressing. After a long moment, Doc stood. "Have you been up on this leg much?"

"As much as I allowed. Too many chores. My woman cain't do 'em all."

"You haven't been cleaning this nor changing the dressing."

"I reckon you did a fair enough job. It just takes time."

A frustrated grunt puffed Doc's cheeks. "Henry, you're a stubborn fool. Your wound is getting infected. I'll have to get a poultice from Sal."

Doc's insult rolled off Henry's shoulders like water on a raincoat. With an answering grunt, Henry shrugged. "I've had worse. I don't see the point in all the fuss myself."

"You don't?" Doc bent until he was at eye level with Henry. "You keep going at this rate, you'll lose your leg."

No emotion flecked across the man's face. "Naw. Not me. It'll get better in time."

"Without that poultice, it won't." Doc pivoted on his heel. "We'll be back in a while. Until then, get out of this bad air and sit in the shade."

Once outside, George drew a fresh, relieved breath.

"Back to Sal's," Doc commanded, the weakness temporarily absent from his footfalls.

As Ginger clopped down the road, dust swirling from beneath her hooves, she whinnied and tossed her head. George tightened his hands on the reins.

"She knows we're headin' the wrong direction. She's anxious to return to the barn for her oats." Doc brushed a fly from his sleeve.

He knew how she felt. He was also heading in a direction not of his choosing. And it didn't seem to matter how much he kicked against it. As though unseen hands controlled the reins of his life, directing him down a path he couldn't stomach.

George stiffened, the thought searing his mind.

"What's wrong, Dr. Curtis? Am I keeping you from other business?"

Clearing his throat, George coughed. "No, no at all."

"I'm one of the sharper tacks in the shed. I can tell when something is needling a person. You might as well be honest about it. These days, I don't have much patience with any beating around the bush. Time's too precious."

Frustration tinged George's face. "Very well. I was thinking how I'm like Ginger. She's going down a path she'd rather not."

"As am I." Doc's soft answer was louder than all the thoughts barraging George.

"I'm sorry, Doc. That was thoughtless of me." *What a dunce I am.*

"No need to apologize. We must make the best of the path we're traveling, with God's help. No need in commiserating or yearning for another reality. I'm learning God's purposes are infinite and beyond our understanding."

George ran a finger around his collar. "And that's another thing. What was the preacher doing there?"

"You might as well get used to it. You'll be running into him often. He does the Lord's work, ministering to their souls. You and I do the Lord's work, tending bodies. The two go hand in hand. Around here, folks call for the preacher first and the doctor second. You'll have to learn to work with Parson Crandall—or at least tolerate him. I saw your hackles raise when he greeted us."

A medicine woman and a preacher. They'd be better off without my help. "I'll be honest. I don't like it, but for now, I'll do what I can."

Doc's gray mustache quirked upward. "Of that, I've no doubt."

26

Ella noted the weary shadows swathing Curtis's eyes as he lifted her into his arms. "You're later than I expected this afternoon. How did your rounds with Doc go?"

She felt his chest expand against her side then fall. "We had a full day." With the toe of his shoe, Curtis pushed open the screen door.

Though no neighbors were near, Ella glanced around. The odd sensation of wearing Curtis's shirt and pants along with Caleb's shoes hadn't worn off. Her legs dangled unencumbered without the layers of skirts.

"Tell me about it."

"I met a medicine woman who hates Yankees like me. I helped birth a foal. Watched Doc deal with an obstinate patient who had an infected leg wound. Miss-licked it with an axe." He descended the steps and turned toward Ella's walkway.

"Goodness gracious."

With a chuckle, Curtis turned his head and stole a swift, tender kiss without missing a step. "I've been waiting for this all day."

Ella's heart skittered, the unexpected caress robbing her breath. She covered it with a huff. "In broad daylight no less."

Curtis's eyes glinted mischievously, and he tightened his arms around her. "Whyever not?"

Ella sputtered for an answer. "It isn't proper."

"Ah, I see." His mustache curved upward. "But according to you, I'm a rude man. And according to me, you're a presumptuous lass. What else can you expect?"

Unable to suppress a giggle, Ella tugged a fingerful of hair at the nape of his neck. She loved when a smile drove the lingering sorrow from Curtis's eyes. More than anything, she yearned to know him and his work better.

"So, you birthed a foal?"

"I helped Doc. I've never seen anything quite like it. I had to stop at my place to change and wash up before coming here."

"When I was growing up, my father would never let me watch, but as soon as it was over, he would call me in the barn to see the new foal." The memory still brought a beautiful ache to Ella's heart. "Douglas left this morning, by the way."

"Did he let Caleb stay? I know his heart was set on it."

"He did, at the last moment. He's so stubborn. He still refuses to have anything to do with Earl."

"It's a hard weight to carry. I ought to know. Don't be too hard on him, Ella. His coming here was a huge step, even if it was for your reputation." He winked, setting her cheeks aflame.

When they reached the railings, Ella tugged his sleeve. "Let me show you something. Put me down."

Curtis raised his eyebrows but did as she bid him. Reaching on either side of her, Ella grabbed the log railing and stiffened her arms as her feet touched the ground.

"I can hold myself up for a few minutes, Curtis."

Taking half a step back, he scrutinized her from the tips of her toes to the top of her head, the doctor's demeanor taking over, gauging weakness and strength.

Her heartbeat pounding harder with the effort, Ella inhaled more deeply. "I practiced earlier today too. Earl helped me."

"That's good. Have you tried taking a step?"

For an answer, Ella lifted one foot with concentration and shifted it a tiny step forward. Letting out a breath, she focused on her other one and lifted it to follow. The muscles in her arms and shoulders started burning. "There."

Curtis's face beamed the happiest she'd ever seen, glowing with admiration and pride.

"Look at you. I'm proud of you, lass."

Her arms quivered a bit.

"That's enough for now." Curtis gathered her up, sweeping the weight away from her upper body. "The more you do this, the stronger your arms and legs will become."

Relieved air expelled from Ella's lips. "A little bit requires much effort. Do you think I'll improve?"

"Without doubt." He carried her the remaining distance through the walkway. "Are you ready to do your exercises?"

"Yes, as long as it's in the shade." Ella retrieved a handkerchief tucked inside her sleeve and dabbed her upper lip.

"I would imagine." He set her on a quilt that he had spread before fetching her. "Time to work."

As Ella flattened her back against the ground, something jabbed her thigh. *The brooch.* Guilt sharpened the sting. Since coming to Valley Creek, she had kept the brooch inside its case instead of wearing it. The closer she grew to Curtis, the more it belonged to the past. She'd slipped it in her pocket for this moment, though.

Her mouth tasted like sawdust.

Sitting cross-legged, Curtis settled at her feet and removed the shoes. He took one of her feet and braced his palm against the arch. "Ready?"

245

Unable to answer, Ella tried to swallow the dry lump in her throat.

Curtis pushed until her leg bent at a ninety-degree angle. "Now push."

Ella wished with all her soul he would take the truth with the doctor's demeanor he was using now. Hidden was the man courting her.

Perhaps he would be gone forever when she told him. The thought froze her.

"Ella?" Concern threaded his voice.

Yanking her thoughts to the present, Ella put her strength into her leg and pushed. "I'm sorry," she mumbled.

While thoughts of the brooch loomed, Ella did the first round of exercises, pushing and pulling against Curtis's strength. For the second round, she turned over on her stomach as Curtis scooted a few feet away.

"Now, I want you to raise your right leg as high as you can. Ten times."

Ella mashed her forehead against her crossed arms. Though she trembled, she lifted it several inches. By the tenth time, she dropped her leg, unable to hold it hardly a second.

"Good. Now do the other leg."

The smell of grass and earth filled her nostrils as her forehead throbbed.

She paused to steady her breathing. "My left leg seems weaker than the other one."

"From what I've read, that's not unusual. You'll have to do a few extra exercises." Curtis's brisk but gentle voice urged her.

Ella groaned and inched it upward. By the fifth time, the remaining strength fled, however. She dropped it onto the quilt and panted as though she had been running.

"I can't move it any further." Her voice wobbled with frustration. "It's no use."

Curtis scooted closer. "Here. Let me help." He slid one palm under her toes and the other under her knee. "I'll lift it a little, but you'll still do most of the work."

"I can't."

"*Can't* isn't allowed in your vocabulary. You can, and you will. Ready, lass?"

She felt the insistent pressure from his hands raise her leg a fraction.

"Ella, darling. You can do it. It doesn't have to be perfect. However long it takes, you'll make it to ten."

Puffing, Ella lifted her leg while Curtis steadied it. *Six. Seven.* Ella's jaw ached while the lower half of her body trembled. *Eight. Nine.* Crinkling her eyelids closed, she gasped at the scorching pain shooting upward into her thigh.

"I know it hurts, but you only have to do one more."

With all her might, she raised it. Curtis's hands kept it from dropping back to the ground. While she groaned, he lowered it onto the quilt.

"You did wonderfully," he said, sounding pleased.

Ella rolled onto her back, blinking back the stinging moisture in her eyes. "It doesn't feel wonderful."

"I know, but you're making more progress day by day." Curtis inched closer until she could better see his face. A sheen of sweat covered it. His well-kempt hair drooped over his forehead, making him look roguish and younger. The sun wove golden threads through those chestnut brown waves.

He held out his hands, and she grasped them. After he pulled until she was sitting up, he rasped his knuckles against her jaw. "Don't let the pain rob you of joy. Remember, it's one day at a time."

"Many long days at a time. Curtis, tell me why it's so important to you that I walk."

A surprised, confused expression dimmed his face a little. "Because it's important to you. I know how you crave independence, and I only want to help you achieve it." His eyes probed her. "I'm not ashamed of you, Ella. I never have been, nor will I ever be, whether you walk or not. Your legs, though they're a part of you, are not the measure of who you are."

His words nearly undid her. "I'm sorry. This whole period of my life is like traveling these hills. One minute, I'm up on top. I can see everything clearly. I'm hopeful. Then the next minute, I'm in a vale with the horizon obscured." Ella bit her trembling lip.

"Whether on a mountaintop or in a vale, I'll be with you." He raised one of her hands to his lips and pressed a firm kiss against her skin.

The beautiful gesture throbbed Ella's heart with guilt as she remembered the brooch in her pocket. She must tell him. Now.

"I wonder." She snatched a deep breath and tugged her hand away. "Curtis, I must tell you something. I should've long ago, but I was afraid you wouldn't understand."

A line puckered between his eyebrows. "What is it?"

Ella wriggled her fingers into her pocket. "This." The dappled sunlight glinted across the golden etchings as it lay nestled within her palm.

"Your brooch?" Curtis searched her face as though trying to understand. "I've noticed you haven't been wearing it lately."

"It doesn't feel right to wear it. Here." She turned his hand over and set it within his. "Open it."

His larger fingers fumbled with a clasp meant for ladies, but he finally managed to release it. He stared at the photograph inside. The silent seconds stretched Ella's nerves thin.

"How did you get a picture of me?" he asked, peering closer at it. "Quite a long time ago. I don't remember this one, though."

"It isn't you."

Curtis's head flew up. "What do you mean?"

Father, help us. "It's Charles."

Without answering, Curtis held up the brooch closer and

stared at the photograph. As she watched understanding dawn in his eyes, the color seeped from his face.

"Why didn't you tell me?"

"I should've. I was afraid." Ella rubbed her arms as a chill shrouded her.

His eyes, wary, darted to hers and seized them. "Afraid of what?"

"That you would draw the very conclusion you're doing now. That I, that I—" Ella choked, waiting for him to interrupt, but he only sat very still, his eyes dark and brooding.

Heat prickled the back of Ella's neck. "I'm sorry, Curtis, truly sorry. I never wanted to hurt you."

His stare never wavered. "Tell me, who do you see when you look at me?"

"You, George Curtis. You." Her vehement voice answered without hesitation. "I don't deny when I first met you, I saw Charles. I was mind-blown. But it didn't take ten minutes in your company to realize the two of you are exact opposites in every single way."

Sighing, Curtis scraped a hand across his jaw. "I know you're not dishonest, but you can't deny that your initial interest stemmed from it. Can you?"

Ella winced. "No."

Curtis straightened his back, his mouth drawing a hard, rigid line.

"By the time I took you to the train station at Valley Creek, my attraction had nothing to do with Charles. I never think of him when I'm with you. Please forgive me, Curtis. I never wanted to hurt you, and I have."

Curtis snapped the brooch shut and handed it over. "I wish you'd told me." Standing, he brushed his knees and retrieved her shoes. He slipped them onto her feet, his touch still gentle and utterly unnerving. He stood, a whirl of thoughts behind his questioning stare.

"What time of year did Charles die?"

"What?"

"You heard me."

Ella's ribs convulsed with her rattled intake of air. How she loathed to answer. "Early spring."

His question, low and insistent, pierced her conscience. "Dogwood winter?"

Rendered speechless, she could only stare helplessly at him.

Wincing, Curtis flexed his jaw. "*An untimely end.* I understand your words perfectly now."

"No. No, you don't." Tears ruptured the barrier of her emotions and gushed down her cheeks, and Ella hated herself for it. For hurting the man she loved. Yes, horribly, irrevocably loved.

A flicker of empathy softened the hard line of his mouth. Without words, he stepped closer and slid his arms under her, lifting her from the quilt.

Ashamed, Ella burrowed her face into Curtis's shoulder and allowed the feelings of the past year to flow. All her efforts to win his heart had failed. Her chin bobbed against his neck as his steps clipped toward the house. Her stomach plunged.

The screen door creaked on its hinges, and the sound of his footfalls thundered into the wide hallway. He turned and entered the parlor. Thankfully, no one else was present to witness her humiliation and grief.

As if she were a china doll, Curtis lowered her into the wheelchair but didn't step back once she was settled. Like a dark cloud, he loomed over her.

Knowing that he was seeking a glance from her, she averted her eyes. Her shoulders quavered.

His large, smooth hands gently framed her face. Through blurred eyes, Ella ventured a peek at him.

No anger filled his face, only confusion and hurt. His thumbs stroked across the stream of flowing tears.

"I'm not sure exactly where I stand with you or if Charles still occupies a place in your heart. I don't want to talk while you're this upset, but we will later when we've both had time to think."

About what? The question lodged in her throat.

Backing away, Curtis headed toward the door. When he reached the threshold, he halted. A shudder rippled across his shoulders.

He ventured a look back at her. Indecision and unspoken questions wrangled across his face.

Ella hiccupped.

Like the sun pushing its rays through a thundercloud, resolution steeled his scrutiny of her. He strode back across the rug. Unsure, Ella seized the armrests of the chair. The tips of his shoes bumped hers.

Once more, Curtis framed her face. Then, before she could blink, his lips crashed into hers; a firm, possessive kiss that took more than it gave. Took her thoughts, took her breath, and took her heart. Never had she been kissed in such a fashion. Like lightning and wind sweeping through her veins.

When he withdrew, he slipped his fingers from her face and cleared his throat. Tearing his gaze from hers, he raked his fingers through his hair, hand shaking.

An instant later, he was treading the hallway and shutting the front door, his steps almost a run.

With a sob, Ella buried her face in her hands.

27

She could've told him sooner. Unsure whether his torrent of emotions stemmed from Ella's confession or more from his feelings for her, George moaned and slumped down on a lichened stump near the little house he occupied. He pressed his forehead into his palms and closed his eyes.

A dead ringer. Of all people, it had to be him. Could he trust she truly saw him rather than Charles? Had she fooled herself into believing it?

He'd fallen into a trap of his own making. Throwing caution to the wind, he had pursued Ella and allowed her to wriggle past his hard shell with her friendship, her wit, her beauty, and that indescribable quality that was wholly Ella.

He needed her more than he'd realized. No, it drove deeper than that. He loved her. From the top of her cinnamon head to the very depth of her feisty soul.

Did she love him?

Or did she love a phantom instead?

A sharp pain seared the side of George's face as he realized he had locked his jaw. His eyelids burned.

"How about it?"

With a yelp, George sprung from the stump. Not ten feet away, Earl leaned against a tree, his arms crossed and face intent.

"Can't you bother warning someone?"

"I wasn't trying to be quiet. I was comin' in the backdoor as you were leaving. Next thing I heard was my sister crying her eyes out." Earl grimaced. "She told me about the brooch. I never knew Charles, or I would've told you myself. He met her after I'd left for New York."

Feeling weak-kneed, George dropped down on the stump once again. "I'm a first-rate fool."

"I agree."

"Why would she care about me anyhow?"

"I sure don't know." A sliver of a smirk curved Earl's mouth.

George scowled. "Aren't you full of good cheer."

Unruffled, Earl smirked wider. "Someone around here has to be." He sobered. "This whole thing is a bump in the road, George. You and Ella will figure it out."

"I wonder. I know Ella believes she cares for me, but what if it's really Charles she sees?" Insecurity writhed in his stomach. "And you know the worst of it? No matter what she feels, I can't walk away."

Earl stiffened against the tree, a sudden spark flaring in his eyes. "No matter what you do, she'll be well-cared for."

Impatience roughened George's voice. "That's not what I mean. Her condition has nothing to do with it. It's me."

"How so?"

A cold tremor tingled across his shoulders, much like the one he'd felt earlier when he walked away from Ella, only to turn back and—

With a growl, George swept the fervid memory aside and jerked to his feet. "I'll be frank with you. I've come to realize I belong with Ella. As if my heart and hers are two sides of the same soul. Sounds crazy, doesn't it? I'm not sure I understand it myself."

The spark faded from Earl's stare as he studied George's face. "Are you sure?"

Without hesitation, George nodded. "What I feel for your sister is something I've never experienced. But now, I don't know if she feels the same for *me*. George Curtis. Not a long-lost dream."

Reaching up, Earl snapped a twig from a branch and twiddled it between his fingers. "You know, you're taking a lot for granted. I can't speak for her, but have you considered Ella's point of view? Do you think she's ever wondered about Lydia?" His pointed stare glinted as he dipped his chin. "Or Lorena? After all, you made your feelings perfectly clear for all to see."

Guilt sank its sharp, unsparing teeth deep into George's heart as the memory of his selfish, imprudent behavior tackled him.

"I can't argue with that."

"Ella puts on a tough front, but inside, she's a tender soul, easily bruised. Sure, she's stung you unintentionally. You bruised her first, though. I'd call it even if I were you." Earl tossed the twig aside. "One thing I've learned: love doesn't amount to much if people fail to put faith in God and each other. Sometimes we have to set aside doubts and act on it. Life's too short otherwise. Look at us. A few years ago, we were young, but middle-age has snuck up on us."

A wistful sigh relaxed the tense muscles in George's face. "We were good friends back then, weren't we?"

"The best. Besides Douglas, I'd never had another friend as close as you." Earl paused as though weighing his thoughts. "I hope it can be that way again between us."

The risk Earl was taking was evident in his open honesty. After all, he was well acquainted with rejection. George remembered Douglas's hostility toward Earl, and it stung because he once treated Earl the same way. No expectation hovered in Earl's expression as he waited.

George took a clean breath of Ozark air and expelled it. "I'd like that. Friendship is sweeter to me now than it used to be."

Earl held out a hand. "Here's to old friends."

A weight rolled from George's chest as he extended his. "The best."

"I HAVE to show Curtis that I care for him and not Charles," Ella said, almost pricking her finger with the needle poking through the fabric of her needlepoint. "There's not much I can do." She gestured to her legs. "But I must do what I can."

The fringes of a headache throbbed against her eyes. A punishment for her wakeful night.

Lorena swiveled around on the piano stool, the melodious notes of *Scenes from Childhood* dwindling from the parlor. "Is there anything I can do?"

"I don't know yet. He has helped me in every way he can, and I need to do the same." She rested the needlepoint in her lap. Her shoulders slumped while she let out a frustrated sigh.

"Whatever you need, let me know."

The shadows from the setting sun stretched long and narrow across the rug. Ella swallowed a rising lump in her throat. "It's well past time for him to be here. I suppose I deserve it."

"Nonsense. I'm sure he's had a busy day. George isn't one to play games."

The door banged, making Ella flinch. The sounds of scurrying feet rapped down the hallway.

"Aunt Ella, Jimmy caught a ten-pound trout!" Caleb nearly tripped over the threshold, staggering into the parlor. Behind him, Jimmy grinned wide and shouldered past Caleb. He held up the dripping fish on a line. Creek water spattered the polished floor.

"Lookie here. Lots of good eating."

"Merciful heavens, not on my clean floor." Lorena dashed from her seat and spun Jimmy around by the shoulders. "Out, young man. We can admire your catch better outside."

Caleb chortled, then looked down at the muddy splotches on the knees of his britches. "I didn't get a bite today, but I will."

Ella smiled. "Of course, you will."

"We saw Dr. Curtis earlier. He said to tell you that he wouldn't be coming today. He still had a lot of calls to make, and it would be after dark 'fore he got home."

"Thanks, hon." Was Curtis trying to avoid her? An idea brewed in her thoughts. Dropping the needlepoint into a basket, she wheeled herself into the hallway as Lorena turned Jimmy and his catch over to Earl. While she returned inside, the boys followed him around the house.

"Lorena, I've an idea. Will you help?"

A half-hour later, while the sun was sinking behind the hills, Earl reined in Crockett and Grits at Curtis's place.

"The place is dark, so he isn't home yet."

"All the better." Ella shifted the heavy basket on her knees. With Lorena's help, she had packed a supper to be waiting on Curtis when he returned.

Earl dashed inside with the basket and lit a kerosene lamp. It bathed the cabin in a warm glow, windows flickering to life. Next, Earl unloaded her wheelchair and placed it inside.

"Come on, sis." Stepping next to the wagon, he reached up for her. After scooting forward, she shifted into his arms. "Do you remember carrying me when I was ten?"

"Fell out of a tree, as I recall."

"Following you as usual."

Carrying her up the steps, Earl grinned. "I tried to tell you, but you never listened to warnings." He settled her in the chair.

She tossed a smirk at him. "Any warnings now?"

"Yep. Waste no time." A wistful gleam invaded his teasing eyes, and she knew he was thinking of the years he had squandered.

Ella chose to keep her tone light. "Then I'd better make haste, or he'll catch me here."

After wheeling herself to the table in the center of the room, she unloaded the basket. Fried summer squash, a mess of fried okra, biscuits, gravy, and bacon. An apple pie. A loaf of fresh sourdough bread made by her own hands.

From the kitchen, Earl carried a plate, fork, spoon, knife, and a pitcher of water. She set them in order. Backing up, she surveyed her work.

"It's fit for a king. You and Lorena outdid yourselves today." Earl rubbed his stomach and eyed the apple pie.

Ella withdrew an envelope from her pocket and laid it beside the plate. "I hope this helps." She wheeled over to Earl. "Time to load your sister up."

Reaching out a sunburned hand, Earl tugged a wayward lock of her hair. "Don't fret. You've not come this far for nothing."

With all her heart, she hoped he was right.

THE TINY HOUSE'S windows winked at George through the tree limbs as his steps trailed into the yard. He'd refused Doc's offer to carry him home, thinking the walk would ease the kinks out of his legs.

It hadn't.

The handles of his black bag bit his gritty palm. He paused, scanning the windows. Had he forgotten to extinguish the lamp? *After the sleepless night I spent, I wouldn't be surprised.* With his limited funds, he couldn't afford to be wasteful with kerosene.

He trudged forward, eager to shake the dust and the day away from himself. Thoughts of Ella pushed through his weariness. Was she all right? Upset? Had she exercised?

George pulled his heavy legs up each step and turned the doorknob. Light spilled onto his feet and swept upward. He squinted, then blinked. Twice.

The table was spread. Glancing around, George eased inside and shut the door.

"Hello? Anyone here?"

Stillness answered him.

Setting aside the bag, he approached the table. The aroma of apple pie made his mouth water. The empty plate sat at the head of the table, waiting to be filled. To his famished eyes, the biscuits glowed golden in the lamplight.

Then he spied the envelope. His name, in Ella's writing, graced the front. His pulse ticked up a notch. Reaching out, he plucked it up and tugged the paper into his hand.

Perhaps we are back where we started. I have waited this long. I can wait forever if need be. Please accept this supper after a long, tiring day.

Yours, Ella

His eyes stung and the words blurred. Friendship was indeed a sweet treasure, but his feelings for this amazing woman struck deeper. Her reaching out to him in this way was another testament to her worth. But then, Ella had always extended her hand to him, even at his worst. He certainly didn't deserve her love.

Picking up a napkin, George covered the biscuits and spun on his heel toward the kitchen. Something more pressing than eating demanded his time. He retrieved a lantern from the cabinet and lit it.

He was bone-weary, but her feelings were paramount. Supper could wait a bit longer. If he knew Ella, he was certain her head was pounding from a sleepless night. He couldn't let her endure more uncertainty. He fetched his bag. After dropping a few pills in his pocket, he grabbed the lantern and trekked out into the inky darkness.

He hardly felt the ache of his feet while his heart carried him the short distance to Earl and Lorena's.

He took their porch steps two at a time and nearly staggered backward when Earl immediately opened the door. Though the shadows obscured Earl's face, George heard the amusement in his voice.

"Runnin' a little behind, aren't you?" He stepped aside, letting George shoulder past him. Earl took the lantern and put it on a shelf.

"I'd like to see Ella if it's all right."

"It's all right by me. She is helping Lorena clean the kitchen." Closing the door, Earl pointed toward the back of the house.

"Thanks."

The ladies' voices hummed toward him, their lively conversation trickling underneath the closed door as he neared. He gave it a light tap and turned the knob.

Both women froze. Lorena's hands paused, submerged in suds at the white porcelain sink while Ella's clung to the stoneware bowl swathed in a dishtowel.

George's collar tightened. He cleared his throat. "Excuse me. I know it's getting late, but I'd like a word with Ella."

Withdrawing her hands from the water, Lorena dried them on her apron. "Of course. I'll go see about Caleb while you both talk."

Ella's fingers cramped where she squeezed the rim of the

bowl. George waited until the door clicked shut before taking a few steps toward her.

"I came to thank you for supper."

Averting her eyes, Ella swiped the bowl a final time and set it on the countertop. "I hope it was to your liking."

"I'm sure it will be. As soon as I saw it, I wanted to thank you first."

"You're welcome." Her fingers fluttered around the towel puddled in her lap.

"I read your note."

Silence.

Look at me, lass. He stepped nearer and took her hand. Her eyelashes swept upward. The luminous ocean of her eyes seized his, and a deep tug within his soul anchored him in their depths. He could stand there forever. To bask in that lovely gaze always and discover a belonging he had never known existed.

Did she feel the same?

His Adam's apple pushed against his collar. "I didn't want you to be troubled, especially after yesterday." His mind grappled for the right words. "We're far beyond where we started, Ella. I might not understand everything yet, but I'm not going anywhere."

Ella's eyes shimmered like starlight scattering across the sea. She pulled in her bottom lip and held it steady between her teeth.

He tenderly squeezed her fingers. "We'll talk at the right time. I think my duties will be keeping me busier. Doc is getting weaker by the day, and I won't see as much of you as I'd like."

"I'm so sorry about Doc. Is there anything I can do?"

"Thank you, but it's beyond human help."

Releasing her hand, he fished the two pills out of his pocket. After fetching a cup from the cabinet, he pumped fresh water from the sink into it.

He set the cup in Ella's hands. "Here. I can tell your head aches. Take this."

Surprisingly, for Ella, she didn't argue. Her mouth popped open as if controlled by a hinge.

Despite himself, George chuckled. "You remind me of a baby bird, lass." He plopped the pills on her tongue. "This will ease the pain."

Ella raised the cup to her lips. After two long gulps, she handed it back. "Thank you, Curtis. Everything you've said and done has been very kind."

He lost himself in her gaze once again. "I'd do anything for you, Ella Steen." As he bent, he cradled the back of her head in his palm and pressed a kiss to her forehead.

"I'll see you as soon as I can."

28

The early morning mist grazed George's face as he stood in the front yard, waiting for Doc. He strained his ears for the sound of Ginger's hoofs but heard only a dove cooing somewhere in the trees. Overhead, the morning stars dwindled into the sky's cherry flush rimming the hilltops.

George snapped open his pocket watch and checked the time. Doc had never been this late. Clicking the cover shut, he slid it into his vest pocket. He tightened his fingers around his bag. Something must be wrong.

He strode out of the yard and headed toward Valley Creek. The walk of several miles would take him to Doc's place on the other side of the tiny town.

The dew dampened the hem of his slacks. Purple shadows pooled around him as he listened for any sign of Doc's buggy. With every step George took, his heart pumped a little harder, dread burrowing in the pit of his stomach.

After a mile and a half, the sound of a buggy's approach crested a hill. George halted, relief spilling over him until the rig came over the hilltop into his view. His relief dissipated.

The driver pulled the mare to a stop. "Dr. Curtis, good

morning." Parson Crandall's mouth widened into a friendly greeting.

Not wanting to be rude, George forced his lips to curve upward. "Good morning, Parson. Out making calls already?"

"I am." He glanced at George's bag. "I see you are as well."

"I'm headed to Doc's first. He's usually at my place by now, so I'm hoping to meet him along the way."

Parson Crandall's brow furrowed. "No one has followed me from town. Hop on. I'll turn around and give you a lift."

Not if I can help it. He'd rather climb one of those summits in the distance. "Thanks, but I'll manage. I'd only detain you from your business."

"Dr. Curtis, I warn you. What I have is catching, but I assure you, it isn't fatal." A wry grin lit the parson's eyes.

A dry cough choked George while the parson laughed, the merry sound echoing through the hollow.

Warmth tingled George's face. "I'm sorry. I meant no offense."

"None taken. I'm used to it." Though Parson Crandall sobered, the glimmer in his eyes still lurked. "I promise not to barrage you with scripture. What do you say? It'll save you a lot of time."

Time meant more than the man knew; Doc might need his help that very minute. His aversion wasn't important. Stepping forward, George climbed into the buggy. "I thank you for the lift."

"You're welcome, friend." Clicking his tongue, Parson Crandall turned the buggy and mare around, setting her to a trot.

On the seat between them, a Bible lay, the worn leather binding crackled from use. The spine seemed to burn into George's thigh. Suppressing a shudder, he set his bag between his feet with a thump.

"Are you here to replace Doc?"

The quiet inquiry jerked George's head around as if he'd been struck. His eyes clashed with Parson Crandall's grave ones.

Parson Crandall sighed. "I've seen death in my time. It's been in his eyes a while. When I saw you the other day, I felt sure he'd sent for you."

Apparently, nothing escaped the man's notice. "No, he didn't send for me. I came to visit the Steens." He held his breath and waited for him to say it was God's doing.

Instead, Parson Crandall shifted his gaze forward. "Either way, I'm grateful you're here to answer the call. I know it's bound to be a relief to Doc."

Instantly, the words swept George to Dr. Benson's visit while he was staying with Mr. Wallace. He'd said something eerily similar. *Promise me this. When the time demands for you to be a doctor again, you'll answer the call no matter where you are.*

No matter where you are.

This wasn't God's doing. Throughout his childhood, his parents had taught him that God brought good things out of hard circumstances. He'd faced hard times but had never seen Him bring any good out of them.

Or had he simply failed to see?

The question rattled his analytical mind trained to study and touch the physical in order to believe. Everything that had happened drove deeper than anything physical. Beyond human sight.

Doest thou well to be angry?

Squaring his shoulders, George cut a glance at Parson Crandall to see if he'd heard, but the man seemed lost in his thoughts.

And then George realized the words hadn't been spoken aloud.

They had come from within.

His memory drifted to his favorite story from childhood.

Jonah and the great fish. How many times had he sat on Da's knee, listening with rapt attention to the tale of the prophet who ran from his calling and his God? The Lord had asked Jonah that question. Was God now asking him?

God hadn't worked things the prophet's way, and Jonah's anger had driven him from the presence of the Lord. After hiding below deck in a ship, he'd been forced to give an account of his actions to the sailors. They'd thrown him overboard, and he'd been swallowed first by the waves of the sea, then the fish. Terrible circumstances. In the end, God brought about good.

But not before Jonah cried out to the God he'd forsaken.

Kneading his forehead with his fingers, George squelched a laugh. Although Parson Crandall promised not to talk scripture, God had made no such promise.

He couldn't outrun God, whether in New York City or the deep hollows of the Arkansas Ozarks.

"IT STARTED LATE LAST NIGHT." Mrs. Brown leaned over the bed, clutching one of the bedposts and peering down at her husband.

Doc's face twisted in pain as George listened to his elevated heartbeat. After a minute, George moved the stethoscope's diaphragm over to Doc's liver.

"That bottle on the nightstand. Need another dose." Doc sucked in a shaking breath. "Helps the pain."

Straightening, George nodded to Mrs. Brown, who immediately popped open the bottle. Two pills tumbled into her palm. She reached for a nearby cup of water.

"Here, hon." She placed the medicine on his tongue and then slid her hand beneath his head to lift it from the pillow. She brought the cup to his lips. Closing his eyes, Doc swallowed then laid his head back. He clamped his jaw, the muscles of his face pulling taut over his cheekbones.

Opposite him, on the other side of the bed, Parson Crandall stood motionless and watched the waves of pain sweep over Doc.

George laid the stethoscope in the bag at his feet. The first rays of morning threaded through the curtains and highlighted the deepening golden color of Doc's skin—a sign of his rapidly deteriorating condition. A sickening weight hemmed George in like a vice.

Utter helplessness.

Doc ran his tongue over his lips and moaned. "Dr. Curtis, take Ginger and do the rounds. Get Sal."

Hating to argue, George kept his voice low and gentle. "I'm needed here for now."

A surge of pain eroded the command in Doc's voice. "There's nothin' you can do. Parson's here."

Parson Crandall's grieved eyes met George's troubled ones. Very true. The man of God could do more good than he could at this point. A lump tasting like bile rose in his throat.

A feather-light touch grazed his elbow as Mrs. Brown leaned close and lowered her voice. "He'd be at ease knowing that you're caring for his people. Please."

George closed one of his hands over hers. "Very well."

Her shimmering eyes expressed gratitude. With a bracing squeeze of her hand, George plucked up his bag.

The hardest part of Doc's journey had begun.

After hitching Ginger to the buggy, George set off for Sal's. Now that Doc could not accompany him, she would have to be his ambassador to these mountain people. Sarcasm twisted his lips. Sal would be thrilled, no doubt. If Doc and Sal accepted him, he might have a chance, but without it, he hadn't a prayer.

What am I thinking? I'm not staying.

When the few miles brought him into Sal's yard, he braced himself. Better to put his best face forward.

A bleary-eyed hound rounded the house and bared his teeth, the crusty, dark hair on the back of his neck rising. The cabin door swung open, and Sal stepped out with the flintlock pistol gripped in her hand.

She rolled her eyes when she spied her intruder still waiting in the buggy. "Oh, I thought it was somebody."

"No, just me." George tipped his hat.

"What ya want?" Sal slid the pistol into her skirt pocket. George exhaled a breath he hadn't realized he was holding.

No need to beat around the bush with this one. "Doc has taken a turn and is ill. I'm to do his rounds."

"And naturally, he told you to come fetch me."

"Exactly."

"Where ya headed?"

"Seven Hollows."

Sal turned her head and spit into a weedy patch of flowers. "The things I do for that man." She spun on her heel and clipped back into the house.

Was she refusing? The reins slackened in George's hands. Should he move on and risk getting his head blown off by some suspicious landowner? Today they were supposed to travel deep into the fringes of Doc's territory. He had joked if strangers ventured uninvited into those hollows, they were never seen again.

Then Sal whisked outside, armed with a rifle and a gunny sack, and shoved the door shut with the toe of her boot.

Without bothering to look at George, Sal strode to the buggy, crammed the gunny sack under the seat, and then glanced back at the hound.

"Up, Jeb."

Promptly Jeb trotted over and jumped into the rig. His wary gaze fastened on George as Sal settled onto the seat. A low growl rumbled in his chest. George schooled his demeanor to hide his nervousness.

"Jeb doesn't like Yanks."

Why am I surprised? "I like a dog with impeccable taste."

Sal's eyes narrowed. "Save your impertinence. I know my letters and what they mean too."

George muffled a laugh and turned it into a dry cough. He flicked the reins. As if on cue, Jeb curled up on the floor between them, his stare still honed on George.

"When we git to Seven Hollers, you let me do the talking. Don't speak unless you're spoken to. Understood?"

"Yes, ma'am."

"And don't git out of the buggy unless I say so. The folks there don't mess around with strangers. They shoot first and don't ask questions later."

"Is that why you brought the rifle?"

"Yep, even though I'm kin to some of 'em. They ain't gonna like seeing me with a furriner." A few stray, wiry strands of Sal's white hair pulled loose from her haphazard bun as the breeze grazed them.

George frowned. "Furriner?"

Sal rolled her eyes heavenward at his apparent ignorance. "For-eign-er."

"I'm not a foreigner, for goodness' sake, Sal."

"Might as well be. For the first several years after Doc came to these parts, he had to take me with him every time we went there. Now I gotta start all over with you." She puckered her lips as though tasting a lemon. "It is what it is." She swiveled in the seat and raked George with her flinty eyes. "You got some mighty big shoes to fill, Yank."

Unflinching, George met her glare. "And I'll never be able to, Sal."

Not one flicker of surprise cracked her expression. She snapped her attention to the road ahead.

"Then mind your step."

"I'm on my way back to Doc's. Will you come with me?" Curtis removed his hat brimmed with road dust.

With a flour sack towel, Ella patted the moisture from her face. "Sure. We've just finished canning for the day." She gestured to the kitchen table crowded with mason jars, their insides stuffed with green beans. "Tomorrow, we do tomatoes."

Curtis blinked as though seeing their work for the first time. A tired smile softened his rather stern expression. "They look delicious."

Laying the towel aside, Ella backed her chair away from the table. "I'll go and freshen up quickly. You'd best do the same. We laundered your clothes this morning. They're folded in Earl and Lorena's room."

Curtis held out his arms and surveyed his crumpled, stained clothes. "Thanks. I could use a change."

"The room is across the hall," Lorena said, rinsing her hands under the pump. She dried them on her apron. "The basin and pitcher are there too."

With a nod and smile encompassing them, Curtis rounded Ella's chair and pushed her toward her bedroom. Only the sound of his footsteps filled the silence between them. When they reached her door, Curtis pressed a hand on her shoulder. "I'll be just a few minutes."

"All right." As Ella looked into his dark, troubled eyes, she sensed the tension simmering beneath his calm exterior.

His few minutes lasted a bit longer than Ella's, though. Determined he shouldn't wait on her, she zipped through washing up and straightening her unruly tresses. By the time he stepped out, he found her waiting by the front door.

Pleasure seeped through her like a warm spring as she

watched his tired face light up at the sight of her. *Somehow I'll show him I'm useful, that he can lean on me.*

"Look at you, all ready to go." He approached and lifted her out of the chair.

"I'll have to hurry and learn to walk because you can't tote me everywhere we go."

"I rather like it." Curtis shouldered open the screen door and carried her into the yard where Ginger stood swishing her tail. "But I can get a buggy that will accommodate your chair."

In the afternoon sunlight, Ella saw more clearly the crow's feet biting a little deeper into his skin. "You've had a hard day."

After rounding the rig and climbing in, Curtis evaded her probing stare, sadness darkening his eyes like a troubled sea before a storm.

"Doc has taken a turn. He couldn't make the rounds today." He clicked his tongue to urge Ginger forward.

"I'm sorry."

Curtis dipped his head. "Nothing can be done."

Reaching over, Ella laid a hand on his forearm. "I'll be praying." In his silence, she watched the emotions tighten his jaw. "Did you make the rounds alone?"

"I had to take Sal."

Ella fished for a bit of humor to lighten the weight pressing against Curtis. He'd told her plenty of the medicine woman.

"I would've bought tickets to watch it."

One corner of his mouth quirked. "It gets worse. We had to go to Seven Hollows; Seven Hollers, as they say it."

"Don't keep me in suspense." She withdrew her hand from his arm.

"No stranger goes into Seven Hollows without an escort, or he probably won't come out again. Sal was my way in and out."

A cold shiver tremored down Ella's back. "I hope you won't ever try it alone."

"Believe me, I won't. Those were some of the coldest,

hardest looks I've ever received. I've no doubt they would've shot me if Sal hadn't been there with her rifle."

Ella listened as Curtis described the weathered, hardened men, the crude houses—often only one-roomed with children seemingly spilling from the windows or peeping from beneath the porches. The patched clothes, dirty faces, and bare feet. The women, old before their time, whose faces had forgotten how to smile, their skin stretched over sharp cheekbones.

He'd worked in silence, treating children's coughs or cleaning ugly gashes on a hand or arm. Nearby, a man always stood watching, his frown rigid, a gun in hand while Sal stood opposite, her stare trained on him.

"No use for small talk in Seven Hollows. Tend to business and get out. Even Ginger had the good sense to hurry out of there. She backed her ears, and I had to hold her back from running until we returned to the main road. You would've thought a hundred devils were chasing after us."

"It's hard to imagine in a peaceful place like this."

"They're hidden in the shadows, and they prefer it that way."

While they traveled, Ella kept the conversation light, preferring to chase away the disquiet of Curtis's demeanor. Something, she knew, lay even deeper than Doc's condition. He was a doctor at war with his calling. Time would force whatever haunted his faraway stares and quiet solitude into the light eventually. Until then, she must be patient.

When they drove into Doc's yard, Parson Crandall and Mrs. Brown stood on the porch talking.

"I guess he stayed all day. Have to admire the man for that." Curtis said more to himself as he reined in Ginger.

While Curtis climbed from the buggy, Parson Crandall shook Mrs. Brown's hand and came down the steps to meet him.

"Any change?"

"The pain is not as bad, but he's weak. How long do you think?" With a somber face, he greeted Ella and turned his attention again to Curtis.

"It's hard to say. A day or two. Maybe a week. Sometimes it can be longer."

"For his sake, I pray it's not." Blinking away a mist in his eyes, Parson Crandall dragged in a ragged breath.

"I'm glad you stayed, Parson. Looks like you need to get some rest."

He set his hat on his head. "I'll be back tomorrow. If I'm needed beforehand, send for me." The muscles in his neck tensed as if words clogged his throat.

As the parson strode toward his rig, Curtis turned toward Mrs. Brown. "I've brought Miss Steen for a bit if that's all right. I thought a change might be good for you while I see Doc."

A relieved, drained smile loosened the strained lines around Mrs. Brown's eyes and mouth. She brushed an ebony wisp of hair, woven heavily with silver, from her forehead.

"I'd be much obliged, Dr. Curtis. Bring her in, and I'll fetch us a cup of coffee."

Curtis reached for Ella, and she leaned into his waiting arms. While he carried her onto the porch, Mrs. Brown stood aside and held the door for them.

"Take her into the kitchen. I've got a pot already going."

Ella stiffened in his arms when Curtis stepped across the threshold. A familiar, unwelcome smell snatched hard memories to the surface of her mind. Memories buried beneath waves of emotion she'd learned how to tread. Faces of Mother, Father, Charles, Douglas's wife, and others. Their voices mingled together as one. Her breathing grew shallow, unwilling to take it in yet powerless to escape it.

One could never get accustomed to the smell of death.

29

"There you are." Doc's raspy voice greeted George as he entered the bedroom. Propped up on pillows, Doc pushed the bedcovers away. "I've been waitin'."

Sensing Doc's intent, George reached him in two strides. "Hold on a minute. You need to stay put."

Doc sighed, his sallow face a bit impatient. "Dr. Curtis, you know the signs as well as I do. I've not much time to waste, and there're things I need to discuss with you while I'm able." He scooted to the edge of the bed.

George grasped Doc's elbow.

Doc paused. "As long as I can walk, I'll do it. I don't intend for nobody else to raise me from this bed until the angels do."

"All right." Backing away, George watched Doc's knees wobble when he stood. Pain creased the deep-set lines in his weathered face.

"Come with me."

Taking a breath, Doc shuffled from the room and led George into his office, through a side door off the parlor. It opened into the waiting area, consisting of a few chairs, Doc's desk, shelves, and oak filing cabinet. Another entrance, from the outside of the house, also led to the waiting area.

A cough racked Doc's shoulders. He cleared his throat and shuffled his bare feet toward the desk. "Over here."

After rounding it, Doc sank into the chair and pulled out a drawer. He withdrew a small cardboard box and laid it on the table.

"I hope you'll forgive me, but I took the liberty of writing Mr. Wallace after you told me of your misfortune. I wanted to know more of your situation. He sent me this box." He pushed it toward George.

"I see." Pulling open the flaps, George willed his fingers not to quiver but failed. Newspaper clippings with ugly headlines lay underneath a letter in Mr. Wallace's handwriting.

"I don't need to see any of this. I know it all too well." He took a step backward, met Doc's yellowed gaze, and knew his friend's liver was failing quickly. "Why would you need this?"

Leaning forward, Doc rested his elbows on the desk. "A simple reason. Once I'm gone, my wife is leaving Valley Creek. We've a daughter in Missouri, and she wants her mother to come and live with them. I think it's best. The house and office will be here, unoccupied. When I wrote Mr. Wallace, I wanted to know just how destitute you were." Doc worked his jaw, his voice growing rough and dry like sandpaper. "I'm sorry for prying into your business, but you're not exactly forthcoming."

Sensing Doc's reasons, George shrugged. "I'm not planning on staying, Doc."

Doc waved a hand, clearly dismissing the words. "We've deeded this place to you. Do with it what you will. Sell it or stay."

George staggered back a few steps as if Doc had cracked an uppercut under his chin. The room blurred and spun.

"You can't do that."

"We did. Mrs. Brown will be well provided for and has no

need of this place. You'd said you lost everything. Though I believed you, I didn't realize the extent of your loss." Doc blinked, anger and disgust glowing like embers in his eyes. "Mr. Wallace thoroughly explained. And the newspapers—to have your reputation murdered, your practice maligned, and your living robbed is a sin of the worst sort. No wonder you've walked away from your calling. However, it hasn't walked away from you, Dr. Curtis."

George squeezed his eyes shut against the wells of emotions churning inside. "I'm overwhelmed. You and your wife are far too kind. I can't accept it. I don't have anything much to give in return."

"Whether you do or not, it's yours as soon as Mrs. Brown packs her things and leaves. It's what we want. If you'd rather sell, you can use the money to help you settle elsewhere."

Stumbling to a window, George laid his head against the sun-warmed glass and clutched the windowsill.

"I've never done for anyone else what you've both done for me. I'm beyond words. I can never repay it."

"You've given of yourself for years. And rightly, you also profited well. A successful city surgeon would achieve no less. But here or wherever else you may go, you'll earn every single floor plank, wall, and nail in this place before you're finished doctorin'."

He couldn't restrain the tide filling him. Tears breached George's closed eyes and surged down his cheeks. Thoughts and words jumbled into a mass of incoherent feelings too strong to stem.

Though all around me is darkness and earthly joys are flown, My Savior whispers His promise: Never to leave me alone.

Ah, Mam. If only she knew. Her voice, vivid in his memory, rolled over him like a wave.

A hand clenched his shoulder. Startled, George peered into Doc's strangely calm face. For a time, Doc said nothing, only gazed at him as if he were memorizing George's features. The fingers on his shoulder tightened.

"Dr. Curtis, kicking against the pricks is a hard thing. I did it for years. Life blooms in the sunshine and frosts in a blinding, untimely moment. Like a dogwood winter. Snatched away much too soon." Doc's gray mustache quivered. "I reckon, throughout our lifetime, we have many such winters. A sudden chilling blast that blights our joy. But then, spring comes again. Quit kicking, my friend, and live. A second chance is waitin' around the corner."

Unable to speak, George reached up and clasped the top of Doc's hand. More minutes passed as they stood motionless, unwilling to move, knowing it would be for the last time.

Finally, Doc cleared his throat. "Come now. I've got more things to show you. My journals where I keep records of all my patients—their history and mine. And my medicine cards; recipes, if you will, of things Sal taught me and will teach you. Then there are my medical books and the medicines I keep on hand. And my equipment. Everything you'll need. And one thing more." Doc paused.

George honestly didn't know if he could handle anything else, but Doc's earnest face compelled him to listen.

Doc stared through the front window where Ginger stood in the shade, her nose tipping the water's surface as she drank from a trough.

"Take her home with you. I had a long talk with her in the barn last evening. Explained everything. Said my goodbyes. She'll be good to you. Though I advise you not to use a whip to kill a fly between her ears."

Doc's weak grin blurred from George's view.

THREE DAYS LATER, just as quietly as he entered the valley all those years ago, Doc departed into a new one while Mrs. Brown and Curtis watched at his bedside.

Sitting in the buggy, Ella edged closer to Curtis, viewing scores of mourners trudge up the narrow hillside road to Valley Creek's cemetery. At the front of the line, the handmade casket was borne on the shoulders of friends—Mr. Mansfield, Earl, Guy, Harley Ray, Mr. Huitt, Mr. Watkin, Andrew Ray, and Mr. Ray.

No one had suspected Doc's illness, and the astonishment deepened the town's stark grief. Many of the ladies, their faces shadowed by their sunbonnets, muted their sobs in handkerchiefs.

"He was quite a man." Curtis's throat bobbed as he laid his arm across the back of the seat and drew Ella closer against his side.

"I wonder how many here he helped bring into the world," she whispered.

"Many of them. Or tended their dying loved ones."

As the last of the mourners passed them, Curtis urged Ginger to follow their ascent. Somewhere up ahead, a man's deep voice lifted and floated through the throng.

There's a land that is fairer than day
And by faith we can see it afar ...

One by one, voices joined until the hillside burst into a melody unlike anything Ella had ever heard. Curtis's arm tightened around her shoulders.

In the sweet by and by,
We shall meet on that beautiful shore ...

Curtis's side quivered against her arm, and Ella mouthed a short prayer for him, for the people, for Mrs. Brown. The voices of those simple mountain folk blended as one, offering up their grief, their love, and their faith to One Who held them and their beloved Doc in His hands.

Overhead, the sunlight gilded the plump, white clouds meandering over the valley, fracturing the heat. When they crested the hill, they followed the procession to a quiet, unassuming spot near the back of the cemetery.

The men set Doc's casket over his resting place and stepped back. Folks circled the area, crowding closely together. After reining in Ginger, Curtis climbed down and stood near Ella's side where she sat, seeming unwilling to leave her alone. Ginger stamped a foot and lowered her head as though she felt the grief permeating the clearing.

Scanning the crowd, Ella found Lane and Edith standing by Lorena and sent them a somber smile. In Lane's arms, Abby babbled and gurgled as Parson Crandall opened his Bible.

At the edge of the woods, a movement caught Ella's eyes. Barely inside the tree line, an older woman leaned her shoulder against a hickory tree. Wayward white strands of hair peeped from beneath a wide-brimmed straw hat. Weathered, narrowed eyes flicked across the crowd. A faded, brown-checked gingham dress draped her angular shoulders and hips without shape.

Angling toward Curtis, Ella reached out and touched the cuff of his sleeve. "There's Sal."

Curtis followed her glance. "How'd you know?"

"I think I'd know her anywhere."

Parson's message was straightforward, like Doc. No frills. An honest outpouring of faith, more powerful to Ella than any flowery speech. After they'd lowered his coffin into the ground, the pallbearers shimmied a large stone at the head of Doc's grave. A stone taken from the mountain—no markings, not even a date, just like many of the other headstones there. Exactly the way Doc had requested.

He'd preferred instead to be written on the hearts of those who loved him.

"DR. CURTIS, IT'S TIME," Harley Ray guided his wagon alongside George's when they reached the bottom of the hill. Behind them, people trailed from the cemetery, where a few remained behind to finish the burying.

George glanced at Edith's flushed face. Sitting up straighter, she rubbed the sides of her stomach and pulled in a breath.

"Let's get her home." George waved to Earl as he was helping Lorena into their wagon. "Get Sal and tell her to come to Edith's."

Nodding, Earl climbed in and popped the reins across Crockett and Grits. The trepidation in Lorena's face mirrored the feelings churning inside George as the wagon clattered past them.

Ella clutched the armrest as he urged Ginger toward Edith's place. "I hope it's different for Edith this time."

"So do I." Thankful they didn't have far to travel, George took a calming breath and worked to clear his mind of the morning. His focus now had to be Edith and her babies. After a mile and a half, he guided Ginger into the yard.

"I'm afraid I'm in the way." Ella dropped a glance at her legs. "You need to get inside."

"Nonsense." After setting the brake, George came around and plucked her into his arms.

He clipped across the yard onto the porch of the wide log home and entered the front room just as Harley Ray was helping Edith toward their bedroom.

George set Ella into a rocking chair. "When I figure out how long it might be, I'll see about someone getting you home."

Ella's soft fingers patted his knuckles. "Don't fret about me. Only Edith and those wee ones."

The cabin door groaned on its hinges as the door swung open. A thin shadow stretched across the floor.

"Yank, you're lucky Earl Steen caught up with me." Sal stepped into the room, her splattered boots spitting chunks of mud in her wake.

Behind Sal, Lorena smothered her face in a handkerchief, no doubt to hide the laughter twinkling in her eyes. Earl covered his mouth with a short cough.

George shrugged out of his suit jacket and handed it to Ella. Uncuffing his sleeves, he began rolling them up as he headed toward the bedroom. "This way, Sal."

Edith was lying on the pillows when they came inside the dim room. Immediately, Sal went over to a window and drew back the curtain, allowing the light to pour inside.

Bending to touch Edith's shoulder, George relaxed his face into a smile, hoping to reassure her. "Are you ready, dear?"

"I suppose as ready as I'll ever be," Edith murmured, her eyes round and anxious.

"We'll be here every step of the way."

Minutes later, after an examination, George stood and washed his hands in a nearby basin. An icy wedge pressed between his shoulder blades, driven deep by knowledge he wished he didn't possess. He beckoned Sal to his side, her stare questioning.

"Feel her belly."

With experienced hands, Sal pressed her fingers along Edith's skin, carefully feeling the two babies within their mother. George watched as the truth dawned on Sal's face. A bland look swallowed the ripple of concern.

"Dr. Curtis, what is it?"

George turned to find Edith's gaze pinned on him. "The babies are all right. One of them, however, is in the wrong place."

"What does that mean?"

"One of them is lying crossways. Like this." He held his hands stretched apart across the lower end of her belly.

"What can be done?"

"A few things." George swallowed. "We can try to move it."

"And if that doesn't work?"

"Let's focus on one step at a time, Edith. Sal and I will do everything we can."

For a time, they worked together. But, no matter how they molded and pushed Edith's belly, the baby didn't change its position.

"Her pains are coming a little harder." Sal swiped a sleeve across her forehead.

Frustrated, George straightened. Time was not being kind. The truth of what he had to do coiled around him with sickening force.

"Please get Harley Ray in here."

As Sal turned to go, Edith reached for his hand. "Dr. Curtis, what's happening?"

George grasped her hand and squeezed. "A bit of a complication, but we'll see it through."

Harley Ray, followed by Sal, rushed to Edith's side, his tall, broad frame casting a shadow across her face. "What's wrong?"

The invisible coil around George's chest tightened as he explained the baby's position. "Unless the baby moves—and soon—I'll have no choice but to operate. It's called a caesarian section. Birth through surgery. A method to save a baby's life."

"Father in heaven, help us." Harley Ray squeezed his eyes shut, scraping his fingers through his hair. "What about my wife?" His eyes, wild with worry, bounced from Edith to George.

"I'll not lie to either of you about the risk. Some women have been known to survive." George swallowed. "Others haven't."

Edith squeezed George's fingers, insistent. "There's nothing else that can be done?"

Deep affection welled up in his soul, but he blocked the

emotion from his heart. Now was the time to think and act, not feel. "Edith, if the baby doesn't move, and I do nothing, the three of you will be lost."

Harley Ray gnashed his teeth against a moan.

"I warn you. I've never done this procedure before. Only studied it."

Biting her lower lip, Edith gasped as a sharp pain coursed through her. After it had passed, she focused on George, her confidence clear and steady.

"Dr. Curtis, I trust God, and I trust you. Do whatever you feel you must." Quiet confidence tempered the anxiety in her voice.

In that blinding moment, Lilith's face rose and shattered his thoughts. George pulled his hand from Edith's and stepped backward.

"Sal, stay with them while I go to Doc's. I'll need some of his things. Try to move the baby again."

The memories chased him from the room and the house. Rushing outside, Earl caught up with him as he swung into the carriage.

"What's going on?"

"Hop in."

Since Doc's place was nearly a mile away, George let Ginger break into a gallop. On the way, he explained the situation. Earl's face drained of color.

"Edith won't survive?"

"She might, but I can't guarantee anything. Can you explain the situation to the ladies when we return?"

"Yes." Earl turned his head toward the mountains and closed his eyes.

30

While Sal scrubbed down the kitchen table, George placed the catgut sutures in a solution of iodine and phenol. On the stove, steam curled upward while surgical tools boiled in a pot.

"We'll need a clean sheet to place over the table." George ignored the roiling in his stomach.

"I'll dry it and find one." Sal set aside the scrubbing solution.

Hands on his hips, George surveyed the kitchen—not at all an ideal place for surgery. But what else could be done? Shaking his head, he strode into the front room and found it empty. The porch.

George pushed the front door open and found Ella, Lorena, and Earl sitting huddled together, unaware of him. He cleared his throat. Their heads jerked upward.

"In about ten minutes, I'll begin." He kept his voice brisk, businesslike, to stave off the fear chilling his insides. "I'll need absolute quiet. No one coming inside."

Earl's and Lorena's faces brought other unwelcome scenes to George's memory. Thomas and Claudia had trusted their daughter to him, and he'd failed miserably. Now his dearest friends were depending on him. Suppose he failed again?

"We're praying." Ella's voice permeated through the fog.

"Please do." Pivoting, George reentered the cabin. *Forget Lilith. You must focus on Edith only. You must.*

After sterilizing the tools and sutures, George laid them nearby on a side table that Sal had scrubbed. Beside them sat a bottle of ether.

George surveyed the kitchen table, covered now with a crisp, white sheet. "Sal, bring in Edith and Harley Ray. You'll disrobe her. I'll stand with my back turned to give her some privacy. After she lies down here, you'll clean and sterilize her abdomen, then cover her with the other two sheets on the counter, leaving her belly exposed. I'll administer the ether."

Without so much as a grunt, Sal obeyed like a well-oiled machine, brisk and ready. Moments later, Edith and Harley Ray followed her into the room, and Sal explained everything as efficiently as any nurse George had ever known. In no time, she had Edith ready, lying flat on the table while Harley Ray stood at the head, his large hand engulfing Edith's.

Turning around, George confronted their pale faces and forced his own to appear relaxed and confident.

"I'll begin momentarily," he said, approaching Edith's side. "Harley Ray, do you think you can handle assisting here? If you can't, you'll need to leave. I can't have you fainting."

Harley Ray shook his head, his brow rigid. "I've seen my share of blood. I'll do whatever needs to be done."

"Good."

A sharp pain rolled over Edith. Gasping, she stiffened and moaned. Once again, George checked the baby's position, but it hadn't moved. The longer he waited, the more danger for Edith and the wee ones.

When the pangs passed, George laid his hand on Edith's

arm. "I'll begin soon, dear. You'll be unconscious throughout, and it'll be over before you know it."

Edith's voice wobbled. "And I'll see my babies then."

With ebony hair plastered against her clammy forehead and her eyes large and dark, Edith looked like a child. Like Lilith.

No.

A chill zipped down his spine. Blinking, George turned to the side table to get the ether.

Dr. Curtis, will I see you in just a little bit?

George closed his fingers around the bottle of ether and froze. His pulse hammered his temples. Cold sweat prickled his forehead.

I can't do it.

All of their faces blurred with Lilith's—Edith, Harley Ray, Lorena, and Earl.

I'll fail them just as I did her.

His stomach spasmed, a bitter taste burning his tongue. He'd known Edith ever since she was born, just as he'd known Lilith.

His lungs tightened and breath thinned. If he did nothing, the three of them would die.

George glimpsed the slight tremor in his hands and flexed them.

Focus on Edith. Only her.

An iron-like hand clutched his elbow. "Yank, we're waitin'."

With dark eyes glinting, Sal hissed low, "I don't know where you drifted just now, but you'd better shake it off, or I'll knock you sideways. You got three lives to save."

George wrung his heavy thoughts the way a prisoner shook chains. "What did you say?"

"I said you got three lives to save. And you'd better do it."

A glimmer of courage pierced through the chill. "Thanks, Sal."

Drawing a deep breath, George reached for the bottle of ether. *God, if You hear me, please help. For their sakes.*

Only his commands broke the silence that pervaded the room. When he made the incision, George shut everything else out except the task at hand.

Minutes later, he withdrew the first baby and handed it into Sal's waiting arms. After George severed the cord, Sal carried the baby to the countertop to clear the child's airway.

"Harley Ray, I'll need you next. Stand ready." George focused on the second child.

A second later, a firm smack sounded behind him, and the first baby squalled. A smidge of relief passed through him.

"That's it, child. Fill your lungs and cry it out." Sal's voice held a note of pride.

George withdrew the second baby and laid it in a sheet draped across Harley Ray's hands. The new father stood as though struck dumb. After severing the cord, George nodded toward Sal. "Give the child to her."

Turning back to his task, George began the process of finishing the surgery. His ears strained to hear the second baby's cry while his fingers worked. Long moments later, it came loud and strong. Without thinking further, he concentrated on Edith.

"First a girl, then a boy. You won't forget this day, Harley Ray," Sal murmured, her gravelly voice soft. "Here. You hold 'em while I help with your wife. Don't worry. You won't drop 'em."

Sal reached Edith's side and checked the pulse in her wrist. "Her heartbeat is steady and strong."

"Good. I'm almost ready to start closing. The bleeding is normal thus far."

Sal stood watchful while he began the longer ordeal of cleaning and suturing the womb. Both babies filled the room with their lusty cries, a very good sign. George paused and glanced over at the young father.

"Sal will help you finish cleaning them up; then you can take them to meet their new family. Edith is holding steady."

"Thank you, Dr. Curtis." Harley Ray's watery voice choked.

George gave Sal a short nod. Immediately, she flew to Harley Ray's side. "Let's get these youngins presentable. Your young wife will be all right. She's got vim and vigor. The Good Man above is here. And she has a good doctor tending her."

WHEN GEORGE FINISHED CLOSING the incision, Harley Ray gingerly carried Edith to bed. A half-hour had crawled by since then. Moments later, Edith's eyes fluttered open, confusion and pain drawing her brows nearly together. Checking her pulse, George bent over and watched Edith's pupils adjust to the daylight. She licked her dry, cracked lips.

"Dr. Curtis?" she croaked.

"The babies are just fine. So are you." He smiled, concealing his worry. The next few days would be critical to Edith's recovery. "You have a daughter and son, and they're quite vocal."

A tiny tear trailed down the side of her face. "God be praised."

"You're not to exert yourself. Harley Ray will assist you with anything you need. You must follow my instructions to the letter so you can recover as quickly as possible. Sal is preparing some medicine to help with the pain."

Edith found George's fingers and squeezed them. "Thank you. I knew, with the Lord's help, you'd pull us through."

With his mind still fumbling for the right words, George quickly pressed Edith's fingers and left. He found Harley Ray sitting on the chair in the living room, holding the girl while

Lorena and Earl admired and cooed over the boy. The joy on their faces had banished the shadows they'd endured earlier.

Ella's cinnamon head was bent over the little girl, her finger tracing the tiny hand. The sight filled George's weary mind, dispelling the turmoil clinging like cobwebs to his thoughts.

Then she raised those glimmering eyes and smiled, holding out a hand to him. "Curtis, they're beautiful. Come and see."

Everyone else's glance flew up and met his with relieved smiles. Approaching Ella, George clasped her hand as if it were his lifeline. "They are indeed, and their mother is awake. She's anxious to see them."

Their unspoken questions showed on their faces.

"Edith is all right," George answered. "Sal and I will stay the night. The next few days will tell how she'll do. She's strong, and I see no reason why she can't pull through."

Harley Ray rose along with Lorena, who placed the little boy with his sister in their father's arms.

"It wouldn't do to keep Edith waiting," she murmured.

In a few strides, Harley Ray was entering the bedroom to see his wife and introduce her to their little ones.

"We can't thank you enough, George." Earl stood and wrapped an arm around Lorena's shoulders. "You saved our girl and her babies."

The unshed emotions glimmered in their eyes. A dry knot that tasted like victory, defeat, and regret rose in George's throat. The presence of Someone unseen hovered closely.

George swallowed hard. "It wasn't me. I couldn't have done it alone."

His voice crumbled like a brick under too much strain. Releasing Ella's hand, he bolted from the room and out into the open Ozark air.

LIGHTNING FRINGED THE HILLSIDES, illuminating the gray haze surrounding Ella and Earl as the wagon clattered to a stop in front of Curtis's door. Thunder rumbled as the first drops of rain speckled Ella's navy skirt.

"It'll be here in a little while." Earl set the brake and hopped down. "George might get caught in it."

Even though the sun hadn't risen, Ella knew Curtis was heading home after a long, wakeful night at Edith's side. In her lap, a warm breakfast waited in a basket. The scent of bacon and buttered biscuits wafted under her nose.

Her wheelchair rattled as Earl swung it over the side of the wagon and carried it inside the tiny house. After a few minutes, lamplight flooded the window.

Before fetching her, Earl hesitated on the threshold and scanned the dark sky, his broad frame silhouetted against the light spilling from the doorway. The thunder growled once more.

"It's still about ten miles out. Time enough for me to get this team in the barn until it passes and split some stove wood for George." He clipped down the steps toward her.

Inside, when Ella was seated in her chair, Earl set the basket in her lap. "I'll leave it to your capable hands."

Smiling her thanks, Ella watched her brother hurry outside. With her hands, she wheeled the chair across the pine floor toward the table, sighing at the sight of it.

"Silly man. Leaving a mess behind."

In the center, papers lay in a haphazard pile. Ella set the basket on the floor and reached to move them. As she swept several into her hand, the top of a page caught her eyes.

Ella ...

"What?" Squinting, Ella pulled it from the others and peered closer.

I yearn to see your face and tell you how much I grieve, but the words choke me.

Like ice water, shock swarmed her heart. Though she was alone, Ella skimmed the room. Should she read it, even though the letter was addressed to her? Why hadn't she received it?

The paper crinkled as she checked the date it was penned. A few months ago. Confusion filled her mind.

Would you understand? Would you turn away as others have done? Would you lay the blame at my feet? There is no need. I have already done it. My guilt knows no relief, night or day.

Lifting a hand, Ella twiddled with the lace collar around her throat. Why hadn't Curtis sent it? She set the letter in her lap and thumbed through the rest of the pile. Four more—fifteen pages total. All of them addressed to her.

"Forgive me, Curtis." She nibbled her lip. "For once, I'm going to pry."

Fingers scurrying, Ella arranged them in order. Her heart rammed against her ribs, squeezing her breath tighter beat by beat. She lifted the first one.

I made a horrible mistake, and a little girl paid with her life.

A gasp escaped Ella's lips. Line by line, she absorbed every detail of that terrible day—the shock and the grief. Then came the days that followed: the lawsuit, the loss of his practice, his reputation, and his friends. Curtis chronicled the gut-wrenching headlines and questioned himself.

Worst of all was his guilt. Through his emotional words, the ink often betraying his quivering hand, Ella discovered how dear Lilith had been to him. The little neighbor who came to him with her injured and sick dollies.

I would give anything to bring Lilith back. My last dime, my last possession. My life. When I hear children laughing, I catch myself looking for her, but she is not there. Then the pain slices through my soul, severing all other thoughts. Human hands cannot move the veil between life and death. I am weary, Ella, with all of it. The nightmares are the worst. My desire to be a doctor died with my little friend.

He described the harrowing dreams that stole his sleep. Goosebumps pebbled Ella's skin, spreading from her scalp to her legs. How had he borne it alone?

A thunderclap rattled the windows, followed by the sudden thrum of rain against the roof in perfect time with Ella's tears.

She fumbled for a handkerchief that she'd forgotten to carry. Ella lifted the hem of her skirt and pressed it against her face. So many times, she'd watched an unspoken thought extinguish the sparkle of Curtis's smile like a blast of wind against a candle. A troubled stillness would settle over him, and he would grow pensive. *If only I'd known.*

The door banged open, a blast of wind and rain hurling it against the wall. Nearly dropping the papers, Ella flinched and snapped her head up.

Curtis stood just inside the doorway. He pushed the door shut.

"I saw Earl. He took Ginger and the buggy to the barn. The rain followed me all the way here."

"You're drenched." Floundering for something else to say, Ella's voice faltered.

"That I am." Curtis surveyed his dripping clothes with a rueful grimace. He removed his sagging hat and hung it on a peg. With a sweep of his hand, he slung aside the hair plastered to his forehead.

Then he spied the pile of letters in her lap. His face clouded, a look of dread darkening it.

"I found them scattered on the table." Ella hated how feeble she sounded. "I saw my name."

"You read them?"

Courage. Ignoring the churning of her stomach, she tilted her chin upward. "Every word."

31

Without answering, Curtis padded toward the bedroom and shut the door with a firm click. Ella heard the wet clothes smack the floor, piece by piece. Then silence. Straining her ears, she heard shuffling. The opening and shutting of a trunk. Soon, the sound of Curtis squeezing out the wet clothes reached her, the stream of water splattering into a washtub.

Ella set the letters on the table and pushed them away as if they singed her fingers. She mouthed a silent prayer for wisdom.

Finally, the doorknob turned, and Curtis took a few rigid steps into the room, scrutinizing her as though trying to read her thoughts. A sleepless night along with the strain of Doc's death had sapped the color from his haggard face. Grief for him panged her heart.

Ella tucked her trembling fingers into her lap. She must say something lest he stare a hole through her.

"I'm sorry I pried. But I'm not sorry I read them."

His mouth twisted a little. "Typical Ella."

Not knowing quite how to take that remark, she squinted, waiting.

Curtis's chest expanded. "Now that you know, how do you feel?"

Ella blinked, surprised. "How do *I* feel? Why I ... I—" She stuttered short of admitting her love for him. "I can't express how grieved I am for you and Lilith's family, even though they tried to ruin you." She spread her hands wide. "Do you really believe it would change how I feel about you, Curtis?"

"Not exactly, but I've been wrong about a lot of things. It's difficult to talk about."

"Come here," she beckoned.

Without hesitation, Curtis came and knelt in front of her. Tenderly, she tunneled her fingers into his hair and brought his head down until it rested across her knees. "Why didn't you send those letters?"

His eyes closed as she felt him relax. "They weren't meant to be sent. It was a way of pouring out my heart to you. And, if you'll remember, you'd already ended our correspondence."

Ella stroked the waves of his damp hair. "I was thoughtless. I'm so sorry. It couldn't have happened at a worse time."

"No need for apology, lass. If anything, it spurred me closer to you. I wanted and needed your friendship. Then, when I saw you and learned how ill you'd been, I couldn't burden you with it."

"I'm tougher than I look."

"I've no doubt. But even so, I can hardly speak of her." He reached up and captured one of her hands in his. "I still have nightmares of that day. Her face."

He shuddered.

"Shhh. I'll help you bear it. In time, we'll make Lilith a welcome part of your memories."

He drew her hand to his lips. A fluttering of butterflies stirred within Ella's stomach.

"Right before I operated on Edith, I panicked. Froze. All I could see was Lilith's face, and I knew I couldn't face it again."

"But you did. What pulled you through?"

"Prayers and Sal. She reminded me I was there to save lives, not cause death. So simple, so obvious."

Worry stirred within Ella as she remembered Edith's pale, weak face after the caesarian section. Her voice lowered to a whisper.

"Will Edith make it?" *Lord, please let it be so.*

"She's had quite a bit of pain, as expected. Sal's medicine helped. Her heart is strong. If infection doesn't set in, she should pull through." Curtis sighed. "Only the Lord above knows. I'm beginning to realize outside of Him, I know nothing." Blinking, he lifted his head and looked up into her eyes. "I must be tired to be talking this way."

"Truth comes when we are broken, if we will listen."

Still clinging to her hand, Curtis rubbed his face against her palm and brushed it with his lips. "I love you, Ella Steen."

Ella's breath hitched. "You do?"

One corner of Curtis's mouth quirked upward, a subtle glimmering in his eyes. "You sound surprised."

"I'd almost given up hearing it from you."

The quirk spread across his lips into a slow smile that melted her heart. "Has this been your plan all along? Your reason for asking to write a crusty bachelor?"

Overwhelmed by his declaration, Ella whispered, "Guilty."

"You are a presumptuous lass." Straightening, Curtis stood on his knees and framed Ella's face between his hands. His gaze roamed her features and settled on her lips.

"If truth comes when we are broken, then I'm one shattered man."

He brought his head down to hers. Ella's arms rounded his shoulders, drawing him closer. Several heartbeats passed, and Curtis pulled back a few inches. "I hope someday you'll feel for me what I feel for you."

"Curtis." A flush set Ella's cheeks afire. "I do. Though I did love Charles for a long time, my heart belongs to you alone. I love you, George Curtis—your spirit, your character—all of you inside and out. We're cut from the same cloth. When I'm with you, I belong. That's the only way I know how to describe it. Please don't ever doubt it."

Eyes darkening, Curtis coiled one of her wayward tendrils around his finger and tugged gently. His voice grew husky. "I've never quite felt this way about anyone."

"Neither have I."

Just as Curtis leaned in again, Earl sloshed inside, the rain trailing down the sides of his face. With a slight grin, he shoved the door shut.

"A man can stay out in the middle of a rainstorm for so long, albeit in the barn." He swept his hands over his sleeves. "I'll dry off as best as I can, then we'll see about setting the table since someone distracted you, Ella."

She nearly missed his slight wink. "Your timing leaves much to be desired."

"I've been told otherwise." Earl swaggered toward the bedroom. "And I'll prove it again in just a few minutes."

Curtis chuckled and stood. "Whatever is in that basket does smell good. Will you both join me?"

"With pleasure."

THE BURDEN BEARING down against George's heart lifted a fraction as he watched Edith creep across the bedroom, her steps soft and careful. "You're coming along nicely. I'm pleased. There's no sign of infection."

Shifting little Curtis on his shoulder, Harley Ray raised his glance heavenward. "Thank the good Lord."

A tender smile spread across Edith's mouth. She reached into the wooden cradle and picked up a fussing Catherine.

"God never ceases to amaze me. I thought for certain I might live long enough to see my babies, but afterward ..." She kissed Catherine's blonde fluff and nestled her against her shoulder. "In a week's time, I'm up, walking, holding my babies. We can't thank you enough, Dr. Curtis. You saved our lives."

George swallowed a lump and blinked. "I'm glad I could be of service."

"Valley Creek could use someone like you, especially now." Harley Ray patted his son's back. "I hear that Mrs. Brown is moving out tomorrow."

"I hadn't heard." Retrieving his bag from the bureau, George ignored the sinking feeling deep inside. "I'd better go over and see if there's anything else I can do."

Ginger's quickened gait shortened the mile to Doc's. George wrestled with the temptation to slow the mare but decided against it. Since the funeral, he had stopped by once to check on Mrs. Brown. Guilt crowded his mind. He should've gone more often, but he hadn't wanted to discuss the arrangements. The leather seat creaked as George squirmed. He didn't want to discuss it now. But he must.

Mrs. Brown was sitting on the front porch with her daughter as Ginger clipped into the yard. Ginger's lips parted in a long whinny.

I miss him too, girl.

While he led Ginger to the water trough, Mrs. Brown stood and descended the steps. The folds of her black mourning skirt brushed the grass.

"Dr. Curtis, I'm glad you've come." She reached out and patted Ginger's neck. "I'm sure you've heard I'm leavin' tomorrow with my daughter."

George tasted the gritty road dust on his lips. "I apologize for not coming sooner."

"I understand, truly." A sad knowing passed between them.

"But the time has come for us to discuss things you'd rather not. Come, let's walk by the creek."

The water whispered and babbled over the rocks, twisting and swirling along its journey while George and Mrs. Brown ambled down the pebbled bank.

"I've placed the deed and other papers in my husband's desk. As you know, I'm leaving most of the furniture. You'll have everything you need."

A sigh pushed through George's lips. "A thank you doesn't go far enough. I owe you and Doc a profound debt."

Mrs. Brown lifted her skirts to step over a mossy log. "No debt. I know Doc pressured you to stay. He was thoroughly convinced God brought you here for that purpose. An answer to his prayers."

George halted, a few pebbles scattering. "And what do you think?"

"It's possible. Doc's conviction was between him and the Lord." She rested a weathered, sun-speckled hand on George's forearm. "I can't speak for them. But from my experience, I'd advise you not to make any sudden decision either way. In the meantime, spend the rest of the summer here. I've canned provisions in the cupboard. I knew I'd never use them, but I had to do something to occupy my mind these months. I intended to give them to friends and neighbors when I left, but you'll put them to better use."

"Your kindness is too much."

"'The Lord gave, and the Lord hath taken away. Blessed be the name of the Lord.'" Her chin quivered. "You'll have to finish tending the garden. There's still plenty."

"Gladly."

The wind rambled among the trees, unfurling the cool creek air. Mrs. Brown viewed the rushing water, the tree-covered emerald hills, the turquoise sky, a faraway look filling her eyes.

"I'll miss this place. We've had hard and good times here. Our roots go deep. It hurts to cut them loose. Saying goodbye is hard. I wish to go like my husband—quietly, without a fuss."

It wasn't to be, however. The next day, as George drove Mrs. Brown and her daughter to the train station, wagons and buggies of every description lined the road from Valley Creek to the depot.

Overall-clad farmers waved their hats while the ladies fluttered their best embroidered hankies in the breeze. Children trotted behind them, some bedraggled with smudged faces, chattering and yelling a fond farewell—the grateful salute of folks whose hearts fiercely loved their doctor and his wife. The scene moved George beyond words.

Deep affection brimmed Mrs. Brown's eyes as she waved. "Dr. Curtis, have you ever seen such a sight?"

"No, not ever."

"Nor will you elsewhere. If you win them, it'll be forever."

AUGUST 1912

"Come, dearie, let these old fingers see what sort of folk you are." Granny Weatherford beckoned with her hand to Ella sitting across from her. For the first time, Ella had accompanied George on his rounds.

Watching, George chuckled. Leaning forward like a child, Ella closed her eyes. "Here I am, Granny."

Granny's gnarled fingers traced Ella's forehead, her eyes, cheeks, and chin. She nodded, her eyes snapping with wisdom.

"You've had your share of trouble, I see. But you're a strong gal, pleasant, and you love to laugh. Good, good. You have a beautiful, kind face. The doctor is a mighty blessed man."

George's heart thudded underneath the envelope hidden within his vest pocket. "If she'll have me."

"She will, all right. Her face gentles when you speak."

A rosy flush scattered up Ella's neck. Granny Weatherford cackled, evidently pleased with herself.

"I feel the heat a-rushin' into her cheeks." With a tiny pinch on Ella's chin, she settled her hands into her lap once more. "You'll do."

Ella snickered, her color deepening. "Thank you. You'll do as well."

Granny Weatherford's shoulders shook as she held her belly. "I'd waste no time if I were you, Dr. Curtis."

A little later, while headed back to Valley Creek, George tugged a finger against his tightening collar. Sweat beaded at the nape of his neck, but the late summer heat wasn't the cause. The envelope next to his heart seemed to burn a hole through his shirt. He tightened his grip on the reins, the blood fleeing his knuckles.

"You know, lass, Granny Weatherford is right."

Ella's russet brows drew closer together. "How so?"

George reined Ginger to a stop. Shifting in his seat toward Ella, he relaxed the straps in his palms, but the nervous wrench in his chest failed to rein in his heart's sudden gallop.

"She said to waste no time, and I've squandered far too much already."

"I see." Uncertainty wavered Ella's voice. She plucked an ivory-colored button on her sleeve. "Time is indeed a precious thing to waste."

"I don't want to lose any more of it, Ella. Do you understand what I mean?"

Solemn eyes held his, but she answered not a word. George swapped one of the reins into his other hand while he rubbed his knee, which was feeling more like jelly while the minutes passed. He cleared a gravelly throat. The lass had no intention of making it any easier for him. *All right, love. I can wait a bit longer.*

"I know what a dogwood winter is now."

Ella blinked, her long, black lashes batting together in confusion. "It's a cold snap that blights a blossoming dogwood."

"No, not entirely. Doc talked to me about it, and I've done quite a bit of thinking. You and I—we've had our dogwood winter: your infantile paralysis and my loss of Lilith. And we've suffered other such winters through the years. No doubt it's blighted us, banished the blossoms of joy into the chilling snow. But then, spring eventually comes, and our hearts thaw in the sunshine. Do you feel it, Ella? I'm beginning to."

The vivid haze of her stare deepened. "Yes, I do." Her husky whisper trembled.

"You once wrote that it felt like a broken promise, but I don't know. Maybe it's a promise instead. A promise of sorrow followed by joy."

The mist spilled over. With a hard gulp, George captured one of her hands. "I'm a poor man. I don't know if I'll ever have much to provide. It's not what I would've chosen for you. But I make you a promise, here and now. No matter what comes, I'll always love you and stay by your side. Will you marry me, lass?"

Ella reached up and cupped his jaw, the wonder of love illuminating her expression.

Deep wellspring bubbled up, the laughter of joy. George reached inside his waistcoat and pulled out the envelope.

"Otherwise, this would be a waste of paper," he teased.

Ella tugged the envelope from his fingers and opened it. "A wedding license. Whenever did you get it?"

"When I took Mrs. Brown to the station. I made another stop after I said goodbye."

She stared down at the document. "I never thought it possible. Are you certain, especially as I am?"

He stroked her cheek with his finger. "I've never been more certain of anything else."

A smile bashful curved her rosy mouth. "In that case, yes, I'll marry you."

"Just one more thing."

Rather than take her in his arms, George fished a ring box out of his trouser pocket, grinning. He flipped the clasp open and withdrew an engagement ring set in emeralds.

Ella gasped, her fingers skimming the sleeve of his forearm. "Where did you get this?"

"It was my mother's, handed down from one Curtis bride to another. It's one of the few possessions I took with me." George slid the ring onto her trembling finger. Holding it out, he admired the glinting stones on her smooth hand.

"A perfect fit. It suits you, lass."

He brushed the back of her hand with his lips. "Thank you, Ella. You have no idea how happy you've made me. I love you."

Drawing her close, his lips hovered a fraction above hers, waiting.

Ella's lips parted, her breath fanning his cheek. Her arms slid around his shoulders. "And I love you."

Waiting no longer, he lowered his head. Moments later, the buggy jostled as the wheels rolled forward. George glanced sideways at Ginger. "I can see I've two headstrong ladies on my hands."

"As long as she and I are at the helm, you shouldn't have any cause for complaint."

"I couldn't agree more." He tugged Ella closer and swept his lips over hers again.

Ginger nickered and tossed her mane, knowing the way to Valley Creek without any help from the doctor.

32

A shadow stretched across Ella's knees where she was sitting beneath an elm. She looked up from *Pride and Prejudice.* With hunched shoulders, Caleb shuffled from one foot to another, his head drooped and hands jammed in his pockets.

"Darling, what's the matter?"

He shrugged, tucking his head lower.

"Come here and let me look at you." Ella gestured her fingers. The boy scuffed a few steps nearer. Reaching up, she inspected Caleb's face. Around his left eye, an angry red ring was rising.

"What on earth happened to you?"

Caleb mashed his lips together and gnashed his teeth.

"You must tell me." Her tone brooked no nonsense.

"Jimmy punched me." Caleb sniveled, scraping a sleeve across his nose.

Though shocked, Ella showed no outward sign to her nephew. "Why would he do a thing like that?"

"We quarreled and fought."

"I see. What about?" She crossed her arms.

Caleb scuffled the toe of his shoe in the grass, avoiding her scrutiny.

"I'm waiting."

"We were playing marbles, and I won his best aggie."

"You were playing for keeps?"

"Yes, ma'am."

Ella exhaled a clipped breath and raised her brows. "We've told you never to play for keeps. Let me guess. Jimmy wanted his aggie back, and you refused."

Ducking his head lower, Caleb shrugged.

A flash of movement near the tree line caught Ella's eyes. She raised her voice. "Jimmy, I know you're there. You might as well come here too."

The sunlight shimmied across Jimmy's golden hair as he trudged toward them, his hands also crammed into his overall's pockets. Jimmy glowered, his left eye sporting a darkening red ring also. With a bare foot, he kicked a stick, sending it end over end.

A tug of sympathy took Ella to the days when Douglas and Earl occasionally bloodied each other's lips. Father's gentle voice filled her memory of times he instructed and reconciled them.

"Come closer, dear," she urged when Jimmy hesitated. He obeyed, standing within arm's reach without glancing at Caleb. Unshed tears clouded beneath thundering brows. Ella sighed. She would try Father's approach.

"You were both playing for keeps. Never a good idea. For that, you're both in the wrong. It led to an argument and then a physical fight."

"Jimmy threw the first punch," Caleb growled.

Jimmy bristled, gritting his teeth. "He took my aggie."

Ella held up a silencing hand. "Enough. That isn't the point. You're both in the wrong because you started badly. You can't go back and undo it."

Both boys blinked. At least she held their attention.

"To ruin a friendship over an aggie is a shame. Over playing for keeps. You boys have enjoyed a wonderful brotherhood these past weeks. I've heard you laughing late into the night after bedtime, watched you play from daylight till past sunset. It would be sad to lose it now, don't you think?"

Though they said nothing, Ella thought she detected a softening in their demeanor. In gentle, low tones, she continued.

"True friendship is indeed a rare gift. You'll be fortunate if you find three or four such special people in your lifetime. They will come into your life, and most of them will go. But a true friend will remain for always, come sink or swim. I'd hate to see you lose it, especially over a game of marbles. Aggies can be replaced. True friends can't. Boys, you should make it right and forgive each other."

Caleb scrubbed his nose with his sleeve once more. Jimmy pulled his fists out of his pockets.

"I reckon you're right, Aunt Ella." Cutting a glance at Caleb, Jimmy thrust out a dirt-stained palm.

Sighing, Caleb reached across and accepted it. While their hands bobbed, their wary eyes summed each other up. Sluggish, measured grins unwound the taut lines around their lips.

"I'm sorry, Jimmy." Caleb rasped.

"I'm sorry, too."

With a wink, Caleb fished the aggie from his pocket and dropped it into Jimmy's palm. "There. I got half a dozen at home anyway."

The queasy feeling in Ella's stomach eased. "I think Aunt Lorena will have something for those two handsome shiners you're both sporting."

Jimmy smacked Caleb on the shoulder, chortling. As they

turned toward the house, Ella spied something dark sticking just above Caleb's collar.

"Caleb, come here. Something's on your neck."

With a confused frown, Caleb bent toward Ella. "What is it?"

Ella inspected his neck and grimaced. "You have a tick. It needs to be removed right away. Let Aunt Lorena take care of it first thing."

"Yes, ma'am."

As the boys jogged to the house, Ella watched them while absently fingering the pages of her book, an unwelcome trepidation seeping like a cold fog around her. *I've become too paranoid.* She'd been bitten by ticks as a child, and nothing ever came of it.

But I also swam in plenty of creeks.

"Are you sure about using these?" Earl raised a quizzical brow, wiping away the barn dust from his old pair of crutches.

Bracing herself between the railing of her walkway, Ella took six tentative steps, each one slow and deliberate. Her bare feet pressed the hard ground, a sensation that buoyed her confidence one footfall after another.

"I believe so. After six days a week and multiple times a day, I think I need to try to venture beyond these rails."

"That may be, but I don't want you to fall."

"Well, neither do I. My arms have strengthened, and I think I can use the crutches to bear myself up. If I get tired and can't reach my chair, I'll plop down wherever I am."

A wry twinkle lit Earl's eyes. "Trust you for that. Show me what you can do."

"Very well." Ella took several more halting steps toward the end of the railing. Inhaling deeply, she bit her lip, twisted, and gripped one rail with both hands. Exhaling, she brought one arm around and gripped the other rail, rotating to face the direction she had just walked.

She felt Earl's eyes on her back, step after step. Her heart pumped beneath Curtis's shirt. Though she was lighter wearing his clothes, her pulse thrummed harder the closer she approached the end of the railing. She halted and closed her eyes. Surely she could make it to the other end. She must.

Behind her, Earl said nothing.

Ella raised her chin and forced more strength into her arms and legs. One step. Another. Closer to the end. She ignored the quiver invading her knees.

I will make it.

She focused her gaze ahead. With every footfall, she pushed against the ground and felt her weight press down into her legs —a feeling exhilarating and terrifying at once. The sensation of learning to trust her legs was altogether unexpected.

Would she ever be able to fully let go?

Only one step more. With it, Ella reached the end. Tipping her head back, she puffed out a laugh. "I did it, Earl. I did it."

An instant later, Earl reached her side. "That you did. Ella, I'm proud of you."

"Thank you, but I'd very much like my chair now," she panted.

She was hardly finished speaking before Earl had retrieved it and set it in front of her.

"Wait a moment," she said when he set aside the crutches and reached for her. "Hold the chair, and I'll lower myself into it."

"Yes, ma'am."

Once settled, Ella raised her arms toward the sky and let the breeze embrace her, caressing away the thrum of heat and exhaustion. She drew the clean, Ozark air through her lips.

"You all right?"

"Very much." The dancing rhythm of her heart thinned her voice. "I believe I'm getting stronger."

"You'll be running races with Caleb and Jimmy before long."

Ella laughed. "That may be quite a while. I'll settle for walking. I can't wait to show Curtis. When he comes this evening, I want to meet him, using those crutches."

Earl's hand rested lightly on her shoulder and squeezed.

A WEARY ACHE seared a trail between George's shoulder blades when he reined in Ginger. Beyond him, the sun slipped farther down the blushing horizon, tiptoeing against the sloping, faraway ridges. The sizzling air scraped against George's sunburned face like rasping sandpaper.

Lightning bugs, as Ozark folk called them, pulsed golden light around the hedges of Earl and Lorena's front porch.

George sighed. Without Doc, an invisible shutter had locked shut between him and these mountain people. They had revered Doc with a fierce devotion that stoked the embers of George's desire to minister to their needs. As a doctor, he'd never experienced such love from his patients—or such yearning to be accepted by them.

Minister. What was happening to him? Stepping down from the buggy, George began unhitching Ginger. Loosening the buckles, his fingers brushed her sweat-streaked sides.

"I thought my days as a doctor were over, girl. But now, it gnaws at me." Moving around to her front, George scratched between her ears. "I'm not sure I like the feeling."

He grabbed the bridle and led Ginger around the house to the barnyard trough. Overhead, pink and lavender streaked the clouds. Lilith's sweet face rose in the fading light and seized his heart.

How can I even consider doctoring? Ever since Edith's twins were born, he discovered pushing Lilith to the back of his mind was possible while tending others. If he concentrated hard enough, he could actually forget for a time. Still, he balked at the thought of devoting himself to practicing medicine again.

Today, though, the pull swept his doubts into oblivion.

He'd entered stark, poverty-stricken cabins and tended the sick. Careworn lines etched the faces with wary stares as he'd given instructions with Sal's herbs. To every child, he'd given a caramel from Huitt's store. Whether chubby or gaunt, their cheeks widened with grins.

Never had he felt more useful or wanted to prove himself so badly. To strip away the closed shutters of doubt and let them see he was a doctor and a friend as well.

George paused mid-step, arrested by his thoughts. How could they trust him if he were merely passing through? He hadn't committed himself to them.

Ginger nudged his back and propelled George toward the gate. With a short cough, George laughed. "Sorry, girl. I know you're thirsty."

He opened the gate and let her through. As she approached the trough, George latched the gate and watched while she dipped her nose toward the water. Nickering and tossing their heads, Crockett and Grits soon joined her.

More lightning bugs pulsed while unanswered questions clung to George like road dust. If only he could dash them away as easily.

Behind him, someone cleared her throat and his thoughts shattered.

George turned. The breath wedged in his throat. There, still wearing his shirt and slacks, stood Ella. With a crutch under each arm, she gripped the handles and straightened her back. A tremulous smile rippled over her lips. She inched the crutches forward.

He waited, transfixed.

She lifted one foot and stepped toward him, and the other foot followed. Again, she swayed the crutches forward. Took one step. Another.

He lifted his gaze from her feet and watched her face. Pure joy radiated from those depths into his soul. He blinked against the sudden pricking of his eyes.

The last time he'd seen her standing on her own was the day they'd let bygones be bygones after she drove him to the depot. His humiliating pursuit of Lorena had blinded him to her. Thank God he'd failed. He would've never discovered the treasure moving toward him now.

Miracles still happened, after all.

With an answering smile, George inhaled the same breeze twiddling the tendrils of her hair until he thought his chest would burst with his love. She drew closer still. Though he ached to reach her, he rooted his feet to the spot. He knew how important this moment was to her.

After several more steps, Ella stood within reach, her shimmering eyes examining his face.

"Dr. Curtis, I presume?"

The poor doctor could take no more. He swept Ella into his arms. With a clatter, the crutches tumbled to the ground while he whirled Ella in a circle. She tipped her head back and laughed like a child.

"Lass, you take my breath away." Slowing to a stop, he rested his forehead against hers. "Look at you, walking when my back is turned. I'm proud of you."

"Truly?"

"Truly. You've worked tirelessly, courageously." He drew his head back and let his eyes meander her radiant face. "I expect you to continue to gain strength daily."

"I can't tell you how good it is to feel the ground beneath my feet, to be able to push my legs against it."

"I'm sure there's nothing quite like it."

"There isn't." Ella averted her eyes and fingered the edge of his collar. "But if it hadn't been for the Lord, you, and my family, I don't know if I could've made it this far. You all pushed and challenged me." Her throat bobbed. "You left New York with a mountain of problems and ran headlong into mine. I owe you a debt of gratitude for not walking away."

"No, Ella, it's not that way at all. I owe you. You've rescued me."

She glanced up, her eyes unwavering. "I love you. Have for a long time."

"For the life of me, I don't know why." Without waiting for her reply, George lowered his lips to hers.

33

"My head hurts, Aunt Ella."

Snatching her attention from the socks she was mending, Ella set them aside as Caleb shuffled to her. He frowned, his forehead puckering.

"Darling, let me see." Ella pressed her palm against his forehead. "You're too warm. I think you have a fever."

"My legs ache too." Caleb rubbed his knees.

Ella reached for the crutches and pushed herself up until she stood. "I'll get Uncle Earl to fetch Dr. Curtis. In the meantime, let's get you into bed."

"Aww, I don't want to. Jimmy's waiting for me at the creek. We're gonna go fishing."

"Not today. I'll tell Jimmy when he comes looking for you." Ella nudged him toward the hallway. "No arguments, please. Let's go."

With a groan, Caleb trudged toward his bedroom while she followed. The twinge of worry she'd felt nearly a week ago eddied around her heart, this time with force.

A few hours later, Curtis confirmed her fears. She, Lorena,

and Earl watched as he finished his examination. After patting Caleb's shoulder, he straightened and faced them.

"I believe you're right. Tick fever. We'll know for sure if he gets a rash, usually after the fever sets in."

Curtis motioned them to follow him into the hallway. With a firm click, he shut the door behind them. "I have tea sachets with a mixture of yarrow, willow bark, and echinacea that Sal keeps on hand. It'll help with the fever and pain. After you brew it, add a little honey and give it to him right away." Concern tugged the corners of his mouth as he lowered his voice. "You need to send for Douglas."

Icy dread stabbed Ella's chest. "No, Curtis," she hissed. Beside her, Lorena clung to Earl's arm.

"I'm only saying it because it's better that he gets here now rather than later. Caleb has a good chance of recovering, but his father needs to know."

"I agree. I'll head to the depot to send a telegram." Earl patted Lorena and moved toward the front door. He snatched his hat from a nearby peg.

"Thank you." Setting his black bag on a side table, Curtis unlatched the top, reached inside, and pulled out a handful of sachets. He handed them to Lorena. "I'm going now to consult with Sal. She may have something else he needs."

While Lorena scurried toward the kitchen, Curtis neared Ella. The professional mask dissolved as he circled his hands around her waist.

"Try not to overworry. You'll do yourself and Caleb no good. And use your chair in between—I can tell you're hurting."

Shifting her weight onto her crutches, Ella's cheeks singed. She thought she'd hidden her discomfort rather well.

"All right," she sighed, trying to decipher the thoughts behind his eyes. "Will Caleb recover?"

A hesitant, pained look flitted through his gaze. "He's young and strong. I wish I could tell you more."

"I know. I'm sorry. We often make the mistake of thinking a doctor knows all the answers."

"Sometimes we know the least." After a quick kiss, he fetched Ella's chair and helped her sit. "I'll return as soon as I can."

After a while, Lorena brought the tea to where Ella was sitting by Caleb's bedside. Steam swirled from the white porcelain cup.

"I hope I added enough honey so he'll drink it."

"You'll need to prop against the headboard, Caleb." Ella pursed her lips and blew across the top of the liquid.

"I hurt." Caleb squirmed and closed his eyes.

"I know, dear, but you must sit up and drink this. Dr. Curtis says it will help lessen the pain and fever."

With a groan, he pushed himself up while Lorena arranged the pillows behind him. He settled back against them.

"Am I gonna die?"

"Why, no. You'll be all right." Lorena's glance at Ella silently begged her to say something to reassure Caleb.

"I heard y'all in the hall. Dr. Curtis said to send for Father."

Lorena's eyebrows lifted. While scrambling for the right answer, Ella handed him the cup and schooled her voice to remain matter-of-fact.

"Of course, he did. That's only expected. Your father should be here, and he would want to be too. You're going to be all right." *You must be.*

Caleb lifted the cup to his mouth and sipped. He squinched his nose with a judder of his head. "Do I have to drink all of this?"

"Every drop."

Leaning his head back, Caleb stared up at the beadboard ceiling. "Do you think Mother knows?"

Ella's expanding lungs jammed against her stays. How could she answer? "I don't know what the Lord allows our departed loved ones to know. But I do know that she loves you. Love is eternal."

"I hope so." Dipping his head, he sipped the tea once more. "Aunt Lorena, could you add a little more honey next time, please?"

A smile touched her lips as she leaned closer and weaved her fingers through Caleb's raven hair. "Gladly."

Two days later, Douglas arrived. Standing on the porch, Ella straightened on her crutches while she watched him swing down from his horse. His brooding eyes swept over her.

"I see you brought your horse," Ella greeted.

Douglas led the Appaloosa across the yard. "He wasn't too fond of riding in the stock car, but he settled down after we arrived at the depot. Took a few miles to get it out of his system." He tied the horse to one of the porch rails.

"It's good to see you standing, Ella Mae."

She beamed a smile she didn't feel. "It's good to be standing."

"How's Caleb?" He took the steps two at a time without pausing to wait for her answer.

There it was. The question she dreaded. Ella tightened her grip on the crutches, her mouth feeling stuffed with cotton.

"Not any better." Maybe a little worse, but she couldn't bring herself to say it.

Douglas's lips flattened. Without answering, he held the screen door open for her to pass through.

Ella moved sideways after crossing the threshold. "Go on ahead, Douglas. I move too slow, and you need to see him."

"If you're sure."

With drooping shoulders, she watched him tread down the hallway.

THE FEVER REGISTERED HIGHER than it had since Caleb became ill. George shook the thermometer and clamped down his rising frustration. Douglas eyed him, the unspoken question evident. George barely shook his head.

Fidgeting with the bedcovers, Caleb moaned and turned his chalky face toward Douglas. "Father?"

Douglas scooted to the chair's edge and engulfed Caleb's hand into his large one. "Yes, son."

"I was making sure you were still here."

"I am. Don't worry your head. I'm not leaving you." With his other hand, Douglas brushed his son's hair from his forehead.

Caleb's eyelids fluttered closed as he drifted into a restless slumber. On the other side of the bed, Earl rose from his chair and approached George, his footfalls sounding hushed like everything else around the house. As if everything held its breath. George put the thermometer in his bag.

"Fever's worse?"

George nodded and latched his bag. Earl followed as he stepped into the hallway. Farther away, near the parlor, Jimmy sat on the floor cross-legged with his chin propped in the palm of his hand. During the past few days, the boy had sat there for hours, waiting for his friend to get better, asking if he could help.

As he passed, George ruffled Jimmy's sandy hair. "You might need to get a breath of fresh air."

"Naw, thanks." No spark of a smile curved Jimmy's lips. "I'll wait here in case they need some help."

"You're a good friend, Jimmy." Earl squeezed his shoulder and followed George onto the porch. The screen door popped against the frame. Puffing out a sigh, Earl leaned against one of the posts. "I was afraid of this."

George set his bag down. "The rash is prominent today on Caleb's wrists and chest. I'm sure it's tick fever."

"It's hard to watch him hurting like this."

"Nighttime will be rougher. There's not much else I can do. We must keep that fever down."

Earl kneaded his fingertips against his forehead. "I know. I'm sorry for my brother. The last thing he needs is to lose his son too."

"There's no need talking that way. This sickness must run its course."

"But it might not end well."

The possibility seized George's heart along with unwanted memories. He curled his fingers around the porch railing and stared hard at the sloping ridges and hills.

"No, perhaps not."

A moment's silence stretched between them, thickening with apprehension. Stealing a glance at Earl's face, George observed the clench of his jaw.

Earl shoved away from the post. "I know Someone Who changes courses if He wills. I'll be back in a while."

"Where are you going?"

"To ask folks to pray."

Earl jogged down the steps and clipped toward the barn. For the first time in years, George wished he possessed the simple confidence to approach God.

"He won't eat." Ella fumbled with George's sleeve, her voice taut. "No matter how much we coax, he says he isn't hungry."

"I've noticed. He must eat," George muttered more to himself than to Ella. The morning sun peered over the mountains and streaked rays across the living room rug. Two slow, excruciating weeks had passed, but Caleb had only grown worse. The boy's constant pain rendered him too weak to get out of bed. His refusing food would only hasten his decline.

George's mind thrashed for anything that might entice Caleb's appetite.

"Where's Jimmy?"

"Sitting on the front steps."

"Excuse me." He pulled gently from Ella's grip, rose from the sofa, and crossed to the window. At George's tap on the glass, Jimmy turned sleepily in his direction. George motioned for him to come inside.

Jimmy scrambled to stand. Seconds later, he dashed into the room. The dear boy had offered every day to lend a hand, but no one could think of anything he could do. Still, Jimmy had faithfully waited every day.

"Jimmy, my boy, we need your help."

His huckleberry eyes brightened. "What can I do?"

George laid his arm around Jimmy's shoulders. "Caleb has hardly eaten the last few days. I'd like you to try feeding him. He won't for any of us, but I have a feeling that he might eat for his best friend. Will you?"

"Yessir!" Jimmy bobbed his head. "Can I try now?"

"You most certainly can." Bracing herself with the crutches, Ella stood, her movements growing stronger each day. "Let's go to the kitchen and fix a bowl of chicken and dumplings. Caleb's favorite."

Jimmy scampered ahead of her. "Those are the best!"

Ella's gaze warmed as she glanced at George. "I'm glad you thought of this."

Standing aside for her to pass, George lowered his voice. "I hope it works."

He watched as they hurried to the kitchen. With soft footsteps, he crept toward Caleb's bedroom, turned the doorknob, and peeped inside. Propped against the pillows, Caleb stared at the ceiling, his flushed cheeks streaked with tears. Moaning, he rubbed his arms.

George's heart shriveled. What else could he do but watch?

Nothing relieved the pain. The fever was equally stubborn, barely manageable with his and Sal's combined knowledge.

On one side of the bed, Douglas knelt, his fingers linked together in prayer. On the other side, Earl also knelt, his voice low and earnest, petitioning the Lord for his nephew.

A stirring of anger rumbled deep within his spirit. Where was He? George gritted his teeth and stepped back, pulling the door shut.

Like an invisible vice, the late summer warmth crushed him from every side. Or was it the shrill silence of the house?

Snatching his bag from the side table, George rushed outside where Ginger waited to take him on his calls. The buggy wobbled as he swung into the seat. Without needing his prompting, Ginger stepped forward, knowing what to do.

George closed his eyes. Lilith. Doc. And perhaps Caleb. Where was the sense in all of it? He clinched the reins tighter. The hopeless flutter within his spirit begged for release like a trapped captive.

The sunlight warmed his forehead, radiating across his eyelids, flowing down his cheeks like the caress of an invisible hand. George opened his eyes and peered into the cloudless blue expanse above him. *I'm doing no good here. I'm more of a bystander than a doctor, waiting for life or death.*

Up and down the hills the miles stretched, bringing George no closer to the answers or the peace he craved. By the time he reached Henry Mahan's place, despair and anguish tightened like a vice. George forced his thoughts to his patient.

Sal's poultices had done the trick. At his last visit, he'd found the infection in Henry's leg almost gone. If Henry had continued using them, it should be healed.

George climbed down and glanced around the yard. No one in sight. His feet crunched across the dead, dry grass, scorched by the heat. A cluster of hens clucked and scattered as he approached the door and knocked. No answer.

Frowning, he walked the length of the cabin, hoping not to run into a gun barrel in the backyard. No sign of life anywhere. Perhaps Henry was at the barn, though it seemed far too still.

As he neared the barn, a muffled sound behind the building met his ears. He crept the remaining steps and peered around the corner.

There, on his knees, beside the woodpile, Henry prayed. Brash, gruff, and often sullen Henry Mahan.

Thunderstruck, George gaped.

Henry lifted his head and flinched, his bushy eyebrows shooting upward. "Mercy, Dr. Curtis. Don't ya know how to *hallo* when you set foot on a place?"

"Apparently not. Next time, I'll remember."

With a grunt, Henry stood. "You'd better, or someone'll blow yer head off." His hairy hand brushed dirt and sprigs of grass from his overalls. "I reckon you're wondering what I was doing." A cherry flush peeped above his beard.

"It's none of my business."

"You right about that, but you caught me red-handed."

George cleared his throat. "You weren't doing anything wrong, Mr. Mahan."

"I know't. A man like me ain't got much cause to pray, but it weren't for me. It was for the young Steen boy."

"Caleb?" Surprise threaded George's voice. "We appreciate it. He needs it. Badly."

Henry's dark eyes narrowed. "I know. Earl stopped by and asked for prayer. Asked *me*. You know something? That's a changed man. I remember when he first came to this valley. He was 'bout as low a wretch as any man could get. Made me think. If the Good Man Above can do something with him, maybe He could do something about the Steen boy. You reckon?"

His piercing gaze burrowed straight into George's gut. He fought the urge to squirm. "I suppose so."

Seeming satisfied with the answer, Henry took a kerchief from his pocket and swiped his sweaty forehead. "If He does, I'll be at church the next Sunday and thereafter. Told the Good Man Above, too."

Far be it from me to tell him not to bargain with God. George gestured his hand. "I came to check your leg."

"It's right as rain. Took the poultice off last night, and the skin was smooth and pink, like new." He hitched up his overall's leg for George to examine it.

"Good." Uneasy, George turned. "I'll take my leave."

"Just a minute." Henry left him standing while he jogged to the nearby stone cellar and disappeared inside. Moments later, he reemerged, carrying a bulging gunny sack. "I knowed you be coming soon, and I need to settle up. These are new potatoes. Best tasting ones around. I thank ya for helping me."

George took the sack, his lips curving in a slight smile. "Doc did the work, not me."

"He's gone, but you done your part."

"Thank you, Mr. Mahan. I'll enjoy these."

Henry hooked his thumbs around his overall straps. Knowing their conversation was over, George headed for his rig.

At the next farm, the scene was similar, except the wife prayed in the barn while her husband prayed on the front porch. Over at the next homeplace, a family prayed under the shade of a hickory tree.

In fact, hardly a farm passed where someone wasn't praying for Caleb Steen. Inside the woodshed, in the hayloft, on the porch, or under a tree. The road stretched through the valley from one praying home to another.

By the time the buggy's wheels carried him from the last farm, George shook the dizziness pervading him in vain. His heart ached. The faith of these people was too much.

And yet, it was the same faith he'd witnessed throughout his life in the souls of people he loved best—Mam, Da, the Wallaces, and the Steens. His faith, however, had been eggshell thin. Broken into a thousand different fragments.

I've never given God a chance to mend it back together.

34

The winding road brought him into Valley Creek, the spicy scent of sawdust from the mill curling under George's nose. The whirling buzz of the saw spilled onto the dirt street, drowning all other sounds.

As Ginger trotted past the buildings, George noticed Parson Crandall's horse tied in the churchyard. Though he tried to forget the scenes of people praying, they clung to his memory. A tug of war tightened in his chest. Unwillingly, he guided Ginger into the yard and reined her to a stop. The parson was the last person he wanted to see, yet he was the very one who might understand.

He swung down from the buggy and approached the whitewashed building. From one of the front windows, a movement caught his glance. Pausing, he peered closer.

Parson Crandall paced across the front of the sanctuary, his eyes raised heavenward while his lips moved in prayer. A heavy weight, like the hillside stones, landed on George's heart, smothering his breath. Quiet assurance touched the parson's face as though the Lord was right there listening and communing with him. Like a friend.

Emptiness yawned wide and deep within George's soul, along with a thirst he couldn't explain. Since when had he ever felt peace like that?

I don't have any business here.

He backed away and turned toward the buggy. When he placed his foot on the side step, the church door creaked.

"Dr. Curtis, wait. I saw you walking away. Is there anything I can do for you?"

George muffled a groan and stepped down. "No, I don't wish to bother you."

"Not at all." Parson Crandall descended the steps. "How's Caleb?"

"Not well. If something doesn't change soon, the worst will come."

"I'm sorry to hear it. We are praying."

"I've noticed. At nearly every stop I made today." George shuffled his hands into his pockets and stepped closer.

For a silent minute, Parson Crandall perused George's face. "I'm guessing you are troubled by it."

"Not in the way you mean. I've never seen anything quite like it."

"True faith at work is a precious, rare thing. I've been heartened to see it. Ever since the tornado nearly destroyed Valley Creek over a year ago, people seem more eager to carry one another's burdens."

"Strange how destruction sometimes makes people better."

"Rather, it's God Who uses hard times to bring us to Him."

Searing heat flooded George's face. "I hope you'll pardon me for saying, but I've had plenty of hard times, but God hasn't brought me to Himself."

"Then why are you here in the churchyard?"

George blinked. "I don't know."

"Don't you?"

"My troubles have broken me, Parson." George balled his

fists within his pockets. "I don't see God anywhere in it. I've looked, but He is far away."

A flicker of compassion touched Parson Crandall's features. "A house is made from broken trees."

What on earth was the man talking about? "Excuse me?"

"What is a house made from?"

"Wood. Boards cut, hewn, and nailed together."

"Exactly." Parson Crandall swept his hand across the landscape. "The trees, magnificent and strong, are cut down, split into pieces, and used to make something, often beautiful. A tree by itself is a wonderful part of God's creation. It's useful on the landscape. And it's invaluable when it's broken." He tilted his head to one side, his gaze never wavering from George. "Though they've been cut down, their purpose remains. God does the same with us. Life hews us down. Tragedy splits us into pieces. Yet our purpose—God's purpose for us—remains. In His grace, He comes to us and puts us back together again if we allow Him. He mends the pieces of our lives, creating a dwelling place for Him to inhabit. An abode in our hearts more glorious than if we continued alone, without His handiwork. And He doesn't stop there. He fashions all of us together. The Lord is building something out of the broken pieces of your life, Dr. Curtis, whether you see it or not. Will you accept it?"

Everything inside George stilled. His stinging eyes clogged the words in his throat. He fumbled with a few coins inside his pockets.

"I thank you for your words, Parson. You've given me something to ponder." With a nod, George moved toward the buggy, hoping his long strides didn't look as though he were fleeing. Though, in reality, he was.

Ginger started without his prompting. The reins drooped in George's hand while he scrubbed his closed eyes with his palm.

Did God's purpose for him yet remain?

———————— 🌿 ————————

"Curtis, he ate for Jimmy. It was only a few bites, but it's better than nothing."

Ella held her voice to a whisper. At his nod, Ella spied the drawn lines digging around Curtis's mouth. "Are you all right?"

"Yes, just tired like everyone else."

He was keeping the worst to himself, as usual, to spare her. Ella tamped her impatience by leaning harder onto her crutches as though it might somehow crush the emotion.

Leaving Caleb's bedroom, Guy and Jimmy joined them in the hallway. The door clicked shut.

"Jimmy, wait for me out yonder." Guy dipped his head toward the door. Still happy from helping his friend, Jimmy smiled and jogged outside. When he was out of earshot, Guy grimaced. "It's not good, is it?"

Curtis shook his head. "There's nothing else we can do at this point. We can't even make him comfortable. I'd like to ask you something, though."

"Go ahead."

"If it's all right with you and Lane, I'd like for Jimmy to stay. He's the only one who can get Caleb to eat. If things take a worse turn, I'll send him home."

A pain in Ella's chest exploded as if a knife had plunged through it. The thought of a worse turn was too hard to bear.

Guy kneaded the back of his neck, the thought apparently hurting him as well. "Whatever Caleb needs, that's what we'll do."

"Thank you. I'm proud of Jimmy. He has the makings of a fine man."

Without words, Guy clapped Curtis's shoulder and squeezed. Nodding at Ella, Guy went to the door.

"Son, Dr. Curtis needs you to stay for the next few days to

help feed Caleb. If there's anything else he needs, you be sure and do it."

"I'll be glad to." Jimmy's sunny face sobered when his glance bounced between them. "Caleb will be all right, won't he?"

Gripping Jimmy's shoulders, Guy tugged him against his chest. "Either way, the Lord will take care of him."

Jimmy blinked up into Guy's face. "Papa Guy, I know, but he's gonna get better. I just know it."

After a long silence, Guy released the boy. "I'll see you tomorrow."

"Kiss Mama Lane and Abby for me."

"Will do." Guy pushed open the screen door without a backward glance and strode toward his horse.

The following two days crawled by the hour, each one more excruciating than the last. The silence so loud Ella often fought the urge to scream. Douglas rarely left his son's side, and then only for a few minutes. He slept on a pallet beside Caleb's bed. On the other side, Earl sat for hours. She and Lorena took care of the household tasks. After his rounds, Curtis stayed and slept all night on the sofa, waking whenever Caleb moaned.

How long, O Lord?

The late afternoon breeze fluttered the curtains through the open window. Ella pushed a needle through the embroidery on a handkerchief while she watched Caleb's listless fingers fumble at the sheet. Earl's eyes, bloodshot from sleepless nights and prayer, caught hers and spoke things she didn't wish to understand. She snatched her gaze from him and focused on Curtis while he felt Caleb's pulse.

Except for a tremor in his jaw, Curtis kept his expression bland. Turning, he went to the doorway and called Jimmy.

The boy shuffled over, stifling a yawn. "Sir?"

"It's time you get some rest. You've been a great help the past few days, but I'd like for you to go home."

What Ella would have given to run away right then.

Jimmy's freckled nose scrunched in a frown. Leaning past Curtis, he peered for a long second into the bedroom.

"No, sir."

"I'm sure Mama Lane misses you."

Jimmy yanked his stare back to Curtis, his eyes darkening. "I ain't goin' nowhere, Dr. Curtis."

The boy and doctor faced each other, and the older, wearier one was no match for the impasse.

"Very well." Curtis dipped his head, his shoulders sagging. "I understand."

Patting Jimmy's shoulder, he stepped over the threshold. Not long after he disappeared from Ella's view, the screen door creaked then slapped the frame.

Ella laid her needlework on the end table and gathered her crutches. She gave Jimmy a quick embrace and made her way toward the porch.

Curtis stood like a ramrod, motionless and unbending as he stared across the hills, not reacting when the door squealed on its hinges. Ella pulled herself to the swing and lowered herself onto it.

Still, he hadn't moved. Ella's heart constricted. For over two weeks, Curtis had worked tirelessly to help Caleb, never showing his frustration or dismay.

For all his painstaking work, it had come to this.

She studied his rigid jawline, the muscles knotted as though he had locked away his thoughts. Unable to unburden himself because everyone else looked to him for the answers that often hurt the ones he loved.

How lonely was it to be Dr. George Curtis?

Ella kneaded her temples with her fingertips. It was pointless to ask what to expect. Why plague him any further? She had seen her share of deathbeds, and it only grew harder.

As though suddenly snapped from his thoughts, Curtis

turned and joined her, the swing rocking beneath their weight. Neither he nor she spoke, words useless to them.

Curtis's arm rounded her shoulders and drew her against his side. Closing her throbbing eyes, Ella nestled her head on his chest, an anchor during this tumult of past, present, and future. The swing creaked with the slow, rhythmic, back-and-forth arcs.

Father, I know You're ever with us, but this is ...

Ella couldn't bear to finish the thought. One hot tear streaked down her cheek, followed by another. Though she squeezed her closed eyelids harder together, they surged through the barrier like waters thundering against a strained dam. A ragged breath shook her.

Shifting towards her, Curtis brought his other arm around Ella. Rather than shushing, he held her while she succumbed to days of caged emotions. His chin lightly rested on the top of her hair as he stroked her back. Moments later, the drip of moisture from his face fell onto her head.

Dogwood winters hovered close these days.

ROUGH, large hands shook George's shoulders. A voice from far away pierced through the cobwebs of sleep.

"Wake up, man." Earl's urgent tone followed another jolting shake. "You've got to come."

George bolted upright from the sofa.

Releasing him, Earl whirled around and jogged toward the bedroom. The sound of Ella and Lorena's crying fully awoke George's senses, and he steeled himself as he followed.

When George crossed the threshold, he skidded to a stop. Blinked. His glance bounced around at everyone—the women holding each other, sobbing. Douglas on his knees at the bedside, grasping his son's hand.

And Caleb, sitting up.

A tentative smile crept across the boy's cracked lips. "Dr. Curtis, I feel all right."

George stumbled forward and felt Caleb's forehead. No fever. His trembling fingers sought Caleb's pulse. Steady and strong.

"Am I well?"

Caleb's eyes were clear; the gray pallor coloring his face had been banished by the flush of life.

"Are you in pain?"

"Not a bit." Caleb drew in a full breath and expelled it. "Feels good to not hurt."

"He was sleeping, and when he woke up, he pushed back the covers and sat up." Douglas's voice cracked. "Said he felt better."

To steady himself, George seized the headboard, shock splintering his thoughts. The boy wasn't dead but very much alive. Alive and well.

Caleb tugged his sleeve. "Dr. Curtis?"

"You appear to be fine. I don't understand it."

"I do!" Jimmy hooted from the doorway. "It's a miracle!" His footsteps bounded down the hallway toward the front door. "God has healed Caleb!"

Caleb's tremulous smile grew wider. "He must have. I thought I was dying, but when I woke up, I felt fine. Like I used to feel. Maybe I'm gonna live, after all."

Within a few hours, the Steen yard brimmed with Valley Creek folk. Jimmy had run all the way home, hallooing the news as he went. Laughter and praise mingled into one voice as neighbors and friends gathered around the house. George soaked in the scene, his eyes watching the laughing faces glow in the light of dozens of lanterns. Sleepy-eyed children peeped over the sides of wagons, blinking at the unbelievable news.

One by one, families filed in to wish Caleb well. He beamed

at them, chortling and talking a mile a minute. Through the wee hours of the morning, the merriment and thanksgiving swelled under the stars. Only hours ago, death shrouded the house, but now, life abounded.

George had braced himself for sounds of mourning. He hadn't prepared himself for sounds of praise.

From the shadowy edges of the yard, Parson Crandall threaded his way through the crowd and skipped up the steps, his dark hair skewed in every direction.

"Brother Mansfield banged on my door and told me." He paused to catch his breath. "Is it true, Dr. Curtis? Does the boy live?"

"Come and see." George nudged his elbow.

Parson Crandall hurried to the bedroom and found Caleb sitting on the edge of the bed beside Jimmy, his arm around his buddy's shoulders. The parson gaped and looked at George.

"Don't tell me you're shocked, Parson." George couldn't resist.

"I'm ashamed to admit that I am," he murmured, lips trembling. "The Lord be praised."

While the parson stepped forward to offer his best wishes, George slipped outside and shouldered his way to a spot beside the fence post. He draped his arm across the top and filled his lungs with a slow breath. Perhaps working with God was better than working without Him. When all was said and done, it came down to Him.

Minutes later, Parson Crandall stepped onto the porch. The crowd lulled as if waiting for him to speak. His broad-shouldered silhouette paused near the top step.

"We'd like to hear a word from you, Parson," called Guy from somewhere nearby.

The parson cleared his throat. "We've all been praying for a few weeks, but I'm sorry to say I'd lost hope after I saw Caleb yesterday afternoon. May the Lord forgive me. He does things in His own way and time. Not ours. I pray this has brought us closer to Him. Shall we sing a hymn of praise? As I raced over here, these words came to me."

His fine voice, neither too high nor too deep, drifted over them. "No, never alone. No, never alone. He promised never to leave me, never to leave me alone ..."

Voices quickly joined until the song overflowed the yard and filled the valley. *When in affliction's valley, I tread the road of care, my Savior helps me carry my cross so heavy to bear; Though all around me is darkness and earthly joys are flown: My Savior whispers His promise: never to leave me alone.*

George's throat tightened. The melody surrounded and embraced his soul in love. The voices carried his memory to the many times the Savior had offered His hand, and he had pushed it away, determined to forge a path without Him.

His choice had led him nowhere.

But the Lord had led him here. To this place. This moment in time. He could either carry on as always, or he could choose never to be alone again.

Everything and everyone blurred from his view.

"Lord," he whispered, "here I am. I'm grateful You've waited. Forgive me, I pray. I'm tired of being useless, tired of fighting what I know is right. My life is Yours. Please use me, if You will, for your glory. I know that I can't do anything without You."

The heavy burden pressing against George's soul lifted as a new Presence filled his being. The peace that had eluded him overflowed as all the wrongs and sins of his past were swept away on the wings of song.

Suddenly, another presence surrounded George. Two hands clapped firmly on his shoulders. Swiping at the tears, he looked up into Parson Crandall's joy-filled eyes.

"The Lord fashions His house beautiful with every broken piece placed in His hands."

35

"Are you going to up and leave?" Sal squinted in the dim hollow, scrutinizing George's every move as he combed the area for herbs.

"I never expected it to be this hard to find." George scanned the moist ground. Though he'd studied the pictures and listened to Sal's instructions, he couldn't see them. "Are you sure ginseng grows here?"

Sal crimped her lips together and heaved a sigh. "We call it *sang* around these parts, Yank." She waved a bony hand. "It's all around you, but I ain't gonna help you see it, else you'll never find it on your own."

A plant near an ancient oak caught George's eye. He hurried over and reached down to grasp it.

"I'd not do that if I were you. That's poison ivy."

He jerked his hand back. Inwardly, George chafed at her smug tone and his ignorance.

"You're lookin' too hard. Close your eyes and wait."

"What?"

"Quit zagging around like a chicken with your head cut off. Stand still, close your eyes, and wait."

George straightened, incredulous.

"Or you can keep bumbling like a blind man. Like my daddy used to say, 'Close your eyes, then you'll see it.'"

No use arguing with her. George closed his eyes.

"Now, listen to the woods. Forget every place you've searched and think about how *sang* looks. Breathe deep and picture it."

The smells of the moist earth invaded George's senses. About a stone's throw away, the creek babbled and murmured through the hollow. Birds twittered overhead. A breeze shimmied the tops of the trees. Farther, in a distant pasture, a cow mooed. While he listened, his frustration slipped away, overtaken by a refreshing calm.

Sal must have known because a chuckle reached his ears. "Now open yer eyes and look 'round slow."

Opening his eyes, George absorbed the details of each plant before looking elsewhere. The leaves, the stems, the color. Then he spied a patch beyond Sal.

"Right there! Behind you." Embarrassment flushed George's face. He sounded like a child hunting Easter eggs.

"You got it, Yank, and there's more." Sal slid a Bowie knife from a sheath at her waist and handed it to him. "Time to dig."

After giving instructions for harvesting the *sang*, Sal pulled the wide-brimmed straw hat from her head and stirred the thick, forest air around her face.

"You never did answer me a while ago."

"About what?" George squatted and carefully plunged the knife into the ground, making sure to avoid the root.

"I don't know what's worse—a man or a Yankee," Sal growled.

George's laughter ricocheted through the hollow as he glanced up into her exasperated face. "Both."

"You're pert near right." Her dark, knowing eyes widened.

Sal reminded him of an owl. Wayward white strands from

her haphazard bun wafted in rhythm with the hat. She looked like a part of the forest in her brown gingham dress, perfectly blending with the surroundings.

Turning his attention back to the task, George sobered in case she decided to thump him on the head. "Don't tell me you want me to stay?"

"Me?" She waved the hat more quickly. "You're the one wantin' to learn all about the yarbs. Seems to me, if you was planning to leave, you'd not care a fig."

Laying aside the knife, George gently extracted the plant and began removing the soil from the roots. "You have a point, but I haven't made up my mind. Fitting in is difficult, me being a Yank and all that." He quirked an eyebrow at her. "I'm not sure people will ever trust me like they did Doc. Besides, I believe it's good to know about herbs. The knowledge will help me wherever I decide to go."

Sal jammed the hat back on her head and harrumphed. Did she actually want him to stay?

"What's your given name, Sal?"

The older woman blinked several times, looking flabbergasted. She opened her mouth and shut it as though she had forgotten it.

"You can't share it with a Yank. Is that it?"

Her scrutiny glinted like the Bowie knife lying at his feet. She worked her jaw as if tasting the challenge. Jutting her chin, Sal crossed her arms.

"Salitha."

"Salitha," George spoke it with reverence. "A strong, enduring name, like these hills. I like it. I think I'll address you that way from now on."

"Pa was the only one who called me that. I ain't heard it since the day he died. Sort of makes me feel ... like old times." Her chiseled features bloomed cherry-red. "I don't know if he would like a Ya ... you ... to call me that."

"But would *you* mind?"

Sal's steely gaze softened, and George caught a glimpse of the young girl hidden deep inside. Widowed young with a stillborn. Tough, life-hardened, but a gem underneath.

Indecision flickered across her face while she ground the toe of her boot against the earth. Her murky stare probed his.

"I reckon you might. Dr. Curtis." With that, she whirled away and tromped to another patch of *sang*.

A feather could have knocked George over. The minutes passed while he watched her deft movements. He had never expected to gain any amount of her respect or friendship. Her grudging acceptance tasted sweet after all the weeks of enduring resentment.

"If ya don't get moving, I'll change my mind," she quipped, without bothering to look over her shoulder.

"Yes, ma'am." George dropped the roots into a burlap sack and turned his attention to another patch of *sang*.

JOYFUL VOICES SINGING *Bringing in the Sheaves* floated upward from both sides of the creekbank. Valley Creek folk, dressed in their Sunday best, stood on the wide, pebbled bank where the creek yawned and deepened, flowing lazily, resting from its raucous journey over rocks and falls.

Silver sunlight danced across the turquoise water, and George marveled how the color rivaled the most beautiful he'd ever seen.

A whimper to his left snagged his attention. With a gentle shush, Edith shifted Catherine from the crook of her arm to her shoulder. Beside her, Harley Ray cradled little Curtis, though his large arms seemed to swallow the baby. Their starched, white bonnets reflected the sun from their tiny faces. George caught Edith's eyes, and they shared a smile. At moments like this, life overflowed with promise.

Beside them stood Lane and Guy, lifting their voices heavenward while Abby sat and squealed delightedly on a quilt spread out at their feet. Her bright eyes watched the faces as though they were singing to her. Right behind Abby, Jimmy and Caleb stretched their legs and snickered, digging their elbows into each other's ribs, no doubt planning mischief.

Ella shifted her weight on the crutches and stretched her back. A quilt lay at her feet in case she needed to rest.

"Are you all right?" George whispered close to her ear.

She smiled without missing a word of the hymn.

Farther beyond them, Earl and Lorena stood underneath the shade of a maple tree with Douglas. When everyone started on another verse, George caught sight of Henry Mahan and his wife. With his beard trimmed and bushy hair combed, Henry looked like a different man. He met George's stare, his somber mouth unwavering. A man of his word.

Near the water's edge, Parson Crandall stood leading the song. He had rolled his sleeves past his elbows in preparation for the baptism.

Since coming to Valley Creek, this was another first for George. He'd never witnessed an outdoor baptism. The beauty and simplicity filled his soul. The Lord felt closer than He ever had to George as the cool breeze from the creek feathered across his face.

As the melody waned, Parson Crandall read several scriptures then directed everyone to sit. After helping Ella onto the quilt, George took his place beside her.

While the parson preached, George focused on every word, but he also observed those around him. Work-worn, often weary faces brightened as Parson Crandall imparted God's Word and lifted invisible burdens.

A feeling of belonging to such a community, becoming one

of them, kindled a desire within George to minister to their needs in whatever way possible. Even during his medical school years, he had never desired it as strongly as he did now. The feeling stole his breath.

Take My yoke upon you and learn of Me. For I Am meek and lowly in heart.

Everything had been stripped from George, including his pride. When he had lacked nothing, his burdens smothered him. Now that he possessed little, he'd never been freer.

Lilith's sweet face rose in his mind, and his heart panged. His little friend was the only thing he regretted losing. Bowing his head, he mouthed a silent prayer for Thomas and Claudia's healing. *May they find it in their hearts to forgive me someday.* Forgiving himself was equally difficult. With God's help, it was no longer impossible.

Parson Crandall called forward those who wished to be baptized. Earl first approached, followed by Guy.

"And to think we're here, witnessing this," Ella whispered, leaning against George's shoulder.

Because of Earl, he was there. All of them—Lorena, Lane, Edith, Douglas, Caleb, and Ella—broken, yet whole together. God had turned Earl's folly and crime into something He could use for His ultimate glory. Like broken trees creating a masterpiece.

Parson Crandall laid his Bible on a nearby stump.

"Before the service, Douglas Steen asked if he could share a few words with you." He gestured for him to come forward.

Surprise and curiosity flickered across everyone's faces as Douglas approached the parson and turned to face them.

Douglas cleared his throat. "I'd like to thank all of you for praying for my son. The Lord heard you all, and I'll be forever indebted to Him and every one of you." Douglas gathered his breath, an unsure expression passing over his face. "I'd also like to say, here and now, that I've been unfair to my brother Earl. I didn't want to believe the change God worked in him. But I know it to be true, and I'm sorry." He turned his gaze to Earl. "Our father never lost faith that you'd repent, but I did. I hope you'll forgive me. Will you allow me to help Parson Crandall baptize you?"

For an answer, Earl reached out and pulled him into a bear hug. With a gasp, Ella yanked a handkerchief from her sleeve and buried her face in it. Many other ladies throughout the congregation did the same.

A sort of homesick feeling, sweetened by the love pervading the place, settled over George. More than anything, he yearned to belong.

Ella laid her hand on his forearm, moving the hankie only a fraction of an inch from her face. "I don't believe I've ever seen anything so beautiful."

"Nor have I."

She tilted closer to him. "Will you marry me? Today?"

Shock juddered through him like a current. "Today?"

Lowering it another inch, Ella bobbed her glance around to make sure no one else heard them. "Whyever not? We have the parson, the license, and we aren't getting any younger."

"Speak for yourself." George couldn't suppress the tease. Like a sunrise, joy rose and beamed inside his soul.

Ella muffled a giggle and tweaked his arm. "Perhaps I'm getting carried away, but I feel like I belong here. Don't you? Being with these people has touched my heart." Her whisper faltered.

Resisting the urge to hug her in front of Valley Creek, George covered her hand with his. "Say no more. I'd love nothing more than to marry you today. Presumptuous lass." He gave her a furtive wink.

She flashed him a watery grin.

George glanced at the creekbank. By this time, Earl, Guy,

Douglas, and Henry Mahan were wading into the creek with the parson.

"I need to do something."

He unbuttoned his vest and shrugged out of it. After laying it across Ella's lap, he stood and strode toward the water's edge, uncuffing his sleeves and rolling them up.

"Parson Crandall," he called.

The men turned to look.

"Might I also be baptized?"

A pleased light came into Parson Crandall's face. "Come on, brother. There's always room for more."

George tugged off his shoes and socks. He stepped into the cool depths, the water swirling around his ankles, the rocks in this part of the creek small and smooth under his feet. With each step, it crept up his legs until it reached his waist.

The men exchanged pleased glances as Parson Crandall lifted his voice for the congregation to hear. Expectation filled the air as everyone on the bank stood and waited.

Looking heavenward, Parson Crandall prayed.

Except for a whisper of wind stirring among the people, everything else hushed while Parson Crandall asked for God's blessing. When he concluded, he turned to Earl first.

A few moments later, the parson and Douglas submerged Earl beneath the water and lifted him back up. Water streamed from the top of his head, down his face, and returned to its place. Earl drew in a gulp of air as his tears mingled with the rivulets.

On the shore, people raised their hands and faces heavenward in adoration and praise to the Savior. Next, Guy was submerged and raised in the same manner. Afterward followed Henry.

Then came George's turn.

The creek lapped gently against his waist, the cold depths prickling his arms and chest while the sun struck his head and shoulders. As the men watched, Douglas wrung out the wet kerchief, folded it, and handed it to George. He pressed it against his nose.

Laying a hand on his head, the parson prayed. George closed his eyes, feeling a Presence surround him while the words of the prayer took root in his heart. Strong hands laid on his shoulders.

"Brother Curtis, I baptize you in the name of the Father, the Son, and the Holy Spirit."

George felt himself tilting backward. His head sank beneath the chilly water, whooshing into his ears, distorting the sounds in the open air above him. Obliterating the world from breath, sound, and view. Just him and the Lord beneath everything else.

A moment later, those same strong hands raised him, and George took a breath, ever grateful for the life God had restored to him.

The congregation worshipped. Overcome by his emotions, George forgot to mop the water flowing into his eyes and across his nose.

Someone tugged the handkerchief from his hand and began wiping George's face. His eyes popped open to discover Earl dabbing his forehead.

The beauty of it struck George speechless. His former friend-turned-enemy restored into fellowship with him.

And I deserve it least of all.

Earl's lips curved upward, his expression reflecting George's thoughts. As he withdrew the handkerchief, Earl clapped George's shoulder and stepped sideways to let the parson lead them back to the creekbank.

Water eddied and sloshed around their legs as they filed behind Parson Crandall. George scanned the waiting crowd. Men and ladies, one after one, nodded to him—some with sober faces, others with pleasant expressions. In each of these, George gleaned the firstfruits of acceptance.

Thy people shall be my people.

He stepped onto the gentle slope of the bank. Creek water rained around his bare feet while the heat from the rocks seared into his soles. Scooping up his shoes and socks, he hurried to the soft comfort of Ella's quilt.

Her admiration brimmed with love as he approached. Ah, she'd never looked more lovely. To think she wanted to marry and share a life with him. His pulse thudded with every step that brought him closer to her.

"Are you certain?" he asked, his tone nearly swallowed by the laughter and conversation humming around them.

"I am. And so is Valley Creek, I think." With a dip of her chin toward his feet, she raised her brows meaningfully. "You'd better hurry up with those shoes and catch Parson Crandall. Invite him for dinner before someone else does."

Chuckling, George crammed his feet into his shoes. "Yes, ma'am."

He glanced around. Everyone else was preoccupied with hugs and handshakes. With one arm, he snatched Ella close and stole a kiss, knocking the wind from them both.

Easing his head up, he waited for her to catch her balance on the crutches. Her delightful lips sputtered.

"And in front of the whole congregation, no less," Ella clamped onto her skewed hat.

George winked and stole another kiss for good measure. Drawing back, he straightened her hat. "I can be presumptuous too, lass."

EPILOGUE

1913
One year later

Laughter cascaded from the overlook into the valley like an invisible waterfall echoing among the rocks. A jaunty melody soon followed. On a nearby quilt, Guy picked his banjo while Harley Ray strummed the guitar. Jimmy pulled a harmonica from his overall's pocket and joined them.

Ella closed the lid of the picnic basket and rose without the aid of crutches or a cane. A slight limp reminded her to take every step with gratitude.

With his back turned to everyone, Curtis stood near the picket fence bordering the edge of the cliff, admiring the unfurled beauty spread out below them. Ella suppressed a shiver as she stepped toward him, remembering the day, a few years ago, when Earl and Jimmy nearly fell to their deaths. Hence the picket fence now barring anyone from nearing the edge.

His deep voice reached her ears and warmed her through and through.

"Someday, I'll teach you all about the yarbs just as Salitha teaches me," he crooned. "And you'll grow to be a doctor like your daddy."

"Already trying to persuade our Lili?" Slipping her arm through the crook of his, Ella dropped a kiss on the infant's downy, reddish curls. Lili gurgled and reached for her father's mustache.

Dodging Lili's grasp, Curtis grinned sheepishly. "Perhaps a little."

After three months of marriage, no one was more shocked than they were to learn a babe was on its way.

"Unca Curt. Up." Abby's chubby hands grabbed a handful of his trousers and yanked.

Curtis shifted Lili and scooped up the toddler with his free arm. "And you, ma'am, will be training alongside your cousin. My medicine ladies."

For an answer, Abby nestled her head into the side of his neck.

Ella glanced over her shoulder. Under the shade trees sat Lane, her waist expanding with another new life. Beside her, Edith sprawled across the quilt to pull a tottering Curtis back within reach while Catherine clapped. How strange yet wonderful it felt to know that her child would grow up alongside Edith's and Lane's. Never in her life had she dreamt such a thing possible.

Leaning against another tree, Earl pulled the bow across his violin and joined the musical fray. Lorena tipped back her head and laughed as the men's fingers flew, trying to outdo each other. Guy and Harley Ray stood little chance against their father-in-law.

Their family. Ella pulled in a deep, satisfying breath and viewed the valley. A distant, silver haze veiled the faraway ridges and peaks. Valley Creek's buildings speckled alongside the main road as it wound through the hills. Farther along, amidst the trees, Ella spied the rooftop of Doc's house—their home.

Gratitude mingled with wonderment and joy. Who knew her bold request to write a lonely, embittered doctor would lead to this?

As though sensing her thoughts, Curtis turned slightly and brushed a kiss against Ella's temple.

"God does all things well, doesn't He?" he murmured into her hair. The remaining Irish lilt from his childhood still quickened her heartbeat.

She tossed him an impish grin. "Aye, that He does."

The End

READER QUESTIONS

1. A snippet of a dream starts the story. What foreshadowing do you see? What is their meaning?

2. How does God use Ella's weakness to bring strength into George's life?

3. Why is it important to confront the things that hinder us?

4. When Parson Crandall says that houses are made from broken trees, what does he mean?

5. In what ways is George like Jonah of the Bible? How is he different?

6. Why is it hard for George to surrender to God's plan for his life? Do you relate?

7. Which character(s) in the book do you relate to? Why?

8. If you could encourage Ella, what scripture would you share with her? If you could encourage George, what scripture would you share with him?

9. The creek itself is symbolic in this story. What does it represent to you?

10. What themes touched your heart?

AUTHOR'S NOTE

A little insider information ... the healing of Caleb Steen is based on a true event. The real story involved a little girl who I'll call Annie. Annie was a friend of my great-aunt. Both little girls grew up in the Ozarks in the 1920's and '30's. One day, a tick bit Annie, and she grew gravely ill. My aunt would walk down to her house and feed her because Annie wouldn't eat for anyone else. She grew steadily worse, in constant pain.

Then the people in the Ozark community began to pray. Late one night, a neighbor burst through my great-grandparents' kitchen door shouting, "Get up! God has healed Annie!" (No one locked their doors in those days) My aunt said that when they arrived in the yard, other neighbors were already there celebrating while Annie sat up in bed, laughing for joy.

The horses in this series are straight from real life. A few years ago, my son started horse riding lessons. Not only did we become good friends with their owner, Dee Henshaw, we became friends with her horses. What a joy to discover their unique personalities. Some of you may remember Crockett and

Grits from *Valley of Shadows*. They also appear in this story, but Ginger takes center stage this time.

Also, the mules, Mag and Huldy, are taken from real life as well. They belonged to my great-grandfather and helped plow many a row on his Ozark farm.

On another note ... my heart ached many times while writing this story. One of these parts was Doc's illness and passing. He had the signs and symptoms of liver cancer, which is what my uncle Randall also had. He was like a second father to me. Writing those scenes was like revisiting moments with Uncle Randall—his courage, his refusing to make a fuss over it, his care for those he loved, private conversations, and the quietness in how he left us. The physical effects of the illness were especially difficult to write. Like Doc, my uncle could be blunt and unabashedly honest, but he had a tender soul beneath that ached for others. He knew the Lord in a way that few have experienced. His life and passing left a gap in my heart that will never be filled this side of Heaven.

ABOUT THE AUTHOR

Candace West was born in the Mississippi delta to a young minister and his wife. She grew up in small-town Arkansas and is a graduate of the University of Arkansas at Monticello. When she was twelve years old, she wrote her first story, "Following Prairie River." Since then, she has dreamed of writing Christian fiction. Over the years, she has published short stories as well as poems in various magazines. Since her teenage years, she has written many church plays. In 2018, she published her first novel *Lane Steen*. By weaving entertaining, page-turning stories, Candace hopes to share the Gospel and encourage her readers. She currently lives in her beloved Arkansas with her husband Aaron and their son Matthew along with two dogs and three cats.

ALSO BY CANDACE WEST

The Valley Creek Redemption Series

Set in the Arkansas Ozarks, this series is a beautifully written family saga with themes of forgiveness, reconciliation, and redemption.

Book One: Lane Steen

by Candace West

To let go of the past, she must confront it.

When Lane Steen discovers her father kidnapped her years ago, her fractured world shatters. A different world and a new family await to welcome her if she'll only take the chance.

Will they love her? Or will she trade one hostile home for another?

Perhaps the journey will only raise more questions.

Who is her father, really? And what happened to him? Will she ever be able to forgive him so that love can heal her heart?

Valley Creek may be her prison, but perhaps it holds the unexpected. True love, purpose, grace, and redemption.

Join Lane on her search for the truth today!

Book Two: Valley of Shadows

by Candace West

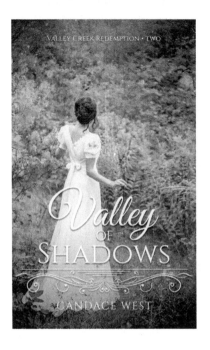

A shattered heart.

A wounded spirit.

A community in crisis.

Lorena Steen gave up on love years ago. She forgave her long-time estranged husband, but when circumstances bring her to the Ozark town of Valley Creek, she discovers forgiving is far from forgetting.

Haunted by his past acts of betrayal, Earl Steen struggles to grow his reclaimed faith and reinstate himself as an upstanding member of Valley Creek. He soon learns that while God's grace is amazing, that of the small-town gossips is not.

When disaster strikes, the only logical solution is for Earl and Lorena to combine their musical talents in an effort to save the community. But even if they're willing to work together, are they able to? Or will the shadows that descend upon Valley Creek reduce it to a ghost town?

MORE HISTORICAL ROMANCE FROM SCRIVENINGS PRESS

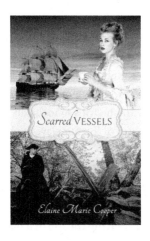

Scarred Vessels

by Elaine Marie Cooper

Winner of the 2021 Selah Award for

Historical Romance

In a time when America battles for freedom, a man and woman seek to fight the injustice of slavery while discovering love in the midst of tragedy.

In 1778 Rhode Island, the American Revolution rallies the Patriots to fight for freedom. But the slavery of black men and women from Africa, bartered for rum, is a travesty that many in America cannot ignore. The seeds of abolition are planted even as the laws allowing slavery in the north still exist.

Lydia Saunders, the daughter of a slave ship owner, grew up with the horror of slavery. It became more of a nightmare when, at a young age, she is confronted with the truth about her father's occupation. Burdened with the guilt of her family's sin, she struggles to make a difference in whatever way she can. When she loses her husband in the battle for freedom from England, she makes a difficult decision that will change her life forever.

Sergeant Micah Hughes is too dedicated to serving the fledgling country of America to consider falling in love. When he carries the tragic news to Lydia Saunders about her husband's death, he is appalled by his attraction to the young widow. Micah wrestles with his feelings for Lydia while he tries to focus on helping the cause of freedom. He trains a group of former slaves to become capable soldiers on the battlefield.

Tensions both on the battlefield and on the home front bring hardship and turmoil that threaten to endanger them all. When Lydia and Micah are faced with saving the life of a black infant in danger, can they survive this turning point in their lives?

A groundbreaking book, honest and inspiring, showcasing black soldiers in the American Revolution. *Scarred Vessels* is peopled with flesh and blood characters and true events that not only inspire and entertain but educate. Well done!

~ Laura Frantz, Christy Award-winning author

of *An Uncommon Woman*

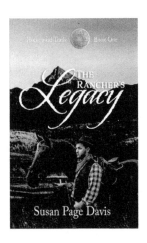

The Rancher's Legacy

Homeward Trails

Book One

Matthew Anderson and his father try to help neighbor Bill Maxwell
when his ranch is attacked. On the day his daughter Rachel is to
return from school back East, outlaws target the Maxwell ranch. After
Rachel's world is shattered, she won't even consider the plan her
father and Matt's cooked up—to see their two children marry and
combine the ranches.

Meanwhile in Maine, sea captain's widow Edith Rose hires a private
investigator to locate her three missing grandchildren. The children
were abandoned by their father nearly twenty years ago. They've been
adopted into very different families, and they're scattered across the
country. Can investigator Ryland Atkins find them all while the
elderly woman still lives? His first attempt is to find the boy now
called Matthew Anderson. Can Ryland survive his trip into the wild
Colorado Territory and find Matt before the outlaws finish destroying
a legacy?

Columbia River Undercurrents ● Book One

Books Afloat

Columbia River Undercurrents

Book One

Blaming herself for her childhood role in the Oklahoma farm truck accident that cost her grandfather's life, Anne Mettles is determined to make her life count. She wants to do it all–captain her library boat and resist Japanese attacks to keep America safe. But failing her pilot's exam requires her to bring others onboard.

Will she go it alone? Or will she team with the unlikely but (mostly) lovable characters? One is a saboteur, one an unlikely hero, and one, she discovers, is the man of her dreams.

Scrivenings
PRESS
Quench your thirst for story.
www.ScriveningsPress.com

Stay up-to-date on your favorite books and authors with our free e-newsletters.

ScriveningsPress.com

Made in the USA
Middletown, DE
07 September 2021